## About the Author

Lexie Winston has been an astronaut, rock star, princess and time traveller. In her dreams. But none of the dreams have lived up to what becoming an author has been like. She gets to live in a world of pure imagination, and her heroines get to do the things she's always wished she could.

When not writing books, Lexie is a mother of two gorgeous teenagers and the wife to a patient and understanding man. They live in Western Australia and are lorded over by a black toy poodle. She loves camping, reading and if her iPad was stolen, her world would explode. (It has the kindle app on.)

And check out my website at lexiewinston.com

Also by Lexie Winston

## The Collectors Division

(Reverse Harem Series)

Guardian

Guardian's Blood

Guardian Ascending

## Arbor Vitae Coven

(Paranormal Romance Series)

Candy Conniptions

Dreamy Delights

Fangtastic Fireworks

## Neighpalm Industries Collective

(Adult Bully Reverse Harem)

Abandoned Girl

Broken Girl

Tormented Girl

Cherished Girl

## Seductive Sins Collection

(Reverse Harem Series)

Glorious Gluttony

Gangs, Guns, and Glory

## Galaxy Circus

(Sci-Fi Reverse Harem Series)

Apprentice

# ABANDONED GIRL

LEXIE WINSTON

NEIGHPALM
PUBLISHING

First published by Neighpalm Publishing in 2020

Abandoned Girl: Neighpalm Industries Collective

Mobi format: 978-0-6487933-2-8
Print: 978-0-6487933-3-5

Cover design by Infinity Cover Designs
Edited by Inked Imagination

 Created with Vellum

*To Mollie, Leslie, Laura and Ashley.*
*Thank you. You guys rock!!!*

## Chapter One

**Harlow**

"Harlow! Are you up here?" My best friend Maxine's husky voice carries up the stairs to my apartment above the barn. She claims the huskiness is due to all the dust and hay from working with the horses every day, but she's had it for as long as I've known her, and that's from before both of us could talk.

"Yeah, come on up," I call back, my eyes glued to the TV in front of me, the noise of her feet on the stairs getting louder the closer she gets. She bursts into the room, and I can see and smell that she's showered. Unlike the smell of horses and hay, which my apartment and I both usually smell like, her scent is spicy and sweet. Probably some expensive designer fragrance that costs a gazillion dollars a bottle.

Looking her up and down, I can tell she's here to harass me to join her for a night on the town. She's wearing a black bodycon dress that hugs her curves in all the right ways. Her dark blue eyes are accentuated by her smokey eyeshadow, and her burgundy lipstick and perfectly tousled pixie cut make her look like Tinkerbell gone wild. Five-inch heels boost her short frame, and you would never know this girl wears boots and jeans most days, handling horses that could easily kill her if things go wrong.

"What are you doing? You want to hit a club?" she asks, going to my fridge and grabbing a bottle of beer for herself. Flipping the bottle top onto the counter, she takes a long pull before heading back over to the couch.

Taking a sip of my own beer, I watch, smiling, as her nose wrinkles when she looks for a clean place to sit. Not that my apartment is *dirty*, but I'm not great at picking up after myself, and books and magazines are lying all over every surface. I've been so busy since I finished college, and I'm too freaking tired to pick up after myself by the time I get home. Also, if they're lying around, well, they're easy to reach when I do want to read something. Reading is the perfect way to escape reality and my drug of choice.

She glances at the TV. "You're not watching those damn abandoned videos again, are you?" she asks, disgust nearly dripping from her words.

"Check this out," I say to her, pointing at the television. "They're visiting this abandoned zoo in Detroit!"

"Huh?" She looks at me, confused, while finally moving some of my vet journals out of the way and taking a seat.

"I don't get it. Why do they leave all these buildings abandoned? Why don't they repurpose them? The zoo would make a great animal sanctuary for the animals that idiots buy but can't manage. Like big cats and huge ass snakes and things." Shaking my head, I take another sip of my beer. "All these places in the world, houses and hospitals and shit, that people have just picked up and left abandoned for various reasons. It's fascinating. And these guys go around checking them out and filming them, discovering all the history. How cool is that?"

The incredulous look on Max's face almost makes me snort my beer through my nose. "Fucking hell, Harlow, you need to get laid. Your obsession with abandoned things is disturbing. Isn't your little menagerie downstairs enough?" Her tone is disgusted, and it's funny in a bit of a sad sort of way. When we were younger, she used to be just as excited as I was to rescue abandoned animals, but as she got older and tried to fit in better with the other kids at school, she slowly lost interest. Whereas mine just grew. Animals were my safe haven against the bullying. Don't get me wrong, she tried to stop our peers' taunts, but in the end, her need to be accepted by them often won out against protecting me. I understood, but that didn't stop me from sometimes resenting her back then. If I'm being honest, some of that lingering resentment flares in and out even now.. She doesn't understand my lack of care about social status, and I don't understand her need to fit in.

"We're going out, and I won't take no for an answer. How long do you need to get ready?"

Looking down at the dirty jeans and fuzzy wool socks that I haven't bothered getting changed out of, I shrug my shoulders. "Nah, it's been a long day. You go and have fun; I'm going to stick to my abandoned, lonely buildings."

The look she gives me is borderline homicidal, but I've faced Max's wrath before, and compared to my mother's hurricane of violence, she's a fresh summer breeze. I'm not scared at all. "Is that supposed to be some kind of metaphor for your life? Because, bitch, I've got no sympathy." She chugs her beer down in one go, dropping it down onto the table in front of her with a dramatic clink. "You're no more abandoned and unloved than I am. My parents think you walk on water, and I would pick you over my own siblings every time."

I roll my eyes at her dramatics, another thing I'm used to. "You have no siblings, you spoiled, rich princess. So there *is* no competition."

"Who cares? It's the thought, right?" She waves

her hand. "I'm giving you half an hour and then calling the car around. If you're not ready, I'll tell Mom that you're up here crying." Christ, Melinda would be up here in a flash nagging me to go out and have some fun. No one ever listens when I explain that this here, what I'm already doing, is my idea of a perfect night. Then she'd sigh and be all disappointed in me, and I'd feel guilty and still give in.

I shudder at the thought and decide to skip the guilt trip, quickly standing up and flicking off the television. "Damn, you don't play fair," I snap at her and stomp off to the bathroom to have a quick shower. "You better be buying the drinks. You know I hate spending money in those pretentious fucking clubs you drag me to with all those damn stuck up people you call friends." I think about the last time we went somewhere. The club was as pretentious and lame as her friends are, and we stood around with drinks in hand while she made catty comments about the rest of the patrons with her friends. I had never been so disappointed with her in my whole life. There are two very different sides to Max, and I really don't like the person she is when she's out with her socialite pals. She shows a side that I know is not her, that I know is all an act.

Maxine is what you would call uber-wealthy. She comes from old, established money and probably has every right to be as stuck up as the rest of the patrons, but her parents raised her to be down to earth and to work hard. There isn't usually a snobby bone in her body unless we're with her friends. Well, not too many, anyway. I'm hoping one day she'll come to realize her own worth and not measure herself against those assholes because if she was real, she'd win hands down.

Max's snort brings my attention back to her.

"Bah, if you didn't keep giving money to that crack whore who gave birth to you, you wouldn't have a problem. You know she's just going to snort it or shoot it up."

Closing the door to my bathroom, a bone weariness crosses my body at the thought of my mother. Never has she been responsible or even partly concerned about my welfare, but I still make sure she has a roof over her head, her bills are paid, and she has money for food. Though Maxine is right; most of the food money goes to drugs.

I peel off my dirty work clothes, leaving them where they fall, and turn on the shower. The bathroom's not huge and is slightly outdated with its tiles from the eighties when it was originally built and its mud brown vanity and sink. The shower cubicle has a curtain that I picked, covered in mermaids, and you would be hard pressed to fit another body in without it being a tight squeeze. But it's mine, and I don't have to share it with anyone, and that's all that matters. Hot steam fills the small bathroom, and I step under the sharp spray, groaning when the heat hits my body. I've been going since very early this morning and basically been in the saddle all day, and my body just isn't used to the grueling hours anymore. Being at college has made me soft, and today was the first day since I graduated that I didn't get a break from riding. Usually, it's only one or two horses a day, but Chuck had us going all day. He's got a few young ones that he's started breaking in basic riding, plus a few that he's been hired to train.

I'm just feeling so tired, and Max's throw away comment about my mother is hitting at nerves that are exposed due to the weariness. Standing there, with the water and steam blocking out the outside world, I give myself five minutes to wallow in sadness.

My mother used to be a personal assistant for Maxine's parents, and they were beyond thrilled when she announced her pregnancy at the same time as Melinda, Maxine's mom. I was an instant playmate for their daughter, and we lived on the estate, so we've been inseparable since birth.

Unfortunately, while pregnant with me, Mom fell in with the wrong crowd. After I was born, Maxine's parents kept her on for as long as they could, but by the time I'd turned two, she was doing hard drugs and not showing up for work. On the occasion she did, she stole from them to feed her habit. They let her go but allowed her to continue to drop me off to be looked after by the same nanny who looked after Maxine while she tried to keep one crummy job after the other. By the time I was five, she was permanently unemployed.

Moving from couch to couch of one sleazy boyfriend to the next or begging her druggie friends to give us a room for the night had child protective services stepping in when Melinda decided enough was enough. I was promptly removed from my mother's care and moved directly into Maxine's bedroom, with a perfectly pretty princess bed to call my own, and welcomed like I was one of them.

Melinda and Charles were everything a girl could want in foster parents, but the children at the schools they sent me to never let me forget where and what I had come from. Maxine was my staunchest supporter, but deep down, a simmering resentment brewed toward the one who should love me above all else; my mother. It wasn't until my late teens, when I did some lashing out of my own and Melinda and Chuck sent me to a therapist, that I came to realize that none of it was my fault. My mother had her own deep-seated issues and was way too selfish to be putting the well-being of a child before her own. That's on her, *not* me.

The one thing I'll always hold against her though is the fact that she would never tell me about my father. She would use the secret as a way to manipulate me, promising to tell me things in exchange for some favor or other, and one day I realized that every story was different every time, so nothing ever added up. That was when I decided she probably didn't know who he was and let go of the thought of ever being rescued. It wasn't long after that that I went to stay with Maxine permanently and tucked that dream down into the recesses of my soul. Mom's always been a stain on my life; on visitation nights, she would drag me down to whichever bar or strip club she was working in at the time, and I would sit in the corner, coloring while she tried to find her next fix. Later on, I discovered she was also finding her nightly meal ticket.

I never told Melinda or Chuck where we went; Mom, or Diane as I try to call her now, took care of that by threatening Maxine with harm if I ever told anyone. It wasn't until I was about fifteen and the men she was trying to score with started to hit on me, that she finally declared our fortnightly visits done with. I didn't see her for three years after that until I had finally graduated high school and was awarded a scholarship to the local university. By then, I was working for Melinda and Chuck on their horse farm and had been for years, being paid decent money. That's when the guilt trip came raining down, and I started paying her money to keep her away from Maxine and her family.

"Hey, what are you doing in there? You didn't fall asleep, did you?" A thump on the doors makes me jump even though I should've been expecting it. Maxine's patience has never lasted long.

Grabbing the soap, I shout back, "Sorry, I was daydreaming! I'll be fast." Making quick work of cleaning myself and my hair, I'm out and drying off when I hear her shout through the door again.

"I've put a dress on the bed. Wear it," she demands, and I groan to myself, but she must hear it. "No, don't complain! I know if I leave you to it, you'll throw on a pair of ripped jeans and a fitted shirt or something. We're *clubbing*, not heading down to the local bar." Sniggering to myself, I wipe the condensation away from the mirror and study my reflection. My skin is sun-kissed from all the time I spend outside, but, as yet, no fine lines are developing. I'm careful to religiously apply sunscreen if I'm going to be outside for any length of time. Using my towel, I rub at my natural sun-streaked blonde hair to stop it from dripping before wrapping it around my body. I grab out the blow dryer and blast the long length until it's almost dry before running a brush through it. It has the windswept tousled look, and I figure that's good enough. I put a hair tie around my wrist in case it gets too hot in the club, and I need to tie the whole lot up.

Unlike Maxine, I apply minimal makeup. Just some shadow, liner to my eyes to make the hazel stand out, and mascara to darken the blonde lashes. A bit of lipstick to my full lips and I'm good to go. Blowing myself a kiss in the mirror and rolling my eyes when Maxine shouts at me again to hurry up, I leave the bathroom in search of what horror she's placed out for me to wear.

Her text notification sounds while I'm stuffing myself into the tight blue number, and it's lucky my work is physical and I'm in great shape because there isn't an inch of my silhouette that this dress doesn't show off. But once it's on, the stretchy fabric allows easy movement, and I don't feel uncomfortable at all.

"That's the car," she tells me, looking up from her screen and giving me a wolf whistle. "Girl, you clean up hot."

Rolling my eyes, I grab my phone and hold it and my wallet up. "Where exactly am I supposed to put these?" I ask her sarcastically. "The dress doesn't have pockets. Why don't they make dresses with pockets? Designers really are letting the female species down."

This time she rolls her eyes. "Put the wallet down, you won't need it, and the phone, just shove it into the top of your dress. Lord knows those things are big enough to keep it safe." She points at my breasts which are looking fabulous in the dress, though she's exaggerating about the size. Really, they're just a little more than a handful for a man with average-sized hands.

Doing what she says, we head down the stairs to the waiting car. "Good evening, ladies," William's elderly voice greets us as we climb in. He's been the

Boston's driver for as long as I can remember and is in his late sixties.

I shoot Maxine a dirty look before replying to him, "William, what are you doing driving us this late? We could have called a cab."

Maxine scoffs at me before he can answer. "Bitch, don't get your nonexistent panties in a twist." My heart in my throat, I look down at my dress to make sure nothing is showing, and she laughs, winking at me before continuing. " I tried to, but he insisted on driving us. When we get there, he's going to return and go to bed, and we'll get a cab or an Uber home." She growls the last bit while looking at him in the rearview mirror.

Wisely, William just nods and smiles. "Of course, Miss Maxine."

He points the car in the direction of Hartford, and we get moving. Maxine has her phone in hand, and her fingers are moving furiously across the screen. "The gang's all there already," she tells me without looking up. "They can't wait to see us." I scoff and sit quietly as I watch the rural area roll by and slowly build up until we're traveling through the city. 'The Gang' are all kids we went to school with. Snobby rich kids who always treated me no better than the dirt at the bottom of their shoe, but Maxine mostly protected me from the worst of their petty bullying. These people are all connected somehow, through business mostly. It all seems so incestuous from the outside, it also means that Max never wants to rock the boat too much. She walked a fine line between being my friend and supporting me and not pissing off the children whose families move in the same social circles as the Bostons. Not that I think Melinda or Chuck would care either way; they have no tolerance for snobby bullshit, but their daughter doesn't know how to survive while adopting her parents' attitude.

William pulls the car up in front of a building glittering with spotlights and a line that stretches back around the block. A neon sign showcasing a horse head and palm trees with a martini glass in the middle is lit up with the words Club Neighpalm splashed across the front. I groan at the sight of that line and look down at the heels that Max made me wear. Unlike her five-inch, mine are slightly lower at about three inches, but I'm naturally taller than Max. I'm also not used to wearing them like she is. She spends an equal amount of time in boots or heels, whereas I try to go barefoot whenever I don't have on my boots. Either that or flip flops. The thought of standing in line for a long time has me questioning my decision to come.

We climb out of the car, thanking William, and he smiles and waves goodbye before driving back into traffic. I start to head toward the back of the line, but Max grabs me. "Where are you going?" she asks, looking confused.

"To the back of the line," I tell her, gesturing down the block.

She just shakes her head and mumbles, "It's like you don't even know me." Then she pulls me toward the door, giving our names to the big beefy bouncer who eyes us appreciatively before stepping aside to let us in.

"Ok," I concede, "I should have known better. How did you get us on the list?"

"You know my grandparents' besties, Grace and Howard?" she says as we walk through the quiet foyer.

"Nana and Poppy Summers?" I reply in confusion, thinking about the kind older couple that visit Nana and Grandpa Boston a couple of times a year.

Nana and Grandpa Boston, Chuck's parents, are an older, refined couple who I've always felt didn't agree with Melinda and Chuck taking in a stray junkie's daughter. They were never outwardly hostile, but they never went out of their way to make me feel like I was wanted.

Nana and Poppy Summers were the complete opposite. They filled a much-needed void when they visited the house. My mother's parents died before I was born, so I had no grandparent figures in my life, but every time they visited, they treated me as one of their own. Nana would bake with me or take me on excursions to museums and the zoo and things. Poppy would slip me candy and chocolate, and when I fell off my pony for the first time, he was the one who picked me up, brushed me off, dried my tears, and made me get back on. "You're not a successful horseman until you've fallen off at least a hundred times," he reassured me. They would always invite me to come and stay with them at their place in California, but that was the one thing I was never allowed to do. When Mom gave me up to Melinda and Chuck, she made them promise I would never be allowed to leave the state. Just another way to control and manipulate me throughout the years. Couldn't let her precious cash cow get too far away from her, and heaven forbid I have some fantastic experiences with the family that took me in, things she wasn't able to provide or down right didn't want to. She would tease me with this regularly.

"Yeah, this is one of their clubs. You know Neighpalm Industries is a huge family corporation, and they have an airline, hotels, record and movie studios, even an energy drink. This is the latest club to open, and they put us on the list when I asked them to. We also get to drink for free tonight. VIPs all night long." She does a little happy dance as we walk, and I shake my head at her, but an amused smile crosses my lips. I love seeing her let loose and not worry about social perceptions, so I savor each moment of 'my' Max until we get in front of her friends and that all changes.

We approach the large wooden doors that also have the Neighpalm logo on them. *Just in case anyone forgot who this club belongs to.* The thud of the music can only just be heard through them, the sound-proofing doing what it's supposed to. We stop, and Maxine turns to me, eyebrow raised, putting her hand on the door. "You ready for this?" Taking a deep breath, I add my hands to hers, and together we push open the heavy club doors and step into a pounding, hedonistic delight.

## Chapter Two

**Harlow**

The club is a sweating, heaving mass of bodies as we enter, practically straight onto the dance floor. We get swept up in the swell of people and find ourselves writhing around, surrounded by like-minded individuals. The smells of sweat and sex are heavy on the air, the flashing lights creating a disjointed, jarring atmosphere, and the smile that crosses my face is huge as I revel in the intoxicating feeling of letting go. It's always a struggle to get motivated to come to a place like this, but once I'm here, I love that the dance floor makes everybody equal. It doesn't matter where you come from or how much money you have. It's about letting go of all the superficial crap and moving with the rhythm.

Bodies are grinding on each other, hands either

in the air or exploring the person nearby. Nothing is inappropriate, just individuals enjoying each other and living for the moment. I let the atmosphere take me, my worries and cares slipping away. Throwing my head back and closing my eyes, I become one with the beat.

I don't know how much time has passed, but eventually, I see Maxine pull her phone out of her dress and look at the screen. She must have been summoned as she gestures to me, and I slowly follow her out of the crowd and up a flight of stairs after being vetted by the bouncer in front of the VIP area. Upstairs is another dance floor, this one a lot less crowded and looking a lot less free. Here it seems like they're dancing to be seen, not for the joy of letting go. It's why I always hate the VIP areas of these kinds of clubs. I want to be downstairs in the anonymous flow of fun-loving bodies, where it doesn't matter who you are or how much money you have. All anyone cares about is whether you have the stamina to go the distance.

But Max is my friend, my only friend really, and she has been there through thick and thin, so of course, I indulge her. *Who am I kidding? If anyone was ever my family, it's Max.* A long bar area and many booths fill the space, and it's within one of these that we find her group of friends. Everyone cheers when she arrives, greeting her enthusiastically and dragging her into the chaos, leaving me on the outside. A few wave and give me polite smiles, the guys mostly, but the girls outright snub me. I smile in return but don't engage. The guys aren't really interested in being my friend; they just hope that I'm easy and a chance to score tonight without much effort. My mother's reputation preceding me once again. Shrugging my shoulders, I head to the bar, passing a waitress with a fake smile heading for the booth. I would much rather order my own drink than have to listen to them be patronizing and rude to the staff. Not Maxine, she's better than that, but she doesn't ever tell her friends to cut it out when they behave like that, and that pisses me off. She knows they will turn on her quicker than she could blink, but fuck it would be nice if she finally stood up to those superficial assholes.

The bar area is through another door, sitting in a glassed-off area where you can still see the upper dance floor and booths, but the noise is significantly reduced; the glass must have noise-canceling properties. The air is much cooler too. I'd tied my hair up on the dance floor to get it out of the way, and I can feel the refreshing air blowing over the sweat-drenched tendrils at the base of my neck. The feeling instantly makes me feel better as I step up to the marble-topped bar and wait to be served by one of the bar staff. It doesn't take long as there aren't that many people standing here. It's a sign of status to opt for table service, so that's what most of these pampered princes and princesses prefer.

Turning, I lean against the bar and look back

through the glass at the VIP area. A small dance floor has a few people swaying back and forth, but their rhythm is off, and it's more about being seen than actually enjoying the music. There's a small mirror ball sparkling above, sending down little sparkles of light all over the wooden floor, and the area must not have a smoke machine because there's no haze in the air like downstairs. Snorting in amusement, I roll my eyes at the thought. I guess smoke would defeat the purpose of people being seen. Deep into the back of the room are numerous cozy, dark wooden booths with tables and deep green cushioned seats for a more intimate experience. I can see some of them are being used by couples for more seductive activities

"What can I get you?" A voice draws my attention, and spinning around, I find a dark-haired, eyeliner-wearing, nose-pierced goth boy waiting for me with a smile on his face.

"I'll have a bottle of water to start with and a Moscow Mule, please," I tell him, handing over the VIP card the bouncer gave us when we gave him our names to come upstairs.

"Sure thing, sexy." He winks flirtatiously at me and busies himself getting my order. He's cute, and I might be tempted to flirt back if I hadn't seen him winking at the person he had served before me. I guess if I had his job, and tips were a major part of my income, I'd be flirty too. Though it is nice to feel sexy. While I wait, I look back out toward the

section where Maxine is. Surrounded by her syco-
phantic friends, she appears happy and comfortable. Smiling then turning back around to wait for
my drink, a movement to my left draws my
attention.

"Wow, what a beautiful tattoo." The deep husky
voice is appreciative as his comment draws my eyes
to my full sleeve. From my shoulder to my wrist, I
have a black and white floral design with roses,
daisies, lilies, and a sunflower. There are a few
vibrant, eye-popping splashes of color here and
there in the form of butterflies amongst the flowers.
In my sleeveless dress, it's on full display, but I often
forget it's there. Smiling, I turn to thank the man
who complimented me, but my voice hitches when I
look into a pair of crystal blue eyes that seem to
glow in the dim light of the club. Mesmerized, I'm
caught in his gaze until, slowly, he blinks long dark
lashes, bringing me back to my senses. He has a
smile on his face as if he was waiting for me to say
something.

"Thank you," I reply, studying the gorgeous man
in front of me. He's taller than I am in my heels but
not by much. His midnight black hair is tousled and
looks like it could have a little wave in it, but it's not
long enough for me to tell for sure. Black stubble
crosses his strong jawline and surrounds his full lips,
but it seems like it's there because he forgot to shave
for a few days, not groomed to perfection. Sharp
cheekbones and a slightly crooked nose lends a

somewhat cavalier look to his otherwise pretty face. My eyes drift down his body. He looks fit; his dress shirt has the sleeves rolled up, showing his sexy tattooed forearms, and his tie is loosened at his neck, the blue shirt stretched across his chest. His black pants sit nicely on his hips, his belt drawing my eyes to his slender waist, but it gives me no hint of what might be underneath. An amused look is in his aquamarine eyes when mine drift back toward them, and I shake my head in embarrassment of my perusal.

"Sorry," I apologize sheepishly. "I can't even blame the alcohol since this is my first one," I tell him as the bartender puts my bottle of water and my Moscow Mule in front of me and hands back my VIP card.

He laughs indulgently, dimples appearing on both cheeks, as he steps closer toward me. "Don't apologize. I don't mind being eye fucked by a gorgeous woman." He waves his hand at the bartender, who nods and starts to prepare him a drink without him even saying anything.

"Is that a tattoo by a local artist? It's amazing work. My brother owns a tattoo studio and would be interested in having an artist who can produce that kind of quality."

My heart sinks a little with the line of questioning. I thought he was just using it as a pick-up line, but no, it seems like he's only interested in my ink. Of course he is, why would anyone actually be interested in me? I plaster a smile on my face and reply, "Yes, Tasha is a local artist. She works at Saint Ink here in Hartford, but I'm not sure if you'll be able to convince her to leave since her boyfriend owns the studio. I guess it wouldn't hurt to ask." My heart races at the thought that he may be interested in offering her a job.

Tasha and I got to know each other really well during the time it took to do my sleeve, and I've got a few more that are covered by my dress. She's probably the only other person that I would call my friend apart from Maxine. Unlike Max's need to fit in, Tasha is more like me. Career-driven and happy with her own company, though I think she has her own issues. I see the way her boyfriend treats her, and I would punch him in his junk if he was mine. Maybe we are more alike than I think in other ways, but we avoid any of that kind of personal talk like the plague. I don't say anything when it happens in front of me because I can tell by the fear in her eyes that it would make it worse for her. He's not only her boyfriend, but her boss, so until she decides she's had enough, all I can do is be there for her, with a few thinly disguised hints at getting another job. I regularly email her open positions, but she hasn't bothered to take any up. Maybe she's scared he may find out. I really wish I could help her more, and maybe this guy might be her way out. I pick up my water and Moscow Mule and give the guy a polite smile before heading back out to Maxine.

The noise of the club is an assault to the ears after such a peaceful break, and I think I've just about had enough of the VIP experience. Deciding I can't be bothered with her vapid friends today, I find a booth on its own tucked back into a corner, and I place my drinks down on the table before sliding in and letting out a breath. I think about sending Max a text to let her know where I am, but she's probably forgotten about me by now, and I wouldn't want to risk that she comes over to find me and brings her friends. This is perfect. Hidden back here, I'm sure it's free because you can't see or be seen, but that suits me just fine. I can just see the corner of the VIP dance floor, where Maxine and her friends have now moved to, but their movements are stiff and thought out. *Wouldn't want to be seen not giving a shit.* I roll my eyes in exasperation. For someone so confident, she does give in to societal norms with little to no fight.

I take a large gulp of my water before I start on my Mule. Taking a sip, I savor the tart bite of the vodka, lime, and ginger beer, and lean back against my chair. Once I finish this, I'm going to head back downstairs and join the masses; I deserve to enjoy my night out too.

"There you are." The husky voice can barely be heard above the music as the man from the bar slides into the booth next to me. The scent of his cologne, something spicy, tantalizing my senses. "I turned around to grab my drink, and when I turned back, you were gone."

"Oh, I thought you only wanted the information about my tattoo artist," I reply in surprise, and a shocked look crosses his face. Now it's my turn to blush again, realizing that I've gotten caught checking the guy out then accidentally snubbed him. *0 for 2, Harlow. Nice going.*

With a rueful smile, he runs a hand through his hair. "God, my flirting skills are rusty. I'm sorry I gave you that impression. I'm Jaxon." He holds his hand out, and I grasp it. It engulfs mine, but I can feel that our palms are similar, rough and bumpy with a few callouses. He must do some form of physical labor for work, a bit surprising coming from the man decked out in a suit at a nightclub.

Smiling, I introduce myself. "I'm Harlow. Don't worry about it; maybe it's my rusty social skills." I look to where Max is on the dance floor, hiding a grimace when I see that they're still acting like the perfect socialite robots. "I don't go out very often, and when I do, my friend Max seems to get all the attention." I gesture to where she's dancing with her group of friends on the dance floor.

He smiles, his eyes turning to where I'm waving, but they come right back to me, not even paying attention to the girls all grinding on each other, unlike many of the other men scattered around. "So what do you do, Harlow? What brings you out tonight?" I study him to see if he actually cares or if he's only trying to get into my pants, but he seems to be interested. He moves closer, and instead of letting go of my hand, he grips it a little tighter, and a tingle rolls through my body.

"I've just finished my last year at Tufts, and I also work on a horse farm." By now, most guys' eyes glaze over, but his smile only grows, making him damningly more handsome.

"Is that where these calluses come from?" he asks, grabbing one of my hands and running a thumb across the palm. I blush slightly. I know my hands are rough and not smooth and dainty. Surprisingly, he can see the faint glow on my cheeks in the dim light because he's quick to offer reassurance. "Don't be ashamed of working hard; I think it's sexy." He lifts my hand to his mouth, his eyelashes fluttering as he places a light kiss on my palm. My blush deepens, equal parts liking the attention and being slightly mortified by it.

"Well, your flirting skills just improved tenfold," I mumble, pulling my hand away, and his smile widens.

"Race horses or equestrian?" he asks as the burn in my cheeks fades.

"Actually, neither. We train them for movies," I tell him, taking another sip of my drink.

His eyes widen in surprise. "Wow. That sounds like fun. Is it dangerous?"

I shrug my shoulders. "It can be, but the people

I work for have been doing it for a long time now, so we have the process down. Sometimes you get a particularly stubborn horse, but patience and perseverance are the keys."

I start to ask him about himself, but before I can get a word out, a gleam enters his eye, and he blurts out, "Now tell me something that hardly anyone knows about you. Quick! Don't think too hard, the first thing to pop into your head."

"I watch a lot of abandoned building videos on YouTube," rushes out of my mouth before I can stop it. Again, my cheeks burn with embarrassment, and I quickly take another drink to hide it. *Fuck! Way to go, Harlow, let the hottie know how lame and weird you are.*

He looks a little confused, and the cutest furrow appears in his forehead when he raises an eyebrow. "I'm not sure what you're talking about. Will you explain it to me?" He smiles encouragingly at me, and I actually believe him. For reasons unknown, I start to feel a little more comfortable, trusting that I can tell him this silly part of me that even my best friend makes fun of. I put down my drink and pull my phone out of the top of my dress, his eyes lingering on where I removed it from, sending a thrill through my body. Opening the YouTube app, I show him the last video I was watching. He leans in close, and I catch another whiff of his intoxicating scent.

"There are these videographers that go around

and explore abandoned buildings. Sometimes it's a house, and sometimes it's hospitals or factories and even amusement parks. They're places people have just up and abandoned for whatever reason. I find it fascinating that there are people who can do that or would do that, and I know this sounds silly, but I feel sorry for the buildings. Just left abandoned, not even cared about enough to clean them up and sell them, sometimes not enough even to clear them out."

The words rush out of my mouth in one go, barely time to take a breath. When I peek up at him, he's looking back at me thoughtfully, but there's no pity or mockery in his eyes even though after that little rant he must realize that maybe I'm a little bit more sensitive than most. The look in his eyes is completely understanding. That he too may know what it feels to be abandoned. Shaking my head, I turn my phone off and shove it back in the top of my dress.

A wicked gleam enters his eye as he leans closer and wiggles his eyebrows suggestively. "Your phone is very lucky." The awkward tension is broken instantly with his silly behavior, and I give his juvenile comment a juvenile reaction by sticking my tongue out at him. We sit quietly after that, talking about nothing particular. It's comfortable, and I find myself leaning into him, relaxing as we sip our drinks, my foot tapping along to the music. He sees it and offers me a hand. "Would you like to dance?"

"Over there?" I ask, nodding toward the VIP dance floor, and he nods, so I shake my head, screwing up my nose. "No, thanks, that's not my kind of dance floor."

A relieved look crosses his face, and he runs a hand through his hair, messing it up slightly and giving him a just out of bed look. "Oh, thank God, me neither. Would you like to go downstairs?" I look at him in wonder, and he must see the surprise because a teasing smile curls his lips.

"Just because I like to drink in peace and quiet doesn't make me a snob." He stands up, grabbing my hand, and a thrill of excitement runs through me. "Leave the drinks. Nobody will touch them, and we can always get fresh ones later."

Tugging on my arm, I stumble after him. He seems to be in a hurry, getting through the crowded VIP area without stopping to talk to the people who quite obviously know him if the shouts of "hello" are anything to go by. *Who is this guy?* Max raises an eyebrow then shoots me a thumbs up, mouthing, "Get it, girl" as we go past. She puts her hand to her ear in the universal "Call me" sign, so I just nod before turning and following Jaxon down the stairs. From the back, his ass is spectacular. Rounded and defined, perfect for sinking your teeth into. If he can dance as well as he looks, he might be worth a night of fun.

He pulls me into the writhing mass, elbowing his way through until he finds a spot that must be dead center. The smell of sweat and sex fills the air as the smoke drifts lazily around. The strobe lights flickering on and off create a disjointed atmosphere, bodies flowing around us, the pulsing beat sending vibrations up through the floor and into my body. He pulls me in, my back to his front, and we start to move with the rhythm. The seamless way our bodies fit and move together blows my mind. We sway and grind in time to the music, his hands on my hips, his breath in my ear—a shiver of desire spikes down my spine to my core. The two of us flow together almost as one, and I'm kind of amazed to have found someone who fits with me so well. Bringing up my arm, I loop it around his neck. One of his hands wraps around my waist and runs lazy circles on my stomach, stoking the flames of desire higher. It's like we're in our own little bubble; the music is still present, guiding our bodies, but the rest of the world is fading away until all focus is brought to each of the places where we touch. The sexual tension between us is palpable as his mouth starts to nibble on my neck, and his hand drifts lower. I can feel the bulge in his pants rubbing against my lower back, so I grind back on it, and his breath hitches slightly. We stay like that for what seems like hours, no words, just complete synchronicity through movement, something I've never felt before with any other person I've been with.

Eventually, he turns me to face him, and we

stop. Both of us breathing heavily from the dancing and the sexual tension, he slowly runs his hand up to cup my cheek. Leaning in, he places a gentle kiss on my lips like he's testing the waters, but I am way too far gone for that and yank him against me hard, my mouth crashing against his, and we become a frenzy of hands, lips, and tongues, wrestling for dominance. A groan leaves my mouth; his leg rubs against my pussy as he tugs me harder against his thigh. I spent my college years having one night stands, avoiding the pitfalls and demands of relationships, but it's been a while, and I'm looking forward to where this may lead.

A voice shouting "Get a room!" finally drags us apart from each other. He grabs my hand and pulls me out of the crowd toward the exit. I stumble a couple of times, and he slows down and steadies me by wrapping his arm around me. We've almost made our way to the double doors of the exit when I think I hear my name shouted. Turning to look, I see Maxine chasing after us, a worried frown on her face and her phone in her hand. Stopping, I tug on Jaxon's hand to make him wait, promptly leaning down to check in with me. "I'll go get us a taxi," he whispers in my ear, and I nod my head in agreement. He disappears through the doors as I wait for Maxine to catch up.

She's breathing heavily when she gets to me. She looks rattled, and Maxine usually isn't fazed by much, so I'm instantly concerned. "I just got a message from Dad. He's asked us to come home right away." My heart starts to beat wildly as we push through the outer doors together.

"Is it Melinda?" She shakes her head, a little bit of panic leaving her eyes although the frown is still present.

"No, he said Mom's fine but wouldn't tell me anything else." We pass the bouncer on the way out, and he nods to us as we enter the street. The line for the club is still huge, and people are milling about looking for late-night transport. Maxine is on her phone, probably ordering an Uber, when I spot Jaxon waving at me from next to a cab. I rush over to him, disappointment forming a lump in my stomach that's only made worse by the suspense of not knowing what has Chuck so upset.

"I have to go; we've got a family emergency. She's just getting an Uber," I tell him, pointing to Max.

"Oh no, I'm sorry. Here, take this one then." The disappointment in his eyes matches how I feel, the brilliant color of his gaze seeming to dim. My desire to get home outweighs my need to be polite, and I take his offer gratefully.

"Thank you." Waving to Max, I gesture to the cab, and she quickly hurries over, canceling her Uber as she does. She smiles gratefully at Jaxon and slides in, her worry overruling her usual politeness.

Kissing him on the cheek, I tell him, "I've had a great time. Maybe we can do it again sometime."

Not waiting to hear his response in case he doesn't want a repeat, I follow her into the cab, and he closes the door before it speeds off. Turning to look out the back window, I watch him standing there, hands in his pockets and a sad look on his face as he fades into the distance.

Suddenly, a thought occurs to me. "Fuck! I didn't get his number." I bang my head against the cab window in disappointment. We didn't talk much, but I'd felt an instant connection with him, a soul-deep kind of link, and the sexual attraction was off the freaking charts. A change of undies is the first thing I'm going to need when we get home.

"I'm sure you'll see him again at the club if we go back." Understandably, Max is all kinds of distracted as she checks her phone for more messages from her dad.

"Yeah. Maybe," I reply, but deep down, I know the likelihood is slim.

## Chapter Three

**Harlow**

**M**ax and I sit up straight when we see the flashing blue and red lights reflecting off the landscape as the taxi drives down their long, tree-lined driveway. The horses in the front paddocks are agitated and nervous, running back and forth along the fence line and kicking up a fine plume of dust that floats like mist in the still, dry night. Light shines through the windows of the house as Maxine pays the driver and we jump out, hurrying up the steps of their home. She pushes open the front door, calling out, "Mom, Dad, where are you?"

"We're in the kitchen." Melinda's voice echoes down the long hallway to the entrance. We hurry in that direction, our heels clicking on the hardwood floors, building the tension in my body. A soundtrack to impending bad news, as what else can a police car at this time of the night mean?

The smell of brewing coffee is strong as we enter the kitchen, and Maxine throws herself at her mom and dad, giving them big hugs. While they're doing that, I study the two police officers sitting at the breakfast bar, coffee mugs in front of them.

"The horses are going crazy out there. Could one of you turn the lights off in the police car?" I ask them, gesturing back toward the front. "I don't want any of them getting injured."

The female officer pushes back her chair. "Of course, sorry, didn't even think to turn them off before we came in," she apologizes. Her standard-issue boots are quiet as she returns to the front of the house to fix the lights. Hopefully, the horses will settle now.

Chuck leaves Melinda and Maxine, whispering to each, and walks over to me, pulling me into a hug. "Good thinking, Harlow. I didn't even realize, and I guess the guys must be out for the night." He's talking about the two stablehands and the foreman that work for him, as well as Maxine and myself. "Take a seat, love." He ushers me onto one of the stools before taking one next to me. "They need to ask you some questions." My heart starts to pound in my chest, and a sick feeling develops in my stomach.

"Me? What's this about?" I ask the remaining

officer. He's older, probably about the same age as Chuck, and he has kind but tired eyes.

"Thank you for returning so quickly. I'm Detective Brown, and this is my partner Detective Jones," he says as the female officer returns to the kitchen. She sits down in front and flips open a notepad, giving me a small nod hello. I return it before looking back at Detective Brown.

"Are you Harlow Stubbs, daughter of Diane Stubbs?" At this question, a wave of anger flows through my body.

Snorting in disgust, I reply, "Yes, what's that woman done this time?"

The two officers look to each other before Detective Brown responds, "When was the last time you saw Diane?"

It's not hard for me to remember the last time I saw her, my back stiffening at the memory, my whole body on alert like it always is when I see her. "She showed up at the farm one morning two weeks ago, smelling of cigarettes and booze and high as a kite with her latest fuckboy. She wanted money." Melinda's gasp of dismay has me turning to face her and Maxine. "I gave her some cash I had and sent her on her way."

"Harlow, honey, we've told you to tell us when she does that," Chuck admonishes me gently while wrapping an arm around my shoulders in comfort.

"That was the day the director for that new movie was coming to check out the horses. I didn't want her to cause a scene," I tell him. "She would've taken any chance to score some more money. You would have paid her to go away, and she knew that."

"And you haven't seen her since then?" the detective asks.

I shake my head. "No, she hasn't been back since. Why are you asking this?"

"I'm sorry to tell you this, Harlow, but your mother was found dead late this afternoon. We think it was from an overdose, but we're waiting on an autopsy." I should feel surprised at this announcement, but I'm not. This news is something that I've been expecting for as long as I knew who and what my mom really was. I just figured this was the way she would always end up, and it was a matter of time before I was in the position I am now. I look around the room, and I can see tears in Maxine and Melinda's eyes, and Chuck rests a hand on me in comfort.

I'm not sure how I'm supposed to react. I think I'm supposed to feel sad, but all I feel is relief. Like a huge weight is lifted off me. Like I don't always have to be looking over my shoulder for her to pop up unannounced. She abandoned me years ago, but finally, it will be permanent. I'm just glad she won't be causing trouble for me anymore.

"Um, okay, do I need to do anything?" The officers look to each other in surprise at my reaction, and I feel defensive all of a sudden, this automatic need to protect myself. "Don't you judge me. You have no clue what the woman has put me through over the years. You don't know my situation; you don't get to look surprised. You don't get to judge me."

They both fidget a little under my gaze, exchanging glances and generally looking uncomfortable at me calling them out. Detective Brown nods after a moment. "Yes, you're right. I apologize." Detective Jones nods her agreement, looking a little ashamed. He continues. "We need someone to come down and identify the body. Could you do that for us? There's also a matter of cleaning out her trailer." The numbness gives way to annoyance. Even in death, she still causes problems.

"Just trash everything; she has nothing that I want," I tell them in a rush of words and anger.

Both officers give me sympathetic looks, but Detective Jones has a note of steel in her voice. "We understand that, but the trailer park owner will not take responsibility for it, and, well, it's better if a family member goes through their personal items."

Melinda walks over and hugs me, and I sink into her embrace, her maternal comfort a warm welcome to my numb soul. "I'm so sorry, baby girl. At one time, I considered her one of my closest friends. I always hated not being able to help her in any way. I tried; she just wasn't interested in it. Let me help you with this. In fact, we'll all help. Chuck can go with you and identify the body with the coroners, and Maxine and I will head over to the trailer and get started. You can join us there when you're finished. We'll have everything dumped, so it's done. Nothing to worry about."

Both detectives stand up. "Again, we're sorry for your loss and thank you for cooperating. We'll see you tomorrow morning," Detective Brown says, and Detective Jones nods her head once more. They both thank Melinda for their coffees and disappear with Chuck down the hallway. Their voices fade the further they go.

Maxine pulls up one of the stools they vacated and grabs my hand.

"Are you okay? Do you want to talk about it?" she asked me quietly. Shaking my head, I squeeze her hand in thanks.

"No, not really, but kind of." Amusement fills her eyes at my indecisiveness, not a normal experience for me. My childhood being so chaotic has made me into someone who likes to be in control. "Am I a bad person because I don't feel sad? All I feel is guilt. Guilt because I *don't* feel sad or upset."

"Oh, Harlow. You have no reason to feel guilty or sad. She burned those bridges many, many years ago." A tear trickles down Maxine's face. "You've got to let it go; you've got to let her stop bothering you. None of that woman's choices were yours. Nor is it your fault. Her lack of backbone and total disregard for anyone else was all on her." She pulls me to my feet, wrapping an arm around my shoulder. "Come on, you can stay in my room tonight. Let's go and get some sleep; you've got shit to do tomorrow."

Wishing Melinda good night, we both head upstairs to Maxine's bedroom. Silently, I remove the makeup from my face and climb into a spare pair of pajamas Maxine laid out for me. The familiar routine is a comfort to my chaotic thoughts, the reminder of more pleasant times when we were still kids and I had finally been taken away from that woman. This was my first place of security, my bed in the room that Maxine and I shared so many years ago. The feelings of finally having a place to belong and to feel wanted soothe my raw emotions.

Sliding into her big bed, I stare at the ceiling, jumbled thoughts running through my head like a screenplay of memories. Thoughts of my mother don't bring me smiles or feelings of joy. Instead, they bring heartbreak and remind me of what it feels like to go hungry and to worry if I'm safe in my bed at night. No, memories of Diane are more like nightmares, and her death feels like I'm finally free.

The next morning, Chuck drives me to the police precinct. We're met there by Detectives Brown and Jones, who escort me into the coroner's lab and a viewing area. The smell of death and antiseptic permeates the room, something I'm familiar with having done pathology labs at my university, and the temperature is cold; a wave of goosebumps appears on my arms. I'm led to a window facing into the morgue where a body can be seen on a table covered by a white sheet.

"Are you ready for this?" Detective Jones asks me quietly. Her voice is tinged with sympathy, and I'm torn. That guilt comes roaring back, reminding me that *I* should be the one upset right now, but there's also a little relief that this is almost over. I nod my head, and she waves her hands to the scrub-clad tech standing next to the table. Leaning down, they pull back the white sheet to expose the face of the body. With detached feelings, I study the person shown to me. My mother wasn't quite twenty-one when she had me, which makes her not quite forty-seven now, but looking at the face in front of me, you can see life hasn't been kind. Lines and divots where the drugs have eaten away make her look closer to sixty. Her skin is sallow and pale, sunken cheeks giving her a skeletal look; she must have resembled the corpse she now is in life as well —the weeks since I've seen her have obviously not been good.

"Yes, that's my mother, Diane Stubbs," I confirm out loud for the detectives. Nodding his head, Detective Brown gestures for the tech to cover her back up.

"Is there anything else you need from me?" I asked the detectives.

"If you just come with us, we can hand you over the personal effects she had on her and sign a few documents so you can be on your way." Detective Brown gestures back toward the front of the precinct.

After signing a few documents, they hand me a set of keys to her trailer. "These were on her body when she was found. Her clothes are being kept as evidence in case, but there was no sign of foul play, and the coroner confirms that she died from a massive overdose of heroin."

I frown at the statement. "Really? I would have thought someone used to doing drugs would have enough experience to not accidentally overdose."

Detective Brown shrugs. "Sometimes it's because they've built up a tolerance, and only a bigger hit will help them achieve the high. Sometimes it's a bad batch of drugs. Unless someone comes forward with some other information, we can only go on what we've found."

Nodding my head, I thank them both, waving off their directions to call them if I have any issues with the trailer park owner. Chuck has been quiet but supportive throughout the whole process, and he wraps an arm around my shoulders as we leave the police precinct.

"I'm really sorry, Harlow. Your mom used to be such a bright, bubbly, giving person, and I'm so sorry you never got to see that. And I'm sorry that you have to do this now." I bump my hip against his and rest my head on his shoulder, a silent thanks for his support. He knows I'm not emotionally capable of much more and doesn't push me. Sharing my feelings has always been very difficult for me, and it's taken a lot of therapy to get me to a place where I don't automatically flinch when I do, anticipating the hit that was always bound to follow when I made the mistake of voicing an opinion to Diane.

He drives me over to the trailer park where Melinda and Maxine are waiting for me in front of my mother's home. The front of the park is full of cheery, well-looked-after mobile homes that have little gardens and white wooden fences around them. People living at the front take pride in the appearance of their homes. As you drive further on, that changes. The homes get older, the painted fences turn to wire and are falling down, and the grassed yards are dirt patches littered in old furniture or cars. Hopping out of the car, I study the surrounding area. The trailers aren't in good condition, and the people keep to themselves, everyone minding their own business. No point in starting something that might get you dead.

Mom's mobile home is one of the worst-kept of

the lot. The steps are sagging, and weeds are pushing up between the gaps in the boards. Her screen door is hanging by a hinge, and the siding is faded and cracked.

Stepping carefully up the steps, I put the key into the lock, but the door just swings open. Bracing myself for what's to come, I step in. The smell is horrendous, and I can hear Melinda and Maxine behind me gagging in disgust. My cheeks tingle with embarrassment, but I take a deep breath and turn around, looking at them. The horrified grimaces on their faces have me snorting. They're both dressed in jeans and boots and have gardening gloves in their hands. Both are used to outdoor work, but they have never struggled for anything in their lives. And even though the Bostons are generous to a fault with charities, they never really see the causes they donate to. This way of living is an eye-opener to them.

"Just be careful. Don't stick your hands into places you can't see; she was terrible at disposing of needles." Their eyes widen in shock, and my cheeks almost heat in a blush of embarrassment. I appreciate their support, but I also would've been happy to never expose them to this facet of my life. "There's probably nothing salvageable; well, there wasn't when I was visiting here. The only place I'm interested in is her bedroom. I was never allowed in there."

They nod their heads, and we walk through the

doorway. The silence is deafening as we look around the trailer. Really, that term is too generous. It's a trash heap. My mood sinks even lower as I study the squalor my egg donor and incubator was living in. At least when I visited, I would clean it. Now, dishes are jammed into the sink. Ashtrays are full of cigarette butts. The trash can in the kitchen is overflowing, and there are empty, dirty take-out containers on every surface. The only sofa is sagging, ripped, and covered in dubious stains. The faucet in the sink is leaking, and the water dripping against the metal is hypnotic in the silence. Drip...drip....drip. The sound of a car backfiring makes me jump and brings my attention back to the front yard.

"Let's get this done before the locals pay too much attention to us."

Shaking off my disgust and melancholy, I step forward, and the floor sags, causing the trailer to shudder and mice to scatter out from under furniture. Melinda screams and hauls ass out of the door. She can't deal with the mice on the farm either.

"I'll call the guys for help removing everything and speak to the owner about dumping the furniture," she shouts back over her shoulder.

Maxine and I laugh as she hurries in the opposite direction. My mother's trailer is not big; it only has one bedroom, a small bathroom, and the living area/kitchen we just stepped into. There is absolutely nothing I want to keep. She's never had any personal items, and the few things in the kitchen are chipped and broken. As far as I'm concerned, it can all go in the trash. We just have to haul it there.

I turn toward the bedroom, intending to go forward, but then stop. A nervous feeling sits at the bottom of my stomach. I'm worried about what we might find, but I'm also worried that there isn't anything to find, and I have my hopes up again. Maxine bumps my hip, knowing me well enough to notice how I'm feeling. "Come on, let's get this done." Smiling gratefully, I follow her into my mother's bedroom.

## Chapter Four

**Harlow**

My mother's bedroom is just as bad as the rest of the trailer. Barely bigger than the double bed it contains, there's an overfull ashtray on the upside-down milk crate beside the bed and what looks like a drug pipe and lighter as well. The musty, sweaty, sour smell brings on more nose wrinkling from the both of us. Suspicious stains spread across the bed sheets that have seen better...decades. "Don't sit down anywhere," I warn her.

"Eww, wasn't planning on it." I can feel my cheeks redden in embarrassment again, and she sees it. Max grabs me by the arms, shaking me in frustration. "Stop it! Stop feeling responsible, or guilty, or ashamed, or whatever it is you're feeling. Nothing that woman did was your fault." She's right, and I hate it. I'm feeling all of those and more. Nodding, I look around and find a small sliding door that must be her closet, and I gesture to it.

"Can you start pulling things out of there? There's not enough room over there for both of us, so put everything on the bed, and I'll go through it. Then, we'll flip the mattress and see what's under the bed." Maxine starts pulling out all my mother's clothes. Half of them wouldn't properly cover a twelve-year-old, let alone a grown woman, but she has slowly withered away into a shadow of her former self, so I may be wrong. One thing's for sure, for someone who always cried poor, my mom has a lot of clothes. Nothing we can donate, though, unless it's going to Strippers-R-Us.

"So who was that hottie last night?" Maxine asks, shooting me a cheeky grin. "Don't think I didn't notice that I lost you as soon as we went upstairs."

I scoff at her. "Your friends are douchebag snobs. Why would I want to hang out with them?" She stops pulling clothes out of the closet, her lips thinning.

"No, they're not," she says quietly. "Have you ever thought it's you who doesn't give them a chance?"

Now it's my turn to get angry, and I hold some of it back, letting loose just enough to be honest without going too far. "I did in the beginning. I was nice to the catty girls and friendly to the guys, but when the guys constantly hit on me, and the girls got bitchy and territorial, I stopped. I was dealing with enough in my life without having to deal with that as well. You know this, we've talked about it before. Just accept it, okay? Why do you need me to like them?"

I grab a handful of clothes and carry them out of the room to where I hear Melinda out front. Outside, she has a heap of boxes, and the ranch's truck has pulled up with a trailer on the back. Chuck climbs out with Luke and Peter, two of the farmhands, in tow. I dump my armload of clothes in one of the boxes at Melinda's feet and hurry back inside. Peter and Luke have always been polite to me, but I think they see me as competition for their jobs, and I often catch Luke looking at me with undisguised lust. It freaks me out; he gives me weird creeper type vibes, and I often find him in the stables under my apartment when he has no reason to be there, so I avoid them as much as possible. I'm also incredibly embarrassed for them to see where I came from, so I'll just let Melinda give them instructions.

Rushing back into the bedroom, I see Maxine has the closet wide open and everything spread out on the bed. She looks up as I walk in, and now it seems that it's her turn to flush, red splotches on her cheeks betraying her own embarrassment. "I'm sorry. I know you're right, but I hate that you are."

Waving my hand, I shake my head. "Don't be. It is what it is, and I'm used to it. I'm happy with my own company, and I have you and Tasha if I need her. I'm used to being alone."

"Yeah, but I'm such an asshole for forcing them on you all the time. I'm sorry. You shouldn't have to be used to being alone." She's in such a state she sinks down onto the bed, not realizing what she's doing.

"I've been such a bad friend all of these years, but you don't realize how cruel they can be." I snort unbelievably at these words, and she immediately looks a little sheepish. "Well, maybe you do, but you know I hate confrontation. I've just learned to over-look their bad behavior in an attempt to fit in. I don't know how you can continue to be my friend." I'm not ready to dig into such a deep subject with her on top of everything else that's going on, so I wave her off for now and gesture to where she's sitting.

"Ewww, oh my god!" she screeches, just like my barn owl, and jumps up, rubbing at her clothes and gagging slightly. I snort again in amusement, her actions breaking the tension.

Looking at the remaining items, I consider going through the clothes and shoes and checking the pockets but figure anything of value would have been pawned a long time ago. "Can you go and grab a box from your mom? We'll put the rest of this crap in it, and it'll make it easier to take to the dumpster. I don't want to go out there; Peter and Luke are here."

A knowing look crosses her face, and she squeezes by me to do as I ask. Leaning against the wall, I blow out a huge breath, looking around. The warmth of a tear trickles down my cheek, but I wipe it away with the back of my hand. Pushing all the feelings down to examine later, I stand up and gather all the clothes together. Voices travel through the central area of the trailer now as they start to shift things outside.

"Fuck, this is *not* livable. They might as well set it on fire; no one will want to rent it," Luke's nasally voice exclaims in disgust. Little does he know the trailer park has a waitlist even for properties like this.

Maxine comes back with the box, and we start to pack things away. "So, you still never told me about the hottie from last night."

I laugh. *I knew she would come back to it.* "Wow, nosy much?" I tease her.

She growls at me, "Since when have you kept secrets?"

I look at her in surprise, knowing she likely meant to tease me but finding her words are hitting a bit of a painful spot instead. "When was the last time we talked about guys or anything other than training schedules for horses? I love you, Max, and you're my best friend, but we don't do much together anymore, apart from work.

We're always too busy to talk about anything else."

She stops what she's doing and looks like she's really thinking about it until a devastated look crosses her face. "Oh shit, Harlow. I'm sorry. You just always project the image of being okay by yourself. You're like an island that no one can breach." I flinch at the description and shrug nonchalantly, hiding how I really feel. It hurts that she sees me that way, but I don't let her see it. I perfected this mask a long time ago, having learned that I couldn't rely on anyone but myself.

"Anyway, his name was Jaxon. He was friendly, funny, and sexy, and boy, he had moves that made my heart pound. But that was then, and this is now. I didn't even get his number, and it's not like I plan on going back to the club. Even if I did, what are the chances I would see him again?"

"I could ask around? I'm sure someone knows who he is. A lot of my friends saw you two head downstairs. What did he say he did? Maybe we can find him through his work."

I think about it, wracking my brain for any detail that might help. "You know, I don't think either of us said what we did. I mean, we talked about me working with horses, but I didn't tell him I was a vet. It just didn't seem important at the time. Leave it be. If it was meant to be, it would've happened," I tell her even though deep down I'm really disappointed that I forgot to get his number and that I've only got myself to blame. I think I subconsciously believed he couldn't possibly be interested, so I didn't make that effort to get his number.

After she drops the subject, we make quick work of putting all the clothes and shoes in the boxes. She carries them back out to the front yard before returning. Looking at the bed, I shudder to think what's underneath it. "You ready?" She hands me a dust mask and slips one on her face before nodding. We go around to the far side of the bed and flip the mattress off toward the door, our faces already stuck in grimaces behind our masks. A few cockroaches scurry for shelter, and the dust is about an inch thick, but apart from a few odd socks and an empty syringe, the only thing sitting under the bed is a shoebox.

"Huh? That was a bit anticlimactic. I was expecting all sorts of illicit things, maybe a sex toy or two," Maxine muses, and I screw my nose up in disgust before smirking at her.

"I guess I was due for a little luck." I step between the wooden slats and reach down to grab the shoebox. Putting it under my arm, I make my way carefully back toward the door blocked by the mattress.

"Come on, let's shove this out of the way and get out of here. I'm just going to pay someone to clean it out."

I go out and tell the others my plans, and

honestly, they all look relieved. Melinda is so happy to get out of here that she tells me to leave it to her. She'll make some calls to get it done. The woman has a well-developed network and can usually get most tasks done with just a few quick calls, so I'm sure this will be no different. The guys leave everything where it is but grab the few boxes of clothes and tell us they'll drop it in the dumpster on the way out of the park. Luke's eyes are on me the whole time, but I pretend not to see him, instead thanking Chuck and giving him a hug before he leaves along with the other two. Maxine, Melinda, and I hop into Max's car and head home. I think they both realize I need some space because the drive back to the farm is silent, with only the radio playing quietly in the background.

I have so many thoughts running through my head and can't even latch onto one. The shoebox is burning a hole in my lap with the need to open it, but if all it contains are the drugs and sex toys that Max was expecting, I'm going to lose my shit. Surely, there must be more to my mother than illegal activities and neglect. Surely, she once had something she cared about apart from where she was going to get her next fix, something like *me*. She must have once, right? There must be some kind of proof of this, and this shoebox is all that is left.

I guess I have more issues than I thought because her death is affecting me more than it should. Not liking the roads that these feelings might bring me down, I definitely add a possible return to therapy to my mental to-do list. Unexpectedly, a song on the radio draws my attention, and I lean forward, breaking out of my mental whirlwind. "I love this song. Can you turn it up?" Max presses a few buttons, and Sanctuary of Chaos' latest song blasts through the radio, the lead singer's husky, sultry voice singing of lost love and finding it again. The three of us sing along, belting out the words as we make our way home.

Although it's only just lunchtime, we all have a glass of wine in hand while Melinda's housekeeper makes us something to eat. The shoebox is sitting on the dining room table, and Melinda and Maxine keep shooting glances at it. I know they're both impatient to know what's in it, but the longer I put it off, the longer I can stave off more disappointment. Max's fingers drum on the wooden table with impatience, Melinda taking frequent sips of her wine, and it's not long before the latter reaches for the bottle to top up her glass. Before too long, Sherry, the housekeeper, places salads in front of us, and we start to eat, both of them staring at the box as if they're afraid it will disappear if they take their eyes off it.

I snort at their behavior, and Melinda startles, shaking her head as if to clear her thoughts. "Harlow, it's okay, honey. You don't have to open it now." Her voice is gentle as she tries to reassure me. I pick at the salad in front of me before putting my fork down and leaning back.

"God, I should be used to all of this. I should be used to this woman disappointing me and resenting her. Every time you guys went on an overseas trip and she wouldn't sign for me to get a passport, every time one of her sleazy boyfriends hit on me, every time she would turn up for money. I *hated* her. There was absolutely nothing about her that I liked, and I don't have a single happy moment to remember her by. She spent her life disappointing me, yet here I am, too scared to open a shoebox because I'm afraid she's going to disappoint me again."

"Redemption," Maxine whispers. I raise an eyebrow in question, and she continues. "In the past, there was always a chance she would clean herself up and beg for your forgiveness. But that's gone now."

What she says hits me hard. Maxine's right. Diane, *Mom*, is gone permanently, and I will never get that storybook moment of redemption and forgiveness. A tear trickles down my face, and I wipe it away again. Standing up, I move my plate to the side and pull the box toward me, praying I'm not about to find my dead mother's vibrator.

"Here, give it to me," Maxine demands. "I'll open it." Breathing a sigh of relief, I pass the box to her and brace myself for the inevitable. She yanks off the lid and stares inside, a puzzled look on her face.

"Huh, not sex toys," she says, almost disappointed, which brings a small smile to my face. She hands the box over, and I look down. There are a couple of pictures of my mom and a really handsome guy. Both seem to be in their early twenties, and they're smiling and happy. In one, the guy has his arms wrapped around my mom, kissing her forehead, a sunset in the background. The other, they're sitting with a group of friends, her on his lap, in a restaurant or bar. I can see Chuck with Melinda on his lap in the background. The guy looks relaxed and happy too, but he's unrecognizable to me, so no one I've ever met before. He's got shaggy blond hair with a full beard and is dressed in beach casual in shorts and t-shirt with flip flops on his feet. He looks like a surf bum, fit and athletic.

She looks so… *healthy* and so much like me. She has long, straight, blonde hair. It's almost down to her ass, and it's washed and vibrant. Her face is full, and there's a sparkle in her eyes. I don't know this woman. I've never known this woman. Placing the photos down, I pull out the next piece of paper, realizing it's a birth certificate. Mine, more specifically, and in the space for Father is a name. *Bradley Cole.*

My heart starts to race. Holy shit, she actually knew who my father was and didn't tell me. And obviously, he didn't know. Or maybe he did, but he didn't want me. My anger at her increases until I'm shaking so hard the paper in my hand is vibrating.

"What is it?" Melinda asks, the concern in her voice making it sound like one of her usual demands. I pass her the photo and certificate, kind of happy to get them out of my hands before I can tear them up so that I can go back to the ignorance I've lived in my entire life.

"She knew," I grind out between closed teeth. "She knew and didn't tell me who he was or anything. Does he know and not want me, or did she keep me from him too, like the spiteful bitch she was?"

Looking up, I can see the sympathetic look on Max's face, but Melinda has turned pale, and a gasp escapes her mouth. Like a cold splash of water, her reaction stops my anger in an instant.

"That bitch!" she snarls, a thunderous look crossing her face. Max and I look at her in surprise, our mouths simultaneously falling open. Nothing about this moment is typical for Melinda. She stands up quickly, eyes darting between us.

"I'll tell you everything I know, Harlow, I promise, but first I need to ask Chuck something." With that, she takes the two photos and my birth certificate and hurries from the room.

"What the fuck was that about?" I ask Max, and she shrugs her shoulders.

"Mom obviously knows something, and right

now, I'm pretty sure if your mom was still alive, mine would be wrapping her hands around her skinny little throat and squeezing." She looks to where Melinda disappeared, and I shudder.

I don't think I've ever seen Melinda that angry. Even when she caught us drunk after that party in our junior year of high school, she was more resigned than angry. She's always been the kind of mom that was disappointed instead of angry, and this fiery part of her is something we've always been spared. "She's scary," I whisper, and Max's eyes are wide as she nods her head in agreement.

"Dude, my mom would totally take your junkie whore mother." That eases the tension, and I laugh.

"I don't know about that; that junkie had some power behind her fist, and when she was jonesing for a fix, she was downright ugly mean." Shame and embarrassment cross Max's face at the reminder of what I dealt with, but again I shrug it off. "Look, if I'm going to try and push away any guilt that I might be feeling, you've got to try to. It's all in the past, and you getting sad every time it's bought up does neither of us any good. Anyway, I was much better off with you guys than I would have been with her, and I wouldn't change a thing."

My nerves and anxiety kick in as we wait for her to return, different ideas flowing through my mind. "Do you think the guy in the photos is my dad?"

She shakes her head, but everything in her face

says that she's unsure. "He looks familiar, but I can't quite place him. Maybe he's a friend of Mom and Dad's? You would think Diane would have told them if that was the case."

I look in the direction that Melinda went and then back at Maxine. "Screw this, I can't wait," I tell her, shoving away from the table and following in the direction Melinda went.

"Damn it. I'm coming too!" Max says, her footsteps hurrying after me.

*I need to get the truth of this.*

## Chapter Five

**Harlow**

M elinda is nowhere to be found in the huge house, so we head outside. The Bostons' horse training business encompasses a vast expanse of land, but the indoor arena isn't too far from the house. Sticking my head through the wide double doors, it's obvious they're not in there because the place is empty. I guess with all my drama today, no one trained any of the horses. Luke and Peter are probably still at lunch, and Chuck might be in the office, working out the afternoon's schedule if Melinda hasn't found him yet.

We head over to the old stable block where the office is kept, my desire to know what's going on only growing with each unsuccessful step. We have bigger and newer stables for most of the horses now, but the old one is still occasionally used for a pregnant mare to foal down in or an injured horse to recuperate. They don't get as worked up when there aren't as many distractions. Unlike the timber and steel design of the new stables, this one is built from red brick and has cute white wooden trim on all the stalls and the beams. Five stalls on each side, making a total of ten stables available, but only four are really in use. An office is on one side, and a feed and tack room is also in there. Two of the stables have been opened up and renovated into a consultation room.

A staircase running up the side leads to the small apartment above. This is where I live, and downstairs is where I keep all the sick, injured, or just plain abandoned animals that I rescue. I'd moved out to live in the apartment above the stables not long after starting college. I'd been doing college-level classes while attending my junior and senior years of high school, so I eased into my freshman year pretty smoothly.

With no friends but Max and no desire to hang with hers, it just made sense to get a head start. Especially when the major I had planned to do was so long.

I didn't move out because I was unwanted. No, the Bostons considered me one of the family, and I was more than welcome to stay in the main house. The move was all me. I had so many issues. Low self-esteem and the inability to trust, to name a couple. I just wanted to get on with my life and do something for myself without having to worry about who I was disappointing or letting down. The lack of distraction out here was also a blessing. No Maxine to pop in and ask me to watch TV or want to talk about boys. Boys that I had no interest in. Animals are my life, and I feel blessed to be able to help so many innocent creatures.

I guess wanting to be a vet stemmed from my own abandonment issues. As a child, I was always rescuing stray animals and begging Melinda and Chuck to let me keep them. They'd indulged me in this, and my menagerie was born. Being able to give them love and be loved in return was soothing to my soul; the animals never let me down. If they lashed out, it was because they were hurt or scared, not because they were jealous or hopped up on meth.

The braying of a donkey greets me as Maxine and I enter the barn, and a little gray head with long velvety ears pops itself over one of the stable doors. My need to find Melinda and Chuck dims slightly as I head over to give Jenny a cuddle. Opening the half-door, I slide in and pull it closed behind me.

Jenny is a recent rescue. I found her malnourished and neglected on a little farm not far from a client's place. She was a pathetic lump of matted hair and feces when I took her from the paddock in the middle of the night. I'd had to calm her with xylazine, a mild sedative, and Luke and Peter helped me move her with the hay cart to our horse trailer, where we laid her down to drive her home.

Yes, I'm guilty of donkey theft. But it was either that or getting the ASPCA involved, and that would have taken days if not weeks to get through the bureaucracy.

When I got her home, I had to clip her down to the skin to remove the caked-on dirt, hair, and shit. Once she was clean, finally, she was a bag of bones, and I wasn't sure she was going to make it. Even using a mild sedative was fairly risky, though her heartbeat remained relatively steady through the whole process.

While Peter trimmed her too-long hooves, I washed her poor skin with soothing lotions, and then, because she didn't have enough meat on her bones, placed a thick cotton blanket on her to keep her a little warmer. Although it's summer, the nights do get chilly, and I didn't want her to get any sicker.

Once the IV fluids I had given had finished, I gave her a reversal sedative, and we just had to wait for it to wear off. I placed a small mash of sugar beets in her feed trough and some fresh water. Not long after waking, she showed some interest in her food, and I knew she was going to be okay. I spent the night leaning against a couple of hay bales, making sure she was fine. At some point, I must have fallen asleep because the next morning, when

Chuck brought me a cup of coffee, Jenny was laying down next to me with her head in my lap. I'm pretty sure she thinks I'm the best thing that's ever happened to her.

Every morning she greets me with a chorus of excited hee-haws and is slowly and steadily gaining weight. She shares her stall and paddock with Devil Spawn, a miniature pony so cute you just want to cuddle her to death. Don't let her fool you though. She has a nasty streak a mile long, and her name was chosen because it fit her too perfectly...and we might've needed to warn people. Many people have tried to get close and scored a kick to the shins. Luckily, she has terrible aim and is reasonably small, and although it hurts, it's not enough to do significant damage.

DS was living with a fool of a woman who thought she could be kept inside like a dog, but she outgrew what that woman expected, and the owner didn't have a fenced yard to keep her in. By the time I got my hands on her, she was already spoiled rotten and had learned if she threatened the lady, she got what she wanted. DS doesn't get away with that here, but we like to let her pretend she does.

I don't have too many rescued creatures at the moment. Living in the dorms and only coming home on the weekends made it tricky, and I didn't want to leave Melinda, Chuck, and Maxine to look after them. So, apart from Jenny and DS, there are five cats in the hay and feed sheds, and they keep the rodent population down. There's also a barn owl that had been clipped by a car in one of the cages in the clinic, and aside from that, I have no steady patients at the moment. I'll also have the occasional horse injury that I take care of for Melinda and Chuck. I just need to decide on what I want to continue doing. I enjoy the horses, but I have a secret dream, one I think is slightly out of reach, unfortunately.

Jenny nuzzles me in the side, bringing my attention back to her, and I pull a piece of carrot out of my pocket. I always have some form of treat on me, and they know it. A moment later, a pair of teeth trying to get a chunk of my ass has me swinging quickly and swatting a hand at DS. Maxine laughs from the safety of the other side of the stable door. DS and Max have come to an agreement. They agree they don't like each other, and it's better for both of them if they don't get too close.

"Damn menace!" I chase her away, but she trots back around, ears flat back. This time, Jenny loses her patience, chasing her out of the stables and into their paddock, and I slip back out of the stall. Leaning against the stable door, we watch them chase each other around, manes flicking and hooves flying as they bolt throughout the large yard. The two skid to a halt before they get to the end of the fence and then throw in a few happy bucks before running off again.

"What do you think your mom's talking to your

dad about? She was so angry when she saw the name," I say to her quietly, my voice full of worry.

She shrugs, brow raised and nose scrunched in confusion. "Like you said, she hardly ever gets mad, so something must be really upsetting her. She's got to have a clue; otherwise, why would she be so upset?"

My stomach rolls with nausea and nerves. This is the closest I've ever been to finding out the identity of my father, and I'm not sure what to do. Is this a can of worms I need to open? Twenty-five, almost twenty-six years of not knowing. Is it going to make a difference now? Maybe he already knows and doesn't care. And if he doesn't, he probably has his own family to worry about. Gaining a daughter my age is going to put a cramp in his style. Maybe we should let the knowledge die with my mother, and I'll convince myself that I don't need anyone other than the Bostons.

Pushing away from the stable door, I head into the clinic that Chuck and Melinda built for me as a graduation present.

"I need to feed the owl," I tell her, and I can hear her trail after me.

"I still say we need to call it Hedwig," she jokes back, and I smile slightly.

"You know I don't like to name the ones we plan on releasing. It's easier to stay detached that way."

"I'm just saying if we keep it, we could train it to carry messages to and from each other! That would be so cool." She becomes a little more excited as we approach the clinic door until she's practically skipping alongside me. Rolling my eyes, I just snort with laughter. She's ridiculous sometimes.

The state of the art clinic's equipped for me to treat both large and small animals, but I specialized in large. It was my way to give back to the Bostons after everything they'd done for me. Now I'm able to take care of their horses as well as treating some from the farms around us. Our closest vet was an hour away, which, in an emergency, made it stressful until they could get there, and we had some close calls that still make me nervous to think about. My little clinic gives a lot of people peace of mind.

Entering the examination room, the sterile smell of disinfectant brings a sense of calm to me. This is what I know; this is what I can control. I let the worries in my brain drift away and concentrate on the here and now as I pull out a small towel and lay it down on the exam table.

"How's it doing?" Max asks quietly from the doorway of the clinic, knowing I need calm for what I'm about to do. Pulling on a pair of cut-proof gloves, I open the cage that I've been keeping the owl in. Reaching in, I drape a towel over him to stop him from biting and flapping his wings before grabbing him by the feet and carefully pulling him out. Securing the towel gently, I pull it back to expose his head. Normally, I would place him between my legs so I could use both hands, but she might as well make herself useful, so I sit down and look over to Maxine.

"Come here and hold it, will you?" Her freaked out face has me laughing slightly, but she gets it together and comes in, taking the owl from my hands. She sits down on a stool next to the examination table, eyes wide and fixed on our patient.

Pulling out some supplies, I fill a bowl with some water and add a powdered glucose solution, stirring it around. Then, I grab some chunks of chopped up mice out of the freezer and set them aside to warm to room temperature. All the while Max coos nonsense to the little creature; it seems to like the sound of her voice. This little guy was clipped by a car, and the driver dropped him off to me a couple of days ago. He didn't appear to have any visible injuries, just stunned, so I've kept him hydrated and been hand feeding him. He seems to be recovering nicely. Today I'm going to move him into an aviary next to the stables for a few days. If he seems to be flying well and eating and feeding on his own, we'll release him back into the wild in the area that he was found.

Now that my hands are free, I pick up a small needleless syringe and fill it with about three milliliters of the liquid solution. Stepping over to where Max and the bird are, I grab the top of his beak, pry it open with my finger, hold the upper mandible out of the way, and slowly release the liquid into his mouth. He's used to the process now, and once I let him close his beak, he swallows instantly. We do that a couple of times until he's had about ten milliliters. This process takes about ten minutes because we don't want to do it too fast and stress him out.

Maxine strokes the top of his head and coos again as I move the syringe out of the way. Bringing over the raw meat, I place the bowl in front of him, and Max starts to gag. Giggling at her reaction, I grab a bit of the chopped up mouse and repeat the same movements as the water, letting him swallow between pieces. This process takes a little longer with Maxine theatrically gagging the entire time.

"Seriously, get a grip," I tease as the owl swallows the last piece, and she shudders.

"It wouldn't be so bad if it wasn't still furry and had its tail on one of the pieces," she says, handing me the wrapped owl. Gently, I unwrap him and place him back in the carry cage. Cleaning up all the stuff I used, I leave everything neat and tidy again. Then, picking up the portable cage, we head outside to the flight aviary.

"Do you think you'll be able to release him?" she asks me as I enter the long aviary. There's a double door set up that allows only one to open at a time, making a bird's escape difficult.

Placing the cage down on the ground, I open the door. "I sure hope so. I don't like to see an animal like this caged if we can avoid it."

This flight aviary is empty at the moment. In the past, I've used it for the rehabilitation of other birds of prey, but I've been able to release most of them or rehome others with a raptor sanctuary. Backing away, I decide to leave him to it. He may not choose to leave the cage until evening, so I'll come back and check on him before I go to bed.

Leaving the cage, we both turn to go, but a screech has us spinning back around. The little barn owl has hopped out of the portable cage and flown up onto one of the bare branches that are sitting under the covered roof. He stretches his wings and ruffles his feathers, getting comfortable.

"Awesome," she whispers. "It must be such a rush to know you've helped."

I smile at her, feeling a warmth that I've only ever gotten from spending time with my animals. "Yes, but there's also the other side too, when no matter what you've tried, you haven't been able to make a difference." Her smile dims a bit, but I just hip bump her, and she cheers up again.

That's when the sound of footsteps gets our attention, and, turning again, we find Chuck and Melinda waiting for us.

"He's looking good, Harlow." Chuck's deep voice sounds pleased, but the strain on their faces is evident. He's got his arm wrapped around her shoulders, and his hand is massaging her shoulder in comfort. Melinda's normally bright eyes are red and her face streaked with tears from crying. My stomach rolls with anxiety at the sight, unable to remember the last time that they both seemed this upset.

"Come on, girls, let's go to my office. We've got some things to talk about." His voice is even, but his eyes are sad when he looks at me, and my previous nerves return with a vengeance.

## Chapter Six

## Harlow

The office is a little bit stuffy when we first walk in, so Chuck leaves the door open as he takes a seat behind his desk, Melinda perching on the arm of his chair. Maxine and I sit on the two remaining seats, but no matter how much I fidget, I can't seem to get comfortable. Both of them have serious faces, and my heart races in anticipation of what they have to tell me. My foot taps up and down with nerves as if the right number of movements might magically bleed out the anxiety that's been building.

"Firstly, I want to apologize for how I reacted," Melinda says to me, her voice full of regret. "It wasn't fair to you, but I needed to talk to Chuck and confirm a few things before I told you anything." I swallow nervously but nod my head. Melinda has been there for me more than Diane ever was, and I don't know if I could ever hold anything against her.

Once they see that I'm not going to freak out, yet, anyway, Chuck takes over. "The man your mother named on the birth certificate, if she's telling the truth, is indeed the man in the photo. He was and still is my best friend. You've never met him, Harlow, because he hasn't been back to visit since that photo was taken. We always flew to them. I couldn't ever figure out why, but with this recent information, I'm guessing your mom may be the reason he's never returned. He may think she still works for Melinda. We never discuss work stuff when we visit. It's strictly banned."

"Holy shit." Maxine's gasps as she turns to look at me with excitement in her eyes; clearly, something has occurred to her, and she's had an epiphany.

"It's also probably why Diane wouldn't approve for you to leave the state," Melinda adds in. "She knows how close our families are. It was another 'fuck you' aimed at us all." She has tears in her eyes, and there's a nervous twist to her hands that shows how much this moment means to her. "I tried so many times to help that woman, but she wouldn't take it. She became a twisted version of the girl I once knew. You know, when she first got pregnant with you, I was thrilled and thought it would help get back onto the right path, but it just seemed to make everything worse. Throughout the whole pregnancy, she was in and out of one rehab center after another. Finally, once you were born and she held you in her arms, she made the choice to stay sober."

Melinda stops and takes a sip of her glass of wine, her eyes glistening with unshed tears. "But that only lasted about six months. It was right around the time your eyes changed from blue to the hazel color they are now. She couldn't look at you without saying that you had *his* eyes. I guess she meant your father, and it was all downhill from there. We tried our hardest to keep her on as long as possible for your sake, Harlow. If you were coming here, I knew you were fed and warm and had all the things you needed. But it just got too much when she stole my engagement ring to try and pawn. She knew I took them off when I ride, and Sherry caught her pocketing it. God, I hated to fire her because it meant I couldn't keep an eye on you, and at that stage we had no proof of neglect. Diane hid it well. By the time we let her go, I hated that woman with a passion I never knew I could feel." Her shoulders sag in defeat, but her eyes now flash with anger before she takes a couple of calming breaths. Once it recedes, she keeps going.

"We know for sure, one hundred percent, that this man has no idea about you. Not long after staying here, he contracted mumps and was told he would never father children, and he was devastated.

When he was a little older, he ended up adopting seven children. I'm not sure whether this is something that will comfort you, but I can guarantee that you would have been loved and wanted." My heart soars at this information, the thought that I would have been wanted, but the fury intensifies now as I realize what my mother deliberately stole from me.

"Why do you think Mom never told him?" My gaze moves between them both as they exchange a glance.

"When Brad was down here, he assumed an alias. Cole is his mother's maiden name. He wanted to have some fun and not be harassed because of his family name and what it's associated with," Chuck explains, "and it worked."

Melinda takes over, adding, "He was able to enjoy his time down here naturally, and he knew that your mom was attracted to him and not his fortune."

"So why all the secrets? Why didn't she track him down?" I'm feeling more confused than ever.

"They enjoyed their time together when the four of us hung out, but Diane also had another group of friends, the ones that partied super hard. There were plenty of drugs and alcohol flowing freely, and while Brad likes a drink or two, he'd never indulge in more than an occasional joint. He liked to be in control. Diane wasn't so restrained. She wasn't willing to give it up, and he wasn't willing to look the other way. Not to mention as the summer wore on, she would go missing for days at a time." Chuck's eyebrows draw together, and his forehead creases in a frown, his disapproval of her behavior clear.

"In the end, Brad called a stop to the relationship, and Diane was gutted. She became abusive and stalkerish to the point that he went home so that he could avoid her. When she turned up pregnant, we didn't even assume it was his because she had been partying so hard, it could have been anyone's. As for why she never told him? Your guess is as good as mine, but the fact that she thought he was just a beach bum and wouldn't be able to get anything from him would've factored in. I also think it was a spite thing. He dumped her, so he was going to miss out on you. That's how twisted she had become by then." Melinda shrugs, looking uncomfortable with how matter of fact she says this all.

"But what she did was rob you of being a part of one of the best families I know." The anger in Chuck's voice is palpable, and there's a steadily rising flush that's creeping up his neck, betraying how worked up he is now.

"What now? Are you going to tell him?" I ask quietly, unsure if I want to know the answer or not. "Do you think he'll want to know?"

Melinda gets off her perch and comes over, pulling me up and hugging me, her grip tighter than usual. "Oh, honey, of course he will, and, well, you've already met your grandparents, and they love you to bits."

Looking at her in surprise, I ask, "What do you mean?" The confusion in my voice is evident, and I pull back to make eye contact with her for this next bombshell.

"Well, Brad's real last name is Summers, so Nana and Poppy Summers are your grandparents." I collapse down into my chair again, my heart pounding at the news, her words echoing in my ear.

"Harlow, Harlow, are you ok?" Maxine grabs my hand and squeezes to get my attention. I feel a wetness on my face, and once I put my hand up to touch my cheek, I discover I'm crying.

"They're my grandparents?" My voice shakes with emotion; my whole body is trembling in this weird and overwhelming mix of joy, shock, and disbelief. "They're mine for real, not pretend?" Their looks of sympathy are just too much, and those sneaky tears escalate into full-blown sobs. Maxine reaches over and pulls me close again, holding me tight in a warm embrace that's exactly what I need.

"Oh, honey, yes, that's what was taking so long. I rang them, and they'll be in the air as soon as they can get their plane ready. They haven't told Brad yet; they want to speak to you first. Make sure you're ok with this and whether you want to go ahead and meet him and his family," Chuck explains. His words fill me with a sense of relief.

The option of having a choice makes me feel a little bit more in control in the midst of this life-altering situation.

Melinda rubs my back in a soft, soothing motion similar to what she would do when I was a kid and not feeling well. "They want you to know that no matter what you decide, they'll keep your secret. But they'll insist on you spending more time with them at least. They also hope you'll consider meeting their son but will leave it up to you."

Taking a deep breath, I pull myself together and wipe my eyes with my t-shirt. "Okay, that sounds good; I can't wait to see them." The smile grows on my face. As a little girl, I would pretend they were mine for real, and now they are.

"What should I do about their son?" I ask, and both Melinda and Chuck shrug.

"That's a decision we can't make for you, sweetie," Melinda says quietly. My thoughts turn chaotic again, and I bite my lip, not knowing what to do, what decision to make. Maxine snorts and then starts laughing, a completely inappropriate but not entirely surprising reaction from her. We all look at her like she's crazy, eyes wide and an eyebrow raised.

"Oh my God, Diane would be turning in her grave if she knew." I give her a confused look while Melinda and Chuck start to chuckle.

"Honey, your daddy is the CEO of Neighpalm Industries and one of the richest men in the US.

That family is worth *billions*. You just went from rags to riches. She used to come and scrounge a couple hundred bucks off you. Could you imagine if she had been able to get at Brad's money?"

Melinda and Chuck stop chuckling and frown at these words, and my stomach turns at the information. She's right. Diane would have worked it to her advantage. "Do you think he's going to think Mom was lying? Should I be prepared for rejection?"

"Nana and Poppy are bringing a DNA sample so we can run it, just to be sure. Not because they don't believe it; actually, I suggested it. It's to cover everyone's bases as we go forward. It's standard practice for wealthy families when something like this happens, and it's as much for Brad's protection as yours." Chuck shrugs, and I nod my okay, a bit of relief flowing through me at the reminder that no matter what Melinda and Chuck have my back. Maybe she's wrong, and this is all a dead end. That's more than likely what's going to happen. My heart drops, but I guess that's my reality.

"You know Poppy Summers always used to say you were the spitting image of their daughter Belinda when she was a child. She passed away when she was a teenager; you have her eyes. He would say how remarkable it was. I think that's part of the reason they were so enamored with you. Not to mention they have a soft spot for abandoned children. We had mentioned all of Brad's kids are adopted, but they also each come from family situations that weren't great. Only two are blood-related, a brother and sister that he didn't want to separate, so he took both. Jacinta's the same age as you. The boys are all a little older."

"She was fun when we were kids," Maxine assures me, "but I haven't seen them in years. I'd stay behind with you when Mom and Dad would go and visit, so you weren't alone with Nana and Grandad Boston. You always looked so sad when we left, and I hated seeing you that way." I lean over and hug Maxine, surprised by this information. I'd always wondered why she stopped going. She'd told me she had better things to do than hang out with a bunch of boys, but now I know that she was looking out for me. My heart warms a bit, thinking about how she wanted to be there for me and tried to protect my feelings too.

Chuck stands up, a determined expression on his face as he joins Melinda, Maxine, and me. "Look, there's no point standing around and thinking about a bunch of what-ifs. It's an almost eight-hour flight from California, so they won't be here until late tonight, and that's if they left straight away. I'm going to guess they may wait a few hours to leave, so they arrive in the morning and can sleep on the flight. Howard is practical like that; he wouldn't want to get here and have to wake everyone up. Why don't we grab a couple of horses and go for a ride? No training, just some exercise. Get some fresh air and forget about our worries for a while. Tomorrow is soon enough to worry about things we can't change anyway."

A little while later, we're saddling some horses to go for a ride. I'm using my favorite of the stunt horses, needing some time with one of my best boys. He's a chestnut warmblood gelding who's popular with the period directors because he's built like a war horse but has a refined elegance to him. Phoenix has been my go-to horse since I sold my own personal mount a few years ago. I was spending so much time at the university and riding the other horses when I did find time to go home, that she was neglected. Midnight was English-trained, and I sold her to a family who was looking to upgrade their teenage daughter to a mount that could take her further in her chosen discipline. The daughter is now doing well on the eventing circuit and has been picked for some junior elite team.

After checking the cinch and putting on my helmet, I lead Phoenix out of the stall to meet the others. Already mounted on their horses, they wait patiently as I lift my left foot into the stirrup and push off with my right before gently sitting down in the saddle. Gathering my reins, I wait for Chuck to take the lead toward the trail we're going to be taking. Maxine and I ride side by side behind

Chuck and Melinda, the latter wearing a backpack that I'm sure is filled with a thermos of coffee and some snacks or something for us to eat at the midway point.

Fond memories of family trips to the pond go back as far as I can remember. Chuck and Melinda had both of us girls on ponies not long after we could walk, and even though I'd moved away when Diane was let go, I always had a pony on the farm. Back then the trips were a lot longer, as the ponies' little legs didn't cover much ground very quickly, and a rest at the midway point was essential for both them and us. So Melinda started packing snacks, and the plan has never changed even though it takes nowhere near as long to get there anymore.

The clip-clop of the horses' hooves and the warmth of the lazy afternoon sun shining down on my face have me breathing out a huge sigh of relief as my body's tension slowly drifts away. We continue like that for a while, the others instinctively knowing that I need the peace and quiet to make sense of all that has happened. The rocking back and forth motion of my horse's walk lulls me into a daze as I try to gather all my scattered thoughts.

Today's revelations have floored me. Never once did I consider the scenario that had been painted. I mean, I'd believed he didn't know and would quite often picture who my ideal dad would be, but never once did I consider that she hadn't told either of us out of spite. I'd just assumed she either didn't know or that she did, and he hadn't wanted me.

Having to change my direction of thinking is throwing me. Now that I know the man exists, and there's a good chance he would like to know me, I have to decide what I want and what is most beneficial to me. I'm an adult now, not a child seeking love and comfort. I have university debt and career decisions to make. Do I have the time to get to know a new family? And speaking of that family, are his adopted children going to be all that keen to get to know me? If they're anything like Max's rich friends, I'm not optimistic. Maybe I should just stick to Nana and Poppy and let sleeping dogs lie.

I'm bumped out of my thoughts as the others move their horses first into a trot and then a canter. Needing to pay attention, I let my turbulent thoughts float away on the passing wind. Ducking some low-lying leaves, the thrill of the ride has my spirits soaring. There's nothing better than flying along a trail, feeling the powerful muscles of the animal beneath you and the thunderous sound of the hooves and wind as it flies by your ears. Crouched down low over my horse's wither, his mane occasionally flicking into my face, I whoop with joy, and the answering sounds from the others has a huge grin spreading across my face. It's times like this, as the feeling of being one of the family warms my soul, that I know I will be forever grateful for Melinda and Chuck and Maxine. For them caring enough not to let me become a statistic, just another unwanted child of a junkie who would go on to become exactly like their mother.

By the time we slow, I'm breathing heavy, and Phoenix has a light sheen of sweat to his coat. The little lake at the back of the large property is the perfect place for a rest and an afternoon picnic. Its surface glassy in the afternoon sun, it looks cool and refreshing. We climb off the horses, removing their tack and releasing them to graze and get a drink. They're trained not to run away and will stay close by for when we want to return.

Pulling off my boots and jeans, I join Maxine in the knee-deep water while Melinda and Chuck set up our picnic, the two of them in deep conversation. The temperature is a refreshing bite on my overheated skin. No words are exchanged; none are needed as we bask in the afternoon sun, and the sound of insects fills the comfortable silence.

"Girls, come and get a drink." Melinda's voice breaks through our moment, and, smiling at each other, we wade out and back up the grassy bank to the shade of a tree. Melinda has laid out a rug to sit on, but we both choose the grass until our legs dry. Once we're settled, she hands me a little plastic cup of coffee. "Do you feel better?" she asks, giving one to Max too.

"Yeah, I needed that," I tell her, taking a sip of the liquid gold in a cup—the coffee warming my rapidly cooling body. The lake water has done the job of cooling me down, and sitting in the shade is now taking it too far.

"Harlow, have you thought about what you're going to do now that you've graduated? Are you going to take Doc Davies up on his offer of a position on his team?" Chuck is going to avoid the obvious elephant in the room, and I could kiss him for that alone, but did he have to ask the one other question I've been avoiding? The three of them wait for my answer, and the pressure makes me squirm slightly.

"Yeah, I guess I probably should. God knows I have enough student debt to pay off. Taking a job with him would certainly start working on that," I reply, Melinda and Chuck nodding their heads in agreement. They offered to pay for university for me, but I just couldn't allow it. I got by on scholarships and financial aid, and now is the time to make good on it. To me, family is here for love and support, *not* for money. I'll make my own way whenever I can. I always figure out how to make it work.

"I mean, I would prefer to work for myself, and you guys have made that an option by adding the clinic, but it would take time to build up clientele, and my loans won't wait for that," I try to explain, but I can just tell by the look they exchange that they're about to offer to take care of them again.

Before I can refuse, Maxine has to add her two cents in. "That's all well and good, but you and I both know that your heart is set on something else."

I shoot her a dirty look, not knowing why I continue to confide in the pushy bitch.

Melinda and Chuck look at her with questions in their eyes, and before I can stop her, she's blurting it out. "Harlow wants to work with exotic animals, zoo creatures and such. It's always been her dream since Nana Summers and Nana Boston took us to the aquarium and the zoos when we were small. You couldn't shake her happy smile after she got to feed the beluga whales, and she almost wet her pants when we saw the tigers." *Wow, thanks heaps, bitch. Share my dream with everyone, why don't you?* My thoughts simmer with anger, but underlying it is embarrassment because there it is. The one thing I'd never shared with anyone else but Maxine. Knowing that getting an internship with a vet that does this is near impossible, it just feels like a joke to have it put out there into the world for other people to know.

"Really? I had no idea." Melinda's voice is full of surprise, and Chuck has a funny look on his face. The two of them tilt their heads, looking at me in a combination of confusion and like they're trying to figure me out.

"You're worried you'll have to leave the state to get one, aren't you?" He's always been able to see right to the heart of the matter, so I answer with honesty. Might as well put it all out there now that Max has opened this up.

"Yes, I'm worried that, after all you guys have

done for me, I'll have to leave, and it will put pressure on our relationship. You guys have been the foundation in my life, and I'm worried my absence will rock that foundation, and I need to know that you'll always be there, always have my back, because without you...I may just crumble." My fears come rushing out in one giant gasp as though my mind hates this idea of being vulnerable and has decided it's now or never.

"Oh, honey, no." Melinda's cry of dismay sounds around the paddock, startling the horses. "No matter where you are or what you're doing, you'll always be a Boston." Maxine's smug face says it all. She's been trying to tell me that for years, but Diane did a number on my psyche, and I always found it hard to believe.

"Well, it's something I need to think about, but I have other pressing worries right now." My words put a stop to the conversation, but I can see in Chuck's eyes he's not going to let it go. He might not say something now, but I'm sure he'll corner me again later.

By now, the sun is starting to sink low in the afternoon sky, so we pack up our picnic, re-saddle the horses, and head back the way we came. The nerves build again the closer we get to the house, causing Phoenix to be skittish. He's obviously picking up my emotions through my body language; horses are so intuitive to people's feelings, you can't fool them at all. But his little jolts and startles don't even shift me slightly in the seat; they just help to keep my mind off the things that are bothering me.

When we return home, I take care of Phoenix's grooming and feeding and wish everyone good-night. As I walk by the aviary, I can see from the outside light that the owl is perched happily on a branch, his eyes wide as he takes in his surroundings. A scuffling sound in the bottom of the cage draws his and my attention. Wishing the field mouse luck, I head up my stairs to my apartment.

## Chapter Seven

**Harlow**

My night is spent tossing and turning, thinking about possible scenarios for the following day. Eventually, I fall asleep and dream fitfully, visions of Diane and all the words of rejection and hate that she ever viciously spewed at me playing like a broken record over and over inside my mind.

I wake early the next morning, tangled in my blankets, covered in sweat, and with tears streaming down my face. *Damn her, how is she still affecting me so many years later?* Her death and the revelations about my father have brought all my issues screaming back; not for the first time, I make a note that maybe I should pay my therapist another visit. For her to torment me in my dreams is one thing. For this to all escalate and make me backslide into the broken little girl I used to be is another. I can't let *that* happen.

Throwing back my blankets, I head into my ensuite and take a quick shower. It's almost eight o'clock already, which may be early to other people, but it's borderline late for me. I must have forgotten to set my alarm before I went to bed, and I guess nobody wanted to wake me for morning feed rounds.

Putting on my regular work uniform, a pair of stretchy riding pants and a t-shirt, I work my hair into a braid, tying it off with a hair tie. Pulling on a thick pair of socks, I head downstairs to find my work boots. After I quickly shove my feet in and lace 'em up, I feed Jenny and DS before heading over to the main house for breakfast and to see if the Summers have arrived

Removing my boots again before I enter, I nudge open the back door, the sound of Nana Summers' sweet voice easily traveling across the space between us. She's already talking about how horrible it was that they had missed out on so much. She sounds like she's been crying, and my heart about breaks at the thought of one of my favorite people getting so upset. I hover in the mudroom, my nerves getting the better of me. Turning around to head back outside, the door slips from my hand in a freak gust of wind and slams shut.

"Harlow?" Melinda calls out. There's no hiding

my entry anymore, so I trudge into the kitchen, head down and shoulders hunched, trying to make myself seem as little as possible. Jesus, I've fallen back on my old habits from those nightmare visits with Mom. Straightening my shoulders, I take a deep breath and look up at the couple.

Tears glisten in Nana's eyes, but she looks happy, and Poppy Summers has a big broad grin on his face. "Hally, my love, come give your poppy a big squelch." With those familiar words, everything falls into place for a moment, and just maybe everything is going to be okay.

I cross the floorboards to be enveloped by him and his strong arms. His familiar designer fragrance surrounds me with notes of sandalwood and brings me such comfort and reminders of some of the happiest memories of my childhood. He's shaking with emotions as he whispers in my ear, "My sweet, sweet girl. You don't know how happy we are to discover you are one of us. We just wish it'd been sooner, and we hadn't missed out on so much time."

"For goodness sake, Howard, stop smothering the girl! Let her breathe, please." Nana sounds exasperated, and I can feel her tug on his shirt until he grumbles but lets me go. A smile threatens to break out, the scene one that I know all too well. For all of her "nagging" at Poppy, Nana loves him so much, and he's always taken it all in amused stride. Before I can say anything else, Nana has grabbed me and wrapped me up in her arms. Her smaller body is surprisingly strong for a woman her age. The tightness of her hug and her familiar violet smell add to the feelings of calm.

She doesn't say anything; she just holds me tight, breathing me in as I do the same. Eventually, we part, and tears streak her face. I pull away and grab a tissue from the nearby buffet cabinet and gently wipe them away.

Patting the seat in between them, they both sit and gesture for me to follow. I study them while coffee is made. I haven't seen them in a few months, but they haven't changed. Poppy is a tall, ruggedly handsome gentleman, with steel gray hair cut neat around his ears and swept to one side across his forehead. He has age lines on his face, though most of them are from laughing, a sign of his generally happy disposition. His skin is tanned from all the outdoor activities they do, but he looks just as comfortable wearing a suit and heading for a business meeting as he does in jeans and boots. Meeting his sparkling brown eyes, he winks at me before putting in his egg order with the Bostons' housekeeper Sherry. It's with that action I realize he has the same color eyes as me, and they're also shaped similarly. A rush of happiness flows through me at this thought.

Turning to Nana, she's looking at me too. Her blonde hair is streaked with gray and is pulled back into a bun sort of thing at the base of her neck. She hasn't got any makeup on this morning, and the fine lines of age she wears so well are showing. Her eyes look a little strained under her elegantly refined blonde eyebrows, but that's to be expected. One of those eyebrows raises as if to say "What?" I shrug my shoulders in response, taking a moment before I answer.

"Just looking at you guys from a new perspective and thanking my lucky stars that dreams do come true." Her lips purse together in shock before a brilliant smile crosses her face. It's true though. I've always wished that they were mine for real. Between Maxine, Melinda, and Chuck, I got the parents and sister that I could only have dreamed of, and knowing I really do have grandparents who are just as wonderful as them brings a lightness to my life.

Breakfast is served, and we chat about benign things until it looks like Grace and Howard are ready to burst.

Chuck starts to laugh, willing to take the lead and get us moving toward the reason we're all gathered here. "Shall we address the giant elephant in the room? Grace, Howard, would you like to start?"

They look at each other, and with a nod from Nana, Poppy starts. "Hally, honey, we would love it if you would come back to California with us and get to know our son and his family. We haven't said anything to him yet because we wanted to see how you felt about it, but it really would make us very happy if you could."

My feelings soar with joy at how accepted I feel

with these two wonderful people, but the doubt and anxiety at how everyone else will react rears its ugly head in equal measure.

"I don't know," I begin, and they start to argue.

Barely a moment goes by before Melinda stops them with a firm, "Hear her out first, please." They nod their acceptance, looking properly chastised though excitement still gleams in their eyes.

"I have so many things going on in my head," I explain to them. I might as well put it all out there. "I have reservations about meeting your son. I'm not a cute baby that he can get to know as I grow. I'm a fully grown adult, with my own life, and, well, what if he doesn't like me?" The words come rushing out now. "And what about his kids? They may feel a bit put out at his biological daughter appearing all of a sudden. Then there's my job offer with Doc Davies to consider and paying off my student loans. If I go to California, I doubt he'll hold a job for me until I come back."

I stop abruptly, noticing they're all looking at me with wild eyes. "Sorry, I didn't sleep much last night, and these are the things I'm worried about."

Poppy pats my hand, a soft smile on his face. "Don't apologize, a problem shared is a problem halved." He always manages to make me smile. He likes to spout off random bits of wisdom, saying they make him seem like he's "sage and deep" as he gets older.

Nana has a look of determination on her face as

she thinks about what I've just told them, and she waves a hand in my direction. "Well, you don't have to worry about your university debt. Howard and I paid for all our grandchildren's schooling, and we'll certainly be paying for yours as well." She takes out her phone and starts making notes. "Give me the next bill, and I will have Brad's PA take care of that." Her words are breezy as her fingers fly across the screen, but I just stare at her with my mouth open. She must realize I haven't responded and looks up at me. "Close your mouth, dear. It's unladylike to stand there with it open."

"But, but, but," I stammer out, and Maxine, on the other side of the table, just giggles. "You do know I'm a vet?"

"Yes, yes," Poppy says, patting me on the leg, "and such a clever one too, getting the first two years of the undergraduate courses done while in high school. I tell you none of our other grandchildren did that, so it must be my genes flowing through your body." He winks at me, and the others at the table laugh, but I still have no idea what to say.

"Look, we have seven grandchildren, eight now, and we made sure each of them got a quality education, even if it was just to fall back on, like Oliver." That must be one of the grandson's names, and when Maxine's eyes gleam and she squirms in her seat, I know that I'm going to hear *all* about him later. "You already got that brilliant education, and we would be poor grandparents if, when we can afford to take care of the bill, we didn't. This way, you're not weighed down with all that debt and are free to make an informed decision instead of one brought about by financial issues." I go to speak, trying to argue my case again, hopefully more successfully, and she holds up a hand. "No, I won't hear another word. It's done. We've already missed so many special moments in your life. Give us this, *please*," she pleads, a tone that I've never heard from this strong-willed woman. Not that she's a terror about it, but Nana's wealth has meant that she really doesn't have to say please to anyone; what Nana Summers asks for, Nana Summers gets, usually quite quickly and with a smile.

I look around the table at the others, not believing what she's just said. The bill is astronomical; that's the whole reason why I've always fought off Chuck and Melinda's attempts to pay. Chuck smiles at me, a teasing glint in his eye. "Just nod your head and say thank you, Harlow. You won't get her to change her mind; the woman is a force of nature." Poppy's nodding in agreement, the surest sign that if I try to fight this battle, I'll lose.

"But that right there is what I'm worried about," I point out to them all. "I don't want your money, and I certainly don't want to be accused of being a gold-digger or anything."

"Pshh." Nana's words are a hiss, so much formidable strength packed into just that one sound. "You're a Summers. You were born into this family, not married in, and anyone who says anything else, send them my way. I'll put them in their place."

This time it's Melinda who's nodding her head with a look of awe in her eyes. "Oh yes, Nana Summers is a feast to behold when she is on the warpath. I remember when I was accused of being a gold-digger..." Melinda had married into Chuck's wealthy family, having come from a poor farming family. Her horse skills were unparalleled, and that's how she caught Chuck's eye, but there were some who were...reluctant to believe their honest love story.

"Goodness, Grace set them straight. I've never seen someone scurry away so fast in my life."

Nana has the classic haughty look of a snob on her face; nose in the air and haughty eyes, her mouth pursed. "Being gold-diggers themselves, those social-climbing bitches wouldn't know quality stock when they see it. But I do." Her face breaks out in a smile, and we all laugh as she blows a kiss at Melinda across the table.

"But what about your son and his kids? I don't want to stir up a happy family, and it's not like we're going to bond like brothers and sisters. That boat has definitely sailed." Nana and Poppy exchange an almost knowing look, and Poppy winks at her, not exactly the reaction I was expecting.

"I think our plan is still possible," he assures her

mysteriously, not giving away anything I can make sense of. She gives him a small nod and stands up.

"You leave the worrying about my family to me. It's time they all got a swift kick up the backside. They've all become complacent, just going through the motions. My grandchildren are almost, dare I say it, spoiled. I think you're going to be just what they need to stir up the monotony of their everyday lives. Now, Maxine gave me a strand of your hair when we first got here, and I had that couriered off for DNA testing. There's no doubt in mine or Howard's minds, but this will stop any of the naysayers."

There's a brief silence before Chuck's deep voice adds in his thoughts. "Harlow, I'm sure Doc Davies will understand if you say no to the position. Let's face it; this is an opportunity you shouldn't turn down." A sly look covers his face. "And, who knows, maybe that other dream you had will have more opportunity out in California, now that you have a family name behind you." While I hate to admit it, this might be the most convincing argument yet. The Bostons have that old-money reputation, and they're looked upon favorably in their world of wealthy businessmen, but the Summers are a whole other level. Neighpalm industries makes them the 1% *of* the 1%. The Boston name can get many doors open, but I'm pretty sure those doors don't even exist when you say 'Summers.'

I can see Poppy's ears prick up at this. Chuck

knew what he was doing, and now he'll be like a bloodhound after the truth. *Ugh, I still love him despite how sneaky he can be.*

"What's he talking about, Hally? Is there something else that you need from Nana and me?"

I shake my head. "No, Poppy, you and Nana have done enough already. I want nothing more from you except for your love." His eyes warm, and he smiles with joy at my response, but I can tell he's not going to let it go and will probably hunt down Chuck later for the information.

"So." Nana has her hands on her hips, that steely look now turned on me. "What's it going to be?" My nerves come racing back, but so does the excitement at the unknown.

Closing my eyes, I weigh the pros and cons. Should I take a chance on this wonderful couple? Everything could be amazing, rainbows and unicorns and shit, but I do run the risk of having my heart broken if things don't go well with the rest of their family. Or do I hide my head in the sand and let the never knowing eat away at the inside until I'm probably as bitter and twisted as my mom?

Opening my eyes, I see everyone watching me with anticipation.

"Will you look after Jenny and DS for me while I'm gone?" I ask Max, and she screws up her nose.

"Jenny, gladly, but the satan spawn can go to the

devil." Everyone laughs, but I know she's only joking.

I look at Melinda and Chuck, not knowing what I'm going to ask, but I guess I'm looking for permission or acceptance. From the look in their eyes, they can see that in the way only parents can.

"This will *always* be your home, Harlow," Melinda says softly. "You will always have a place with us, but I think this is something you need. You need to go and discover all about the other side you always wished you knew. We're only a flight away if you need us."

"Come on, Hally," Poppy teases, "I never took you for being chicken."

With those words, I straighten my spine and take a deep breath. "I'm in!" I tell Nana, and a large smile crosses her face.

"There's my brave girl." Poppy pats my thigh again in encouragement.

Nana claps her hands together, her excitement spilling over in a very unrefined way which is not like this woman, and picks up her phone again. "Excellent! Chuck, can Howard and I use your office here at the house to call Bradley? We really should tell him about this. I'm not quite evil enough to spring it on him; though his face would be priceless, I want to spare Harlow that extra drama. He'll want to tell the kids, I'm sure, and who knows how long it will take to get a hold of all of them."

Chuck tilts his head, raising an eyebrow in question. "I thought they all still lived at home. None of them are married, are they?" he asks her, and she shakes her head.

"No, none of them are married, though God knows enough gold-digging whores have tried."

I duck my head at the venom in her voice while also fighting a reaction at her choice of words. She sees my actions and shakes her head, giving me a stern look. "Shoulders back, sweet pea. You are not and never will be one of those women, and don't you dare flinch when someone says that. Summers women are cool and collected in the face of insult, and we are adept at sly social innuendos ourselves. I will give you a lesson about that on the plane on the way home," she assures me before turning back to Chuck. "They all still live at home, but they're also often away on business, and this is certainly something you don't want to blindside them with. Men have such fragile egos, and Jacinta, well, let's just say she has her own hangups." She sniffs, making a show of looking away from her husband in jest.

Poppy stands up, grabbing my hand, and pulls me with him. "Why don't you do whatever it is you all do as normal, and when we've made the call and some plans, we'll come and find you, and then we'll go from there. Sound good?" he suggests, and everyone else starts to get up and ready for the day. Max and Chuck are both dressed similarly to me, ready for a day's work. We've got a couple of horses that are due to head out in a week or two to a movie set, so we need to work with them, make sure they're ready for what's required.

I nod my head and kiss him on the cheek, more than okay with getting a few more hours of normalcy before my whole life changes. "Sounds good, Poppy!" Leaving him with a smile a mile wide, I follow the others out the door to where I left my boots and head to the stables to check on the owl before joining the other two.

# Chapter Eight

## Harlow

Maxine could not wait to get me alone the first night Nana and Poppy had arrived. Not long after I'd finished for the day and had just taken a shower, she arrived on my doorstep with a bottle of champagne and a couple of crystal flutes that she'd obviously stolen from Melinda. She popped the cork with a twist of her wrist, poured us both a glass, and handed me one while holding up hers to toast me. "Congrats on becoming wealthy!"

I take the glass but screw up my face at her. "Really?"

She blows out a sigh of air and flops onto one of my couches, managing, in a way that only Max can, to not spill a single drop. "Yeah, I know, so not you, but you've got to admit the world has just opened up to you. Oh, and let me tell you about your new family. Brad's great in a 'he's a cool uncle,' dorky kind of way. Kind and generous to a fault but a little awkward. He's a genius and has never been great at social interaction because his brain's always got so much running through it. Actually, that's probably why you tested out in a lot of your courses. You get that from your dad."

That word has me freezing, the glass halfway to my mouth. *Dad*. I roll it around in my brain before trying it out loud to see how it sounds. "Dad." It feels...weird, and Max is looking at me like I've lost my mind. Shrugging, I take a sip of the champagne. "It feels funny; I'll stick to Brad for now."

Her confusion clears in her eyes, and she nods sympathetically. "It will be a huge adjustment. Imagine going from living here to living in a house with ten people."

Ten people! How could I forget that part? Apparently, I have six adopted brothers and an adopted sister. Of which none are blood-related except for one of the brothers and Jacinta.

"Don't worry though! They're all so busy with their lives I don't think they're all there at once," she reassures me as she grabs a vet journal from the coffee table and flicks through it.

My curiosity gets the better of me, and I give in to this weird and slightly uncomfortable drive to know more about the people who will become my new...family. "How do you know all this? I thought you hadn't seen them in years." She gives me a pitying look, throwing the journal back on the table.

"Harlow, you need to keep up with social media. It can answer everything at the touch of a button."

I screw my nose up in disgust. "No, thank you, social media is for posers."

Now she just looks annoyed, her face all frowny and her lips pursed like she tasted something sour. "No, it's not. Yes, there are a fair amount of posers on it, but it's a realistic way of keeping in touch in the twenty-first century. It's also a great marketing and networking tool." She puts down her glass of champagne and pulls out her phone. Her fingers fly across the glass before she turns it toward me. Taking my own glass of champagne, I sit down next to her and bring my legs up underneath me, getting comfortable. Groaning with the stiffness that is settling into my body now that I've stopped for the day. An especially sharp pain in my knee makes me take notice, but when I stretch the leg back out, the ache eases. Might as well be comfortable as I settle in for my "lesson" with Miss Maxine.

On the screen in front of me is a tall, elegantly dressed woman with jet-black straight hair and blunt bangs that sit just above her piercing aquamarine eyes. Her makeup is flawless, and she's dressed in a fitted knee-length royal blue sheath. She, too, has a glass of champagne in her hand as she watches a catwalk show surrounded by other similarly dressed women. The photographer must have timed it perfectly to catch the full-frontal shot as she had turned her head from the show in front of her. It looks like she's staring straight at the camera. There's a smile on her face, but her eyes show a different story. Those eyes look wary and on edge, as if she's always prepared to put on a show for whoever is watching.

"That's Jacinta, and from this photo, I know she attended the Chanel show at Paris Fashion week, and she sat next to Evangeline Masters and Selena Cross."

The names are familiar, but I'm not sure exactly who they are. Maxine can see me struggling, and she rolls her eyes with a soft sigh. "God, you're so out of touch; animals and college are all you've known for years. I swear this trip is going to broaden your horizons, or I hope it will." She mumbles the last part before pointing to each of the women. One, an icy blonde with a look of disdain on her face. The other is a redhead with a riot of curls and a smile a mile wide, giving a friendly and open look. Maxine swipes her finger, and in the next photo Jacinta and the redhead are laughing at something, their heads huddled close, and the icy blonde's disdain just seems to get deeper. "Evangeline and Selena are two of the hottest actresses in Hollywood at the moment. Selena," she points at the snooty blonde, "is rumored to be involved with

Declan Summers, head of Neighpalm Productions."

Again, her fingers fly across the screen, and this time, the image that comes to the screen has me looking twice. This guy is smoking hot. He's wearing a suit and is talking to an older man, who I do recognize as an actor I've seen in a movie, but I can't put a name to the face. He's an older gentleman that has been followed by scandal throughout his whole career, and if I recall correctly, he has a penchant for younger wives. However, despite his obvious starpower, he's completely overshadowed by the man next to him.

Even through the photo, this guy oozes power. Declan can't be in his thirties yet, but he has the presence of a seasoned businessman. His suit is designer, and the cufflink I can see is probably some expensive stone. A chiseled, clean-shaven jaw lends an intense look to his face, and his dark hair is pulled back into a short ponytail, not a lock out of place. The angle is wrong, though, and I can't see the color of his eyes, but I bet they're mesmerizing.

"Neighpalm Productions produces movies and also works as a talent agency. This guy could make or break your career, and rumor has it, it's the only reason Selena ever got anywhere." The words rush from Max's mouth, full of speculation and a giddy pleasure that comes from years of being in the 1%. When you grow up with money, reputations are something that can come and go pretty quickly, and it's almost like a soap opera when you have a front row seat to watch it happening.

"See, even though I haven't seen them in years, I know everything I need to about your new siblings," she declares smugly, her lips curled in a triumphant grin. It's the one thing I hate about Maxine. When she knows something you don't, she gets smug about it. She's been that way since we were kids, and it's caused more than one small argument.

I hold a hand up. "Yeah, no. You're the only sibling I need; you are more than enough. I just hope that we can establish some sort of friendship." My stomach rolls at the thought that we may not be able to, but I quickly brush it aside.

"Who knows?" she says breezily with a shrug. "But with Grace and Howard on your side, you'll be just fine. Howard's father started Neighpalm Industries with a couple of hotels and some real estate investments, and through Howard and then Brad, it's grown to be one of the biggest companies in the US. Mainly thanks to Brad and his business brain." She taps her empty champagne flute against her temple then stands up to get the bottle before returning to her seat.

She pours some more into my glass before she empties the bottle into hers and lets it drop to the floor. Taking a sip, she continues. "Neighpalm Ink is the latest venture. That's Oliver's baby. He's the tattoo artist, the one who studied business as a backup. It's not huge yet since there's only one shop in California, but last I heard they were going to do one of those tattoo reality shows to showcase the talents of the artists. Drama sells, baby, and I'm sure Declan is producing it." She chatters on about the rest of the brothers, but my mind drifts off into my own turbulent thoughts.

How am I ever supposed to have anything in common with these people? All of them are mega-wealthy, with impressive careers and friends if Jacinta is anything to go by. How does the daughter of a junkie whore ever fit in? Sure, I've been with the Bostons for a long time, but Mom was always a part of my life. I was always looking over my shoulder, waiting for the other shoe to drop, even in college. She would occasionally turn up there too to demand money from me, making sure to throw some more threats at Maxine and her parents, assuring me that she knew people who could "fuck them up," and quite often she was accompanied by whatever grubby biker she had hooked onto for a while. She used to terrify me, even then, but thinking back now, all I feel is hollow. There's an empty space where the love of a parent should be. It's been slowly eaten away until nothing remains. To be honest, I have no clue if Brad is going to fill that space or if he's even going to want to. It sounds like we may be just as awkward as each other, so this could be a perfect fit or a perfect disaster.

A text message to Maxine's phone drags me

from my musings. Looking at it, she declares that the pizza she ordered is here, followed by a totally unsurprising plan to raid her parents' fridge for more alcohol.

Standing up, she holds out a hand and drags me to my feet when I take it. My body screams in protest with the movement, and I barely manage to suck in a gasp at the pain. We'd been practicing jousting with a couple of the horses today and all the different kinds of moves they're required to make. As good as we both are as riders, both of us took falls today, and even with the safety equipment we wear and the fact that we know how to fall, it doesn't stop the bruises from forming or the muscles from screaming once you finally quit.

I don't do it very often, but Maxine often works with the horses as a female stunt rider in movies. I look at her enviously; she isn't even walking stiffly. She bounds down my stairs with a bounce in her step and the empty champagne glasses in one hand, while I follow slowly behind. My knee shouting in agony with every step

She turns around to look back up at me. "Jesus, Harlow, you're walking like an old lady. You haven't been putting in enough hours on horseback."

I grunt my reply. "It's not being on horseback that's the problem; I fell oddly when Samson reared. I think I twisted something in my knee."

The teasing smile drops from her face and immediately becomes concerned. "Why didn't you say anything? Should we head to the ER to get you checked over?"

Shaking my head, I finally get to the bottom. Pulling up the leg of my sweatpants, I show her my knee, cringing when I realize it already looks worse than when I'd first inspected it. It's swollen and purple, and a whistle escapes her mouth when she sees it. "Holy shit! I didn't even realize you did that."

I wave her off, not wanting a full-on Boston freak out over whether my knee will ever be the same again. "It wasn't too bad until I stopped and sat down. I think I should probably ice it."

She nods enthusiastically and grabs one of my arms, wrapping it around her shoulder to help support me to the house. I just laugh in response. "You're a midget; that's not going to help." She sticks out her tongue, unfazed by the teasing that's become normal for us ever since I hit a growth spurt years back.

Pulling a set of keys off a hook in the wall, I hand them to her. "Could you drive me over to the house on the ATV, please? I'm not sure I'm going to make it on my own." Jenny snuffles her greeting as she pokes her head over the stable door to see what's happening but quickly loses interest in favor of the hay in her feeding trough.

Maxine disappears, and before long, the lights shine through the stable doors as she pulls up next to it, and I climb gingerly onto the back. Letting out the brake, she slowly eases us forward until we're moving steadily toward the house. Neither of us tries to talk over the sound of the engine, but when we get there, she shoves on the hand brake, turns off the machine, and leaps off running into the house.

Confused, my eyes follow her up the steps as she disappears. The confusion clears up not five minutes later when Chuck and Poppy follow her out of the house, faces lined with worry. "Harlow, why didn't you say anything when this happened?" Chuck gently chastises me as he and Poppy support me, one on each side, and help me limp into the house. Once inside, they guide me to the living room where they assist me onto a sofa there with explicit orders to stay put. Melinda meets us with some over the counter medication, and Nana with an ice pack in her hand, brows furrowed in concern, and pursed lips as though she's holding back from a lecture.

As I get settled and put my leg up, I realize Chuck is still waiting on an answer. "To be honest, I didn't even notice it at the time. When you've got 1,600 pounds of horse flesh heading in your direction, you don't stop to think about anything else. I just know I wasn't quite as quick as normal, and Samson must have realized because he shifted in mid-descent, so he missed me completely." Nana's mouth opens, and I revert to bad habits, preparing to cringe and desperately apologize, but before she can say anything, Poppy stops her.

"Now, Grace, don't say anything. The girls have been doing this for years, and just because Harlow is now ours does not mean we can start dictating what she does with her life. They are careful and take all the necessary precautions. They wear helmets and back vests and padding, but things happen."

She squeezes onto the couch next to me and brushes my hair back from my face. Her hand is soft and gentle against my skin, and I close my eyes and revel in the loving feeling for a moment.

"As long as you're okay?" she asks again, and I open my eyes and nod at her.

"I am, and Samson got an extra scoop of grains in his feed for being such a clever boy." Turning to Chuck, I say to him, "Whoever they put on his back during the shoot should be safe as a house. He's a pleasure to ride." Chuck's pleased smile eases my worries.

"If anything, it was my own fault. I've got so much going on in my brain that I wasn't paying enough attention. You can't let your guard down when attempting those maneuvers because that's when things do go wrong," I tell Nana and Poppy, and they look at each other, guilt showing in their faces.

"Oh, I didn't tell you that to make you feel bad. It was mostly about Mom." My words seem to ease their feelings slightly, and they nod, Nana patting my hand as though she can't stand having some distance between us.

"Harlow, I think maybe you should head into the hospital and get that checked just to make sure you haven't done any damage." Melinda's quiet, sensible words set everyone into motion. Before I know it, I'm in the back of Chuck's Land Rover, and we're headed into Hartford to the emergency room. Poppy in the passenger seat and Max in the back with me. She's got a sneaky bottle of vodka in hand, and we keep taking sips. Me, not too much in case I need to take some stronger painkillers, but it's giving me a nice warm feeling and taking the edge off the twinges of pain in my knee.

Thanks to Poppy and Chuck's influence, the wait isn't long, and after being seen by a fairly hot doctor that Max keeps flirting with, I'm told that I've tweaked some of the ligaments in my knee. There's no tear, but some solid rest is recommended for a few days. I hobble out of the ER with a set of crutches to relieve any weight-bearing to the knee, a prescription for some strong painkillers for the first couple of days, and instructions to alternate heat and cold compresses.

I used to worry about taking painkillers or about how much alcohol I consumed, not wanting to become addicted like my mother, but the shrink helped me come to the realization that Mom's addictions were a symptom of much deeper issues.

The therapist brought me to understand that as long as I stayed aware of it, I could indulge in moderation and feel comfortable doing it. I tend to avoid recreational drugs, not worth the risk, though I did smoke a bit of weed during college.

Max, now with the doctor's number in her phone, runs into the pharmacy for me, and not long after, we're headed for home again.

## Chapter Nine

## Harlow

I t's not until a couple of days later that we manage to leave. The DNA results have come through and confirmed that I am a hundred percent match to Bradley Summers.

When the limo we're in pulls into the airport and onto the private airstrip, my mouth drops open in shock. The Bostons are wealthy, but the Summers take it to a whole new level. Nana said we were taking their private jet back to California, and I was expecting a smallish private plane. That is *so* not what we're parked in front of. This is like a full-sized airliner the public would fly on. It's a pristine, shiny white, with the Neighpalm logo on the tail in green and black and a green stripe running the length of the plane.

"Close your mouth, dear. Remember what I

said. It's unladylike, and a fly might go in if you're not careful." She takes my crutches from me and hands them to the attendant who's standing at the bottom of the steps.

"This is Chris; he's the co-pilot on this aircraft." Without missing a beat, she introduces me to him next. "This is my granddaughter Harlow. Be a dear and carry those up for us." He's a handsome man in his late twenties, and he shakes his head, a slight smile on his face.

"How about you carry them, and I bring Harlow?" he suggests, handing my crutches back to her. Before either of us can say anything, he sweeps me up into his arms and carries me up the staircase.

"Oh, well, yes, that is much more preferable," Nana titters behind us, and when I look back, she winks at me. Chris' arms and chest are solid, and I feel secure, if not a little awkward in this stranger's grasp. But it *is* preferable to hobbling up all those steps, and he's not too bad to look at either. Goodness, it's like the president boarding Airforce One.

When we get to the top, there's another man and a woman waiting for us. Chris sets me gently down on my feet and steps to the side, taking the crutches from Nana again. She pats his arm, giving him a warm smile that I usually see directed at the Bostons and me. "Thank you so much, Chris." She turns to the others, and her eyebrows raise in surprise when she sees the woman, but she quickly clears her face and smiles at the man when he greets them.

"Welcome aboard, Mr. and Mrs. Summers, nice to see you again." The pilot's voice is warm and reassuring, and, like Chris, he's nothing but smiles for all of us. "Did you enjoy your trip?"

"Thank you, James, we did!" Nana replies graciously at him. "This is our granddaughter Harlow." She turns to me. "James is the pilot of this plane. Both of them have been with us for a few years now and exclusively fly this jet for whoever needs it." She turns back to him, and I shoot him a quick smile, hoping it doesn't convey the over-whelmed feeling that's threatening to take hold. "I believe you've just fetched Jacinta from Paris Fashion Week, is that correct?"

He nods his head while the flight attendant turns to me. "Welcome, Miss Summers. I hope you enjoy your first flight with us." She's a pretty, little, dark-haired woman, but the look on her face brings a negative twist to her otherwise pleasant appear-ance. There's a slight sneer twisting her lips like I smell bad or something. Discreetly, I sniff my armpits before her words penetrate my brain, and I give up on that particular mystery. *Miss Summers.* My feet stop moving in shock, and I look at Nana and Poppy with panic in my eyes. *Holy crap, that's my name now, or it could be. What should I do?*

"It's up to you, Harlow," Poppy reassures me, knowing what's going on in my brain. "We'd love it if you changed it, and we can get our lawyer started on it straightaway, but it's completely up to you."

"Can I think about it?" My voice is quiet, the sound of the jet engines almost drowning it out.

"Of course, you can," he replies. We follow the dark-haired flight attendant past a couple of doors and then into a huge open lounge section with a bar and comfortable plush seating. Stopping in surprise, my mouth drops open in shock again, and Nana just puts a finger under my chin, pushing it closed while tutting at me. I hurry to keep up with the attendant, who hasn't stopped, and she moves past the lounge to another seating area. On one side, there's seating for six around a table, and on the other side is four around a smaller table. Nana slides into the seating for four, and I sit down next to her. Poppy slides in across the table from us.

"This is where we sit for takeoff, but we can move once we're in the air," she informs me before turning to the attendant, who's handing Poppy a newspaper from a compartment above us.

"Where's Jilly, Veronica? She's usually the flight attendant on our private jet."

Veronica purses her lips like she ate something bad before blanking her face and replying, "She's off on one of her vacations for a week or so." Though she's saying something quite normal, her voice is thick with disapproval, making it sound like Jilly must be doing something horrible.

A sly smile crosses Nana's face, and she replies

with enthusiasm, "Good for her! I admire a woman who takes control of life and doesn't march to the beat of everyone else." This time Veronica's mouth starts to part in shock, her eyes widening slightly, before she informs us to strap in for take-off, and that she'll return with refreshments once we're in the air. With that, she flounces back to the front of the plane. Poppy laughs at her as he opens the newspaper he had been given, the sound just loud enough for us to hear.

I quickly try and work out how to put my seat belt on, but my hand is shaking so badly I can't get it in. Nana's small soft hand on mine stops my frantic movement, and she gracefully helps me. Then, she pats her hand on my leg, the gesture soothing me a bit like it did back at the Bostons' house.

"Jilly, our normal flight attendant, leads an exciting life," she starts. I know she's trying to distract me, so I indulge her. "She works for us and flies all over the world. Did you see Veronica's face screw up in disgust?"

"Terrible poker face," Poppy adds in from behind his paper. "Not good for private clients. I'll have to talk to Thomas about putting her back on the public flights," he grumbles.

Nana just laughs. "Silly girl, she doesn't like things that buck the norm," she explains, and my curiosity gets the better of me.

"What do you mean, Nana?"

"Jilly's bisexual," she confides in me, and I just shrug because that's no big deal, but she continues with something much less ordinary. "She's also polyamorous and has different lovers in every city she visits. That girl is living the dream." She sighs after giving me a wink, and Poppy's newspaper drops. Despite his frown, she waves at him nonchalantly, totally unfazed about admiring Jilly's love life.

"Hush, Howard, you know you're my one true love." That's so super cute; they still love each other so much after all these years. He smiles, and his newspaper goes back up. "But if I were young again, I certainly wouldn't be settling for one if I could have more."

The newspaper drops again, and his face is so shocked that it sends her into peals of laughter, but she sobers quickly. "Imagine if I hadn't had to choose between you and Edward. You and he might have stayed best friends instead of drifting apart as you did. You did everything together, but none of us considered that you could've shared me as well."

A sad look crosses Howard's face as he thinks about his old friend. "I wonder whatever happened to Edward."

"You should find out. It's high past time that you two put aside your issues." He nods thoughtfully, the frown now gone.

"And I'm still not opposed to sharing either," Nana cheekily finishes, and her eye sparkles as he chokes on a cough at her words, but a gleam enters his eye too. *Oh my word. These people.* I chuckle to myself, once more basking in the luck that out of all the grandparents in the world, these two officially belong to me. I fall more and more in love with them every day. Nana pats my leg to get my attention again.

"See that as a lesson. Don't make decisions that you're going to regret. Jilly grabs life by the balls and gives a good yank; you should too." Nana's crude words make laughter fall from my lips, but she may have a point.

"Are they one night stands, or are they regular things?" I ask, my curiosity growing.

"Oh no, dear. She's in committed relationships with these people. They may have others too, but they're open with each other. Communication is the key in any kind of relationship, but it's particularly important in an untraditional arrangement like Jilly's. She travels so often and isn't in one place for long, so she can't fully commit to one person who expects her to come home every night. Jilly, I guess, has it easy because not often do her various relationships interact. The only one who may is James." She nods at the front of the plane, and my eyes widen in surprise.

"He's with her too?" I ask, and Nana nods while Poppy's newspaper comes down again.

"Goodness, Grace, you're such a gossip." Despite his words, there's an amused undercurrent to his words, and she sticks out her tongue at him.

"Howard, you old gossip, you're just as bad as me," she scolds him, but he doesn't look embarrassed.

"Rumor has it, Veronica tried to become one of James' partners, but he wouldn't even consider her. It's why she's so bitter," Poppy whispers, and Nana looks surprised at this piece of news. Poppy smiles in satisfaction. "See, you don't know everything, woman."

Just as he tells me this, my stomach dips in protest, and I realize while we've been gossiping, we're taking off. My hands grip the plush leather seat underneath me, and I hold my breath.

"Breathe, Harlow. It's fine," Nana soothes and rubs my leg, and before long, the plane evens out.

My knee starts to throb, and I look around the plane having not paid too much attention to it before. Poppy sees where I'm looking, and he puts down his paper and stands up, stretching. "How's that leg feeling? Fancy a tour?" Even though it aches, I still want a tour, so I unbuckle and stand up.

"This is an Airbus A350 and our family's private jet. As you know, Neighpalm Airlines is one of our companies." Poppy and Nana had given me a rundown of the companies in the Neighpalm Group, but a lot of it went in one ear and out the other. I was so overwhelmed by it all, but I do remember the airline.

"We have a smaller one for United States travel

that we usually use, but this had just landed when I called Brad, so he refueled it and sent it our way. To be honest, I think he was trying to impress you," he confides to me, and a smile crosses Nana's face as he says it.

"He's very nervous but excited to meet you," she explains, and my heart accelerates with nerves.

Poppy leads me back the way we came, and I hobble after him as he continues to talk. "So we have this plane and a smaller one, and we also have a couple of helicopters. A couple of the boys have their licenses, and it's an easy way for them to quickly get from the estate into the city without having to wait for all the traffic." My eyes just about pop out of my head at his words. I don't even own a car. I used to travel back and forth from the university with Max or on the bus if she was busy. Sometimes, William would drive me back and forth. To be able to travel by helicopter blows my mind.

"The kids use this one for their international travel, and they'll often take a lot of people with them, staff or friends. Like Kai and his Neighpalm extreme sports team. If they're going to competitions or whatever, there's a large storage hold for luggage in the very rear," he tells me, leading me through the lounge area.

Kai's the brother who runs the Neighpalm Energy branch; that leg of the company produces energy drinks and sports-related products. There's also Thomas, the airline dude, Jacinta's the fashionista, and Declan, the movie executive, whose picture Maxine showed me. There are three more brothers, but I can't remember their names off the top of my head or which business they belong to.

We go past the two doors from earlier and pass by the closed boarding entrance, through what looks like a galley, and to where Veronica looks to be making something. She glances up at me, staring as we pass through. We get to a closed door, and he pushes it open; daylight assaults my eyes. I throw my hand up to protect them.

"Oops! Sorry," he apologizes as he rubs at his own eyes, "forgot it was daytime." It's only now that I realize all the windows in the cabin were covered.

"Hi, Mr. Summers. Have you brought Miss Summers up for a look?" Chris asks, climbing out of his seat in the very futuristic-looking cockpit and gesturing for me to sit down. He then inches past Poppy as he leaves, and I watch as he heads to the galley to make himself a cup of coffee. Veronica fluttering her eyes at him all the while.

"Come on, Miss Summers, take a seat," James says, patting the vacated chair. "You can be my co-pilot for a little while."

Poppy smiles and nods at me when I look at him, so I climb into the chair. "I'll just go and have a coffee with Grace, and I'll come back and get you in a bit, so we'll finish the tour." Once I'm settled, he leaves, pulling the door closed behind me.

"Just call me Harlow, please, James. I'm not sure

how I feel about Summers yet." He gives me a sympathetic look and smiles to show his acceptance.

"Alright then, Harlow. Ever been in the cockpit of a plane before?" His change of subject is appreciated, and it's easier than I thought to get comfortable sitting next to him.

"Actually, this is my first time on a plane ever." I blush at the admission, embarrassed by that fact. "It's all a little overwhelming."

He whistles and then laughs. "What a first time experience. You won't find many jets that are quite as fancy as this one." Pride is evident in his voice, and he even seems to sit a little straighter with those words. The view out the window is nothing but blue skies, so my eyes drop to all the gauges in front of me.

"It looks like something out of *Star Trek*," I admit, gesturing to them all, and he laughs again.

"Yeah, this thing practically flies itself. So, what happened to you? How come you needed Chris to carry you up the steps?" He lounges back in his seat, face bright with curiosity, and I actually don't mind talking about myself even though he's a stranger. He's got a way about him that makes you feel instantly comfortable. Maybe it's because he's so open and friendly.

"Horse stunt went wrong," I tell him ruefully, and his eyes widen in surprise.

"Oh, you ride horses, do you?" I can tell he's genuinely interested and not just being polite, so I relax back in my seat too, careful not to touch any of the buttons or knobs or anything.

"Yeah, my foster parents train horses for movies, and I've been riding for them for as long as I can remember. But at the beginning of the week, I fell funny, and my knee has been giving me grief ever since."

"And is that what you want to do with your life?" he asks.

"What? Train stunt horses?" He nods. "No, I've recently graduated from vet school." His eyes widen in shock, his mouth drops open, and a snort escapes my mouth.

"Aren't you a little young to be a vet?" He looks me up and down, and I return the favor.

"Aren't you a little young to be flying a big jet?" I return saucily, and he smiles, amusement and joy clearly shining through.

"Nah, you can get your pilot license at 18. I got mine flying planes in the Air Force. I went to high school with Tom, and when he heard I got out, he offered me a job."

"Tom? Oh, you mean Thomas Summers, right?" He nods again, and I can see his brain whirling behind his eyes. He takes a breath, and it looks like he's reached a decision.

"Can I ask some nosy questions?" he asks politely, and I pretend to think about it. I know what he's going to ask, but I have some questions of my own.

"Yes, but I get to return the favor afterward." He thinks about it and nods his head in agreement.

"Deal. So, you didn't know anything about your dad?" I laugh at the first question, unsurprised and completely aware that this will likely be the first thing that everyone wants to know.

"Wow, gossip sure travels fast." He has the grace to look slightly ashamed, but that doesn't last long as he waits for my answer.

"No, I didn't. I only found out about a week ago, though I've known Nana and Poppy all my life. They're best friends with my foster father's parents, and they've always been part of my life," I explain to him, my eyes tearing up slightly. "To find out that they were my grandparents for real was... amazing."

The look in his eyes softens too as he smiles. "Yeah. I could imagine it would. They're great people. They never treat us like employees; we're just one of the family. They insist we call them Howard and Grace, but when we're flying, especially with others around, I like to show them the respect they deserve." I can see Nana and Poppy being like that, just by the way they welcomed me as one of the family so many years ago.

He takes a deep breath, his eyes intent on me and my reactions. "Does Brad know about you yet?" he pushes a little more.

"I've been told that he does and that his children will know by the time we get there." A grimace crosses his face at my words, and my heart sinks.

"You can't look like that without explaining the reason," I plead.

"Look, Tom's my friend, and the rest of the family are great too, but they're not good with outsiders. They like their inner circle, and to break through that is tricky. I can't tell you the number of times the guys and Jacinta got burned through high school. They learned to build thick skins, and trust is very thin until you've proven your worth. They are incredibly protective of each other and have a bond not often seen in biological families, let alone a made family. They would always choose one another over a friend if they needed to, and they all worship the ground Brad walks on. He can do no wrong in their eyes, and you existing is going to push a lot of buttons."

I wave my hand at him as though that one motion can somehow dismiss the not so optimistic news he's just given me. "Look, I'm there to get to know my biological dad. That's it. If his kids want nothing to do with me, that's no skin off my nose. I have a family and career prospects back home, so if it doesn't work out, I'll just return." I deliver this breezily with my best poker face, but deep down, the possibility of more rejection terrifies me. There's only so much a girl can take.

## Chapter Ten

**Harlow**

Thankfully, he changes the subject after that and asks me about being a vet. We chat about that for a little while, but I know Poppy is going to come back for me soon, so I've got to squeeze in my own nosy questions while I have the chance. "Okay, my turn for the personal questions," I tell him, and his face lights up with anticipation.

"Shoot," he replies with no hesitation. It's my turn to blush, and he laughs, a knowing smile on his face. "I bet I know what you're going to ask."

"You do?" He nods. "Yes. I bet Grace told you about Jilly, didn't she? She seemed surprised to see Veronica."

"Yeah, she did. You're in a polyamorous relationship with Jilly?"

He's smiling when he responds, none of the blush I know I'd have staining his cheeks. "Yeah. I think Grace is just a little envious of Jilly." I roll my eyes, but I can't stop the smirk at his too-true words.

"Ew! Yes, I had to listen to Nana and Poppy discuss the possibility of adding a friend to their relationship," I tell him, screwing up my nose, and his eyes jump in surprise.

"Really?"

"Yes, but let's not talk about that." I shudder, his laughter filling the room. "What's that like? Are you jealous? Do you have other lovers too?" I fire the questions at him faster than I'd intended, and he holds his hands up in defense.

"Whoa! Slow down." He's still smiling, so I know I haven't upset him. He holds one hand up and starts counting off on his fingers.

"It's fine; she and I are open with each other and who we have in our lives. Our partners are not casual one night stands. We all know about each other, and we respect each other. Communication is the biggest thing. We don't hide things from each other. If she wants to add to her partners, she talks to all the others first, and we can then tell her how we feel about it."

He holds up his next finger. "Do I get jealous? No, both of us were upfront with each other from the start. We're both bisexual, and neither of us is willing to give that up and commit to one sex.

And that leads into question three..." He holds up a third finger, and it's my turn to laugh. "Yes, I have another lover. Chris is my other partner. He and I are always together, so that works well, and when Jilly is on the flight, then we have her as well."

"Oh, so the three of you are together?" I gesture between him and the door, and again, he nods.

"How does that work when you're in cities with her other lovers?" He shrugs, completely nonplussed.

"She visits them, and we have our own time." I shake my head, trying to wrap my mind around it. I couldn't even successfully manage one night stands, let alone more than one other person in the relationship. Nor do I really want to. My trust issues are like a deep-flowing river; sure, I look good and calm on the surface, but underneath, the currents are fast and furious

"It's hard looking at it from the outside in, but it works, trust me. There's a big polyamorous community in Cali and lots of support if needed, but communication and trust are definitely the keys."

As he finishes telling me this, the door opens, and Chris and Poppy return. "Ready for the rest of that tour, Harlow?" Poppy asks, and I hop out of Chris's seat, not quite ready to look Chris in the eye.

"Thank you for letting me sit there," I say to him, and, turning to James, I hold out my hand, and he shakes it. "Thank you so much for talking to me about everything. It's been nice getting to know you."

He winks, harmlessly flirting with me. "Anytime, sweetheart, looking forward to seeing you next time you're on the plane."

"I'm not sure when that will be, but I look forward to it too," I tell him, my answering smile as genuine as his.

Following Poppy, the door closes behind us. Veronica meets us in the galley with a smile on her face, but it looks a little forced.

"Mrs. Summers wanted to know if you would like something to drink? They've just had coffee." Her words are scornful, and combined with a roll of the eyes, I get her message loud and clear. She thinks I should have had coffee with them too, instead of wasting her time now. Holy crap, she really doesn't have a poker face. Poppy was definitely right. She isn't really suitable for customer service, unless it's just me, but I can't think of anything I've done to upset her.

"Sure, I'll have a cup. If you can pour it now, I'll take it with me." Poppy has walked further on and can't see her, but she rolls her eyes and pulls a cupboard door open. Taking out a cup, she slams it down and sloshes some coffee into it before offering me creamer and sugar.

"No, that's okay," I reply, pushing them back toward her. "I take it black. Thanks so much for this; I appreciate it," I add, trying to make nice, but she just huffs her response as I move past her. I don't know what the fuck I've done to her, but the attitude is beginning to get annoying.

Poppy is standing in front of one of the doors, and he jumps right back into the tour when I reach him. "Back there is the galley as you saw. There are also crew rooms through that door. This door is a master bedroom with an ensuite, and the next door is a private office." He starts walking, and I hobble behind, careful not to spill my coffee. Now that I get a chance to look around, I can see the plane is fancy as fuck. Entering the lounge area, I find Nana has moved to the plush couches. Looking around, I notice everything is beautifully appointed, with a muted color scheme of grays and blues—both relaxing and inviting. The bar is a beautiful rich reddish wood that contrasts nicely with the muted colors, and the shelves behind it match. They're lined with bottles recessed into the shelves to help hold them steady if the plane experiences any turbulence. "Oh, there you are, dear. Did you have a good visit with James?" Her eyebrows are raised in question, and her face lights up in what seems to be her default reaction when she sees Poppy and me together.

"Oh, yes. James is a fascinating man," I tell her before taking a sip of my coffee.

A sly look crosses her face, and she winks. "Yes, he is." Hmm, Nana's acting funny. *Is she trying to set me up with him?* Not sure I'm ready for an open relationship when I've barely had any relationship to begin with.

Poppy huffs impatiently, "You can gossip later. Come on. I want to show you the rest of the plane."

I put my cup down on the coffee table in front of Nana and follow him easily. He's walking slowly, so I can keep up. We pass the seating area we used for takeoff, and he opens another door leading to a surprisingly large conference room with seating for eighteen around a large table. Then there are couches in each corner for more people.

"This is for dining or conferences on long haul flights. Sometimes we use the plane for business meetings; clients get a kick out of it, makes for good schmoozing." We walk around the table and chairs to another door, and a galley greets us, this one bigger than the last one.

"This one is for preparing the meals. We would have a bigger crew on if we were going to use this and have meals served. We have a chef that would come on board and prepare the meals for us. There's also another sleeper cabin and bathroom for the crew."

The next door opens, and we come to another corridor with six closed doors—three on either side and then one in front.

"These are another four bedrooms, all with desks for business and attached bathrooms. There are also two more toilets." Walking down the corridor, we don't open any of the doors, except the last one that's at the end of the hallway.

"This is the last room before the luggage hold," he tells me, pushing it open and walking through. My mouth gapes open again, and he laughs. "Don't let Nana see that." I snap it shut, not ready for her to call me out on 'catching flies' again. It's like I've walked into a five-star movie theater. Seating for about twenty people, but all the chairs are those fancy reclining ones and super comfy. A big screen is on the wall just waiting for a movie to play.

"It makes long flights pass quite quickly, and the seats are also a great place to take a nap." Poppy grins as he says it, and I know he's totally done that before. "So, that's it." My feelings are all over the place as I sit down in one of the recliners. Looking at Poppy, I decide that I can tell him some of it. He's never let me down in the past. I pat a seat next to me, and he sits down.

"This is all very overwhelming for me," I start, unable to look at him. "I can't connect to this kind of wealth, and I'm worried that I'm going to be so out of place."

"You very well may feel like that." I look up in shock at his words, and his eyes are full of sympathy. "It *is* a very different world. People judge you by superficial means as opposed to the type of person you are. There are some very bitchy, catty people in our world, but you'll learn how to deal with them. Grace and I tried to raise both our kids to value humility and hard work." Sadness crosses his face before he continues, clearing his throat as though he needs that second to keep himself composed. "Brad's the only one left, but I like to think we were successful with him, and he's tried to do the same thing with his kids. Granted, they got a little more spoiled than Brad did, but all of them came from difficult homes, and he wanted to make their lives as easy as possible." He pats me on the leg before standing up. "Whatever happens, you've got Grace and me to come to for advice, and our door will always be open to you no matter what you decide." The look on his face tells me he knows I may decide not to stay, but it also makes me feel comfortable in whatever choice I make because they'll still be there for me.

"Come on. Let's go and finish your coffee, and if you want to watch a movie after, we'll put one on." I stand up, my knee aching so much I wince. Poppy looks down at it. "You can take one of those painkillers too," he insists, and I screw up my face.

"They make me tired, and I'll want to go to sleep."

He laughs. "Well, there are plenty of beds to sleep on, so I don't see the problem. The flight is still at least another six hours to go, and that's a decent sleep. We'll arrive mid-afternoon and then travel to the estate by car. If you nap now, you'll have the energy to meet the family later."

My stomach rolls with nerves again, and a

grimace crosses my face.

"Poppy, you should know by now I'm not all that social. There's no party or anything organized, is there?"

He blanches, looking alarmed at my suggestion. "God, I hope not." A shudder follows, and I'm grateful that at least someone in this family will always understand me. Turning, he hurries back toward the lounge, leaving the hallway doors open for me and my slower pace. I close them all behind me, and by the time I get back, he and Nana are arguing about something.

"He didn't?" Poppy's voice is horrified, and that sinking feeling appears in my gut again. "He can't do that to her. You get on the phone and tell your son to pull his head out of his ass. This is to be a family-only affair," he orders, but Nana shakes her head.

"He wanted to celebrate this. He's excited," she argues with him, and I grab my stomach. I feel like I'm going to throw up, and the thought races through my mind about how much it would cost to clean the upholstery on one of these fancy chairs.

"No, I'm putting my foot down. He can do it in a week or two when she's met everyone, and they've all gotten used to each other. This is just as traumatic for the other kids too. God, sometimes I wonder about his so-called genius brain." He's muttering angrily now, and Nana gets up, heading for the office at the front near the main bedroom.

"Alright, I guess you're right. I don't see the harm, but maybe it would be better to settle in for a few days before throwing a party."

"Nana," I call, and she stops, turning to look at me. "I wouldn't want him to announce it and then get embarrassed if I don't decide to stay. Better to keep it private for now," I tell her gently, but she flinches at my words, and I go over to her.

"You know there may be a chance that this won't work out. Please don't get ahead of yourself. Everyone may hate me. I can imagine his kids are going to be at least annoyed at me; it's to be expected, and it's not like I haven't experienced plenty of rejection. I have thick skin, and if it happens, well, I'll just go back to my normal life," I reassure her, but at the same time, I need to hear these words for myself too. My insecurities are enormous, and I'm rethinking the whole thing now.

She pulls me tight into her embrace, and she whispers in my ear, "I know I have no right to ask this, but be patient. If I know my grandchildren, they're going to try and make you jump through hoops. They haven't always had it easy, and you may find you have a lot more in common with them than you expect." Though she starts off gently, her voice turns fierce as she orders, "But don't take any of their crap; you give as good as you get." She releases me, continuing to the office, and I flop myself into one of the lounge chairs and grab my coffee cup. Taking a sip, I grimace at the now cold liquid.

"Is it cold?" Poppy asks before pushing a button on the arm of the chair. He then sits next to me on the sofa, but a little further down, not wanting to crowd me. "These buttons call the cabin crew," he tells me just as Veronica appears at the front of the lounge, a smile pasted on her face. "What can I get you, Mr. Summers?"

"Ah, Veronica, please take Harlow's cup. It's cold now. Can you bring us another, and maybe a plate of those little pastry things I like so much?"

"Of course, Mr. Summers, it won't be long." She walks over and takes the cup abruptly, a little liquid spilling over my hand. "Oh, I'm sorry; I'll bring you back a napkin too," she says with forced politeness. Turning on her heel, she heads back to the galley, leaving me with spilled coffee on my hand. Looking around, I don't want to wipe it anywhere, but I can't see any tissues. "I'll grab you a napkin," Poppy says, shaking his head at her behavior. "I'm going to speak to Thomas about her. I'm not even sure she should be serving the public. She's never been this rude before."

"That's okay. I have something," I tell him.

Reaching down to my feet with my clean hand, I grab my backpack that Poppy had carried on board for me. There's not much in it except for my purse, cell phone, and a book that I threw in, along with a packet of tissues and my painkillers. Grabbing a tissue, I wipe at the mess on my hand before putting it back in the bag and pulling out my medication. I think I'm going to take one and rest. That'll get me out of my head and make the flight seem not quite so long.

Poppy sees me taking them out of my bag, and he gets up and goes behind the bar. He bends down, and when he stands up, he's holding a bottle of water. "These fridges are fully stocked with water and soft drinks as well as alcohol, please help yourself," he tells me, coming back around and handing me the bottle of water.

I place the medications on the coffee table and take the bottle of water from him. "Thank you, I will, but I think I'm going to take your advice and have a nap. Is it alright if I curl up just here? I like being around you and Nana, and I'd feel funny in one of those big bedrooms on my own." He smiles again, and it's full of joy.

"Harlow, honey, you go right ahead. If it were up to me, I wouldn't let you out of my sight for a few years, but I know that's not possible, so I'm going to be selfish and take all I can get now." Again, the warmth in his words is reassuring and helps settle the anxiousness I feel. "Would you like me to grab you a comforter off one of the beds? They're really cozy. Jacinta insisted we get them. She wanted to be comfortable, not like hotels where you get just a blanket and a fancy cover. These are fifty-fifty feathers and down and are like sleeping with a cloud wrapped around you." He looks like he's considering a nap too while he describes them.

Nana comes back from the office while I'm thinking about it and sits down next to Poppy, and he wraps his arm around her shoulders automatically. The two of them are drawn together like magnets, each movement seeming natural, as though they don't even take a moment to think before reaching out for the other. "All done." She sighs. "You didn't need to worry, though, because apparently, Jacinta gave him a lecture for the same reasons. I guess we were being a little unreasonable. We would have been giving all those bloodsucking society people cannon fodder to gossip about." She spies my medicine on the table. "Are you in pain?"

I shrug my shoulders. "A little, but these should take care of it."

"I'm trying to convince her to use one of those wonderful quilts off one of the beds," Poppy stage whispers to her, and she laughs, rolling her eyes at him.

"You do love those things, don't you? Of course, you can use one; I'll get Veronica to fetch you one." She goes to press the button, but Poppy places his hand over hers.

"She should be back any minute now with our coffee; you can ask then."

Just as he says that she does return, carrying a tray with a couple of cups and a plate of delicious-looking miniature cakes and tarts. Placing them on the table, she hands me a napkin. "For your mess," she says, smiling as I just take it politely while Poppy snorts. Nana raises her eyebrows, having missed our earlier interaction but clearly finding Veronica's words to be a bit disrespectful.

"Veronica, can you grab Harlow a quilt off of one of the beds, and then you can just relax until lunchtime?" She smiles her thanks and disappears. She's back not two minutes later, throwing the quilt at me. Before I can even get comfortable, she starts to sit down in one of the lounges opposite me, but Nana raises her eyebrow at her again.

"I think in crew quarters would be more appropriate, don't you, dear?" Nana's voice is kind, but her eyes are telling a different story. Veronica blushes and quickly hurries away.

"Why would she think she could sit here?" Nana asks Poppy, confused, and Poppy raises his eyebrows in surprise.

"I'm not sure, dear; maybe she's been allowed to in the past?" Nana's forehead deepens in a frown, and she growls a little. I jump, hearing the sound come out of her mouth, and Poppy pats me on the leg. "Nana gets riled up sometimes, just ignore her, but between you and me I wouldn't want to be one of her grandsons when she gets a hold of them."

Oh, okay, it finally occurs to me why she might be sitting in the lounge, and I shudder. *I guess that's one way to guarantee your job.*

I pop one of my tablets out and take it before I

have my coffee and cake. That way, it's almost working by the time I finish. We sit in comfortable silence while we have morning tea. Poppy has his newspaper again, and Nana talks to me about their estate and where they live. Nana and Poppy live in the same house as my father and his children, but they have their own wing. Sometimes they don't see each other for days.

"It's nice. We get our own space but can also see whoever is around whenever we want. Bradley has offered many times to build us our own house, and of course, we could too if we wanted to, but this arrangement suits us all."

"What about when your grandchildren start to get married and have families of their own? I guess they'll get their own place then," I say to her, and she smiles, but her eyes sparkle with deviousness.

"Not if I get my way," she says back to me, and something tells me she has a plan in the works, but I don't pay much attention to it. In fact, I'm kind of relieved. If she's busy matchmaking her grandchildren, then she'll stay out of my love life, non-existent as it is.

Finally, the pills start to work, and I curl up on the couch, pulling my blanket up around me.

"Sleep well, dear," Nana says.

"Thanks, Nana. I love you," I mumble back, the pills affecting my inhibitions as well as my energy, and as I close my eyes, I see a tear of joy trickle down her face.

## Chapter Eleven

### Harlow

I sleep for a few hours and wake when Veronica serves a late lunch of steak salad with blue cheese dressing, a side of fresh fruit, a chocolate pecan brownie, and a glass of a California Cabernet red wine. When the plane lands, it's two-thirty in the afternoon. Again, the plane stops in the middle of the tarmac, and there are a considerable amount of steps to climb down.

Leaving the plane, James and Chris are there to see us off. Veronica, on the other hand, is nowhere to be seen, but I'm not worried about that; her passive aggressiveness has worn very thin. Nana and Poppy say thank you and goodbye and head down, while I stop to talk to both pilots.

"It was nice meeting you, Harlow." James holds

out his hand, a smile on his face. "I look forward to flying you again." Returning a grin at his genuineness, I shake it.

"Thank you so much for the talk. I look forward to seeing you next time." Turning to Chris, I'm about to ask for my crutches, but I notice he has them in his hand already. Instead of passing them to me, he hands them to James and again sweeps me off my feet.

"I love to help a damsel in distress," he tells me, winking cheekily, and he carries me down the stairs. James is grinning broadly, following behind.

"You know you don't have to do this," I assure him.

Without missing a beat, he replies, "Honey, I think you've got enough on your plate at the moment; let someone else take care of the small things if we can." His words strike a chord, so I just hold on tight until we get to the bottom, and he places me down.

"I look forward to getting to know you next time, and thank you," I say, kissing him on the cheek as James hands my crutches to a waiting driver who places them in the back of the limo for me. Waving goodbye, I climb in next to my grandparents, and the driver closes the door behind me.

Settling myself, Poppy hands me my backpack, and I get comfortable. They told me earlier that there's a forty-five-minute drive to the estate.

Apparently, Poppy's father bought the thousand-acre land for a steal, subdivided it, then sold most of it off. That was how they'd made their money to start with. But he was smart, and when he divided it, he made it so there was only one other estate close by, and he gave one to each of his children, Poppy and his sister. But the sister had a falling out with her father and sold the land to an eccentric Transylvanian millionaire as a way to get back at him. I was fascinated, and Nana promised to tell me more about that story, but not when Poppy was around. It still bothers him that his father disowned his sister. Apparently, she now lives in Nevada and runs a successful business out there, but they didn't elaborate on what kind of business. I get the feeling it may be the reason her father disowned her, but Poppy still speaks to her once a week, and I'm told I'll meet her at Christmas if I decide to stick around.

The estates face each other, and they're about 100 acres each, but there are no other houses in the vicinity. The drive passes quickly, and all I've done is stare out the window and bite my lip to pieces with worry. Nana and Poppy have left me alone, somehow knowing that I needed the quiet. The car slows down as it enters through a big fancy gate and drives slowly down the road. On the left-hand side, the gardens, bushes, and trees are overgrown, but from a gap in a clearing, I can see a gothic mansion peeking through. It's thick with ivy and looks like some of the windows are smashed. With a gasp, I lower the window to see if I can get a better look.

"That's the mansion the Transylvanian million-aire built," Nana tells me. "Used to say he was a distant relative of Vlad the Impaler." Poppy harrumphs at these words.

Turning, I look at her. "Dracula?" I ask excitedly.

She shrugs, a twinkle in her eye, lightly elbowing Poppy until he drops the grumpy look from his face. "Yes, he was harmless and fun, but poor Ivan died with no heirs, and it has sat empty ever since. Sad, really. It used to be such a grand place, and he threw wonderful summer balls." She turns to Poppy with a nostalgic smile on her face. "Remember, Howard, we would dance all night until the sun came up?"

"Yes, dear, I do remember. I also remember what else a lot of the people would do." Nana's cheeks pinken with a blush as Poppy continues. "Crazy he might have been, he also made his money through drugs, and there were always party favors at his parties. Quite often, they would devolve into orgies," he tells me, and I look at Nana in shock.

"Don't look at me like that; we were all young once, dear, and liked to let our hair down." I've learned so many things about my grandparents in the last few hours that blow my mind. I can't see how they could be friends with the laced up too tight Boston seniors.

"Anyway, he was a fan of exotic animals and had a miniature zoo in there." Poppy looks at me, knowing that will have me even more interested. Damn it, he must have gotten that extra information from Chuck. "He had lions and tigers and bears, and all sorts of things. When he died, all the animals went to zoos around the country, but all the facilities are still there."

"And it's abandoned? No one lives there?" I cross my fingers in hope. I would love to explore it just like those guys do in the videos I watch.

"I believe there's a caretaker, but I don't think he's been there in a while; everything seems to be quite badly overgrown," Nana says, peering over my shoulder, trying to get a better look.

The limo makes a turn right and starts up a driveway, and the mansion disappears behind some trees. I turn around and sit, but I can't wait to get some time to go exploring. I know what I'm doing first. Settling myself again, I look out the other window at this new leg of our journey. This drive is a stark contrast to the other side. Tall poplar trees line the driveway with beautifully manicured lawn stretching as far as the imposing old mansion that we're now approaching. Garden beds filled with in-bloom roses line the house as well as one garden bed in the middle of the driveway. There looks to be a fountain in the very middle, but it's not on at the moment. This makes a convenient turning circle for cars.

The limo glides to a stop in front of the stone steps leading up to the double entrance door. The mansion is straight across at the front, but I can see two large wings stretching out behind it on either side, like a large U without the rounded edges. Built from stone, it has limestone-colored window frames and a balcony over the front door with two columns framing the entrance. The roof also has window frames, so it looks to be three stories high.

Nana points to the right-hand side of the house. "That wing is mine and Howard's. Now that the kids are older, Bradley has also moved to that wing. Goodness knows it's still too big for the three of us, but we make do." She gestures to the straight-ahead area. "That's the main living quarters; all the social rooms are in that section, and over there..." She gestures to the left wing with a sweep of her hand. "Is where the children's bedrooms and areas are. I think Bradley had a room made up for you on each side, so you need to decide where you're going to stay."

That thought terrifies me, and it's also a bit of a no brainer. "Your side, please," I answer quickly. I know that's rather gutless of me, but at least if we don't all get along, that will allow us our own space. I don't want to force these things. I used to hate all the new boyfriends my mother used to force on me, so I have firsthand experience having someone thrust into your space while you're expected to deal with it. Mostly they were customers, but she would tell me they were going to be my new daddy. I shudder at the reminder, but then something occurs to me.

"Brad never married?" I ask her, and she shakes her head, looking sad. "No, he's had a few lady friends now and then, but at the start, he was very busy with all the businesses, and when the children came along, he liked to spend all his free time with them. The women he dated didn't like to compete with that, so they would give him an ultimatum, expecting him to get more nannies."

Poppy butts in, laughing. "Boy were they shocked when he would give them the heave-ho instead." He chortles to himself, but that makes my opinion of my father creep up even more.

"He's still young. Why not now that they're older?" I ask.

Nana shrugs. "He hasn't met the right person yet."

The driver opens the door and is waiting with my crutches in his hand much sooner than I'm ready to get out of the car. Handing Poppy my backpack, I edge my way out. Taking them, I thank him before putting them under my arms and moving out the way. The cobblestone driveway is uneven underneath them, so I place the crutches carefully so as not to fall over and do more damage. I think I can probably do away with them soon, but

Nana insisted on bringing them. It seems her and Poppy are quite unwilling to take any chances with my health.

While I wait for Nana and Poppy to hop out of the car, the front door of the mansion slams open with a bang, making me jump in shock. All three of us turn to look, and standing there on the porch is an older, cleaner-cut version of the man in the photo with my mom. He's aged well, still handsome and healthy with only some gray streaks in his blond hair.

He's fit and tanned, but it's his eyes, which are an exact match to mine, that draw the most attention. They look half-terrified, half-excited, and I know exactly how he feels. When they meet mine, his mouth drops open in shock, and I hear, "Fuck."

That is so unexpected, I can't help myself, and I burst out laughing. Seeming as unsure about our next steps as I am, he runs his hands through his hair, looking a little embarrassed as he comes down the steps holding out his hand for me to shake. I'm so relieved he doesn't want to go for the hug that I shove one crutch under my arm, so it doesn't move, and I take it with enthusiasm.

"I'm sorry," he apologizes. "It's just you look so much like your mom. I was a bit surprised. I'm Brad. It's so good to meet you, Harlow." His voice is kind, and he sounds sincere. I'm still unsure how everything will work out between us, but if he's good friends with the Bostons, at least I can likely trust that he's as good a man as they say.

"Thanks. Melinda has always told me how much I look like Mom when she was younger." My mention of Melinda has a frown crossing his face as we let go of our hands.

"Yes, Melinda and Chuck. I'm so glad they were able to give you some sort of stability. I don't like to speak ill of the dead, and I'm sorry for your loss, but your mom robbed us both, and I will never forgive her for that." His words are angry by the end, and I don't blame him. I also don't want our first meeting to be tainted by rehashing my mom's failures as a parent and partner, so I do the only thing I can.

"Brad, I've spent many years being angry with my mom, and this is just the icing on the cake. What do you say we don't even mention her again?"

His eyes widen in surprise at my response, and I smile to show him there's really no hard feelings here. At least none directed at him. "It's taken me a lot of therapy to get to where I am, don't worry," I reassure him. "It's a waste of time hating someone and wishing we could change things; let's just look to the future." He looks impressed at my mature take on things, and I'd like to think that means I'm already starting off with a pretty good impression.

"Alright then, Harlow, I'll let you set the example. But I would like to hear about everything when you get comfortable enough with me to tell me." After greeting his parents, he gestures to the front door. "Shall we head inside?" He starts up the steps but stops and turns around, looking at my crutches and my knee.

"Mom told me on the phone you'd hurt your-self. Do you need a hand?" I appreciate the gesture and that he's already trying to be attentive, but I shake my head and maneuver myself up the stairs slowly.

"No, thanks, I'm fine," I reassure him. He looks dubious, but he doesn't push it, and I'm grateful. Grateful that he's not going to force a relationship and that he's going to let it develop organically no matter which way it may go.

He leads us inside, and we follow after him, Nana and Poppy staying quiet for the moment, letting us have our first meeting.

"My children are all here. Did Mom and Dad tell you about them?" Brad asks me, and I nod.

"Yes, but with so much going on, I'm afraid I can't remember all their names," I admit, and he shakes his head.

"Don't you worry about that. I'll introduce them all." He stops abruptly in the hallway and turns back to face me. "This has been a shock to all of us, and, well, they haven't said anything, but I think the fact that you're my biological child has ruffled their feathers slightly. Now, I don't see them as anything different than you; they're my kids, and I love them all equally as I will love you, but society gave them a hard time growing up, and I'm afraid it has left some scars. Same as how I'm sure you've some scars of your own." His eyes show that he has some knowledge of my upbringing, so I nod my head, glad that, for the moment at least, I don't have to explain my past.

"I understand, but let me tell you this, I have no intention of trying to replace them in your life. That said, I won't tolerate outright abuse either."

He looks shocked at my words, eyes flicking between me, Nana, and Poppy as if trying to figure out how my mind made that jump. "Abuse? God, no." The pity in his face as he realizes what I mean is almost enough to make me turn around, but Nana's hand on my back makes me steel my nerves.

"I just meant it might take a little while for them to warm up to you." He starts to move through the house again, and I'm so nervous I don't take notice of any of my surroundings. *This place is huge. I'm going to need a map before I try to get anywhere on my own.* My crutches thudding on the wooden floors echo through the large entrance, which has a lovely old-fashioned chandelier hanging in the center. On either side of the entrance are two sweeping stair-cases leading up to the next level, but we're headed to a door underneath them.

"Now, I know this might be a little overwhelm-ing, so I think a signal that we all know, if it becomes too much, might be the best idea," he suggests, and Nana and Poppy snort in laughter. I look at them, wanting to know what's so funny.

"Bradley gets overwhelmed easily too, and he has a signal that the kids know. If he does it, whoever is with him has to send a text message to one of the others to call him so he can excuse himself from whatever he is doing."

I look at my dad, and he's shuffling his feet, not looking at me. "Some of those meetings are so tedious," he complains, and when he does meet my gaze, there's a twinkle in his eye. I don't think my dad is as socially inept as everyone thinks he is. I think he's just a brilliant man who knows how to get out of boring meetings, but I'll keep his secret for him. I continue to study his face as he looks at mine, and then he winks slowly. *Yeah, that's what I thought.*

"How about if she pulls her hair back in a pony-tail?" Nana suggests, gesturing to the elastic band around my wrist. I'd left it out for the plane trip but still put one on my wrist just in case. Looking down at my comfy leggings and oversized off the shoulder sweater, I kind of wish I'd worn something a little dressier now, but Nana insisted I was fine.

"Good plan?" Brad looks at me for confirmation, and I agree. "Alright, then." He pushes open the door, and we're greeted by another long-stretching corridor with a few closed doors on either side. We walk the length until we get to the end where it opens out into a wide spacious living area. He's slightly in front of me, but as he steps to the side I can see a comfortable-looking open plan living area. But what draws my notice are the seven adults seated in various places throughout it. My heart skips a beat, and my stomach rolls with nerves as goosebumps prickle my skin. Now I really wish I had worn something fancy because I feel like I just stepped onto the set of *The Vampire Diaries*. So many beautiful, lethal-looking people, and all their eyes are on me.

## Chapter Twelve

## Harlow

With so many eyes on me my nerves are getting the best of me. My crutches dig into my armpits as I lean heavier on them in a subconscious attempt to make myself smaller, trying to be more easily overlooked, a throwback to some of my worst nights with Diane. Cringing internally, I hate that I've instinctively dropped back into those self-defense measures again. I don't know where to look, so I settle for the only pair of feminine eyes and give a slight smile. They're aquamarine and so similar to ones I've seen recently but can't place. This must be Jacinta, and she's even prettier in person than she in the photos Max showed me, something I hadn't thought possible. Her familiar frosty blue eyes sit under perfectly sculpted black eyebrows that match her long black hair. Thick straight bangs frame her naturally pale face, which has perfect cheekbones and pouty red lips. She's like the embodiment of Snow White, and she's looking me up and down with a frown. From the haughty look on her face, I don't measure up to her standards.

Brad finally steps forward after what seems like hours but is probably only seconds. "Harlow, I'd like you to meet my kids. This is Jacinta, Thomas, Declan, Oliver, Holden, Kai, and Jaxon." My eyes swing from one to another, not really taking them in until I get to the final figure, and my heart skips a beat.

Those familiar turquoise eyes are looking at me, and I finally put two and two together, feeling incredibly stupid all of a sudden. *Jaxon, of course.* I smile at him in the hope I have one friend, but he just sneers at me, and when he opens his mouth, his voice carries enough venom to strike me down if the crutches weren't insisting I stay upright.

"Wow, you really had me fooled. Pretending you didn't know who I was when I guess you had targeted me all along." His words spear an arrow straight through my heart, and I visibly flinch, hating that this situation is now even *more* awkward than it would have been otherwise. Brad inhales deeply next to me in surprise, but I think he's frozen in shock as he doesn't come to my rescue, or I hope that's the reason. Looking down at the floor, I have to swallow the tears that suddenly well up. Not wanting to need Brad for assistance, I take a deep breath, push the sadness and heartbreak down, and pull up my old friend, anger.

Before I can say anything, he hurls another barb in my direction. "What did you do? Research us online? Maybe you pumped your foster parents for details on us. Or even Nana and Poppy. You've got them so blinded that they never even considered you had an alternative agenda. Found out about the club and weaseled your way to the VIP area in the hope you would meet one of us?" The poison he's spouting is irrational and feverish; the glint in his eye manic. His anger radiates from him and is echoed by the look in his siblings' faces. All of them eye me as if I'm a snake in the Garden of Eden, and by the time he finishes his tirade, I'm practically vibrating. My emotions on a hair trigger, and I've completely switched into fight mode, no part of me thinking how I can solve this smoothly.

Looking him in the eye, I fire my attack right back at him. "Are you fucking stupid? *You* approached *me* with your lame ass pick up lines. I thought you were just interested in my tattoos, and I walked away. You chased me after that. Also, I didn't find out any of this until days after I'd left the club. That emergency I was called away to was my dead mom." He flinches at my words, but his gaze doesn't soften at all. "So how about you pull your overinflated ego out of your ass because you're not that hot."

A snort escapes one of the others, but I don't know who, and I don't care. Just as I'm about to ask Nana to show me to my room so I can breathe, another woman enters the room. This one has her long chestnut hair pulled back into a bun and is wearing a pencil skirt and jacket that emphasize her rail-thin body. She's holding an iPad in her hand.

"Oh goody, is this another one of your kids who's going to accuse me of being a gold-digging whore?" I wave my hand in her direction, throwing my words at Brad, who's red with embarrassment and shooting a look of fury at Jaxon. The woman gasps and holds a hand up to her chest like I've offended her, but I'm at that no fucks left to give stage. *Huh, that didn't take long.*

"No, this is my PA, Cecelia." He holds out a hand for the envelope she's carrying under the iPad, and she passes it to him with a smile before looking down on me with a frosty smile. *Yeah, she's not going to be an ally either.*

"I organized for you to have a card linked to our accounts and a credit card set up in your name." At Brad's words, Poppy just groans, and my mouth drops open in disgust.

"Are you serious?" He nods his head, looking pleased with himself and definitely not hearing the anger in my voice. I gesture around the room in disbelief. "I can tell by the looks on every one of your kids' faces that they think I'm doing this for money. God, one of them *just* accused me of stalking him! It's a look I'm familiar with. One I faced every day from the kids at school while growing up with the Bostons. I was always the poor junkie's daughter, being looked after by the wealthy family. And you think handing me cards with my name on them is the right thing to do?" My head is full of steam now, and Bradley just has unfortunate timing, but he's going to wear it all. Closing my eyes, I take a deep breath, trying to calm myself so I don't scream at them all. I knew it was going to be bad, but never had I considered that it was going to be like this.

With deadly, deceiving calm, I sneer at him. "You can take those cards and shove them up your ass. I don't need your money, nor do I want it. I came in the hope of getting to know you and possibly your kids. I can see now that the kids want nothing to do with me, and that's fine. I couldn't care less either way." I hope they can't hear the lies in my voice as my eyes look round the room at all the handsome faces with cold eyes.

They're not willing to give me a chance; I should've guessed they weren't ever going to. Inside, my heart breaks in two, but I close my eyes and take a deep breath. Ignoring the stretched out hand and Brad's incredulous and wounded face, I turn to Nana and Poppy. Before I can say anything, Poppy is hustling me into his arms. Not a moment later, after looking at his grandchildren in disgust, he helps me out of the room. As we leave, I can hear

Nana chastising the bunch of them. It's sweet of her to try, but I'm feeling pretty hopeless about this whole situation. .

"I am so very disappointed in all of you. I want you to think very carefully about your first few days here in this family and how that felt. Imagine if Poppy and I had been as unwelcoming as you all are and how that might have made you feel. And Jaxon, I am so ashamed of you right now. I don't know where all that venom is coming from, but you need to take a good hard look at yourself. I've known Harlow for many, many years now, and she has *never* been one to approach a boy. Maxine was always lamenting her lack of game." I shudder in embarrassment as Nana over-shares, but her voice fades as we move further away, and I'm relieved I don't have to hear the rest of it.

As we walk back the way we'd come, Poppy doesn't say a word; he just holds me tight. He can feel me shaking with anger, and he's obviously learned that sometimes you just need to let a woman be. Nana has trained him well. On our way, we go out the door under the grand staircases, and an older gray-haired woman hurries up to us. She's plump and round, and with her rosy red cheeks, she could play Mrs. Claus just perfectly.

"Harlow, this is our housekeeper and all-round lifesaver, Mrs. Hayton. Anything you need, she's the woman to speak to about it." Before I can say hello,

Mrs. Hayton has pushed Poppy aside and wrapped me up in her arms, holding me tight.

"Oh, my poor girl, thank goodness you were found! Anything you want, you just ask me. We've got you now." Her voice is gentle and kind, and a lump forms in my throat at her kind words. Her hug is exactly what I need right now, tight and reassuring. Tears start to stream down my face as this total stranger gives me the kind of welcome I wish I could've gotten from the people who're supposed to be my new family.

She pulls back, frowning when she sees them. "What is this? Who has made you cry already?" She has an accent, but I can't pick up from where. Maybe German? She starts to mutter in another language, and she stalks off in the direction of the room where we'd left my new venomous siblings. I go to stop her, but Poppy grabs hold of my arm.

"I learned very early on that Gretchen is going to do her own thing, and we just need to let her be. Trust me, between her and Nana, those kids and Brad are going to have the hide torn off them. Come on, let's go find your room."

Beyond the staircase, on the right side, is a door leading to their wing. Again, I don't pay attention to my surroundings, my thoughts a violent storm of sadness and hurt that suck me in with no promise of letting go. I just make sure to look where I place my crutches to not damage anything on the way.

"Nana asked for a bedroom on the ground floor

for you, so you wouldn't have to worry about nego-
tiating any more stairs," Poppy says, pushing open a
door. "And this one has an exit out on the patio,
too, so you don't even have to go through the house
if you don't want to." I step inside with a sigh of
relief and lean my crutches against a wall. My
shoulders and armpits ache, and I'm more than
prepared to hobble around the room to give them a
break.

The room is decorated in happy lemon and
cream colors and has a large king-sized bed with
what looks like another quilt similar to the ones on
the plane. This one has a cover that has daffodils on
it, but that's not what catches my attention. Laying
directly in the center is a fluffy cream and brown cat
that's looking at us, her blue eyes blinking drowsily
behind the chocolate mask her marking makes it
look like she's wearing.

"Oh, aren't you a pretty thing," I coo, allowing
my mind a reprieve from all the turmoil. Sitting
gently on the bed, I reach a hand out and stroke it.

"Don't ..." Poppy calls out, his voice laced with
worry, but I pay no attention. Stroking between its
ears, it starts to purr and nuzzle into my hand, so I
move further down her body.

"Well, I'll be!" Poppy's exclamation sounds
bewildered this time. "I'm not sure how she got in
here; maybe one of the maids left the door open.
That's Princess, Declan's ragdoll, and she doesn't
usually like anyone but him and the other grand-

kids. I'm afraid she's even worse at the moment." Just as I stroke over her belly, I can tell why.

"How far along is she?" I ask him as I gently stroke over her swollen belly.

He shrugs. "Not sure, exactly, but Declan would know. It's her first litter, so he's been pretty anal about the whole process." After one more pat, I leave her be. Declan Summers, the hardcore movie producer slash talent agent who has the ability to make or break a career. Who would've thought he would be into cats? I would have guessed he was a dog person myself. Or not into animals at all, seeing them as not worth the mess or irritation of looking after them. I guess we all have preconceived notions.

Shaking my head, I push the curtains aside and let myself out onto the little outdoor patio. It's covered with hanging honeysuckle, and the pretty cream blooms are heady with their intoxicating fragrance. Sitting down on one of the cushioned chairs, I take in my view. This room faces some wide open paddocks with a few trees clustered here and there. A herd of horses graze peacefully while a gentle afternoon breeze stirs the leaves on the trees. Poppy takes a seat next to me, and I breathe in the fresh country air and lean back on my chair.

"I'm sorry, Harlow," he starts to apologize again, but I hold up my hand.

"Don't. None of it is your fault. I was half-expecting it anyway." I sigh in frustration and disappointment, not satisfied with being right this time. We sit in silence for a while as the sun starts to set and the sky darkens. A noise inside my room has us both turning to see who it is, my body tightening for another attack, but it's just Nana. I guess she's finally finished ripping her grandkids new ones.

She slides into the remaining seat and blows out a deep breath. "Harlow, come in and have dinner. I promise it will be better." I snort at her declaration, and Poppy joins in. Before long, the both of us are laughing uncontrollably.

Nana just huffs, exasperated at us both. "You don't need to be like that," she complains.

We sober ourselves up, and once I've caught my breath, I say to her, "I'm pretty sure it can't get much worse than what it's already been."

"Don't be too sure," Poppy mutters, but I choose to ignore him. Getting up, I stretch my body, the pull of my muscles reviving me, and we walk back into the bedroom. Princess is still fast asleep on my bed, and I leave the door cracked open in case she needs to move.

Grabbing my crutches, we head back toward the living area. Nana tells me they eat in a formal dining room on special occasions; otherwise, they usually just eat at a table in the living area. She turns and walks backward, so she's facing me, her voice animated. "It's been so long since we sat together as a family. The kids are always busy with their businesses these days, and I can't remember the last time we were all together like this. Although it's strained, I'm glad to see all my family in one place." Her face is expressive and filled with joy even though I can see the toll the situation is taking in the lines around her eyes, and I feel sad that I have helped put them there.

I don't say anything, and she turns around and continues leading the way. When we finally get to the dining room, my heart drops as I notice I'm the center of attention again. Everyone else is already seated, including Cecelia, the PA. Everyone's eyes turn to me as I hobble into the room behind Nana and Poppy. Not meeting anyone's gaze, I look for a place to put my crutches while we eat.

Before I can do anything, one of the boys gets up and comes over to me. This one has reddish-brown hair that has a slight curl in it. His eyes are a vivid green, and the stubble on his face matches the hair on his head, maybe a little redder. He's wearing blue jeans and sneakers, with a long-sleeved Guinness t-shirt. He has a forced smile on his full lips as he reaches out to take my crutches from me. "Oh, uh, thank you..." *Shit, I can't remember who this one is.* It all happened so fast, and Jaxon was the only one I'd paid attention to.

"Thomas." His voice is a little gruff, and there's a faint accent. Ah, the airline magnate James was telling me about. He takes them over to a wall and leans them against it before returning to the table. Normally, I wouldn't want them so far out of reach, but I guess I can't cling to them if we're all pretending to give this civil dinner a try. Poppy helps me over to a vacant seat, and he and Nana sit on either side of me, comforting me with their mere closeness. As soon as I sit, Mrs. Hayton bustles into the room, followed by a couple of smartly dressed maids? Servants? Waiters? I don't know what to call them, but they're placing plates of food on the table, and everyone starts to fill their plates.

The room is filled with the sound of voices chatting, silverware banging on plates, and then the general commotion of a family dinner, but I just sit there. It's all a little overwhelming, and when I look up, I meet a smirking face and challenging brown eyes behind black-rimmed glasses. This one has an eyebrow piercing, and his pushed up sweater sleeves show off his impressive tattoos on each arm. On one arm it looks like he has the words 'family first' in a pretty black scroll followed by the black and green Neighpalm Industries symbol. On the other arm there looks to be a white tiger done in black ink, its bright blue eyes the only bit of color.

"How did you hurt yourself, Harlow? Is it bad?" he asks, curiosity in his voice along with amusement. I bet he's expecting me to tell him I fell off a stripper pole or something.

"Horse riding accident," I reply, and his eyebrows raise in surprise. *What an asshole.*

"You ride?" he asks, disbelief entirely undisguised, and Nana snaps at him.

"Oliver, you idiot, of course, she rides. Chuck and Melinda Boston are her foster parents. It wasn't *just* a horse-riding accident, Harlow, stop talking yourself down. She fell off while practicing a stunt for a new movie their horses are going to be in." Ah, of course, Oliver, the tattoo artist, the black sheep of the family. I can see how a reality show starring him might just sell tattoos, but I try not to let the appreciation show on my face. The gorgeous outside doesn't seem to be matching the shit-stirring inside.

"You're going to be in a movie?" a deep, sinful voice asks me from the end of the table. Turning, my eyes meet the piercing green eyes of Declan Summers, and my ovaries squeal in excitement. *Holy crap, this is my adopted brother. Down, girls.*

Shaking my head, I answer his curiosity-filled question. "No, not me, I just work with the horses on the farm. Maxine's the one who will travel with them and ride them if needed." Declan's eyes glaze over at that information, and he goes back to his food. *Asshole number two.*

Jacinta claps her hands, the ice queen facade breaking for a moment. "Oh, I haven't seen Maxine in so long! I must ask her to come out here for a ride next time she's in town." Well, ouch, that snub certainly hits its mark—*asshole number three.* I wonder if we're going to go for a full seven tonight. The meal continues, and I sit quietly, eating the food that Nana had placed on my plate. She, Poppy, and even Brad try to include me in the conversation, but it seems like the siblings are doing everything in their power to change the subject every time I'm asked something.

Finally, Brad has had enough. "Right, that's it!" His voice thunders across the room as he stands up, placing his hands on the table. His children flinch as if they're not used to this kind of reaction from him, and Cecelia looks smug from her place by his side as if the thought of his children getting into trouble pleases her; I must remember to ask Nana about her. The table falls into silence, the anticipation for what's to come making it awkward and uncomfortable.

"This is what's going to happen. Harlow is going to spend the day with each of you. Getting to know you and all about your part in the family business." They all start to protest, all pretense of kindness gone.

"Silence!" Brad bellows, holding up his hands, the man seeming to be at his wit's end. He runs his hands furiously through his gray-streaked blond hair, his hazel eyes looking tired. "You will do this for me. You will do this because I am begging you to give her a chance to see how wonderful I know you can be. Please, Harlow!" he pleads, turning to look at me, his voice almost breaking under the weight of today's emotions. "I know they're not earning it right now, but give them a chance."

I look around the table, and I see his kids

squirming. They don't like that they've upset their dad, and it's the first sign of a warm emotion I've seen all night. This gives me hope, but then one by one, I meet their eyes. I can see the malice and the blame, and my heart sinks even further; apparently, I'm the only one who thinks they're the cause of their father's upset. This is *not* going to be fun. Regret sweeps through me, and I'm filled with just one nagging thought. *Maybe I should just go back home tomorrow.*

## Chapter Thirteen

## Kai

Holy shit! I watch as Harlow rakes my brother over the coals, and my cock is as hard as a rock. She is fierce, taking none of his crap. Her eyes are flashing with anger, and her chest is heaving, drawing my eyes to her perky breasts. Her nipples are peaked through the shirt, her emotions subconsciously showing in her body. Drawing my eyes back up to her face, her plump lips are all I can focus on as she gives as good as she's getting.

My mind flashes back to Jaxon when he first came back from Connecticut. He'd been on cloud nine, raving about a girl he'd met at the new club over there and how he couldn't wait to go back and look for her again. He'd talked about how hot she'd been and how off the chart their chemistry was. The best thing was she'd had no clue who he was.

Then it flashes to the day Dad told us about his biological daughter. I can't say it didn't cause my heart to skip a beat and that insecure part of me to worry about whether he was going to replace us now that she was around. But I quickly snapped out of it. I know Dad has enough love for all of us, and when he told us about the situation she was coming from, my heart nearly broke for her. The poor girl suffered the same as we all had before Dad rescued us, but she was unlucky enough to have to suffer longer than all of us put together. I decided then and there that I wasn't going to make waves and would welcome her with open arms.

But I was the only one. When Dad had finally left us on our own, my siblings turned feral.

*"We* cannot *let this happen," Jacinta says from where she's sitting on the couch as soon as Dad gets out of earshot. Her eyes flash with anger, and her body is rigid and tense. "Who knows who this woman is and where she came from. Probably some gold-digger who read about us in the tabloids and thought we'd make an easy target. Well, she's not going to know what hit her." Her body is shaking with so much emotion that Jaxon puts his arm around her in comfort and squeezes tight. He starts to whisper words to her, too softly for me to hear. Although she's angry, I can also see the scared little girl inside, and I watch as his hugs finally make her crack. Tears start to run down her face, and she quietly sobs into our brother's chest. I stand there, helpless in that moment*

*at the sight of her tears. Jacinta's tough and doesn't cry often, so this must be really digging at her insecurities.*

*"Now hang on." Oliver stands up and walks over to the nearby cabinet, picking up his tablet he'd left there. "Let's do some research before we get too upset. I'm friends with Maxine on Facebook. Let's see if we can do a little social media stalking." He sits back down on the couch next to Declan and starts to run his fingers across the screen.*

*"I think we should hire a investigator." Declan is the picture of calm sitting next to Oliver, and if you didn't know him well, you wouldn't be able to see that he was upset, but I can. His jaw is clenched, and there's a vein throbbing in his temple. Declan has abandonment issues similar to Jacinta and Jaxon. In fact, we all do, but his led to always needing to be in control. He doesn't like it when things don't go his way; it throws his little world into chaos. So this offer stems from that.*

*"Why don't we hold off on that for a bit?" I suggest. "I wouldn't want Dad to find out you're investigating her. Didn't you see how thrilled he was about the idea of her? He's already devastated about her mother and the situation the girl's been in. Come on, man, you'd break his heart."*

*I can see him mulling it over in his head before he gives me a quick nod. "Fine, I'll wait and see what she's like when she gets here. But we're definitely revisiting that option the moment something seems off."*

*Breathing out a sigh of relief, I turn to my other brothers. Holden and Thomas have been quiet, and they didn't show much reaction when Dad had told us, but I can see the strain in both of them as well. The tension around the eyes and the* taut muscle in their bodies. Before I can talk to them about how they're feeling, Oliver finds something.

"Here! I found her. Her Facebook page is private, but I've got a photo of her and some basic information. She's twenty-five like Jaxon and Jacinta, and she goes to Tufts University. It doesn't say what she does there, but it does give her relationship status as single, and she lists the Bostons as her family. That's pretty much it, though there are a few photos of her with Maxine. Man, she's smoking hot." His eyes gleam with appreciation, and Declan leans in to have a look. Completely shocking me, the iceman's eyes heat with appreciation, his tongue coming out to brush across his lip. That's quite a reaction from him, and Thomas and Holden must see it too as they all leave their seats and move around so they can look over their shoulders. Unable to resist the temptation, I follow them.

The picture shows a beautiful blonde girl with high cheekbones, cat-like hazel eyes, and plump lips. She and her friend are smiling naturally at the camera, but you don't even notice the friend over her presence. A whistle escapes Thomas's mouth. "Holy hell, she is hot," he mutters, his Irish accent thickening on the words.

Across from us, Jacinta scoffs while wiping the tears from her face. "God, that's so typical of you lot. A pretty face and a impressive rack and you go gaga. Haven't you learned your lessons over the years?" Her barb hits a direct shot, and we all shift uncomfortably. She's right. All of us have been fooled by a pretty face before then discovered alternative motivation. Most of our past relationships have crashed and burned as soon as we realized our significant other was just trying to get to one of our siblings or some of the family's money or advantages.

"Show me," Jaxon barks, holding out his hand. I can tell he's already made up his mind by the set of his shoulders, but he was never one to be left out. She's upset his sister, and that automatically makes her public enemy number one, no matter if Jacinta is being oversensitive or not.

Oliver passes him the tablet with the picture, and as soon as he sees it, his frown deepens, and his lips curl back with a snarl. "Fucking hell. That bitch." He's shaking his head in disbelief. "Well, she certainly had me fooled." His fury eases, and it's replaced by a disgusted look.

He throws the tablet on the coffee table in the middle of all of us. "That..." He points to the picture. "Is the girl that I met at Club Neighpalm in Connecticut."

"The one you were so into?" I ask him, surprised, and he snarls again.

"Fuck, I'm such a fool. She must have known who I was." He runs a hand through his hair in frustration before it drops back down again.

"But didn't you approach her?" Oliver asks. "Twice, from what you told me?"

"Yes, but it had to have been a set-up. She planted herself right in front of me," Jaxon growls. Fuck, there we go with the conspiracy theories. I roll my eyes internally. Jaxon and Jacinta are so freaking dramatic at times, but they'd continued to trust people a lot longer than the rest of us and got burned for it. That last bit of trust got spectacularly shattered by the last person they'd ever suspected.

"But how?" I question him, and he shakes his head.

"I don't know, but it's just too much of a coincidence, isn't it?" This time, he sounds unsure, a little of the disgust softening from his gaze. I go to respond, but before I can, Holden does. He's been quiet all this time, listening and taking it all in.

"It really doesn't matter if it is or not. She's part of our lives now, and we have to decide what we want to do about it."

Jacinta sits up straight at his words, her eyes wide. "We'll get rid of her, of course. No one gets to make a fool of our family and not pay for it."

The others are nodding their heads and murmuring their agreements, but I can't meet their eyes. I don't agree; I don't think we should do anything until we know more, and Oliver seems to be on the same page because he's not saying anything either. We're both certainly more easygoing than the rest of our siblings. I'm not sure if that has to do with our individual businesses just not having the kind of pressure the others are under, or if it's got to do with the way neither of us take life too seriously. Both of us never settled down with any one girl in particular through school and college, so we weren't burned like the rest of our family managed to be. I tell you what, the Summers family certainly knows how to pick 'real winners.' Even Dad, if this new daughter's mom was anything like the rest of them.

Just as I'm about to speak up, Declan puts me on the spot. "Oliver, Kai, you're both quiet. You know what the rule is."

"Family first," Oliver replies quietly, and my blood starts to boil at his easy capitulation.

*I start to argue, but Declan's firm "Kai" stops me in my tracks. Huffing out a breath, I nod my head, and as they start to make plans, I make a promise to myself. I'm going to give the girl a chance. I just won't interfere with what they do.*

My thoughts come back to the present, and my dad's fury practically pulses through the room. At some stage, Poppy and Harlow exited the room, leaving behind Nana and Dad and their scathing anger. I don't think I've ever seen either of them that angry before, not even when Jaxon totaled his first car after he lost control joy riding. They were just relieved he wasn't injured.

As they both lecture us on our behavior, I can see, by the glint in their eyes and the set of their bodies, that it has no effect on my siblings. They're in it for the long haul, and all I can do is hope that our family comes out of this intact on the other side.

## Harlow

Dinner didn't get any better; it was an awkward, stilted affair, and I escaped back to my bedroom as soon as I could, Brad's plea running through my mind on repeat. I'm not sure why he wants me to learn about the different businesses. Whether he hopes I'll take a genuine interest in his company, or if it's a way to force his children to get to know me. But it had been decreed that Jacinta would be the first person to show me her little corner of the Neighpalm business. I think Brad had hoped we might bond since we're both women, but I could tell by the look in her eyes that wasn't going to happen. And let's face it, they only have to look at me to know I'm not any kind of fashionista.

My bag had been dropped in my room when we first arrived, and I find that someone had unpacked it while I was at dinner. Gulping in horror, I frantically search for my backpack until I discover it next to my bed. Grabbing it and throwing it on the now empty bed, I search the inside zipped pocket. Sighing with relief, I pull my favorite vibrator out and slip it into the top drawer of the bedside table. Max had made me pack the damn thing, saying I'd need it to hold me over until I could track down my mysterious dance partner back in Connecticut. I guess that won't be going anywhere now, so I guess it's lucky she packed it. God, I wouldn't have been able to face any of the staff if they had found it and put it away for me. I shudder with the thought.

Grabbing some sleep shorts and a tank out of the drawer, I open the door to the ensuite bathroom. I'm super pleased I decided to stay on the same side as Nana and Poppy, so I don't have to deal with noisy room neighbors in the other wing.

Stripping off, I leave my dirty clothes on the floor and turn the faucet to hot. A veritable waterfall comes pouring down, and, looking up, I notice there's one of those wide showerheads built into the ceiling. Shivering with delight, I step under the flow of water.

Groaning, I feel the tension leach from my body and flow away, just like the water flowing down the drain. Leaning my head against the wall, I let the water batter my shoulders and ease the aches and pains caused by being so stressed today. Before I think about all the negatives, I try to focus on the one bright spot aside from Nana and Poppy. Brad seemed pleased to see me, and I feel like there was a spark of connection there. I'd like to see where we can go with that. See if we can build something that may eventually resemble a father-daughter relationship.

As for his kids, that was a big fat fail. I'm pretty sure that Brad would be open to coming to Connecticut to visit me, or maybe we could meet in a neutral location. That just seems a more sensible idea than going through what I did today. Shaking my head to clear my thoughts, I do make one decision. I'm not going to make any decisions today. I'm just going to take each day as it comes, and if it gets too much, I'll book myself a flight home.

What I'd really like to do while I'm out here is organize the use of a car and visit some of the local zoos. See if I can make some inquiries regarding internships. I know it's possibly farfetched, but I might as well give it a go. With the way things went with my "siblings," who knows the next time I'd be in California. I'd also like to get down to San Diego and check out the killer whales and other aquatic animals at SeaWorld. I watched that documentary *Blackfish* a while back, and I've always been fascinated with them. This will probably be the only chance I'll get to see them up close. Maybe I could steal Brad, Nana, and Poppy away for a day, and we could make it our first mini family trip. Other than that, there are a lot of touristy things I want to do while here, and if I'm stuck shadowing Brad's kids, I'm not going to have a lot of time to do things like that. I'll wait and see how tomorrow goes, and then I can always discuss it with him.

Grabbing the shower gel and loofah that was in the shower, I give myself a quick wash. Using the provided shampoo and conditioner, I wash my hair with something magical that smells like apples and springtime and instantly makes me feel better. Turning off the faucets and squeezing the excess water out of my hair, I climb out, grabbing a towel and rubbing my hair vigorously to dry it more before wrapping it around my body.

When I walk back to my bedroom to find my body moisturizer, I don't get more than a step out of my bathroom before there's a hand over my mouth and an arm wrapped around my chest. It pulls me back against a hard body. I struggle, but he has me in a vise-like grip, and I can't scream with a hand over my mouth.

"Stop wiggling," Jaxon commands, and my body stills instantly. "Don't scream if you don't want Nana to find you like this." His voice is low and hostile in my ear, and I nod as his hand slips from my mouth to wrap around my throat where he puts on a little pressure. "I don't know what your plan is here, but I want you to know I'm watching you. You may be able to win over some of my family members, the more gullible ones, but most of us know trouble when we see it." His breathing is rapid in my ear, each exhale causing goosebumps to pebble on my arms and legs. His hand tightens around my throat, and my core throbs with desire, my pussy becoming wet with need. I shudder with both lust and shame as pure want runs through my body at the memory of this man and his seductive moves on the dance floor. *Oh my God, there is something wrong with me that this turns me on.*

A groan escapes his mouth, and, looking down, I realize my towel has started to slip thanks to my struggling and is now sitting below my nipples, which are both peaked to hard points. *Screw this!*

I start to struggle some more, and my ass makes contact with his crotch. From the feel of it, he's not as unaffected as he pretends to be. Jaxon loosens his grip, and I manage to rip myself free from his arms. Juggling the edges of my towel, I try to save my modesty, but it's a losing battle, and it falls to the ground, puddling at my feet. I'm left standing naked, my back to Jaxon, as a hiss of breath escapes his lungs. Turning to face him, I put my hands on my hips and raise an eyebrow. My heart is galloping a million miles an hour, and my bravado is an act, but I can't show any weakness. He's like a wild animal who will pounce if he suspects his prey is getting ready to run.

"Happy now?" I ask him, using sarcasm as a shield for how unsettled his "visit" has made me. "Let's add battery and sexual assault to your list of offenses, now shall we? Well, Jaxon, I will tell you, you're making my mother look like a real peach now. She might have abused me, but she never sexually assaulted me."

He blanches at my accusations, and his face pales even further, which is an amazing effort with his lily-white skin. His eyes roam my naked body, pausing at both the junction of my thighs and level with my breasts. By the time his eyes meet mine, the bulge in the front of his jeans gives away that he likes what he sees. But the words that escape that mouth cut to the quick as surely as any blade.

"How much would you have charged me, Harlow, that night at the club? A man likes to know these things up front, not after."

With a step forward, I crack my hand across his cheek and growl at him, "Get out! You make me sick!"

He puts his hand in his pocket, not even rubbing his now red cheek. Sauntering out of the room, he takes one final shot. "Let me know when you decide. With that banging body, it might be worth a few dollars to have a go." I pick up a lamp off the bedside table and throw it in his direction, but in my anger, it hits the wall next to the door, nowhere near him, and crashes to the floor; luckily, the carpet muffles the sound.

Picking up my towel, I forget the moisturizer and quickly put on my clothes for bed in case I get any more unexpected visitors. My sobs echo through the bathroom as I leave the towel in the same place as my dirty clothes. I'll worry about them in the morning. I'm too upset to do anything now.

Throwing back the quilt on the bed, I climb underneath and pull it up and over my shoulders. My body and mind are a riot of feelings. My body is turned on by the touch of him and the look in his eyes, but my mind feels ill. His words are a vicious lash of innuendo and speculation, cruel taunts that hit a direct bullseye. Fury overwhelms any other feeling, and my body tenses, the roiling anger driving me to shake. How dare he compare me to that woman. He knows nothing! Spoiled, pampered little prince wouldn't know what it was like to live like I did.

I toss and turn for what feels like hours, my mind creating scenarios in my head, playing them out and giving me options. How I could have responded, and what I would do next time something like that happened. I should have just kneed him in the junk, but with my luck, I would have only aggravated my ligaments and done no damage to him.

Finally, I can't stand it any longer. Although my mind has calmed, my body is wound tighter than a grandfather clock. Rolling over, I pull the bullet vibrator out of the drawer and bring it under the quilt. I shove it down my pants to rest on my clit, running it through the wetness that coats my pussy lips before turning it on at a gentle speed.

I almost hate myself when my mind goes to Jaxon's strong arms wrapped around me, his hand against my mouth and then around my throat. The almost possessive squeeze of his hand and the memory of the violence in his voice causes me to tremble with want. As worked up as I already am, the vibrator doesn't take long to get me to where I need, and as I shudder through the explosion that sets fire to all my nerve endings, it's Jaxon's fucking name that leaves my lips.

Panting through the final waves, I wipe away the sweaty tendrils of hair that have settled on my face before I get up, walking to the bathroom. There, I wipe over the bullet with a cloth, which also joins the clothes on the floor, before returning it to my drawer in the bedroom. Finally feeling relaxed for the first time since coming back from dinner, I'm ready to head to bed when scratching at the door has me opening it and looking out. Not seeing anyone, I've gone to close it when something soft brushes past my bare legs. Looking down, I discover Princess, who moves into the room and sits in front of the bed looking at it patiently.

Closing the door behind her, I move to where she is, carefully pick her up, and place her on the bed. She proceeds to stalk back and forth across the foot of the bed until I climb in and lay down. It was like she was waiting for me to get comfortable because as soon as my head hits the pillow, she comes up to the head of the bed and curls up on the other side, closes her eyes, and starts to purr. The sound is a gentle soundtrack that eases me into oblivion with not a care in the world. Or not too many, anyway.

## Jaxon

The thud against the wall as I leave Harlow's room has a feral grin crossing my face. Heading back to our wing of the house, I make my way to my bathroom. Quickly shedding my clothes, I turn on the shower and hop in, wrapping my hand around my throbbing cock.

Imagine my surprise when the woman I haven't been able to get out of my head turns out to be my father's biological daughter. What are the odds? Pretty fucking slim, I would think. My anger makes my grip harder and my strokes rough, and that makes the pleasure so much better. Groaning, I think about the luscious naked body that she didn't attempt to hide from my sight. That body was made for sin. Long, lean muscles on her legs, arms, and stomach made feminine by rounded hips and lush perky breasts with pebbled nipples that made my mouth water. And to see her bare pussy...I just about said fuck it all and took her there against the wall. The way she responded to my hand at her throat, the glaze of desire in her eyes when she turned and defiantly faced me. She was like a goddess.

Furious with myself and my body's reactions, I set a punishing pace, and it's not long before that familiar tingling flows through my body as my balls tighten. Cum explodes, painting the shower walls, my knees buckling at the intensity while I moan Harlow's name as she smirks at me from inside my mind. Putting my other hand against the wall to hold myself upright, I slowly stroke to extend the pleasure, the sensation bordering between pleasure and pain, causing shivers to wrack my body.

Groaning, I think about her. My disappointment when she'd had that emergency that night was the strongest it had been in ages. I don't get attached to women. They're useful to relieve some tension, but then I send them on their way, so they don't become too attached. All of us boys have learned our lessons about clingy women. Or the ones who want to cause tension in the family. Or the ones who are jealous of Jacinta.

We've just altogether learned it's easier not to get attached, but Harlow had been different. I thought she'd had no clue who I was. I thought we'd had a genuine connection. But she truly played me perfectly. And then for her to accuse me of sexual assault was like a knife being driven straight into my heart. Fuck! Scrubbing my hand through my hair, the tiles are cold where I lean back against them, disgusted with myself. Comparing me and her mother was a low blow, but I'm pretty sure I deserved it after letting my temper get the better of me. There's just something about her that makes me feel so much… anger.

Banging my fist against the tiles, I stand upright, washing myself and turning off the shower. Grabbing a towel, I dry myself before climbing into my bed naked.

When Dad had announced that a biological daughter had been discovered, I can't say that the shriveled up tiny bit of doubt that we'd all held when we were first adopted hadn't reared its ugly head. That doubt that made us question if the situation was too good to be true after so many rejected foster homes.

But Nana, Poppy, and Dad had squashed the doubt almost as soon as we'd all been brought home. They made us feel wanted and loved for the first time in our short lives, and not once had that doubt ever risen its head again until *her*. But now that little noxious feeling is like a small flame caught by a gentle breeze, slowly being fanned into something more.

My sister has been particularly affected. She's "daddy's little girl," and now there's another one coming into the picture. Jacinta and Dad are so similar in many ways. Both of them share a love of horses, and both are homebodies, preferring to stay at home and read rather than socialize with fake self-important people. She'd just gone to Fashion Week, solely because of her business responsibilities, and usually needs a week to decompress after an event like that. Quite often, when we're home, you can find them curled up in the library, Jacinta knitting her latest sweater, Dad reading a book or working on something for the business. No words are needed; they just like each other's company. But this new announcement has thrown her for a loop, and she is not reacting well.

I have a feeling tomorrow is not going to be particularly pleasant for Harlow, and an admittedly evil grin crosses my face at that thought. Though there is that kernel of doubt, the one that took root when she claimed that her mom had died only after we'd met. Is she telling me the truth, or is it a convenient lie? Nana sure ripped us a new one earlier, and if her words are correct, then maybe Harlow's are also. But I just can't bring myself to trust in them. I can't let that sway me. I need to stay the course and teach Harlow what it's like to try and make a fool out of a Summers man. *She's not going to know what hit her.* With that promise to myself, I roll over, plump my pillows, and wait for sleep to take me away from my confused mind

## Chapter Fourteen

## Harlow

I'd set my alarm for the next morning, but it hasn't even gone off when my door slamming open startles both me and Princess. Standing in the doorway, dressed in a pair of designer jeans, heels, and some fancy wraparound top that shows her body to perfection, is Jacinta. If she had a pair of wings, she could be a warrior angel out of one of my paranormal romance books with the fierce scowl she has on her face.

Her eyes widen in surprise when she spots Princess. "What's she doing in here?" she snaps, pointing at the cat.

Rubbing the sleep from my eyes, I sit up in bed, peering at her with blurry vision. "Fucking hell! What time is it?" She doesn't answer; she just starts to tap her foot against the floor impatiently. *Oh, right, the cat.* "She scratched on my door not long after I went to bed, so I let her in."

"Declan's going to be pissed. He's been looking for her all night." Princess gets up and stretches her body, kneading at the blankets, before she walks over and headbutts me for some attention. I give her ears a little rub before she saunters to the end of the bed and leaps to the ground. Tail in the air, she walks past Jacinta, who reaches down to pat her. Instead of the warm greeting I got, Princess hisses and swipes at her hand, narrowly missing her. Jacinta quickly pulls her hand back, a surprised squeak leaving her lips.

"What did you do to that cat?" She looks accusingly at me like I've somehow tainted her precious brother's pet. I snort, throwing back the blankets. "Jacinta, I am many things, but bewitching a cat is beyond even my capabilities. Have you ever thought she's just hormonal due to carrying around a belly full of babies?" Climbing out of bed, I stretch my tired body and test the limits of my knee today. It feels better, so I'm going to leave the crutches behind. *One less way to stick out like a sore thumb.*

She eyes me like I'm a science experiment that she doesn't want to do, equal parts disdain, disgust, and judgment. "Well, hurry up! We're going to be late." Crossing her arms, she leans against the door frame, obviously prepared to wait right there for me.

"I guess it's lucky I showered last night," I

mutter to myself before asking her. "How come we're starting so early? I was under the impression we weren't leaving until nine."

I reach for the bedside table where I'd placed my phone when I'd plugged it in to charge overnight. Messages from Max continue to flash across the screen, even though the sound has been muted. If I dont ring her today and give her an update she may fly over here herself. Maybe I won't mention what happened between Jaxon and me, though.

A throat clearing behind me draws my attention. *Oh, right, clothes.* Unplugging and throwing my phone in my backpack, I open a drawer and grab a pair of ripped jeans and a fitted pink shirt that I know looks good against my tanned skin and blonde hair. Quickly, I pull them on before brushing my hair and heading into the bathroom to clean my teeth and put some mascara on my light lashes.

When I return to the bedroom and sit on the bed to put on my Converse, Jacinta has her phone out with her fingers flying across the screen. I wonder if she's snitching on me to Declan or something else entirely, but the blank, haughty look on her face gives me nothing to go on. Lacing my shoes, I stand up, throwing my backpack over my shoulder.

"Okay, I'm ready," I tell her. Looking up from her phone, her top lip raises in a sneer as she surveys my outfit. *And I'd thought her expression couldn't get any worse.*

"What's all of.... that? You represent the Summers family and the Neighpalm brand now; you can't be going around looking like... trash." I flinch. Her words make a direct hit, which I know is what she was aiming for, and I hate giving her that satisfaction.

"I don't own much of anything formal or designer. This is who I am," I explain, shrugging my shoulders.

Rolling her eyes, she huffs, "That will have to do. I don't have time for you to change." She takes off down the hall, her heels clattering on the wooden floors, as I grit my teeth and follow her. I hope she doesn't get too far ahead because I can't quite keep up. I'm still limping slightly, favoring my knee. One of the things I'd decided last night was to give them a little bit of slack, so I don't call out and remind her that it's hard for me to match her pace. No, I won't put up with hostile attacks like Jaxon's, but Jacinta's passive-aggressive disdain is easy to deal with. I've got the experience. I mean, it can't be easy having a complete stranger waltz in and disturb your tight-knit family.

We don't stop for breakfast, and I also don't see anyone as we leave the house. I'm not sure what time it is, but it can't be much past six-thirty. I'll have to check my phone when we get to wherever we're going.

Outside, the daylight is just breaking over the treeline, so I wasn't far off on time. There's a big black limo waiting for us in the same spot Nana, Poppy, and I were dropped off yesterday. The driver is wearing a suit and cap and politely says good morning as he opens the door for Jacinta. She just ignores him and slides in, while I smile and say good morning back. He frowns at Jacinta slightly before clearing it and nodding his head, a smile lifting on one side of his mouth.

When I get myself seated, the door closes with a sharp bang, and I watch him through the tinted windows as he makes his way to the driver's seat. Seamlessly, we start to move down the driveway. Jacinta has a tablet out, stylus in hand, and she looks to be drawing on it, but I don't pay too much attention. As the limo leaves the estate, I roll my window down to get another look at the abandoned mansion across the road. I need to start doing some exercise, so I might walk down and have a look next time I get five minutes. It's also on my list to find somewhere to buy a camera and a chest harness. I'm going to film my adventure. You never know what I might find.

"What are you doing?" Jacinta snaps at me, the contempt in her voice alerting me to the fact that I've once again offended her. "For God's sake! Close the window; you're messing up my hair." Turning to look at her incredulously, I can see there's not a strand out of place, but I don't want to spend the whole day fighting, so I do as she demands.

Pulling out my phone, I search the internet for any information about the old mansion and its eccentric owner. There are some cool articles about his famous parties in the seventies as well as a few others about his mysterious disappearance. It seems that he and his illegitimate son from an affair gone wrong went missing twenty-five years ago. No bodies were found, and the only suspect was the son's pregnant girlfriend, but with no evidence, they had no choice but to let her go. She disappeared, and the place has been empty ever since. Lawyers for the state have said there were rumors that the pregnant girlfriend was carrying the son's children, and those children would inherit anything if they came forward, but no one has claimed it as yet. *Wow, how exciting!* YouTube has no video footage of the castle, so unless it's lurking somewhere deep in the internet, it's likely no one has ever officially explored it. "God, could you be any more annoying? What are you smiling like a loon about?" Looking up, Jacinta's unfriendly gaze meets mine. In my excitement, I forgot she was in the car, and I guess I wasn't hiding my enthusiasm for my plans.

"Oh, ah, nothing really." I'm definitely not sharing it with her; the last thing I need is to give her more ammunition to mock or criticize me. So, putting away my phone, I change the subject.

"What are we doing today?" I ask, trying to make conversation.

"We're going to a photoshoot for my new line of lingerie and sportswear. There will be investors and buyers there, as well as the photographer and the models. Please don't do anything to embarrass me. Just find somewhere quiet and out of the way to sit, and if anyone asks you, just tell them you're an intern or something." She shudders, her Disney princess looks marred by the sneer that I'm starting to think will be her default expression around me. "The last thing I need to get out is that you're Dad's illegitimate daughter, and your mother was a junkie whore. That publicity would kill me." She looks me in the eye when she says that, and there is not one ounce of kindness in her cold blue eyes. Such a shame, I was hoping we might have been able to build at least a tolerance for each other, but I guess that's not how this is going to go.

After she fires that shot, she goes back to whatever it is she's doing, and I pull out my paperback that Maxine packed me. Reading the blurb on the inside, I chuckle at the words. *"This book is a reverse harem story. As such, the female main character will not be choosing a love interest, and there will be multiple scenes with group sex in them."* What has Max given to me? Looking at the front, there's a picture of a woman surrounded by six bare-chested men. *Married to the Pack,* the title says. I haven't had a chance to read in a long time. Between college and work for the

Bostons, and course practicals, I can't remember the last time I sat down with a good book. I especially love anything paranormal, and this looks to fit the bill. Settling myself in, I open the book and start the story.

I've been reading for about ten minutes when I hear her snort again. "What is it this time?" I ask, exasperated.

"Of course, you would read a book about a slut," she snaps, her words acidic and harsh.

"Oh, for fuck's sake, really?" I ask. "You're going to call a woman being liberated and not feeling the social pressure to choose a slut." I roll my eyes. "I would have thought a woman in big business would be liberated enough to see that this woman has got the right idea. Why should she have to choose? Do you call Jilly, the flight attendant on your jet, a slut? She has multiple partners." Jacinta's eyebrows tip down, and of course she's pretty even when frowning, but I can see her mind at work.

"I've never really had a relationship before. Men always expected me to be as loose and easy as my mom, so I avoided that as much as possible, and the one or two times I've had sex, well, I didn't really know what the big deal was. But if I found someone who could rock my world, or even better, a couple of someones, I would hold onto them tight. Everyone else could go screw themselves. Life is too short to be trapped under pressure from society. I want to look back when I'm old and never regret a thing."

Her frown has disappeared, and she's looking at me with slightly more interest now, but when she catches my eye, she scowls again and huffs, ignoring me and going back to her tablet. *Well, okay then, nice chat.* The drive into the city is quiet after that, but we do stop on the outskirts at a Starbucks, and Jacinta asks the driver to go in and get her a coffee.

"Don't be silly. I'll go and get it. What do you want? " I ask her. The limo can't park anywhere, so the driver will circle the block for me until I get back.

"I just want a chai latte, please," she says, and I'm surprised her order isn't more complicated.

She tries to hand me some money, but I just shake my head, holding up my purse. "I got it! It's fine." I also ask the driver if he wants anything, happy to get his tall flat white no sugar for him. The poor guy's been up at the crack of dawn right along with us. So when the limo stops, I jump out and quickly hobble in. It's not too busy considering what time of the morning it is, and I only have a five minute wait once I've placed my order.

When my name is called, I take the tray and run back just as the limo does another lap. The driver has his window down, so I pass him his coffee in return for an enthusiastic thanks. I guess it was an early start for him too. Hopping into the back, I carefully pass Jacinta her chai before taking out my caramel frappe and taking a long sip of it. Although I usually drink black, I sometimes indulge in this icy, sweet goodness that gives me a much needed boost. I take my little indulgences where I can get them.

The drive is a little slower now as we hit the traffic, but it's not long before we're pulling into the parking lot of a red brick warehouse which has a discrete Neighpalm Industries plaque next to the entrance. The rest of the area looks like it's made up of converted warehouses too, a trendy refurbished spot in a former slum area.

"What is this place?" I ask Jacinta as she packs away her tablet into a large leather satchel that she swings over her shoulder.

"This is my warehouse. I have my design office here, and we have a few seamstresses on the premises. It's also where we shoot a lot of our print ads. It made more sense than hiring a studio every time I needed to work." She places a large pair of dark glasses on her eyes, and it looks like she has to fortify herself with a deep breath before she gets out.

That's weird. It's almost like she doesn't want to be here. She goes on, explaining, "The Neighpalm building in the city is where I deal with clients, they expect it, but out here is where I spend most of my time." That little snapshot into Jacinta Summers tells me a lot. It's what I thought; there's more to her than meets the eye. I just need to try and chip away at the ice cold exterior to see what's on the inside.

"Come on, and remember don't talk to anyone." Her voice is cold and commanding again, and any snippet of hope that sparked a moment ago is quickly snuffed out.

*Or maybe I just won't try.*

## Chapter Fifteen

**Harlow**

The lower level of the old building is quiet, and the cutting tables and sewing machines are free of people, but Jacinta leads me over to a set of wrought iron steps that lead up to a mezzanine level that's bustling with sound and activity. I slowly make my way up the steps, my knee protesting slightly, and when I make it to the top, I stop to take in my surroundings. In front of me is a large white backdrop that's surrounded by equipment. Jacinta walks up to a guy with a camera wrapped around his neck and starts a conversation while various assistants run around, adjusting lights and these umbrella-looking things that I think are the flashes.

Off to the left-hand side is obviously hair and makeup, with a couple of chairs filled with what I'm assuming are the models with people fussing over their hair and faces. On the right-hand side is a long table filled with various snacks and a coffee machine, and it's there that I head. Grabbing a few pastry things, I put them on a plate, find a chair tucked away behind some panels, and settle in with my book and my snacks. Hopefully, Jacinta won't be able to fault me if I stay out of the way. Pulling out my book, I get sucked back into it, the background noise a dull rumble in my ear. Occasionally, I can hear Jacinta issue instructions, but for the most part, I'm able to block it all out.

That peace comes to an abrupt halt when a man walks behind the panels; he must not have noticed me in the corner as he drops the terrycloth robe he's wearing and flashes me the most magnificent naked body I've ever had the pleasure of seeing in person. Golden blond hair, with long, lean, sculpted muscles that ripple as he pulls on a pair of what look like ladies' leggings. My eyes run down his tattoo-covered body, to his washboard stomach, and a squeak escapes my mouth. He's stuffing his well-endowed package into them and pulls them up over his hips, adjusting his cock to sit a certain way. His head snaps up at the sound of my voice, and although his eyes widen a bit in surprise, he maintains this cool confidence that must come with the experience of being drooled over by people on a daily basis.

"Huh, didn't know anyone was back here."

A searing blush crosses my cheeks. "I'm so sorry. I didn't realize this was for changing; I was just trying to stay out of the way."

He winks at me, looking much less perturbed than I would be in his shoes. "No harm done. I'd be a pretty poor model if I found people looking at me upsetting. Who are you, and what are you doing hiding back there?"

"Ah, um..." What should I tell him? I know Jacinta doesn't want anyone knowing who I am, and I don't want to upset her, but on the other hand, screw the bitch. "I'm here with Jacinta."

His eyebrows raise, and a knowing look crosses his face. "Are you the new sister?"

Now it's my turn to look surprised, and he snorts. "Oh, honey, that's the worst kept secret ever. Everyone knows about it. I'm Alexander." He holds out a hand, and I take it, shaking firmly.

"I'm Harlow."

"Why are you hiding back here?" he asks. Raising a sculpted eyebrow, his face is filled with curiosity. Overall, he has a kind, open look to him, and while many others would be giving out the vibe of a petty gossip, he seems like he might just want to get to know me a little. Before I can answer, another knowing look crosses his face. "Queen Jacinta doesn't want anyone to know who you are, does she?"

"Ah yeah, apparently, my sense of style doesn't meet her standards," I tell him, gesturing to my outfit. "But to be honest, I think that's just an excuse."

He nods and sits down in the chair next to me, and I struggle to keep my eyes on his face. He sees the struggle and smirks before continuing. "Yeah, the Summers family are tough ones to crack. Burnt too many times, and when you're that wealthy, I guess you've got to wonder if it's all about the money or not." We sit quietly for a moment before he sighs deeply. "So, does that mean you don't know anyone here?"

"Nope, but you know what, I've got my book; I don't need anyone else." He looks down at it before reaching over, yanking it out of my hand, and reading the page I was on.

His face crosses with a wider smirk. "Oh, honey, I think you do need someone if these words are doing to you what they're doing to me."

He reaches down and adjusts his generous package, but before he can say anything else, a woman with frizzy black hair and tawny skin pops her head around the panel. "Alexander, are you ready to go? What's taking so long? It was just one pair of pants!" Her voice has a touch of annoyance to it, but she tempers it halfway through her questions as if realizing she shouldn't be mouthing off at him. Turning from him to me, her brows draw together in confusion. Crossing her arms, she demands, "Who are you, and what are you doing back here? She's not bothering you, is she?"

I look at him in panic, and he quickly replies for me.

"She's an intern, Lindy. I asked her to rub some oil on my body, but she didn't know where it was."

Her face clears, and I guess this is somehow an acceptable answer. "Oh, I can do that for you," she offers, and a change comes over Alexander. He stands up and adopts a different manner, both his body and voice transforming from how he'd carried himself just a moment ago.

He stands with his hip cocked, and he puts his hands on them. "Oh, darling, that's okay. I know how important you are, and you don't have time." His voice has an effeminate tone to it, and he simpers, fluttering his eyelashes at her. "If you could just get the oil for Harlow, she can get my body oiled up, and I'll be all ready for Shane."

She blinks a couple of times like she's dazed by him before shaking her head to clear it. "Of course, I'll get that right away, and then let Shane know you're almost ready." She hurries away, and I look at him, a combination of confused and stunned.

"What the fuck was that?" I wave my hand at him, gesturing to all that he is. He drops the pose and rolls his eyes.

"People expect male models to be gay, so that's the person I give them. I book so many more jobs now because of it," he explains.

"That sucks; it must be exhausting," I sympathize with him, but he shrugs his shoulders.

"Nah, it's half-true, some might say. I'm bi, but the fashion industry is surprisingly narrow-minded. I get other jobs as well, like book covers and things, and they don't care, but to get major fashion jobs, I needed that little bit more."

"Jacinta is like that?" I question, surprised at the revelation, but he's shaking his head.

"Actually, she's not. She doesn't handle the booking; one of her people does. She doesn't seem to care either way." He looks thoughtful, and I can see the want in his eyes, and something clicks.

"You're hot for her, aren't you?" An adorable blush crosses his face, and he ducks his head, embarrassed.

"Yeah. I know you've probably seen the worst of her, but every job I've ever done for Neighpalm Couture, she's been supportive, kind, and caring to all her people. And seriously, have you seen her?" I roll my eyes but nod as he continues. "But like all the others, she thinks I'm gay and doesn't look at me any way but as an employee. It doesn't help that I have a male partner at the moment as well. He's interested in her too. We wouldn't mind making her the meat in our sandwich, but she doesn't seem to notice either of us. She has walls built so high and blinders on when it comes to everyone around her unless you're family." Poor guy. God, I know what it's like to be attracted to someone and for them to see you as something you're not.

"Well, since you're the only person who's talked

to me like I'm a normal person who's not after their money, I guess that makes you my new bestie since I had to leave my other behind. What do you say we make a spectacle of ourselves, see if we can get her to notice you?" Plucking my book out of his hand, I throw it in my bag. "Or at least get her to notice by pissing her off. Which works for me anyway." I laugh and grab him by the hand as I tow him out from behind the screens, bumping into Lindy on the other side, a bottle of body oil in hand. Grabbing it from her, I thank her enthusiastically.

"Thanks so much, Lindy! I can't wait to do this; it's got to be the best part of my day, you know, getting my hands on all those gorgeous muscles!" My voice carries across the room, bringing people's eyes toward us. Some of them are amused at my words, but one particular set of turquoise blue ones look furious.

Turning to Alexander, I mutter to him, "Well, she took notice of that. Are you still game?" I raise an eyebrow to check if he's up for this, and he nods his head emphatically.

"Okay then, follow my lead, and let's see what kind of reaction we get from this." I pour a small amount of oil into my hand and rub them together to warm them before placing them directly over his pecs. Stroking my hands over his ripped body, I start to babble.

"Wow, your body is so sculpted. You must work out really hard!" Again, my voice is loud, and a tittering of laughs can be heard behind me, but I ignore them. Yeah, the guy's hot, but I know he's into Jacinta, and God only knows I don't need any more issues with her.

My ears catch the sound of heels clicking against the wooden floors, and I shoot him a wicked smile before continuing my babble. "I'm new to L.A. I'd love it if someone would show me around."

He smiles a genuine grin, and I don't think he's acting when he responds, "I'd love to show you around. How about I get your number before you leave today?"

A clearing throat has us both turning around. Jacinta stands there, arms crossed, eyes flashing with fury and her mouth pursed as she says loudly, "Harlow, are you bothering our models? You know I told you you're not to do that." She steps close and hisses under her breath, "I knew you were as bad as your mother; hitting on complete strangers is low." Alexander's eyes widen, and he loses the easy grin in favor of a clenched jaw that betrays his anger at her comment.

"That's a bit harsh, don't you think? How else is someone supposed to get to know anyone if they don't make an effort?" he admonishes her quietly. A wicked smile crosses his lips, and he speaks louder.

"She's not bothering me at all. In fact, she's doing an amazing job at rubbing in the oil; her hands are magic if you know what I mean."

Reaching a hand down to adjust his package, his words take on a suggestive tone that has me completely amused but also convinced that fire might come out of my new sister's eyes next. He winks at me as I step away. "All done? Great, thank you." He places lingering kisses on both my cheeks before pushing past Jacinta and walking toward the photographer.

"I'm sorry I took so long, Shane!" He flutters his eyelashes at the guy who looks a little bemused at everything. "We couldn't find the oil, and you know how I like to be rubbed all over." He slaps Shane on the ass as he passes, and Shane snickers with amusement. I smile at his antics, and Jacinta's bemused expression has me squealing internally. At least until she turns to me and pierces me with her blue eyes.

"See, his boyfriend probably doesn't appreciate you hitting on his partner." Looking over her shoulder, I can see the photographer watching us with appreciative eyes. I know it's for her and not me, but I can fuck with her a little more.

"I don't know...he seems to be fairly interested." I wave my fingers at him over her shoulder, and she turns fairly quickly to see a smile cross his face at my antics. He winks before turning back to concentrate on the shoot.

Lindy walks up to us with a frown on her face. "Jacinta, is the intern bothering you?" she asks, shooting me a look of annoyance. "Go and make yourself useful; get me a coffee," she demands, and

I wait for Jacinta to pipe up and tell her who I am, but a wicked grin crosses her face instead. *Damn it, here comes her revenge.*

"Well, girl, hurry up and do what she says. In fact, you can be her assistant all day. Use her how you wish, Lindy," she directs, waving her hand at me. "God knows everyone else does." Her words are laced with purposeful innuendo and her face filled with malice as she turns and strolls back to the action, knowing exactly what reputation she's setting out for me. And there it is, the payback.

"Hurry up then! I don't have all day. I want it black, three sugars." Taking a deep breath, I go and get it for her. I don't want to make a scene, and I know that's what she wants, so she can go home and complain to Brad. So for now I'll suck it up.

I spend the next few hours running my ass off for Lindy and anyone she offers my help to. Alexander is not the only model here today. There's another male one named Josh who's friendly and leaves me alone, but then there are three females whose names I don't care enough to remember. You can bet your ass I'm going to remember their faces. Those bitchy cows had me do things like taking the gum out of their mouths when it was time for their shoots and dab at the sweat they developed under the lights, with huge grins on their faces the whole time.

Alexander tried to stop them once, but I just shook my head. It's fine; I can suck it up for a day, and at least I can say to Brad that I made an effort without having to lie about it. While I've been running about, Alexander and Shane have exchanged numerous glances when I've been ordered to do something. I'd seen Alexander whispering to Shane earlier, and they had both turned to look at me, pity crossing Shane's face, so I guess Alexander filled him in on who I am. They both look at Jacinta to see if she's going to do anything, but she just watches with glee, her fingers flying across her phone. What's the bet that she's messaging her brothers to share my pain with them?

When one of the female models tells me to go and get them all sushi from a specific restaurant, conveniently far from the warehouse, Shane has finally had enough; he steps in.

"Actually, I will be making use of Harlow for the rest of the afternoon. That's if you don't mind, Lindy?" He phrases it as a question, but there is no room for her to wiggle at the tone of his voice.

She shakes her head enthusiastically, all smiles now that she's talking to someone important to her campaign. "Oh no, Shane, use her how you wish." *How kind of her,* I think sarcastically, but his eyes heat as a cheeky smile crosses his face.

"I just might do that." His words are suggestive, and he scans me from head to toe. "You know, I'm not feeling all this." He waves at the three models. "It's not working; they just don't have the right look." There's a challenge in his eyes when he turns back to me, and I've got at least enough common sense to know I might not like what's coming. "Now, Harlow, on the other hand, I bet she'd look amazing in your lingerie line. She's got a banging body, and men will drool over her more, dare I say, sexy figure." The models' faces blaze with fury at that dig, but they keep quiet, knowing better than to piss off the photographer. He turns to Jacinta, whose mouth is pursed in annoyance, but a wan smile crosses her face as he waits for her response.

"I told you that I would work with your vision. If that's what you wish, I'll find her something to wear." She stalks off in the direction of the clothing rack, and Alexander hurries over to me and drags me back behind the curtain.

"Strip," he commands.

"What are the two of you doing?" I ask as I start to take off my clothes. I'm not shy or ashamed of my body. I know it looks good. I just choose not to flaunt it regularly.

"Shane is right. Those models were too athletic. They were great for the sports line, but they don't fit for the lingerie. Jacinta needs sensual and sexy, not 'I work out as hard as you do.' We originally had another model booked for this but she's out 'sick'"

He rolls his eyes at his words, and mutters about drug addicted anorexic supermodels. *Whoa*

He eyes my body now that I'm standing in just my underwear, his up and down glance assessing. "And he's right, that's exactly what you are. You can see that you look after yourself, but you've got curves that make a man's mouth water. You're every man's wet dream, and every woman wants to be you." The look in his eyes says he likes what he's seeing, but only from a professional point of view. There is no interest there at all. Jacinta must really do it for him; he has it *bad*.

"This is a way to get back at all those bitches out there, Jacinta included. They've been appalling to you all day, and you haven't deserved that treatment. It's like they all decided you were fair game once Jacinta called it open season. If they knew who you were, not one of them would have put a foot out of line." He looks disturbed at the thought, and it's kind of scary that he has a point. *I wonder how much of their behavior was natural or whether Jacinta might have pushed them over the edge.*

Lindy bustles around the corner, throws a small scrap of lace at me without a word, and disappears again. Holding up the g-string and demi-cup bra, I shake my head. It's the same shade of pink as the shirt I was wearing, but it's got to be the smallest thing she has. It's like she's deliberately trying to make me feel uncomfortable, but when you've had your arm elbow-deep in the back of a cow, there's not much that makes you uncomfortable anymore.

Alexander turns his back as I slip off my underwear and put it on. "I was serious about getting your number. In fact, how about Shane and I take you out for dinner after all this? We can drop you back off afterward," he tells me over his shoulder.

"Can you do this up for me?" I ask him, turning my back, and I feel his warm hand against my skin as he does. "I would love to, but you know it's quite a drive to the Summers' estate."

He turns me back around and winks at me. "I know, but I've always wanted a look." Laughing, I follow him back around to the set, which is now decorated with a huge bed covered in white sheets.

"What about her tattoos?" Lindy frowns, gesturing at my sleeve. One of the other girls had tattoos, but they'd covered them with makeup, and both guys do too. "Shall we cover them?"

"God, no! They're hot as fuck. Leave them," Shane orders. "Okay, Harlow. I want you and Josh and Alex on the bed. You're going to roll around like you're having a threesome." He starts issuing instructions, and I follow along. Who am I to complain about rolling around on a bed with two sexy men? Closest I've gotten to getting laid in months, and they're both smoking hot.

We spend the next two hours following his instruction, and I make several outfit changes. Both guys go out of their way to make me feel comfortable, and we end up laughing a lot. Shane must be pleased because all he can do is shout praise while his finger furiously clicks the button of his camera. Jacinta and two of the models stare at me, frosty-eyed, through the whole shoot. The other one was so upset she stormed off the set and went home.

Finally, Shane calls an end. "I think we're done guys; I got some great shots. Why don't the three of you go ahead and get dressed?"

Climbing off the bed, I move behind the panels. The guys are kind enough to let me go first and give me some privacy, but Lindy stands just outside the whole time like she's afraid I'm going to steal the clothes. When I hand them back to her, she just huffs and snatches them out of my hand. As I step out from behind the screen, I can see Shane and Jacinta in a heated discussion. I mean, I can't hear the words, but the gestures make it obvious that sister dearest is definitely displeased. Alexander steps in front of me, blocking the view, and he's already managed to get clothes on. He must have had them somewhere else or knows some secret model magic.

"Still want to go and have dinner with us?" he asks, putting his hand on my arm. Jacinta approaches me, her eyes locked on the hand.

"Are you ready yet? We need to go." Her tone is impatient, and she can't look at Alexander. If she weren't' trying to hold onto some semblance of professionalism, I'm sure her foot would be tapping and her arms would be crossed. *Hmm, maybe she's not as unaffected as she pretends.* Perhaps she's more interested than he thinks she is. I jump up and down internally, cheering for my newest friend to find some happiness even if it's with the ice queen.

"Actually, I'm going to get something to eat with Shane and Alex. They'll drop me off later." Her face freezes, and she slowly blinks before nodding and turning on her heel then stalking away. Alex blows out a whistle, and I release the breath I had been holding, feeling some of the first moments of relief for the entire day.

"Well, that went well. I think I'm going to need a couple of drinks," I tell him, and he wraps an arm around my shoulder.

"It's alright, princess. We'll look after you." He leads me over to Shane and makes me sit after he notices me hobbling. My knee has held up well throughout the day, but now it's starting to throb. While Shane finishes packing up, Alex finds me some painkillers and a glass of water, and then the three of us head to dinner.

## Jacinta

M y blood practically boils as I watch her roll around on the bed with the two models. I know they're only acting, but seeing Alex pretend to worship her makes my skin crawl. It's common knowledge that he has a boyfriend, and he and Shane are very open in their affections to one another, but I've also seen the interest in his eyes when he thinks I'm not looking. I've caught both him and Shane giving me heated looks in the past and have always wondered if they're bi, not gay. There are certainly enough rumors flying around the modeling world to question it.

Alex seems to have two personalities depending on who's watching. There's the supreme campy, effeminate one who flaps around a set like a drag queen who's lost her sequins, which I'm sure is all an act. Then there's the one who has quiet intelligent conversations with me when we both have a break. The one who is super attentive and brings me a cup of coffee for no reason or makes sure I eat during a busy fashion show. The one who touches me for no reason, a touch that brings goosebumps to the surface of my skin. Shane is very much the same when he's on a photo set or at a runway show. He always goes out of his way to come over and check on me or give me a bottle of water or a little shoulder massage. These guys are sending me signals that I thought I could interpret as interest, but now, watching them both with *her*, maybe I'm not so special after all.

And that's another strike to the gut.

First, she catches my brother's eye and throws him for a loop. Thank god he discovered her true nature before anything could happen. Then she arrives and takes my place as Dad's only daughter, and from what I can understand, she has many of the same interests that *I* share with him. And don't think I didn't notice the gleam of interest in my other brothers' eyes when they first saw her. Oliver and Kai seem particularly reluctant to get rid of the tramp.

It's a shame, really. I had to try especially hard this morning not to laugh when she bit back at my retort about Declan's cat, and I would love to borrow the book she was reading in the car once she's done with it, but I have to settle for remembering the name because there's no way I'm asking that gold-digger for anything. It incenses me even more to admit that I think the two of us could be good friends if the circumstances were different. Giving myself a mental shake, I remind myself that I have to steel my heart no matter what. Family first, always, and that gold-digger is *not* my family.

I saw her disappear when we first got here, and I'd thought she was finally doing something right, staying out of the way and not drawing any attention to herself. But then Alex found her, and he couldn't leave well enough alone, too damn kind for his own good. Thankfully, Alex passed her off as an intern. I wouldn't have been able to deal with all the gossip mongers today, and then it was fun to see her run off her feet doing menial tasks for those bitchy models, though I did feel a twinge of guilt as I saw her limp now and then. In the end, though, it's her fault, isn't it? She could just give up and leave, and then there'd be no cause for any extra pain.

When Dad told us about her and how awful her mom had been to her, my mind flashed back to our own mom. I don't have many memories, but the few I do have are *not* pleasant. I remember how I could never do anything to please her. Jaxon could, he was her angel, but vivid echoes of her telling me I was useless and worth nothing to her bounce around my mind. Not to mention her insistence that I'd ruined her body because carrying twins had been a nightmare, and maybe if she'd only had Jaxon, my father would still love her. Four-year-old me didn't really understand the words, but that didn't stop my brain from absorbing them, and adult Jacinta certainly knows how badly our mother was trying to hurt her.

I later found out through some stealthy eaves-dropping that the woman was bi-polar and manic depressive, and she'd actually approached Dad in a lucid moment and begged him to take Jaxon and give him a good life. I'm not sure what she had planned for me, but I shudder to think of what would have happened if Dad hadn't insisted on having both of us. I've got a feeling a sum of money may have exchanged hands as well since we never saw her again, but I don't care. There's not a single bit of me that wants to know what happened to her.

So of course I feel sorry for Harlow, and if she was becoming a member of any other family, I would be thrilled for her and them, but I can't and won't accept her into mine. All of us have been through too much to have our well-balanced life upset and thrown into chaos because her junkie mother finally OD'd and she discovered who her father is. Let's face it, if the mother was still alive, we would all be living our lives in blissful ignorance.

As I continue to watch the tramp roll around on one of the first men who has shown genuine interest in me, not my fortune or my business, I swear to make her wish her mother had never died.

## Chapter Sixteen

**Harlow**

We have dinner in a cute little Mexican restaurant not far from the warehouse. The hostess had shown us to a little corner booth out of the way, and after delivering a pitcher of margaritas for Alex and me, and a beer for Shane, the waitress takes our food orders. I study Shane and Alex across the table from me while she's engaged with them, taking advantage of this moment where no one's paying much attention to me. Shane is a striking man, maybe a little older than Alex, I'd say mid-thirties, whereas Alex is the same as me, twenty-five. He has dark brown hair, which is streaked with gray already, as is his neatly trimmed facial hair, and he has deep ocean blue eyes that sparkle when he smiles, especially when looking at Alex. He's tanned like he spends a lot of time outdoors, which I guess could be true if a lot of his photoshoots are outside. I'd say he's ruggedly handsome compared to Alex's beautifully handsome.

When the waitress has finished with them, she walks away, having taken my order first. Shane sits back in the booth and puts his arm around Alex's shoulders before saying to me, "So, Harlow, tell us about you. How did you hurt your knee?"

"Oh, I fell off a horse," I tell him, waving off the question as I pour both Alex and I a glass of the frozen tequila drink. "Twisted my knee the wrong way. It's already much better than it was." They don't push any further, but judging by the way he's wiggling in his seat, Alex is busting a gut to ask me more questions.

"Look, just ask what you want to ask, okay? Better we get it all out in the open and move on." Shane looks impressed, though there's a slight edge of warning in his gaze like I don't know what I've just released. Alex lets out a sigh of relief before firing off the first one.

"Is it true you didn't know you were a part of the Summers family, and you grew up with a junkie mother who killed herself, and now you're coming in to steal all of the kids' businesses away from them?" His voice rushes out of him in a flurry of words, and my mind takes a moment to catch up to both the speed at which he spoke and the absurdity of that final question. Shane and I stare at him, me in amusement and Shane with a barely disguised disgust.

"Where did you hear all that garbage?" Although his tone makes it clear that he's seeing the nonsense in those rumors, the look he gives Alex is equal parts affection as it is exasperation. He just rose even more in my esteem.

Alex blushes a little but refuses to shrink down under our scrutiny. "That was all the gossip on set today. Everyone was chatting about it, out of yours and Jacinta's hearing, of course," he tells me, his eyes full of sympathy. I just shrug it off.

"How did everyone know who I was?" Jacinta never introduced me to anyone, and I certainly didn't say anything. My eyes narrow in on Alex. He was the only one who knew who I was today, and he must have shared it with Shane. Did he share it with everyone else? He sees where I'm going with that line of questioning and quickly holds up his hands.

"Oh, no, they didn't," he assures me. "They were just gossiping about the situation. I promise no one knew who you were. They would have been groveling at your feet if they had, not treating you like dirt." Giving him another moment of close scrutiny, I decide to take his word for it and think back to what his questions were.

"Alex, I've been talked about my entire life in one way or another. My mom made sure of that little detail. I've become immune to general gossip, but I'm worried about what the Summers family thinks," I explain to them. "No, I didn't know about Brad. My mom kept it from both of us. I only found out when I had to dig through her belongings after she overdosed. And that's the answer to your next question. Yes, she was a junkie. Apparently, she managed to stay fairly clean while pregnant with me, but it was a downhill battle after that until eventually, I was moved into foster care." I deliver all of this as factually as I can, keeping a tight lid on any latent emotions so the parts of me that are still a tiny bit raw aren't exposed.

Tears well in Alex's eyes, the big softie, but I wave them away. "No, don't be upset. My foster family is amazing. You hear all sorts of things about foster care, but I didn't suffer at all. My life was so much better than it would have been had Mom retained custody. In fact, my foster dad is best friends with Brad Summers. It's how my mom met him. Grace and Howard Summers were regular visitors in our house, and I've always felt a connection with them. It was awesome finding out they're my grandparents for real."

Shane's looking at ease, accepting the well-adjusted front I'm putting on and probably thankful he's not dealing with a crying, screaming mess. I've learned how to fake it with the best, but I can see that I'm not fooling Alex. Maybe there's a kindred spirit there; he seems to be affected more than someone who was raised in a normal, well-adjusted family would be.

I take a sip of my margarita, enjoying the cool frozen goodness with the kick of tequila and lime. "And the business one?" Shane pushes, his curiosity getting the better of him. I just about snort my drink through my nose as I laugh, putting the glass down carefully on the table and looking him directly in the eye.

"Quite frankly, Shane, I couldn't give a fuck about any of their businesses. I have a career, or the start of one anyway. I came out here looking to make a family connection. None of Brad's kids have shown any inclination toward wanting one, so I'll spend a little time making Brad happy before heading back to Connecticut and getting on with my life."

They both look a little skeptical at my words, but I don't hold it against them. Most people would be. It almost sounds like a fairy tale that someone could find themselves to be related to the Summers' wealth but not want any of it. "Look, from the small snapshot I got of that family and listening to the conversation going on around the dinner table the other night, none of them seem particularly happy. They're all stressed over one aspect of the business or another and had nothing else to talk about except that. I didn't hear anything about hobbies or likes or dislikes; it was *all* business. That's not a way to live. Where's the fun and joy in life?"

Both of them stare at me wide-eyed like I'm a

creature they've never seen before. "But, but, surely all that money..." Alex stammers.

"Money doesn't make you happy, Alex. The Summers prove that. It just makes you paranoid and gives you trust issues." The table is quiet as they contemplate my words, and I sip my drink, the silence becoming awkward until Shane shakes his head and changes the subject abruptly. It's like he realizes how uncomfortable I've become and has decided that we need to try and save the rest of the night.

"So, what is it you do?" he asks me. "Because I could get you booked for a whole heap of modeling work while you're here if you want. You were amazing." The frown clears from Alex's face at Shane's words, and an enthusiastic look blooms in its place.

"Girl, you were hot; those shots are going to be amazing!" This time he's bouncing up and down in his seat in excitement, and I can't help but smile at his energy. There's something about him that just feels so friendly and welcoming, almost like he's a puppy stuck in the body of a hot male model. "I'm sure you could get representation. I'm represented by Neighpalm..." He trails off, and I snort with laughter.

"Yeah, not sure *that's* going to happen. Declan could barely disguise his disdain when he looked at me. Getting signed by his agency is not an option."

"Well, you'll need to be paid for those shots,"

Shane declares, "Jacinta is going to make a killing from them."

"Guys, I don't care. Look, Nana and Poppy just paid for my college. That's all I needed, and I honestly didn't even ask for that. They insisted!" They both eye me skeptically, but not as though they don't believe the sincerity in my words. It's more like they're waiting for me to declare myself some kind of alien life form.

"Girl, everyone needs money," Alex pushes.

"Yeah, money's nice, but I'll probably open my own business when I get back home, so I'll be alright," I insist, and Alex's face falls at the mention of me going home.

"You're not allowed to leave," he says, reaching across the table for my hand. "You're the most down to earth person Shane and I have met in ages. I'm sure you're supposed to be our new bestie." Shane smiles at his enthusiasm but doesn't disagree.

"Yeah, someone always wants something from one of us. My help for their career or Alex's help with his dick." This time, I choke on the drink going down, and Alex needs to pat me on the back as I wipe the tears from my eyes. Shane's eyes are sparkling at my reaction, and he winks at me.

"Well, it *is* a pretty impressive one."

I look at Alex, and he has a cheeky grin that reads as nothing but fun flirtation. "I can show you if you want, love," he jokes, but I know he's not serious. Even though both he and Josh had to adjust themselves occasionally during the shoot, I know it was purely biological; neither of them made me feel uncomfortable. I mean, I was pretty turned on myself, rolling around on a bed with two mostly naked guys, but every time I closed my eyes, the face that I was picturing had wicked blue turquoise eyes and a sneer of disgust. *I'm sick in the head.* But I'm pretty sure Alex was picturing my adopted sister the whole time too.

"If only you were serious," I tell him, "but I think it's a different Summers you're after, not me." He and Shane exchange a glance and both shrug. "Well, we definitely got her attention today. You may never see me again after you drop me off," I joke, but they look worried, and I wave them off. "Relax, I can handle myself."

The waitress arrives with our food at that moment, so we're quiet as she places our meals in front of us. I've ordered chicken enchiladas, and both the guys have some sort of quesadilla in front of them. Before she's even walked away, I start to devour my food. "God, rolling around on the bed with you for a couple of hours works up an appetite," I joke around a mouthful of food, and the two guys just grin at me.

"And we weren't even doing anything strenuous!" Alex winks again, sipping his margarita.

"So, Harlow, what's this career you keep talking about? What are you going to leave us to go back to?" Shane probes smoothly as he swipes a corn chip through some of the queso dip we're all sharing.

"Oh, I'm a vet." The silence that follows my announcement has me looking up from my food. Both have their, thankfully empty, mouths wide open in shock, and a giggle explodes out of me.

"Get the fuck out!" Alex whispers, eyeing me like I'm some strange creature again. Shane shakes himself out of his shock and keeps eating, an indulgent look on his face as he lets Alex have his moment. "Holy cow, Harlow, you're the whole package, beauty, brains, and kindness." Even with that compliment, I sense nothing from him but friendly interest and enthusiasm, and it's such a relief that I've just felt safe every moment I've been with them. I really like these guys. They seem to have morals, and their sense of loyalty isn't easy to find. They're crushing on Jacinta, and not just any pretty face is going to change their minds. Good for them, sticking to their guns. I couldn't be happier with our friendship so far.

"You're awfully young to have finished vet school, aren't you?" *Why does everyone keep saying that?*

"Ah yeah, I tested out of a few classes during junior and senior years of high school and started college early. I've just graduated, and the Bostons, they're my foster family, put in a clinic on the farm for me. I've been treating a few patients there, as well as all their horses. I've also been offered a position with a nearby vet, but I haven't decided if I'm going to take it."

Their eyebrows raise, and their eyes widen at my words. "So, not just small animals?" Alex asks, sounding like he knows what he's talking about.

Shaking my head, I reply, "No, I prefer large animals. Actually, I thought while I was out here, I might see if there are any internships at any of the zoos that I could apply for; my dream is to work with zoo animals." I share my secret shyly, my face blushing red in embarrassment as my voice unconsciously quiets with the big reveal. I can't believe I just told them that! I hadn't shared that with anyone until Max forced my hand the other day, and here I'm sharing it with these guys, practically strangers, but they've just made me feel so comfortable. Now and during the shoot. We talk for the whole meal, me grilling them on their interests and likes and them grilling me in return. I tell them all about my fascination with abandoned things, Jenny, DS, and about the gothic mansion near the Summers' place that I want to explore.

"That reminds me I need to do some shopping! I want to get a GoPro, so I can film it, and then I'm going to load it to YouTube like all those other videos," I tell them, excited about the prospect. "I wonder if Nana will take me shopping," I muse out loud.

"Pshh," Alex admonishes me, "I'll come and pick you up, and we'll make a day of it. We can pick a zoo or two to visit, and we'll do some shopping and see some sights. It will be fun! Shane will be editing those shots for the next few days, and I've got nothing booked until next week, so I'm all yours."

My heart swells with his words as optimism fills me that perhaps this visit won't be so bad after all. "Really? That would be awesome. Just let me check with Brad if he's lined up for me to 'visit' with any of his other kids, and I'll let you know."

We finish another pitcher of margaritas between us, and Shane moves onto water. *Smart man.* Dessert has Alex and me giggling through churros and different kinds of sweet dips before we settle the bill and head out into the fresh night air. The guys insisted on paying, and Alex has been trying to convince me to stay with them tonight so we can keep drinking, but I make my excuses.

"I need to get home. I don't want to make a bad impression with Brad, Nana, and Poppy before they get to know me." I had already received a text message from Nana asking where I was. Jacinta had failed to tell anyone, and they'd been worried. I rolled my eyes at her childish behavior, and the guys pushed me to tell them, causing frowns to form on both their faces.

"We had no idea she could be like this. Today's the first time we've seen her act any way but pleasant. She doesn't have a reputation of being hard to work with or a diva. Everyone in the industry always says how nice she is. It's rare," Shane explains as Alex nods his head. "Honestly, her reputation and the way she acts on set are part of why we're interested in her. She seemed like one of a kind."

"We all have some sort of facade we put on for other people though, guys. The way you talk about it and other people have also told me," I think of James' words, "something is always wanted from them. It must be exhausting. I'd adopt a cool, collected persona too. Never letting anyone too close to see the real me. I didn't appreciate the way she treated me today, but I also understand why she did."

As we're talking, we make our way through the parking lot until we get to where Shane parked his car. It's a nice-looking BMW, but that's all I know about it. Climbing into the back, I give him the address that Nana sent me for his GPS. The ride home is filled with quiet conversation and even quieter background music, and I'm feeling the most relaxed that I've felt in days.

"Thanks, guys. I needed this, especially after this morning." My knee is starting to ache a little again, and I massage it as they turn past the big wrought iron gates that block the two estates off from the main road. It's completely dark now, but this road has a few street lights that make seeing the entrance easier. The driveway is lined with cute, little old-fashioned lanterns I hadn't noticed when we arrived. Their warm yellow light leads a path to the house.

"Wowwee." A whistle escapes Alex's mouth. "I had heard it was fancy, but this is something else."

I laugh at his words. "Yeah. I had somewhat the same reaction but had to be cool, you know what I mean." Shane guides the car to a stop in front of the steps leading to the front door. I'd planned to sneak around to my side door, but Nana opens the front one just as I'm getting out of the car and puts a stop to that. Alex and Shane climb out with me, and I introduce them to her.

"Thank you, boys, for looking after my granddaughter." She gives them both a kiss on their cheek, and they look surprised but pleased at the gesture. "It gives me a little bit of relief that she's making at least a few friends." I roll my eyes at her words but smile at her concern. It's nice to be fussed over, though I might abstain from admitting that out loud.

Something catches my eye, and, looking up at the second-story window, I can see Jacinta staring down at us. Smiling to myself, I turn and throw my arms around Alex and then Shane, giving them both quick kisses on the mouth, which they return in surprise. They look at me quizzically, but the minor crinkles in their noses would be hard to see from where Jacinta's watching. "We're being watched," I mutter as their eyes clear, and they smile.

"Text me and let me know about tomorrow," Alex reminds me.

Waving goodbye to us, both of them climb in the car and leave as Nana turns to see what I was talking about. She sees Jacinta, and she turns back to me with a skeptical look on her face. "What are you doing, Harlow, my girl?"

"A little bit of payback mixed with some possible matchmaking. Maybe, who knows." I shrug my shoulders as she tucks her arm through mine, and we head inside.

"What was Alex saying about tomorrow?" she asks as we head to our wing of the house. No one else seems to be around, and I'm relieved.

"Oh, he offered to take me sightseeing, and I wanted to buy a camera to take some photos and video," I explain, "but I wasn't sure if Brad had organized anything for me tomorrow."

She pats her hand on mine, the gesture comforting and familiar. "You go and have fun with your new friends. I'll smooth everything with Bradley for you. I've got a feeling today wasn't easy, was it?" She eyes me carefully as we get to my bedroom door, and there's a bit of a challenge in them as though she's just daring me to try and lie.

"I've had better days, Nana," I tell her honestly before pushing my cracked open door.

"Hmm, I could tell what with the way Jacinta came home in a fierce mood. I now know why, I guess." The older lady doesn't miss much, and I just

LEXIE WINSTON

wink at her as I notice the ball of fluff in the middle of my bed again.

"Oh, Princess, you're going to get me in so much trouble!" I tell her, but I leave her be, missing the companionship of all my animals back home in Connecticut. Nana smiles at her, her expression holding as much fondness as when she looks at her grandchildren.

"Well, she obviously knows she and her babies are in safe hands with you," she praises me, proud of my achievements. "Good night, sweetheart. Glad you made it home alright. Just hang in there; things will get better." Nana kisses me on my cheek and leaves me.

I close the door behind her and quickly send Alex a text asking him what time he's going to pick me up in the morning. He replies just as quickly, telling me he'll be by to grab me for breakfast. I feel a little guilty at the distance he will be driving, but he assures me it's okay, plus he's looking forward to marveling at the Summers' home in the daylight. Plugging my phone in to charge, I shoot Max a quick message, telling her I'm busy but everything is okay so she doesn't worry. I grab a quick shower before collapsing on the bed next to Princess. Her gentle purrs lull me to sleep once more.

## Chapter Seventeen

**Harlow**

The following morning, the door crashing against the wall of my room has me bolting upright in bed and Princess making a mad dash under my blankets. "What the fuck are you doing with my cat?" a voice growls as I blink my eyes a couple of times to adjust to the light.

A pair of green fury-filled eyes are staring at me, but they quickly warm to desire as he continues to look, his gaze drifting downwards. Glancing down, I quickly pull the blankets up over my chest, a squeak of surprise escaping my mouth. Shit, I was so tired last night I climbed into bed as soon as I got out of the shower and had dried myself, not worrying about clothes. With the shock this morning, I just gave Declan a full frontal view of my tits.

"Why is my cat in here?" he persists as Princess pokes her head out of the blankets at the sound of his voice. She pushes her way out from where she was hiding and saunters down the bed toward him, tail in the air, purring like a motorcycle.

It's my turn to ogle him as he strokes his cat's back, cooing words to her with a softness that will never be directed at me. The man is topless with just a pair of sweatpants on, and good lord, he's going into the spank bank memory. His body is not overly bulked like someone who works out religiously, but he has long lean muscles with washboard abs, and that defined v leading into his pants. He has a few tattoos, but the one that draws my eye is the name Princess tattooed over his left pec in a scrolling script. Oh my God, he got his cat's name tattooed onto his heart. *Fuck me. I* close my eyes to the visual and steel my heart.

"Don't you growl at me," I snap at him, and his eyes widen in surprise. "She's been in here when I've gone to bed, and, well, I won't kick a pregnant cat out of my bed for you or anyone. Maybe you should find out who's been in my room and keeps leaving the door open," I fire back at him now that I'm more awake and super annoyed at being woken up so early.

"And, what the fuck is the deal with you and your siblings just waltzing in and not knocking? Do you not have any sense of common decency? That's three of you now, and I'm fed up. I'm going to ask for a damn lock to be installed." My head is full of steam, and I don't think what I'm doing as I throw back the bedsheets and climb out of bed.

His throat-clearing has me freezing, and a wash of cold common-sense comes over me, dulling my anger. *OH fuck, I'm naked.* Not wanting to let on that I made a mistake, I stand up straight and push my shoulders back. Turning around, I wave at Princess. "If you would so kindly take your cat with you, I would appreciate it."

He blindly waves his hands around to pick up his cat, but his gaze is locked on me, more specifically, my naked body. Looking back at him, I can see a tent forming in the front of his sweatpants and feel a thrill of excitement. It seems he's not so unaffected by me after all. But then his eyes turn cruel.

"Put some fucking clothes on! Your transparent and pathetic attempts at seduction are wasted on me. Naked temptation isn't going to sway my opinion, but it does go to prove you're as much of a whore as your mother was," he jeers as his eyes leave my body. With a gentleness he shouldn't be capable of, he carefully picks Princess up off the bed, cradling her in his arms.

His words are like a knife in my chest, but I calmly turn, giving him my back, and saunter toward the bathroom. "Don't let her out of your sight. I don't think she's far off from having those babies," I call over my shoulder.

"What would you know?" I hear him mutter,

but in the bathroom mirror, I see him look down at the cat with concern in his eyes before he turns and hurries out of the room. What an asshole, but his love for his cat is a small redeeming quality. Not sure it's enough, though.

Not bothering with another shower since I'd had one before bed, I pee and brush my teeth and hair before pulling out something to wear. I'd brought a cute little sundress with me that has a fitted bodice, so I don't need to wear a bra. I'm just pulling that over my head when an appreciative sound has me snapping my head toward the door. *For fuck's sake. Another one?* Standing in the still open doorway is the brown-eyed, blue-haired tattoo artist. He must have dyed it yesterday because the night before it had been bleach blond. His eyes follow the dress as it flows down over my body before they scan their way back to mine.

"That's some pretty sweet ink you have on your body." His voice is gravelly with appreciation and his eyes heated with desire. "I wouldn't mind getting your artist's number off of you if you don't mind?"

I scoff, rolling my eyes. *How unoriginal.* "Yeah, I've fucking heard that before."

Turning my back to him, I pull a pair of panties out of a drawer and slip them on under the dress before turning back around. Honestly, I'm not sure why I turned around; it's not like he didn't just cop an eyeful. Damn it, that's three brothers I've flashed the goodies to now.

Across my torso, I have a tattoo of a collage of zoo animals done in black and white. It sort of sits under my boob and down as far as my hip, wrapping around my side. I got it at the beginning of my last year of vet school, a reward for making it so far. On the opposite thigh to my sleeve, I have a fantasy animal collage with a unicorn, a dragon, and a phoenix. This one was to show my love of reading, especially paranormal and fantasy. Then there are a few others scattered here and there. I love tattoos and the ability to express myself through pictures. I wish I could have been a tattoo artist, but I can't draw a stick figure, unfortunately. All of them have been done by my talented friend Tasha.

He's looking at me expectantly. *Oh, he was serious.* "Ah, yeah. Tasha works at Saint Ink in Hartford, Connecticut." He nods his head in thanks, but I don't stop. "Do none of you ever feel the need to knock? Are you all so freaking privileged that you have no manners?"

He holds his hand up. "Hey, sweetheart, slow down. The door was already open," he defends himself, and I grunt my annoyance.

"That's because your damn brother left it wide open once he had finished yelling at me." Curiosity crosses his face at my words, and he lifts an eyebrow in question.

"Which brother would that be, and why was he here?"

"Pick one," I mutter, but I continue, louder.

"The asshole who reamed me out because his blasted cat keeps snuggling up to me at night." The annoyance filling my words is a bluff. I love having the cat snuggle with me every night, but he doesn't need to know that.

The curiosity turns to amusement, and a little smirk twists his lips before he answers. "So you managed to ruffle the ever in control Declan. Good for you! I just came to let you know you're with me next, but Nana tells me you have plans today?" He raises an eyebrow in question, and I raise my own in reply. I'm not sharing with him. Although he hasn't been particularly hostile, I'll stay wary until proven otherwise.

"Well, be ready to come in with me to the shop tomorrow morning. I've got a tattoo artist to interview and a couple of appointments; you can keep me company for the day. That will keep everyone else happy that you're out of their hair." Rolling my eyes, I nod my agreement, and he turns and walks away.

"Oh, and Harlow, I like your penguin tattoo." Smiling ruefully, I think of where that tattoo is. I'd lost a damn bet with Maxine, and she wanted me to put it directly over my pubic mound, but I had won out and put it off to the side. He obviously looked closely enough to see it because it's not big. *Perv.* Tingles run through me at the thought of his eyes studying me so closely, and I huff out a deep breath.

*How can I be attracted to so many of them? Maybe Jilly does have the right idea.*

Grabbing my phone off the charger, I see that I have a thumbs up and a kissy face message from Max in reply to mine from last night, and another forty minutes before Alex is picking me up, so I decided to do a little snooping. Not inside. I shudder at the thought of running into one of the siblings, but I'd noticed some stables out the back, and I miss the smell of the horses and hay.

Slipping on a pair of Converse, I grab my backpack with my things for the day and slip out my patio door in the direction of the barn. When I get there, I push my way through the big wooden doors and inhale deeply. The musty, manure-filled scent is familiar and relaxing, and some of the tension that I already felt this morning melts away.

The large barn is made from brick and timber and is in immaculate condition—everything's neat and tidy, so similar to the barn at the Bostons'. I can even see a hayloft. I must remember that when I need to hide away with a good book.

Horses stick their heads out of their stables and nicker their hellos. Peering in at each of them, I make my way down one side and then back up the other. There are ten horses in here, and all are amazing examples of good breeding. When I get back to the first stall on the right, I stick my head in, and a rounded palomino mare is standing there, her beautiful big brown eyes observing my every movement.

"Well, hello there, pretty lady! You look a little too rounded to be just fat," I coo, sliding into the stall so I can run my hand over her extended belly. Yep, there I can feel a little hoof, not to mention when I bend down to look, her nipples are swollen slightly. "Oh, Mama, you haven't got long to go either, have you?" She nuzzles my side in search of a treat, and the sweetness of the familiar gesture makes my heart clench from missing my own horses. "I haven't got anything, but I'll bring you something next time I come down."

Hearing the big doors open, I exit the stall, pushing the door closed behind me.

It's Brad's surprised face I see as I turn around, but it quickly turns to pleased as a smile lights up bright enough to reach his eyes. "Harlow, what a surprise, but it really shouldn't be, I guess." He moves forward and wraps his arms around me for a quick hug, but lets go, not holding on for long enough that I become uncomfortable. *Yep, definitely more socially adept than people think.*

Smiling at him, I reply, "I hope you don't mind; I noticed it the first day I was here, and I've been missing the animals."

"Oh no, of course not," Brad assures me. "You're welcome to go wherever you want. It's just nice to see you. I missed you yesterday, but Mom says you made some new friends. I'm pleased about that." He walks down the aisle to about the third stall down and opens it up, grabbing the halter from the hook outside. When he exits, he's followed by a large brown gelding with a shiny coat and long black mane.

"Western or English?" he asks conversationally as he hooks the halter onto two crossties and grabs a couple of brushes from a room off to the side. Must be the tack room.

"Oh, ah, both," I reply as I step forward and stroke my hands over the beast's velvety soft nose. He must be about seventeen hands high and solid. "But I enjoy English. I love show jumping and dressage, but then I love a good canter over an open field too. So it doesn't matter to me."

He smiles again, and I can't help but be drawn to those eyes that are so similar to mine, his joy evident. "Me neither, I ride both styles. We've got a great cross country course through the property if you'd like to join me someday. There are various heights," he assures me, but that doesn't worry me too much.

"I would love that," I exclaim, and his face lights up even more. It's nice to know we have something in common, and I'm glad I didn't hold back the enthusiasm I felt about his offer. A moment later, just when I'm about to ask him more questions about the animals housed here, my phone beeps with an incoming message. It must be Alex.

"I have to go," I tell Brad. "My friend's taking

me shopping, and we're going to do some sight-seeing too. I'm supposed to go with Oliver tomorrow, but how about the day after, if you're not too busy, we go for that ride?" He beams in response, and I make a note to buy some riding pants and boots. I didn't think to bring any with me.

"That would be great. Will we see you tonight for dinner?" he asks, no pressure in his voice.

"I'm not sure what Alex has planned, but I'll message Nana and let her know." The edges of his smile dip the tiniest bit, and I realize that maybe I can extend a little bit of an effort here too. "Actually, why don't you give me yours too, and I'll message you as well if you'd like," I offer, and the smile turns even wider as he rattles off his number and I program it into my phone.

"I'd like that, thanks." I wave goodbye to my beaming father and run toward the front of the property, slowing to a power walk when I remember that I shouldn't be pushing my leg that much. As I get around the corner of the building, I smile internally. He's leaning against Shane's car, looking like a million bucks, but that's not what makes me smile. Both Jacinta and Jaxon are on the front porch, talking to him. Both seem to be questioning why he's here, but he's holding his own under their ruthless questioning.

I run up to him, kissing him quickly. "Sorry, I was in the barn and lost track of time." Turning, I smile brightly at the twins. "Good morning. Have a great day!" I call out to them and clamber into the passenger side of the car as Alex climbs into the driver's seat. He waves a hand at them, and we take off down the drive. Turning, I look back over my shoulder and giggle at the identical furious looks the siblings are sporting.

"That was fun." I laugh, and Alex joins in with a sound so smooth that I'm nearly speechless. *How can someone that handsome even* laugh *attractively?*

"Let's show you some sights. I think the closest camera store is first, and then we can hit the Santa Ana Zoo; that's the closest to here." From what I understand, the estate is smack dab between LA and San Diego, but I really don't know exactly, and I'm grateful for a local's knowledge showing me around.

"Sounds awesome. Thanks again, Alex." I lean in and kiss him on the cheek before sitting back and enjoying the drive and the company.

## Chapter Eighteen

**Harlow**

Breakfast was at a cute little bistro, where we were both treated to a huge breakfast with the works. There were fluffy, fresh pancakes with maple syrup and crispy bacon and scrambled eggs with toast and hash browns. Freshly brewed coffee permeated the air and had a kick like a mule, all a perfect start to the day.

After that, we drove around until we found a Best Buy. Luckily, a tech-savvy teenager pointed us to the best camera and mounts for what I wanted to achieve once I explained my goal. He was really interested and told me he'd really like to see it when I'd filmed it and to make sure I uploaded it to YouTube when I was done. This sent another thrill of anticipation through me, and I couldn't wait to get started. Not to mention that I felt like texting Max to rub it in her face that I had at least one other person interested. From there, we headed on to the zoo, the big breakfast and easy conversation lulling me into a comfortable place once again.

The warmth on my face from the sun as we walked around the zoo made me wish I had thought to bring a hat, but the smells and sounds of the animals quickly distracted me from my thoughts. We strolled down meandering paths, checking out the various exhibits, talking all the while. Everything just felt easy, like there was no need to have any limits on what we shared with each other, and we touched deeper on what I wanted to do with my degree and where I hoped to see myself in ten years time.

As we patted the pony in the children's zoo and my heart ached with missing DS, Alex also talked about what he'd like to do once his career as a model ran its course. His question the other day about being a large animal vet finally made sense to me, opening my eyes to why the two of us got along so well. Apparently he volunteers at animal shelters in his spare time and has a love almost as big as mine of animals. He said because money isn't really an issue anymore, he'd like to start a not for profit organization, encouraging the sterilization of cats and dogs so there are less unwanted animals. Thrilled at his idea, I told him to count on me for my services if I'm still around when he does this. I'd happily donate a couple of days a month helping to make this happen.

After a few hours, while we're standing in line to go on the conservation merry-go-round, a cool old-fashioned style carousel with endangered creatures as the mounts, my phone rings. Chuck's name appears on the screen, and my heart goes into overdrive.

"Hello, what is it? Is it Max? Melinda?" I fire questions at him, and he starts to chuckle, my tension dropping with the calming sound.

"Can't I just be calling to check on my girl?" His voice is warm and familiar and brings a smile to my face as my heart stops racing.

"Yes, I'm sorry. I think panic is just my default mode at the moment. Hi. How are you? I'm sorry I haven't called to speak to you earlier. I've been a little overwhelmed," I admit, feeling guilty that I haven't spoken to him.

He chuckles again. "Relax, Harlow, you're fine. We knew you would be in good hands, so we haven't been too worried. I just rang you to ask you a favor. I've got a couple of the horses being shipped out to LA next week for that new movie, but the director is behind on the schedule and doesn't need them just yet. I've spoken to Brad, and he's okay with them being delivered to his place. Will you work them for me over the week that they're there? Put them through their paces so that they're fresh and ready when the director needs them?"

"Yeah, sure, but isn't Max coming too?" I ask him, worried about my friend.

"She is, but she's been asked to work as a fill-in for another movie. The actress they hired promised she could ride when they offered her the role, but she can't, and they needed a stunt double quickly. So she's going to do that while waiting for the other director's schedule to get to where it needs to be."

"Ok, cool. No problems then," I assure him. "Who are you sending?"

"Samson, Delilah, Hercules, and Zeus." A smile crosses my face as my favorites are mentioned, and I do a little jump of excitement that has Alex nearly breaking out with a laugh at my expense. "Thanks, Harlow, I'll send you a text the day before they'll be there." We chat a little more about mundane things, and I ask about Melinda, Max, Jenny, and DS. Tears fill my eyes as I hang up, and Alex grabs me and pulls me in for a hug.

"I'm okay. I just miss them. They've been a constant fixture in my life forever, and it's just weird not seeing them every day."

"Come on," he urges, pulling me out of the line. "You didn't really want to go on that, did you?" he asks as he drags me to the exit. I shrug, not caring either way.

"Well, I have another idea. Let's go to the beach!"

Without any other planning, he drives us to the coast, to Newport Beach, where we proceed to walk along the sandy shore watching a few surfers ride the rolling waves that are crashing against it. Shoes in hand, I breathe in the salty air and rub my toes into the grainy sand. Seagull calls float on the breeze, and the sun warms my skin, and for the first time since I got to California, I'm at peace. No one's going to jump out and accuse me of something here. There's no pressure to be on my best behavior so that they might like me. Here, I'm just me. Not the gold-digging whore trying to usurp their positions with my father. The thought of all that is just exhausting, and I try to remind myself that it'll all be worth it if I get my own relationship with Brad out of all this awkwardness.

After getting tired of the sand, we stop and get a table at a little seafood restaurant not far from the pier. Sitting on the balcony, we can still watch the waves and the people walking their dogs or riding their bikes along the beachfront. "So, are you definitely going to look for an internship while you're here? Ready to make that leap?" Alex's questions bring me out of my musings. I had explained everything to him today, the pros and cons that had been piling up in my mind. Not wanting to leave the Bostons after all that they had done for me and the worry about not getting too close to the Summers in case the attitude from the children is a permanent thing.

"I think you should go for it. You don't want to

look back in twenty years and wish that you had done things differently." Our conversation pauses as the waitress comes by, and I mull over his questions, nearly bungling my order since I'm so distracted. After the waitress takes out lunch order, he pulls out his phone and slides it across the table to me.

"Google some jobs now and see if you can line up an interview or something. I'm sure some program would love to have Brad Summers' daughter on board even if it's so that they can drop his name." At his words, I screw up my nose in disgust and push the phone back toward him, my stomach dropping at his words. That's exactly the reaction I'm trying to avoid, and I'm a little grossed out that he suggested it.

"Yeah, no, I'm certainly not going to use him like that. That would make me exactly what his kids think I am. I'll do it but use my own name. If I can only get a job because of him, then I think I'd rather go home."

He huffs out an annoyed sigh, rolling his eyes in a dramatically playful way that makes it clear he's not truly upset with me. "Fine, do it your way, but just do it." He waves his hand at his phone, and I grab it, googling AZA, which is the Association of Zoos and Aquariums. Their website shows job listings throughout the country, and it's one of the best resources for anyone who wants to work in the industry. I've already missed this year's matching program as I wasn't sure what I wanted to do after graduation, but if I'm lucky, maybe someone has pulled out.

Scrolling through the entries, I send myself some emails with the ones that catch my eye. My laptop is sitting in my dresser drawer back at the estate, so I'll dig it out when I get home and put some more effort into it this evening. Just as I finish and hand the phone back to him, mine rings in my backpack. I quickly scrounge around to find it and answer with definitely more calm than I had before.

"Harlow, honey, how's your day going?" Nana's voice is sweet and gentle over the phone, and I smile, putting it on speaker.

"Hi, Nana. I've got you on speaker. It's going well; Alex is a great tour guide." He rolls his eyes again but smiles at my words.

"Well, that's wonderful, you're a good boy, Alex. Listen, I'm calling to tell you about the event we're all going to tomorrow night. It's a movie premiere for one of Neighpalm Productions' newest releases. I know everything has been a bit overwhelming, but we like to attend these things as a family, and it would mean so much to Poppy, your dad, and me if you would join us. Declan was supposed to tell you about it this morning, but I hear he got sidetracked by Princess." Her voice is rueful with a touch of annoyance as she tells me this last part, and now it's my turn to roll my eyes.

I snort in response, muttering under my breath, "More like he got sidetracked by my tits." Alex just about spits his beer across the table at my words, but Nana doesn't seem to hear them.

"Anyway, some of the kids bring dates if you'd like to invite Alex, or, if not, your dad also said he'd be happy to escort you." She trails off, and I look at Alex, wanting to ask him but also feeling kind of excited that Brad had expressed an interest in escorting me.

"Alex, would you mind if I went with my dad? I feel like I've hardly had a chance to talk to him yet." He shakes his head, smiling, and I'm once again glad that he decided to adopt me during my stay here.

"Of course not."

"Alex, how about I arrange for you and Shane to get tickets too, and you can join us for a meal afterward?" Nana suggests, and he beams with delight.

"That would be great! Thank you, Grace."

"Have you got suitable wear for a premiere? I assume you do since you're in such demand." Alex blushes slightly, and I eye him with confusion.

"What do you mean by that, Nana?" I probe gently, and Alex seems a little uncomfortable. While the happy look is still present on his face, he fidgets around in his chair with an air of uncertainty that I haven't yet seen in him.

"Alex is one of the most sought after models for our agency at the moment. I'm surprised you haven't been mobbed today." Looking Alex up and down, I realize that explains the low key jeans and shirt combo with a pair of Chucks, shades, and a beanie. I wondered why he wore it while it wasn't too cold, but I thought maybe that was just me being from the east coast.

"Yes, Grace, Shane, and I are fine for evening wear, thank you." Alex blushes a bit, his cheeks tinting in a barely there pink; we will be delving into that interesting tidbit when I finish on the phone with Nana.

"I don't have anything to wear though," I tell her, getting excited at the thought of dressing up and going to a movie premiere even if it is with the siblings that loathe me.

"Don't worry about that; I've pulled something from Jacinta's collection for you. You're practically the same size, and she's never worn it, so it will be perfect."

"Great, thank you. Oh, and Nana, can you tell me where I can get some riding clothes from? I didn't think to bring any with me, and Brad and I are going riding in a couple of days, and Chuck's sending some horses that he needs me to work until the director is ready for them."

"Oh, yes, dear, if you go to LA Riding Wear, we have an account there. Get what you need, or you can order online, and they'll deliver it tomorrow. I'll message you the address."

"Ok, thanks, Nana." She says goodbye and

hangs up, leaving me looking at Alex, eyebrows raised.

"Shane told you yesterday that someone always wants something from us and how nice it was just to be Alex and not 'Alexander the hottest thing since sliced bread.'" He laughs, but it's kind of awkward, so I jump out of my seat and give him a quick hug before going back to mine.

"Yeah, I understand. It seems there's a lot of that going around." I change the subject, wanting to give him some of the acceptance and relief that he's given me in my short time of knowing him. "Alright, shall we try and find this LA Riding Wear or just order online?" He looks at the watch on his wrist, and my eyes get stuck on it. There's something familiar about this now that I realize it's a TAG watch.

"Sure, we have time," he tells me, but my mind can't seem to move on. I think back to the TAG ad campaign that Max and I had ogled over and over when she bought one for Chuck for Christmas last year.

"Shit, you're the TAG guy! I rolled around on a bed, almost naked, with the TAG watch guy. Fuck me; I can't wait to tell Maxine! Do you think Shane would give me a copy of one of the shots where it looks like you're ready to ravish me? She'd be green with envy!" I'm babbling, and he cracks up, putting his hand out and grabbing hold of one of mine.

"Girl, if it weren't for Jacinta, I'd be all over

you. Why haven't you got a boyfriend who worships the ground you walk on?"

Now it's my turn to blush with embarrassment. "To be honest, during high school, I was that charity case that the Bostons took in, and anyone who did try thought I was an easy lay like my mother, who had taken to whoring herself to pay for her next fix. It's not like I had any close friends besides Max, but word still got out about where I'd come from. When you're in one of those preppy schools surrounded by the kids of the 1%, privacy just doesn't exist." His eyes fill with sympathy at my words, his hand squeezing mine a little harder. The little voice in my mind whispers that I can just stop there, but I ignore it and keep going. "I messed around during college, but with my course load, I didn't have time to be a committed, steady girl-friend, and that put guys off. I found a couple of regular booty calls for when I was horny; that worked well for all involved. None of us wanted the strings that came with a real relationship. I even had a threesome with two of them once when they both called me on the same night." I smile, thinking about how hot that night was. "That was fun, but that's all it was."

"Are you sure there aren't any other reasons for avoiding a real relationship?" he pushes, seeing deeper than I like or had honestly expected him to.

"Yeah, I guess not wanting to get too attached to someone and get abandoned when they didn't like my long hours or the way I dress, or even the fact I'd prefer to stay home and watch movies than go out. Don't get me wrong, the occasional night out to drink and dance is fun, but I am *much* more of a homebody. Lots of guys don't like that at our age. They want to party hard and make the most of their youth." None of that appeals to me at all. I want someone who's got their head on straight and knows exactly what they want from their lives. Someone who wants me as much as I want them.

Not wanting to talk about it anymore, I drain the rest of my beer and throw my napkin on the table.

"Come on, let's get out of here. We'll go and find the clothing store, and then you can take me home. I guess I should put in a little effort of my own with the family even though they're all as prickly as cactuses." Thankfully, he runs with the change in subject, and the two of us head back to the car. We find the address Nana sent us, and he drives me to the store, losing ourselves over the next hour as I try things on. Honestly, I didn't need to. I know what sizes I wear, but Alex wanted a show, so while he and the store clerk flirted, I tried on a few different pairs of breeches and boots and then paraded around the store.

While strutting like I'm on a fashion runway, a saddle catches my attention. Walking up to it, I run my hands across the soft seat, breathing in the smell of quality leather. It's a hand-tooled, hand-stitched, black leather dressage saddle that I bet is as soft as butter on your ass. It has a beautiful fleur-de-lis motif stamped into the panels. It's truly love at first sight, and I'm more tempted to buy it than I've been to get anything in a long time. Looking at the price tag has me gulping in shock and walking away. Yeah, with no horse to put it on, I can't justify that kind of money. I end up grabbing a couple of pairs of pants, one long and one short pair of boots with gaiters.

The flirty clerk bags it all for me, but when I tell him to put it on the Summers' account, he purses his lips and eyes me up and down. "And why would I do that?"

Alex frowns, all sign of the flirty man gone now, and he crosses his arms. "Because she told you to."

"Yeah, I'm going to have to check on that with my manager." He grabs the phone from under the table, and I just wave him off, blushing with embarrassment. "You know what, don't worry about it. I'll pay for them myself." I hand Alex my phone to hang on to while I dig around in my bag for my purse.

"Grace, it's Alex." My head shoots up as I hear him speak, and I realize he has my phone to his ear. *Sneaky bastard.* "They're giving Harlow a hard time at the equestrian apparel store. Do you think I could put you on Facetime, and you could speak to the guy directly?" He looks at the clerk condescendingly, a bit of the attitude coming out that I recognize from when Max's friends look me up and down. "You do know who Grace Summers is, don't you?" The clerk nervously nods his head, and when Alex swipes his hand across the screen and turns it to face him, he pales considerably.

"Good afternoon, Mrs. Summers. It's lovely to see you."

Her voice is frosty as she replies, "I wish I could say the same. Why am I having my afternoon interrupted for such a trivial thing? Put my granddaughter's purchases on our account, and you can be sure I'll be speaking to your manager about this." Her voice has taken on an imperial quality like a queen telling off her subjects, and I smile slightly. Nana is kickass, and I have *got* to learn how she turns that persona on and off with a breath. He nods his head furiously and starts shoving my purchases into bags, apologizing profusely. Alex turns the phone back around and air kisses Nana before he hangs up, handing it back to me.

I lift an eyebrow. "Really?"

"Yes, you shouldn't let people walk all over you anymore. Even if you don't care about the money, own the reputation." He grabs my bags and stalks off, leaving the clerk gaping in surprise as I hurry after him.

# Declan

Even at work, a few hours later, my cock is still hard and bloody uncomfortable in my suit pants as I sit behind my desk. The sound of my buckle as I open the belt and pull down the zipper is loud, but I don't fight the need to try and relieve some of the pressure. The naked sight of my father's new daughter is seared into my memory, and I'm having trouble shaking it. Long, lean, limbs, rounded hips and breasts with a slender waist and all that sun-kissed tattooed skin making my mouth water. I'm so disgusted and angry with myself at my visceral reaction to her. No one has stirred me like that in a long time, and she is 100% off limits. Even if I wanted to indulge in a quick roll in the sheets, my siblings would kill me. What is it about her that draws my interest? I mean, even my damn cat likes her, and she doesn't usually like anyone, but I found her snuggled up next to her, just like I want to be. *Do* I want to be snuggled up behind her? Hell yes, I do, and I'd slowly slip my cock into her wet heat and give her a good morning she'd never forget.

That thought has me stopping suddenly, and I realize I've released my cock from my pants and have been stroking it as my mind wandered. "Mr. Summers, you have a call on line one. It's Mr. Simpson, and he doesn't sound very happy."

My secretary's voice has me jolting with surprise

and ripping my hand off my still throbbing cock, pre-cum glistening at the tip.

"Fuck!" I quickly jump up, shoving it back down and doing up my pants, the guilt and shame I feel making my cheeks warm.

"Mr. Summers?" my secretary probes again.

I push the button on the intercom. "Sorry, Liz, I was on my cell. Just give me a couple of minutes to finish up this call, and I'll talk to him. If he doesn't want to wait, tell him I'll call him back in a moment." My voice is steady, but my hand shakes on the button.

What was I thinking, doing that at work? How had I not even noticed that I was? This woman really has me in knots; in fact, she has the whole family in knots.

I know I promised Kai that I wouldn't investigate her, but maybe it's time we did. Maybe I just need to make a few discreet inquiries myself. Maybe about her mother, I never promised not to investigate her.

My cock is still throbbing behind the fabric of my pants, and I consider taking care of it in the bathroom, but my secretary's voice rings through the room once more. "Mr. Simpson is waiting, and he told you to hurry the fuck up." She sounds a little harassed this time, and there isn't much that flusters the older woman, so I skip the self-pleasure and get my mind back on business. *Jesus, she's even affecting my work ethic.* Scrubbing my hand through my hair, I sit back into my office chair and press the button on line one.

"Frank, how are you? What can I help you with?" I keep my voice light and business-like, picking up a pen to fidget with while I chat and possibly make notes if needed.

"Declan," the movie producer's voice bellows through the speaker, and I cringe at the anger. "What the fuck have you sent my way?"

"Frank, you're going to have to be more specific," I tell him patiently. The man is a blowhard, and the fastest way to make him explode is to lose your calm. I do my best to keep my voice measured, even, so that there's no hint of what I'm really feeling right now.

"Selena Cross," he growls, "does not know how to ride a horse! In fact, she won't even go near them because she's allergic."

My heart sinks at his words, and my hand tightens so much around the pen, I crack the plastic sleeve. "She assured me she could ride and never mentioned being allergic." My rage seethes at the thought of being made a fool of by yet another woman. No wonder I have such trust issues.

"Was that because she was riding your cock at the time?" His anger is palpable, and I can feel the depth of it in that question as he usually doesn't make throw away comments like that.

"Leave it with me, and I'll figure something out." I try and soothe a few ruffled feathers.

"Fuck no, I'm behind on filming now. I'm going to make my own arrangements, but let me tell you if this happens again, I will *never* take another one of your recommendations for future projects," he threatens before hanging up on me.

Picking up an empty coffee cup off my desk, I throw it across the room. "Fuck!" I yell as it smashes into the wall and shatters.

Dropping my head into both hands, I rub my face as the office door flies open and Liz steps into the room.

"Everything ok in here?" she asks carefully.

"Can you get legal on the line for me and get them to bring me up Selena Cross's contract?" I ask her, not looking up. My anger is giving way to annoyance now, and the thought of more work that shouldn't need to be done if people would only tell the truth is doing nothing to give me any sense of internal calm. "And when you're done with that, get me the numbers for a few reputable private investigators in the area." She quickly agrees despite the second, likely odd, request as she quietly closes the door behind her after picking up the pieces of the coffee mug. In the moment of quiet after she leaves, I look down into my lap and realize my problem has finally disappeared. *Well, at least Selena was good for one thing.*

## Chapter Nineteen

**Harlow**

Alex delivers me home after that and kisses me despite the lack of an audience this time. Before he leaves, he promises to see me at the movie premiere the following night. "Of course we won't miss it. We'll be your moral support," he swears and drives off, gravel flicking up from his tires. His car disappears down the driveway, and dread starts to build within me. There's nothing I want more than to stay out of this house for just a little bit longer, but I know I need to suck it up and do it. So, taking a deep breath, I climb the steps. Opening the door, I make my way inside, the house almost silent except for the faintest murmur of voices.

"Harlow, darling, is that you?" Nana's voice

echoes from somewhere. I look around, trying to figure out where it came from, but I have no luck.

"Where are you, Nana? I don't really know where I'm going," I call back.

A flurry of heels on the floorboards tracks her movements around the house as she hurries through the open door under the stairs.

"Oh, honey. I haven't shown you around, have I?" She grabs one of the bags from me and starts waving her hand around the entrance. "You know that's our wing, and that's the kid's wing," she explains, pointing at either side, "and upstairs is the ballroom and the library." That has me pricking my ears up. I must have a good look at the library when I get a chance, and I might even sneak a peek at the ballroom. I mean, it's a ballroom. When will I ever get the chance to do that again?

"Down those stairs," she continues, indicating a door off to the side I hadn't noticed before, "leads to a gym, the indoor swimming pool, and a wine cellar, as well as what the boys call 'the ultimate gaming room.'" She starts to walk toward the door she came from, her steps practiced so that she barely needs to watch where she's going. "Behind these doors, there's a bathroom, a couple of offices, and of course, the formal dining room that we had dinner in the other night." Nana leads me back into the open plan living room, which has huge glass windows overlooking a deck area with an outdoor swimming pool and spa.

Without walking over, she draws my attention to the other end of the room. "That's the conservatory down there. I spend a lot of time playing with my orchids and plants; if you're ever looking for me, that's a great place to start." Her love of that space becomes clear in the ways her eyes shine and the subtle smile that uplifts her face even just when talking about her plants. She waves in the opposite direction. "That's the kitchen and laundry down there. If you need laundry done, just leave it in the hamper in your bathroom, and one of the house-keepers will grab it and have it done." Finally, she seems to take in the confusion that's surely written all over my face. I try to smooth the furrow I can feel creasing my forehead, but I'm definitely not successful before she notices. With a warm smile, she tilts her head in the direction she'd first come from. "We're just having a cup of coffee and deciding what we should have for dinner." *Crap, who's we?*

She guides me to the living area, which is sump-tuously decorated, where a high tea spread has been laid out on the coffee table in the middle of the room. Sitting stiffly on one of the sofas, her face definitely not reflecting Nana's warmth, is Jacinta. Nana leads me to a sofa opposite and sits down, pulling me next to her. She places the bag on the floor, and mine joins it as she pulls the coffee pot toward her and starts pouring the coffee into dainty, flower-covered china cups.

"Did you have a good day with Alex, dear? Jacinta was just telling me about yesterday's shoot and how you were roped into appearing in the photos," Nana says as she pours the coffee, not looking at either of us. My eyes meet the frosty blue ones in front of me, but I refuse to blanche.

"Oh, she did, did she?" I raise an eyebrow in her direction, and her eyes take on a challenging look, a smirk on her face like she's daring me to tattle on her bad behavior. Without much thought needed, I decide not to lower myself to her level.

"I had a great day both yesterday and today. Who knew it was so exhausting rolling around on a bed with two hot models while another handsome man took photos?"

"I bet your mom knew." Jacinta's words are barely audible, but I do hear them, and Nana's head comes up so swiftly that I'm pretty sure I'm not the only one.

"What was that, dear?" Her words are sharp, but the ice queen just pastes on a smile.

"Nothing, Nana." She's saved by both her and my phones beeping. Scrambling around in my backpack, I pull it out and open the message. It's from Shane, and the pic that appears has me blushing redder than a tomato. *Holy hell! Who knew I could look like that?*

The picture is of me wearing the first bright pink set Lindy had thrown at me. I'm on my back, and Alex and Josh are on either side of me, both of them with their hands on my body. My tattoos are vibrant against the white sheets, and you can see the penguin low on my hip toward the crease of my thigh. With my eyes hooded with lust, mouth open in a pout, and messy sex-hair, I look like I've been having a very, *very* good time. I must have been staring too long because Nana pulls the phone out of my hand, and a whistle echoes across the room.

"Good lord, child, you look like you've been well ravished! Shame it wasn't for real, right, Jacinta?" I swear, if the ice queen could shoot laser beams from her eyes, I would be a puddle of goo at Nana's feet. By the look on her face, she must have received the same photo from Shane.

Nana continues, oblivious to the tension. *Or she's playing some sort of game.* "They got some great shots for your campaign. Maybe it was lucky that Astor was sick that day. Harlow looks fabulous. She makes your clothes look amazing! I can't wait to see how she looks in the dress I picked out for her for the premiere." Nana digs the knife in just that much further without even realizing, and Jacinta flinches.

"Yes, she really does," Jacinta manages to grind out between gritted teeth, her smile looking more like a shark's every second.

Nana hands me back my phone and finishes with the coffee pot. "Do you take sugar and cream, Harlow?" she asks, passing me the cup and saucer.

"No, thanks," I tell her, putting my phone in my backpack and taking the offered cup. I'll send that photo to Max when I go to my room. A wicked grin threatens to break out when I think again about what her reaction will be, but I force it back, not wanting Jacinta to think I'm laughing at her instead.

"So, show us what you bought at LA Riding Wear." She looks excited to see my purchases, so I indulge her. "I can't believe Alex had to call me. I had already rung them and told them you were coming." She pats my knee, a bit of the haughtiness she'd directed at the poor clerk coming briefly back to her face. "I wouldn't have left you hanging like that," she reassures me.

"You ride?" Jacinta's voice is like a whip cracking as she fires the question at me, and Nana just looks at her quizzically. We'd already talked about my horse-riding accident, but she obviously hadn't cared to listen.

"Ah, yeah, I do. I haven't owned a horse for a few years though. College took up too much time, but whenever I was home on the weekend, I rode one of the Bostons'. Actually, that's why I needed the clothes. Well, apart from Brad asking me to go riding with him." Jacinta gasps at this information, and her eyes look shiny for a second. Crap, maybe I should have kept that to myself; I'm guessing I definitely just messed up somehow. Knowing it's too late now, I barge ahead. "Chuck's got some horses coming out west for a movie, but the director is behind schedule, so he asked Brad if they could stay here until he needs them. He's asked me to put them through their paces because Max is going to be filming another movie while they wait."

"Who's Max?" a gruff voice asks from behind, and I spin to see Declan standing in the exit from the hall. Oh, my poor ovaries, I think they just sighed in awe. The man's dressed in a gray suit with a green tie and black shirt underneath, and he looks amazing. His black hair is tied back, but a few tendrils have pulled free to frame his face. His tie makes the green of his eyes pop, and that stare is locked onto me.

"Oh, that's Maxine," Nana tells them while I'm still tongue-tied by this exquisite specimen of a man. That has me thinking about his bare chest this morning and his Princess tattoo, which makes me smile. Shaking my head, I tune back into what she's saying. "I sometimes wonder if any of you listen to a word I say. Remember, she used to come out here during the summer holidays when she was younger?"

"Yeah, I remember," Jacinta mutters, the bitterness strong enough that this time I can't hold back my wince; her lip has even curled back in a snarl. "That is, until she stopped coming. Couldn't leave her precious Harlow home alone."

"I didn't find that out until recently. She told me something different all those years." I try and defend myself to Jacinta, but she's not interested. Most of those times were when I had visits with my mom, and when she wasn't around, I was stuck with Nana and Grandad Boston. She could see how much I hated it when they left, so she stopped going.

"We always use their horses in our movies," Nana reminds Declan, and he nods in acknowledgment.

"Yeah, but I usually deal with Chuck. I hadn't remembered Maxine's name until you mentioned it." He walks over to the sofa with Jacinta, loosening his tie on the way, before removing his jacket and undoing the buttons on his sleeves. Rolling them up, he exposes his forearms, insert ovary sigh again, as he makes himself comfortable, putting an arm on the back of the chair and crossing one leg over the other.

"Would you like coffee?" Nana asks him, pouring some into one of the dainty little cups before he can answer and sliding it over to him. He reaches down, his forearm rippling, and my eyes locked onto it, unable to look away. There's just something about a man in a dress shirt with rolled-up sleeves.

"Harlow," Nana calls, her sharp voice startling me and leaving him smirking as I turn to look at her.

"Ah, yes, sorry, what?"

She studies me carefully before a small smile crosses her face. "Well, show me your purchases."

"Oh, ah, ok." I grab the bags and start pulling

out the riding pants. She oohs and ahhs over them with far more enthusiasm than I'd expect her to have, but I guess she dotes like this on all of her grandchildren. "I got dark colors because they show the dirt less," I tell her, and Jacinta snorts, though I'm not sure what I've said to earn her disdain this time. "I only really wear white for competition since they're so not practical. Especially when you wear them day in and day out."

"And what else did you get?" Nana is like a kid in the candy store, and Declan is smiling at her with love in his eyes. Damn it, the man loves his Nana as much as he loves his cat. Pity he's a douchebag. Not letting him and those delicious forearms get the better of me again, I show her the boots and the gaiters, and she gushes over them too.

"Why did you get both pairs?" Jacinta asks, the accusation in her voice telling me that I'm already losing no matter what reason I give her.

Turning, I face her. "You ride, don't you?"

She nods her head, and Nana interrupts, "She does, but her horse is pregnant at the moment, so she's not riding very often."

"Oh, was that the sweet, pregnant, palomino quarter horse I saw in the barn this morning?" I ask, and she nods her head stiffly. "So, you ride Western then?" It's safe to assume that because that's what quarter horses are generally for. We have a few for Western movies.

"I prefer Western, but I do ride English, too." Her voice is stiff as if she's reluctant to engage

"Ok, well, I mainly ride English for pleasure; I use the long boots for that, but when I work with the stunt horses, I like the movement and freedom in my ankle I get wearing the short boots and the gaiters." She actually looks impressed and interested in my words, but she must remember who she's talking to because her eyes freeze over again. "So, I bought both." The room falls silent as both siblings share a glance, their eyes unreadable for the moment.

"When will Chuck's horses arrive?" Nana prompts, breaking the awkward silence. "And who's he sending?"

"He said in a couple of days. He's sending Delilah , a pretty gray Lipizzan mare who's perfect for a female character. Hercules and Zeus are big Holsteiner warmbloods, so they make great warhorses, and the fourth is my favorite. Samson is a big black Friesian stallion. He's so very handsome and such a great animal," I ramble. "The film is a medieval story with knights and jousting and such, and they're going to look amazing."

"Samson? Isn't that the one you fell off when you hurt your knee?" Nana asks, sounding concerned.

"Ah, yeah, but it was an operator error, I'm afraid. It was all my fault, and it could have been a lot worse. Actually, I need to ask Chuck to send all my protective gear with the animals. Don't want to take the chance that I get hurt any worse."

I stand up, gathering my things together and groaning at the pull of pain in my knee from being on my feet most of the day. Nana looks at me with worry in her eyes, but I just wave her off. "I'm okay, just stiffened up now that I've finally stopped moving," I reassure her. "I'm just going to take these back to my room and message Chuck. Can I help with dinner when I'm done?"

Nana waves her hand as though I've asked a completely silly question. Which, considering the amount of money these people have, I guess I did. "Oh no, that's fine. The chef's done most of it already, and Brad and the boys like to do the grilling. Why don't you come back in an hour or so, and we'll have a drink before dinner," she suggests. "Declan, help Harlow take her things to her bedroom."

"Oh no, that's okay! I've got it," I protest, but he's already jumped out of his seat and is picking up my bags with the boots.

"Of course I will, Nana." His smile is sly, but Nana doesn't see it as she's already turned back to talk with Jacinta. He quietly follows close behind me, and I can feel his gaze boring into the back of my neck. Pushing open the door to my room, I find Princess on my bed again and cringe, knowing whatever happens next won't be fun for me.

A quiet growl escapes Declan's mouth, and I

put my bag down, holding my hands up in defense. "Dude, I haven't been here all day, and I know I shut my room when I left this morning because I went out the side door. You're barking up the wrong tree." He places my bags down and strides toward me; his fury-filled face has me backing up until he's got me pinned against the wall, a hand on either side of my head, his body pressed into mine.

"Just because you've managed to fool a sweet old lady doesn't mean we don't see right through you. Were you happy spending all that money on our account? You're just like your mother. Don't think we haven't looked into you, Harlow Stubbs, made some inquiries into your life. We're watching you." My heart thunders in fear at his words, somehow finding this violation of my privacy worse than him invading my personal space. He runs his nose along my jawline, inhaling as he goes before he pulls his head back and meets my eyes. Unlike Jacinta's ice, his contain a blaze that just might burn me alive...the worst thing is, I'm not sure that I'd stop him.

"We're watching you, waiting for you to fuck up this little act, and then you'll be gone. Just like all the rest that tried to weasel their way into this family. Just like all the rest who saw us as a meal ticket and nothing else." He's breathing heavily now, and his eyes are full of anger and hurt. "We all learned the hard way that family is all you can trust, and you will *never* qualify as that."

Tears well in my eyes, and I push him away, a stabbing pain inside my chest proving that words can hurt. Not looking at him, I move to the bed. "Please, just take your cat and leave," I ask him quietly. There's no point in getting upset; he's not going to change his mind.

Without another word, he tries to gather Princess, but she hisses and swipes a paw at him. "Fuck!" He pulls back, and I mentally high five the cat, loving that at least someone in the room was able to express the feelings overwhelming me right now. He tries again and gets the same reaction, so with another look of hatred aimed in my direction, he spins on his heel and storms out of the bedroom, leaving me to my loneliness and hurt.

## Chapter Twenty

**Harlow**

When I finally wake from my pity party for one, a fit of searing anger flows through me. *Fuck him.* I've done nothing; I'm not the people from his past, and to judge me by their actions or my mom's actions is crap. Wiping the tears from my cheeks with the back of my hands, I pull my laptop bag out of the dresser drawer where it's been staying and settle myself on the bed next to Princess, the soft rhythm of her purr helping to settle something inside me. I'm not going to let them make me uncomfortable or allow them to put me off achieving my dream. I'll contact some of the zoos here in California, and if I get a job at one of them, I can reassess my living arrangements. Alex said he and Shane have a spare room in their condo that I'm welcome to, plus I have a little bit of savings for a deposit on an apartment. If I get an internship in San Diego or San Francisco, I'm going to be okay.

I read through the job descriptions and submit my application and resume via email, a jolt of exhilaration hitting me when I realize what a big step I've just taken. There are three or four that I apply for, and to be honest, I'm not all that hopeful for a couple of them since they want experience, but there's one advertised at the San Diego Zoo that looks promising.

It's a rotating internship that allows you to shadow a different vet from a different specialty every six months. The pay is crap, and I would possibly need to get a night-time job to support myself while doing it, but I'm sure it would be worth it in the end. Maybe I can find a twenty-four-hour horse practice that needs a night vet or an on-call vet for the weekends. That should help to supplement my income. I send out a few more resumes to the local equine vets and cross my fingers that I hear back from one of them soon.

After that, I pack away my purchases into the walk-in closet and splash some water on my face. It's been probably close to an hour now, and the pressure of heading out to dinner is looming larger and larger behind me. "What do you think, Princess?" I ask the dozing cat, and she, of course, doesn't respond, but I know in my head she's telling me to get on with it.

So I brush my hair, tying it back in a ponytail, and wander back to the main area for dinner. When I get there, the big windows are sliding doors, and they're all open, letting in the evening air. The smell of horses and hay drifts through the breeze in a comforting aroma that makes me feel more at home than any other experience I've had in this house so far. Making my way onto the deck, I've just stepped out of the doorway when I hear, "Pull!" There's a clicking sound and a loud bang bang that scares the shit out of me. I jump nearly a foot into the air, and when I turn to see where the noise had come from, I can see Jacinta with Thomas, Holden, and Kai, the three brothers I haven't had much to do with. They're all holding shotguns over their shoulders and have safety glasses on and protection over their ears. They're all also snickering at my reaction.

"You bloody twits." Poppy's annoyed voice drags my eyes to the grill where he's standing behind it, an apron tied around his waist. "You could have warned me; I just about dropped a sausage I was turning on to the ground!"

Brad's standing next to him, but his eyes light up when he sees me, and he makes his way over to me. "Harlow, come and have a seat, what would you like to drink?" he asks, leading me over to a large round table. Nana, Declan, and Jaxon are already seated at the table. "Would you like a glass of wine or a beer? Nana is having a Cosmo if you prefer that."

"Make her one of these, Bradley," Nana commands. "She needs to relax a little. Poor girl is so wound up; it doesn't help that those idiots frightened her." She waves her glass at the clay pigeon shooters, a balance of irritation and amusement in her eyes. Turning, I watch reddish-haired Thomas line up his rifle, his eye down the barrel of the gun.

"Pull!" he calls, and Jacinta does something to the machine, causing two clay discs to come flying out. He tracks their flight through the air before *bang, bang!* They both explode into dust, and Holden and Kai clap him on the shoulders while Jacinta keeps score on a chalkboard behind them.

"Have you ever shot clay pigeons before?" Nana asks. "Thomas is a fiend at it; he loves to go hunting during duck season. He says it's good practice."

I shake my head in response. "No, I haven't, but it looks fun." Oliver joins us at the table, and he and Jaxon exchange a glance. Oliver's eyes are calculating behind his black-rimmed glasses, but there's markedly less hostility than I'm used to seeing in Jaxon, Jacinta, and Declan's eyes.

"Would you like to have a go?" he asks, and Jaxon and Declan snigger like teenage boys. I have a feeling there's a trick somewhere in here, but I'm game.

"Yeah, actually, if you wouldn't mind," I tell him, and Jaxon leans back into his chair.

"Have you ever fired a gun before?"

"Yes, I have," I answer, feeling awkward, not

wanting to share the story of how I came to know how to use a weapon.

"Oh, when?" he prompts when he sees me squirm, and I look to Nana for reassurance.

"It's okay, Harlow. You don't have to talk about it." Nana's face is wreathed in sadness, and that makes the boys latch onto the subject even harder. I guess their love for Nana and consideration for her feelings doesn't surpass their hunger for any opportunity to make me feel uncomfortable, or they're oblivious to her feelings. No matter which, it's not going in my favor.

"Oh no, we'd love to know," Jaxon pushes, his eyes as cold as his sister's. My stomach sinks, and common sense pokes its ugly head out to ask me how I could have ever found him attractive.

"When I was about fourteen and still visiting my mother once every two weeks for the weekend..." I start, not wanting to tell them the rest, but I know they won't let it go. Their eyes have already perked up, brightening as though they're sharks who've found the first drop of blood in the water. What makes it worse is Bradley returns with my drink, placing it in front of me and taking the seat next to me.

"What are we talking about?" he asks, and Jaxon can't help himself.

"Oh, Harlow was just telling us how she learned to shoot." That's it. The asshole, I hope he feels terrible once he hears this story. Declan just sits there in brooding silence, his eyes on me as he waits for the tale.

"As I was saying, Mom had me every second weekend for two nights. I would go and stay at her trailer with her, and I was about fourteen when one of her nicer..." I stop and look at my dad, wincing. "Sorry about this... One of her nicer clients took an interest in me." Dad's face turns white, and Declan sits up straight in his chair. I make sure to lock eyes with Jaxon. "Not in a creepy way, but he knew he wasn't the only one using mom's service, so to speak, and that she wasn't stopping just because I was there. He showed up one afternoon, and while she was busy, he took me out the back of the trailer and lined up some cans. He pulled a gun out of the back of his pants and proceeded to teach me how to use it. He also gave me a couple of clips and a box to keep it all in and told me to keep it next to me while I slept at night." By now, all of them are looking somewhat ill, and I'm shaking. Nana pats me gently on the hand, and from the way she's much more collected than Brad, I think Chuck and Melinda must have told her this story.

"Anyway, I learned how to use it, but it wasn't long after that, Mom's clients started noticing me more than her, and after a couple of close calls, she decided she didn't want me around anymore. I took the gun back to the Bostons', and when Chuck found out about it, he made sure I knew how to use it properly, clean it, and all the rest. I still have it in a safe back home, but I've got a feeling it's probably not legal, and there's a good chance it may be linked to a crime. The guy who looked after me was the leader of the local MC gang, so anything is possible."

I peek at their faces, doing my best to not meet their eyes in the process. Brad looks decidedly green around the gills, and the other three don't look too happy either. The triumph that Jaxon had before is definitely less sharp, and I can't say I'm unhappy about that. "But I've had experience with a few weapons since then, so can I have a go or not?"

This brings their minds back to the present, and a smirk crosses Oliver's face again. "Care to make a little wager on it?" he asks. Ah, here it is, what does he want?

"I'm listening," I fire back, letting a healthy amount of competitive attitude seep into my voice.

"Tomorrow, I've got a tattoo artist coming to interview. If you hit the target, you get to pick the tattoo that she does and where it goes on me." He gestures to his body, and I nod, happy with the arrangements so far. "If you miss, I get to pick one and where it goes on you." He waves at the sketchbook in front of him. "I have the perfect idea already; it's going to look so good," he crows, sure of his win.

"Hang on, I don't know about this," my dad speaks up.

Jaxon, the ass, is quick to scoff, "She's a big girl,

Dad, let her decide. You let Jacinta hold her own with us. Isn't Harlow supposed to be one of the family?"

You know, I'm just about sick of his attitude, and I show that in my cold look before turning to Oliver. "You're on, but nothing vulgar or offensive." He nods his agreement to the terms and rubs his hands together. Opening his book, he picks up a pencil and starts sketching, immediately losing himself in it.

"Hey, hang on, don't I get to miss first before you get too happy?" He ignores me and keeps drawing. Nana just smiles serenely at me as I stand up and walk down to the other end of the patio, Declan and Jaxon at my side.

"Do I have to worry that one of you is going to take a shot at me?" I mutter under my breath now that we're out of earshot of the elder Summers.

"You're not worth jail time," Jaxon grinds out, another direct hit to my soul, but I keep smiling as we approach the others.

"New sister," Kai shouts out and waves his gun around. That has us all ducking for cover, but I see that it's broken and in no danger of firing.

Declan smacks him in the back of the head. "You idiot, put it down if you've been drinking! Go and sit with Nana." He takes the rifle from him and pushes him in the direction of the table. Kai stops to give me a kiss on the cheek on the way past, his friendliness a welcome change. I watch him walk away; he swaggers with the confidence of a handsome man who knows it. He's obviously of some Islander descent and has chin-length black hair with golden skin and black eyes, his build is athletic and a little on the bulky side compared to his brothers, so he obviously works out. My eyes drift to his ass before a clearing throat brings my attention back to the others. All of them are eyeing me with cool disdain.

"So any brother will do, I guess." Jacinta nudges Jaxon, and I blink in surprise.

"Oh, why don't you all fuck off? I've had enough. I don't know who did a number on you all, but I'm not that person, nor am I my mother, so why don't you cut me some slack?" Their mouths drop open in shock, but they quickly school their expressions into hungry smiles. I'm thinking that bantering back with them might just do me more harm than good, but there's only so much I can take. Yanking the rifle out of Declan's hands, I storm over to the table full of ammunition. The rounds are heavy in my hand as I load them into the gun, the steps reassuringly familiar as I try to calm my breathing. In through the nose, out through the mouth. I'm not going to have any sort of accuracy if I don't get my emotions under control, and this is my chance to finally fight back at them just a little. Once loaded, the click of the gun is loud in my ear as I ignore everything else around me and concentrate on the task at hand.

Placing it carefully on the table, I reach for Kai's discarded safety gear and block out even more of the surrounding noise as I pull the ear muffs over my head and situate them correctly before sliding the safety glass over my eyes. Picking the gun back up, I move over to the line on the deck where Thomas had been standing. The weight of the gun in my hands and the feel of the butt in my shoulder, brings my mind back to learning how to do this originally, and I smile at the memory of how excited Chuck, Max, and I were when we first hit a target through the bullseye. I know the circumstances of me learning to shoot sound sad to the rest of the Summers, but to me, it's a moment that marks someone caring about me, someone noticing that I might be in danger and doing what they could to give me a way to protect myself. Maybe it *is* a little sad, but when you grow up with a mother like Diane, you learn to cherish the moments when someone takes the time and goes out of their way to keep you safe. Squinting, I line up my right eye with the sight and move the weapon in a practice arch, getting a feel for the motion.

"Go, Hally girl! You got this!" Poppy cheers for me from behind the grill, a broad grin on his face.

Taking a deep breath, I yell, "Pull!" The mechanism whirls, and I track the flight. With a quick repetitive *bang*, I fire the shots, but only one of the discs explodes, while the other continues off to wherever.

"Fuck." I drop my head and turn to face the music, but they're all looking at me with stunned expressions. "What?" "You hit one," Holden says, sounding impressed. "No one ever hits one first go." Well, that makes me feel a little better as I place the gun on the table and remove the safety equipment before moving back up to the dining table, leaving the others behind as they whisper between themselves.

"Woo hoo!" Kai cheers and salutes me with his fresh beer. Brad and Nana also give me my congratulations, but Oliver has a puzzled look on his face. "What's wrong, Oliver?" I ask him, and his brown eyes meet mine.

"Well, I'm not sure how to call that. You hit one, and you missed one. So we both lost then." He scratches his blue hair with his pencil in confusion.

"Or you could say we both won," I respond, hoping to make a little bit of headway. His brown eyes sparkle again, and from the corner of my eye, I catch Kai's small grin at my words.

"I guess this means we're both getting new tattoos tomorrow." He resumes his sketching, lost in his artsy dreamworld once more.

"Yes, Oliver, yes, it does." Something in my voice has him looking upward and frowning. I wink at him, and he swallows slightly before continuing with his sketch. I know exactly what his tattoo will be and where it's going to go. Tomorrow can't come soon enough.

"Food's ready!" Poppy calls as he makes his way over to the table with a tray of meat. He plonks it down in the middle. The others make their way down to the table, and everyone starts helping themselves. I watch the feeding frenzy, similar to feeding time on the farm. Baskets of bread are being passed around, as are bowls of different types of salad and corn on the cob. I don't actually reach for anything but still end up with a plate of food. I look on, bemused, as Brad fills my plate for me and feel my heart skip a beat at the fatherly gesture.

"Before everyone starts," Brad says, standing up, "I'd like to propose a toast. I never thought I would be lucky enough to have kids after I had the mumps, but adopting you guys was the highlight of my life and still is. Finding Harlow is just the sprinkles on the sundae of my life, and I wanted you all to know how very glad I am for you all and how much I love you. My hope is one day, Harlow will also know the love of this family." His eyes have turned a little frosty while his gaze moves from each of his children. Brad's not as oblivious as they all think, but he's not willing to intervene just yet, and for that, I appreciate him.

General conversation flows around the table. Oliver gets quizzed on the new artist he's interviewing tomorrow, and Jacinta gets asked about the photos from yesterday's shoot. No one interacts with me, and I'm fine with that. It's been a long day, and the passive aggressiveness of this family is truly tiring.

I find myself sitting next to Kai, and although he doesn't talk to me, his hand has brushed mine a few times, causing me to shiver. He doesn't say anything, and neither do I, but he has a wonderfully calm and welcoming vibe that I haven't gotten from any of the others. The relief I feel just sitting next to him and being able to relax is immense. I don't feel like I need to be constantly on alert for wicked barbs or insults, that he's happy being friends with me. A warm feeling sweeps through my body, and the tingles move towards my groin as I watch his handsome face. The animation he has about his job and the people he sponsors is amazing, and I'm grateful that he keeps the conversation light and away from any possible triggering conversations. He's telling a story about one of his team members when I find my eyes drifting closed and my head lolling to one side, landing on his shoulder. Someone snorts.

"Huh, bet that's never happened to you before, Kai. Harlow just fell asleep during one of your amazing stories." That sounded like Thomas again, his Irish accent making me think of green rolling hills, four-leaf clovers, and little pots of gold at the end of the rainbow. Thank god I don't say any of that out loud. I can only imagine the scorn that would be directed my way if I did.

My eyes are too tired to open, and I hear Nana

say, "Carry her to bed, Brad. Poor dear must be exhausted. It's all a bit much to take in." I get lifted into someone's arms, and the rocking motion has me feeling even more sleepy.

When I finally get laid down on the bed, the blankets are pulled back over me, and a pair of lips presses against my forehead before Oliver whispers, "You and me tomorrow morning, sweetheart, don't forget."

## Chapter Twenty-One

**Harlow**

The next morning I manage to escape being woken by one of the Summers siblings, but that doesn't mean I don't get woken obnoxiously. My phone, next to my bed, starts to ring incessantly at six-thirty am. I ignore it the first couple of times, but whoever it is isn't giving up. Rolling over and managing to avoid Princess who's snuggled into the curve of my back, I grab it, glaring at it through bleary eyes.

Swiping my finger across the screen, I snap at my best friend, "For fuck's sake, this better be good. It's still early here."

Max's chuckle warms my soul, and some of the irritation fades away at that little glimpse of home. "I'm sorry. I forgot about the time difference. Right now, I'm at the airport waiting to catch my flight.

I'm flying out to stunt double for Selena Cross. Apparently, she told the director of her new film that she could ride, but not only can she not ride, she's allergic to the horses."

I snort at the audacity and sheer stupidity. "How did she think they would never find out?"

"Rumor has it, your new brother may have vouched for her," she says conspiratorially. "And she never thought she would have to do any riding; she assumed she would get a stunt double."

I sit up straight in bed, bleary eyes now open wide. "Who? Declan?"

"Yep, and it's making him look *bad*," she tells me.

I snort again, getting a little bit of satisfaction from the whole scenario. "She may have said he did, but even though I don't know him very well, I can guarantee you he wouldn't have if he knew the truth. So either she lied to him, or she lied to the director. I don't know him very well yet, but even I can see that he's wound tighter than a grandfather clock and won't like being made a fool of."

"Anyway, that's what I'm doing. I'm going to do all her action shots and body double for anything that involves horses."

Now it's my turn to chuckle. "I know CGI is good these days, but how the fuck are they going to manage that? You're practically a pixie compared to her."

"Shut up," she teases. "But get this, the story is a

reverse harem tale, and the main female character doesn't have to pick which man she likes the most! It's just like that book I gave you to read. How's that going, anyway?" Her voice turns sly as she adds, "See any future harems in your life?"

My laughter cuts off abruptly. I can only wish that the men I'm lusting after would be interested in something like that, but they can't even stand the sight of me let alone the thought of sharing. *Most sharing they'd probably want to do is splitting my plane ticket home.*

"Uh oh, what's going on? You went silent instantly."

"Meh, it's not going well. You remember the guy at the club that night?"

"Who, Jaxon?" There's a pause of silence and then a sharp intake of breath. "Fuck, Jaxon! Oh, I'm sorry! I didn't even get a good look at him, not that I would have recognized him necessarily. I haven't seen them in years."

"Yeah, well, he hates me. Thinks it was all a set-up. In fact, they *all* hate me. Although Kai and Oliver have been somewhat tolerable, I don't think they're going to go out on a limb and be nice despite how their siblings feel. Holden and Thomas are non-entities at the moment; I've barely said two words to either of them. But Jacinta, Jaxon, and Declan loathe me with an impressive passion." My voice hitches on the last sentence as tears well in my eyes, and there's no way she could miss the emotion.

"Oh, Harlow, I'm so sorry," I sniffle and wipe away a few stray tears that have escaped, shrugging my shoulders even though she can't see them.

"I kind of expected it, but they've been brutal. I spent the day with Jacinta so far. She told everyone I was the intern, and they used me as everyone's bitch."

"No, she didn't?" Max's disgusted gasp echoes through the phone.

"Oh, but hey, I did have a good part to that day. Hang on, I'm going to send you a picture." Pulling the phone away from my ear, I forward her the pic Shane sent me and then put it back to my ear. "I made a new friend."

There's silence while the message sends, then, "Get the fuck out! You bitch! That's the TAG guy!" She's yelling by the end, and I giggle madly. "And look at your tits! They look spectacular."

My heart warms on the inside; I really needed this phone call. "God, I miss you." I giggle sob, and I hear her sigh.

"Maybe you should just come home," she suggests, and I consider it, weighing the possible internships and relationship with my father against the drama that seems par for the course in being the outcast Summers sibling.

"I'll stick it out until your dad's horses leave, and then I may just do that. Not sure I'm cut out for this family thing. Letting in more people with the capability of cutting me to shreds just doesn't seem sensible to me."

We talk for a little longer before saying our goodbyes and hanging up. Checking the time, I have a long hot shower and get dressed in an ombre yellow maxi dress for the day. I'm not sure where Oliver wants to put my tattoo, so I don't want to wear restrictive clothing. Brushing my hair, I pull it into a high ponytail to keep it out of my face and apply some mascara to my blonde eyelashes. Studying myself in the mirror, I look tired and worn out, the ever see-sawing emotions taking their toll on me. I close my eyes, taking a deep breath in and letting it out, preparing to head into breakfast and the next wave of hostile battering I'll probably face.

When I open my eyes, the girl that looks back at me is resigned but determined. Turning away from the mirror, I pick Princess up off my bed and cradle her against my chest. She doesn't do anything but blink at me with sleepy eyes, an edge of sadness in her gaze since I'm disturbing her rest.

"Come on, sweetheart, let's go before your dad comes and shouts at me again."

When I get to the living area, I place Princess on one of the sofas and head over to the dining table. Mrs. Hayton is bustling around and placing out platters of food, but she seems to be the only one around. "Oh, Harlow, *mein liebling*." Her accent is as strong as her enthusiasm, and the warmth in those few words is just so nice to hear. She pulls me in for a hug, and I realize I hadn't seen her last night.

"Hi, Mrs. Hayton," I push out, the greeting slightly muffled against where she's pressed us together. She pulls away and pats me on the cheek, her pale blue eyes seeing way more than I'm comfortable with.

"You hang in there." She puts both hands on my cheeks, hands slightly calloused, showing she's always worked with them. "They will come around. The poor ducklings have had many a hurt themselves over the years and have fortified strong defenses. I believe you will blow those defenses to smithereens, and all will be balanced within the family again. They just need a little time." She pats my cheeks lightly after her mysterious words and bustles away to finish setting breakfast up.

"I didn't see you last night?" I question her as I take a seat at the table, and she brings me over a cup of coffee.

"No, I gave you all time as family." Her English drops slightly with the rush of words. "But of course, those assholes like to play their games, she says, part with affection and part with exasperation. I blink at her words and laugh slightly; she's obviously heard about the bet and the guns.

Reaching for some toast, I hear a voice behind me. "That's what I like to see. Glad you're eating so that we're not tattooing you on an empty stomach."

Turning, I find Oliver standing just behind me. He's dressed in a pair of distressed jeans that mold to his body nicely and a Neighpalm Ink t-shirt stretched across his chest, his tattooed arms standing out against the black fabric. Waving his sketch pad at me, he teases, "Got the drawing right here. Can't wait to get in and get started."

I frown at him, feeling less confident with the idea of him being so in control of the tattoo. "I thought you said the new artist was going to do it."

He smirks, and his eyes light up with delight, sending a shiver of desire through my body. I try very hard not to show any outward signs of it, but his smirk gets even wider, so I don't think I was too successful. "I did, but I've decided I want to do it myself. I can't trust my masterpiece to just anyone."

"Fine, but you better be going through with yours. You're not getting out of it. I hit one of those targets fair and square." A resigned look crosses his face, and his eyebrows pull down as he sighs.

"I won't renege. I have honor." His words are laced with innuendo, but I ignore it, telling him cheerfully

"Well, eat up then, no tattooing on an empty stomach." He sits down across the table from me and starts to pile his plate high with food. As he does, the room seems to explode into noise as other people all join us for breakfast. Declan is looking immaculate in a dark gray suit, black shirt, and lavender tie, phone to his ear as he seems to be arguing about something.

"No, she told me she could ride. Swore black and blue, I would never have vouched for her if I knew she couldn't." I snort at his words, realizing Max was right. He's getting into trouble for Selena Cross' actions. Wonder how that's going to affect her career. His eyes shoot to mine, cold and calculating, as he hangs up and throws his phone next to him on the table.

"Where's my fucking cat?" he growls, and I wave in the direction of the sofa, showing him his sleeping Princess. He huffs but smiles at Mrs. Hayton as she puts a cup of coffee in front of him.

"What do you know about what I was just talking about?" he demands, his voice laced with suspicion, like I may have something to do with it. I roll my eyes, not overly amused at his assumption that I have nothing better to do than mess with his life.

"I spoke to Max this morning, and she was just getting on a plane to head to that set. *She* told me all about it. Apparently, she's going to fix Selena's lies." He just huffs again and proceeds to ignore me completely, asking Oliver about his plans for the day.

I tune out Oliver's gloating and watch as the two brothers I've hardly had anything to do with grab cups of coffee from Mrs. Hayton, both kissing her on the cheek in thanks.

Holden, the record executive, is also dressed in a suit. His is navy blue, and he's paired it with a lighter blue shirt, and a gray patterned tie. His dirty blond hair is styled messily, slightly longer on top and shaved at the sides. I can see a tattoo on his neck but can't make out what it is. The little glimpse I'm getting has a lot of black and gray shading. He has a similar build to Kai, stocky and tall, kind of like Vin Diesel. I bet he and Kai pump iron together; they would get all sweaty, and their shirts would come off, and their muscles would ripple as a drop of sweat rolls down their skin.

The picture is so vivid in my mind that a sharp "Harlow!" has me jumping. Shaking myself out of my daydream, my eyes meet his hazel ones. Oh wow, they're similar to mine.

"Sorry, what did you say?"

"Well, while you were busy eye-fucking my brother, he asked you what you had planned for Oli's new tattoo." Thomas' accented words have me flustered, and I can feel a blush cross my cheeks from a combination of being caught fantasizing about his brothers as well as just what he sounds like. It's not strong, just a faint hint, but it's undeniably sexy. What is with these men and their suits? I guess being the CEO of their respective businesses means dressing up every day, but they may be more than my poor heart can handle. This is my first breakfast with them, and I'm not sure if I'm going to survive to my second. Thomas has on a deep green suit that sets off his messy red hair and green eyes perfectly; he looks like a sexy elf. His build is long and lean like a swimmer, and he sits in a seat across from me, an expectant look on his face. *Oh, right, the tattoo.*

"Oh, it's a surprise, and you'll all just have to wait and see when it's done." They all frown at me, and I guess they're not used to being told no. Mrs. Hayton's bawdy laugh rings out across the table.

"You all should see your faces." She slaps a hand on the table, her mirth causing me to giggle. "Good on you, child! They need to be told no more often. All they hear is yes, sir. Buck up, boys, it's good for the soul." Jacinta and Kai enter the room, both with smiles on their faces as they see Mrs. Hayton laughing.

"What's so funny?" Jacinta asks, smiling, and her eyes have a warmth to them that I've only seen when she looks at everyone but me. The housekeeper's laughter is contagious.

"Oh, Harlow just put the boys in their places, and that didn't go over well." Jacinta's smile drops at those words, and it looks like she's going to join her brothers in annoyance even though she has no idea why they're annoyed. It's another show of solidarity against me as an interloper. Looking around the table, I'm met by frowns and pursed lips or ugly sneers on all the boys present until Kai's laughter has them all turning their heads to look at him.

"Cheer up, you miserable assholes." He grabs

Mrs. Hayton in a big hug, lifting her feet off the floor with his enthusiasm and those muscles that I am definitely not going to fantasize about again...right now. "Breakfast looks awesome, thank you." Kai is dressed in a pair of sneakers, a loose pair of shorts, and a t-shirt.

"Not going into the office today?" she asks him. He pushes his chin-length hair off his face as he shakes his head.

"No, the guys have a photoshoot at Newport Beach that I'm going to supervise."

"Oh, I was there yesterday, and the waves were amazing! There were a few surfers out in the water, and it just looked magical," I add to the conversation before my brain catches up to my mouth. *Why, Harlow, why would you invite their attention?* All talk stops, and as one they all look at me like they're shocked I had something to say. But Kai smiles, coming over to sit next to me at the table.

"Do you surf, Harlow?" he asks, showing some genuine interest, and I snort.

"Hardly." Brad and his perfectly put together PA, Cecelia, have walked in just as I'm talking. "No, going to the beach was not something that Diane would have allowed."

Kai raises a confused eyebrow. "What do you mean?"

Sighing, I look at Cecelia. It's not really something I want to share with outsiders, and I'm debating whether I answer or not since I barely want to even tell my "siblings" anything else about my life with Diane. Everyone's eyes follow mine, and she sees us looking at her, waving her hand at me before smoothing back her hair. "Oh, don't worry about me! I'm practically family," she simpers. That gets an interesting reaction from the kids. Eye rolling, a couple of snorts, and what sounds like gagging from Jacinta. *Hmm, is she implying that she and Brad are an item?*

"She's also got an ironclad NDA," Brad adds in absently as he puts food on his plate, which draws an annoyed look from Cecelia before she quickly smoothes it away.

"Harlow," Kai prompts me, bringing my attention away from the PA.

"Oh, well the Bostons had custody of me, but I'm not sure it was technically done through all the proper legal channels. I think it was an under the table thing because Diane dictated a lot of the rules. I wasn't permitted to go on any kind of vacation with them, and until I got accepted to college, I hadn't left our hometown."

I don't add in that after I had turned eighteen and could do whatever I wanted, she kept me close through blackmail and manipulation. That might be just a bit too heavy for breakfast conversation. My eyes meet Brad's, and his eyes shimmer with tears, a bit of guilt hitting me that this is two consecutive meals that I've managed to upset him in some way. He walks over and places a kiss on my forehead. "I'm so sorry, kid."

I shrug my indifference. "It's all in the past, and you didn't know." Everyone else loses interest in the conversation, but Kai's eyes are shrewd as if he knows there's more to my story than I'm saying.

"Okay, what's on the agenda today?" Brad asks, taking a seat, and Cecelia sits next to him. "Where's Jaxon?" he asks, looking around the table for the missing brother before his eyes land on Jacinta.

"Oh, he had to go out to Vegas for the day for something with the hotel; he'll be back this evening. He doesn't want to miss our first premiere as a family," she says, waving her piece of toast in the air, her words laced with sarcasm that Brad seems to miss. The siblings exchange wicked grins, and I squirm uncomfortably in my seat. Damn it; something is definitely going on. Looking at Kai, he won't meet my eye, so the nice guy façade only goes so far. I'll have to keep that in mind.

"What about everyone else?" Brad continues.

"Well, the billboard is going up today for the shoot we just did. We should all get to see it tonight. It's just across from the movie theater." She sounds excited at the prospect as her cool blue eyes meet mine. "I think you'll be pleased with what we've done with it, Harlow." Her fake smile has me twitching, my mind running through all the mischief she might be planning for me.

Brad is frowning, his brows furrowed. "What's Harlow got to do with it? Why would she be pleased?" I wiggle even more in my seat at his words, but Nana and Poppy walk in, saving me from answering.

"Oh, the photographer thought Harlow was beautiful, which she is, and decided she was more suitable for the shoot than the hired models." Nana runs a hand over my head on the way past, and I smile up at her. Poppy leans down and kisses me on the cheek before going around and giving Jacinta one as well. Thank goodness she jumped in; there was no way I was explaining that Shane was saving me from all the bullying.

"I've got to deal with the fallout from Selena's lies and kiss a director's ass. Hopefully, I can do it via video chat, but if he's a temperamental bastard, I'll have to get on the jet tomorrow and go and straighten it out," Declan informs his father, and Brad nods before looking toward the next son.

"Meetings for me," Thomas tells him, "but I may have to fly to London and check on our British branch in a few days. There's been talk of industrial disputes from the cabin staff." Brad frowns but again nods his head.

"And I've got a boy band imploding." Holden groans, his elbows resting on the table, head in his hands, and my ears prick up in interest. "Ninja Starfish needs some mediation, and I have to be involved in the talks. I don't know what's going on, but they're good guys, so it's the least I can do. I don't want to lose one of our number one selling artists." Ninja Starfish is a cool funky little boy band outfit; a cross between One Direction and Imagine Dragons. They sing, dance, and play instruments. I'd love to know the gossip, but he doesn't share any more information.

When everyone has finished the schedules for the day, Cecelia stands up. "Don't forget tonight's premiere; everyone is expected to attend." She starts handing out tickets to each of them. "These are your tickets and a plus one if you need it." She gets to me and hands me an envelope, but I look down at it in confusion.

"I'm sorry. I thought I was attending with Brad?" I ask, looking up as the table falls silent.

Cecelia waves at me. "Oh, no. I *always* attend with Brad." She titters at my mistake while Nana clears her throat.

"Actually, why don't you hang on to Harlow's tickets. She will be attending with Brad tonight, and you can use hers. Maybe bring a date. One who is more age-appropriate." She mutters the last bit under her breath, and Poppy barely holds in a chuckle at her snark.

Turning to Cecelia, I see her eyes flash in anger, and she lets out a quiet huff in outrage at Nana's comment before she quickly schools her face again, a small smile appearing. "Of course, Grace, that would be lovely." Looking around the table, waiting to be blown up at for attending with their father,

I'm surprised that the kids seem pleased about something for a change. I guess Cecelia is about as welcome as I am. Maybe she's sleeping with my father, or maybe this is just another example of that Summers' hospitality for outsiders. If he's a little friendlier when he's away from the rest of them, I'll ask Oliver today.

At that thought, he stands up, wiping his mouth with a napkin. "Come on, Harlow, we need to get going." I drain my coffee, taking his lead. Wishing everyone a good day, I follow after him, Nana's call of good luck and have a nice day, echoing after me.

## Chapter Twenty-Two

### Harlow

After grabbing my backpack from my room and forsaking the crutches for another day, I follow Oliver through a door I haven't seen before. It leads us to a huge garage with the faint smell of gasoline fumes and oil. It's big enough to house their eight cars, I quickly count, with a couple of empty spaces. I also see some pretty wicked motorcycles on the far side, but it's a silver Aston Martin Vanquish in front of me that catches my eye, a whistle escaping my mouth.

"Whoa, that is a seriously nice car!" I say out loud. Oliver presses something on his key fob, and the lights flash once as a beeping sound echoes through the garage.

"Hop in; we need to get moving." He climbs into the driver's side, not acknowledging the compliment, and I just about have a panic attack at the thought of sitting in a car this gorgeous. As the garage door lifts, I run around to the passenger side and jump in.

I've barely sat down and closed my door before we're shooting out of the garage at a rapid pace. The car flies around to the front of the house and down the driveway, the rose bushes a blur of purple and pink. As we fly by, a rush of adrenaline that spikes through my body, waking me up even more. I'm no stranger to a little adrenaline, and I can't say that I don't appreciate the burst of energy. He has some classic rock playing softly in the background, and as Lenny Kravitz screams about an American woman, I watch for the old mansion through the trees. Straining my neck, I try to catch a glimpse of the gothic monstrosity, but we fly by too fast. Disappointment runs through me, and I decide my next free day, I'm going over there to explore. I just hope there really isn't a caretaker on the premises anymore.

Turning my head, I examine Oliver's profile as his hands grip the steering wheel tight. His citrusy scent has dug itself into the car, and the smell reminds me of summer afternoons by the lake back home. A part of me wants to enjoy the familiarity while I can, knowing that our time one on one might be just the chance for me to finally make some headway with one of Brad's kids.

"So..." Screw the tension and the silence; I want

to know more about this man. Let's see if I can get any. "Black sheep of the family or just no business for you to take over?" My words are nosy and kind of mean, but I'm hoping that they'll get him to engage, and he does strike me as the type who might appreciate some blunt words.

He snorts, "Hardly!" *Hook, line, and sinker.* "I could have run the clubs and hotels with Jaxon, or Productions with Declan, or even the energy drink company with all its different sponsored teams. There are more than enough businesses to go around; those three especially are often flat out busy."

That's fascinating information. They're all hell-bent on not wanting me around, yet the businesses are busy enough I could slide in anywhere if I really wanted to, or if that's what Brad's intentions are. That does make it seem like their personal issues have to be even more deeply rooted than I'd first thought. I'm truly no threat to their wealth or status in the family enterprises, so this might be harder than I can handle.

He's quiet for a little while before he keeps going. "I was a sullen, withdrawn kid when Dad first adopted me. My home life had sucked, but Nana realized I had a knack for drawing and bought me my first art supplies. It calmed me like nothing else did, and with some therapy, I managed to channel my emotions into my art." His hands are tight on the wheel, and his body is tense. The ripple of muscle in his tight forearms makes his tattoos dance with the movement, and I squirm slightly with desire, but I quickly check my inner hornbag. Telling me those things was difficult for him, but it makes me feel like he's opening up, and it's honestly more progress than I've made with any of Brad's kids so far. My hormones are certainly not going to get in the way of making the most of this connection. I put my hand on his thigh, low enough that I'm not getting too personal, and his gaze leaves the road to look at my hand before going back to the road. Afraid I've pushed too far when all I wanted to do was show some sympathy, I pull it away slowly, but he grabs it and keeps it there.

"By the time I was a teenager, I had a fascination with tattoos, and Nana organized for me to meet a tattoo artist friend of hers. I wasn't allowed into the shop because I was a minor, but he would come out to us and give me drawing lessons once a month. He gave me my first gun six months after I started lessons with him, and I would practice on pig skins Nana would get from the butcher for me. Occasionally, I could talk one of the guys into letting me use them as practice dummies. When I turned eighteen, I started an official apprenticeship with him. Three years of hard work and no pay, but by the end, Frank told me I was the best apprentice he'd ever had. And that guy was hard to please, let me tell you." A rueful smile crosses his face at the memory, but there's also a soft affection in his eyes that I feel like I've seen before in Declan's and some of the others. It's the look the Summers seem to get when they talk about or spend time with someone they genuinely care about. "He made me work hard for it, but I stayed on with him for another two years before I opened NPI. Dad was thrilled I was expanding the Neighpalm empire, and he, Nana, and Poppy have been nothing but supportive."

His story warms my heart. They're such loving and supportive people; these guys are so lucky to have them.

"And the new artist today?" As soon as I change the subject, his body language transforms. His grip on the steering wheel loosens, and his whole body slumps slightly in his seat, relaxing. *Okay, well, that clearly defines some boundaries. Good to know.*

"We have the one shop here in LA, but we're looking to expand. We're opening a store in San Francisco, and we're also opening one on the east coast in New York, so we're interviewing a whole heap of artists. I'm flying to the east coast to do some interviews out there in a week or two." He looks at me, his eyes covered by reflective glasses, so I can't read his expression. "You should come with me, visit your family, or whatever," he suggests, and a huge smile crosses my face.

"Really? Yeah, that would be awesome. I'll have to wait and see where the horses are by then, though," I remind him. He gives a quick nod of his head but doesn't seem bothered by the need to put business first; I guess that *is* a Summers trait, after all.

"So, what are you looking for today in the artist?" I probe, interested in his thought process and wanting to take advantage of every moment where I'm being treated like a real human being.

"Well, talent, of course. I want to see their set up and break down. Even though there will be an apprentice for those kinds of things, I want to see their process. You can tell a lot by the way an artist sets up their station," he explains to me as the outside scenery flies by, getting busier the closer to the city we get.

"Also want to see what their interaction with the client is. Will they talk to them and interact, or will they just sit there doing the job, all awkward silence? I want to see them make their client as comfortable as possible, and they need to be able to read what the client wants. Some like to babble their way through a tat to keep themselves distracted, but some need the silence, sinking into a meditative state. An artist's bedside manner and their ability to tailor it to their client is a huge factor in building up their clientele and the loyalty that keeps people coming back."

Nodding my head, I think about what I like to do, realizing I don't have a preference. I've read and talked my way through most of my tattoos, but once I just about fell asleep. I have a fairly high pain threshold, and tattoos aren't a big deal for me.

"We're going to be doing a reality tv show around the business; it was Declan's idea. Good publicity for the company and excellent viewing for an audience. They've proven to be popular in the past, so it won't hurt if the artist is attractive."

"A reality show sounds like a fun idea. I wish I could draw; I would have loved to have been a tattoo artist. Unfortunately, I can't even draw a stick figure." He smiles slightly at my words, and we fall into a comfortable silence, some of the most peaceful time I've had in days apart from my hang-outs with Alex and Shane. Reaching into my back-pack, I pull out my paperback and start at where I'd left off at the photoshoot the other day. I can see Oliver looking over from the corner of my eye, but I don't pay any attention to him.

"Do you have a boyfriend?" he asks suddenly.

"Nope," I reply, popping the p. I'm a little surprised at his line of questioning, but he hasn't called me a gold-digger or a whore yet, so that's a lot of progress.

"Girlfriend?" He sounds curious, and a smile crosses my face.

Putting my book down, I look at him. "No, Oliver, no significant other. The closest I've come to getting laid just recently was rolling around on the bed with Alex and the other guy at the fashion shoot. The only action I see is in my books." I wave the novel at him, waiting for a joke about the rippling men on the cover, but none comes. But a frown has creased his forehead at the mention of the photoshoot, and he doesn't say anything else, so I go back to reading my book.

A while later, the car starts to slow. Looking up, I find us in a funky little urban area, with cute clothing stores and trendy cafes and bars. One building has the Neighpalm Ink Logo on it, just like Oliver's shirt. He pulls around the back of the building while I stuff my book back into my bag.

"Come on, she should be here soon, and I want to get this printed onto transfer paper before she does." He gestures to his sketch pad that he's grabbing off the backseat.

Oh, it's a female artist; for some reason, I was expecting a male. A wave of jealousy flows through me at the thought of her putting the tattoo on him where I want it, and I contemplate changing the position. But I shake my head at my silliness, chastising myself. *Girl, you don't even know if he has a girlfriend. You shouldn't be feeling territorial. He's your adopted brother, not to mention he's been a bit of a dick.* But when I think back, Oliver really hasn't done anything apart from the bet. The door opening knocks me out of my musing, and Oliver offers me his hand. Taking it, I step out of the low sports car.

"Why thank you, kind sir," I say to him in my best British accent, but he just rolls his eyes, a laugh escaping his mouth. He closes the door and sets the alarm before walking toward the building, pulling out another set of keys.

"My turn to ask. Girlfriend?" He just snorts but doesn't answer verbally. I'm going to take that as a no.

"Boyfriend?" I ask casually, my voice raised in question, and he turns around. Pulling off his glasses, his whiskey brown eyes are full of amusement as he walks toward me, backing me up against the wall. The bricks are rough against my exposed shoulders, the spaghetti straps of the maxi dress offering me no comfort. His chest is hard against my breasts as he leans down, his breath tickling my ear as he whispers.

"No, sweetheart, I won't say I haven't experimented, but I much prefer a hot, wet, tight pussy wrapped around my thick, hard cock." My breath is coming quickly now, and his eyes are on my mouth. Just when I think he's going to make a move, he backs away and sticks the key in the lock, throwing on the lights as he walks into the back of the shop. He might think I don't notice it, but I see the deep breath that he takes right before he's fully turned from my view.

Leaning against the wall, I wait for my heart rate to slow down. Holy crap, I hope he doesn't want me to get a tattoo around my pubic area because my panties now have what is possibly a very visible wet patch.

Heaving out a huge breath, I follow him into the store. The back rooms have an office and a storage room, as well as what looks like a staff lounge. It has some comfy plush sofas and a large fridge and kitchen area with a TV. Peeking in the storeroom as I pass, I see supplies. Lots of medical-looking things, but there are also piles of paper and bottles of ink.

Moving out onto the main floor, the store is pristine and clean. Four cubicles are set up for four artists. Each partitioned area has a tattoo table and a chair off to the side for the client. It also has a rolling workstation and chair for the artist. The floors are wooden throughout the store, and each station has a TV screen set up with Bluetooth headphones placed on each of the tables. The walls are decorated with prints of different artist's art and lots of framed flash pictures. *I wonder which ones are Oliver's.*

In front of the four cubicles is a large counter with what looks like merchandise inside, and I walk close to get a look. There's a range of shirts and hats, but there's also a selection of piercing jewelry.

"You have a piercer?" I ask him. He's standing at the end of the counter, running his sketch through the printer that's set up there as well as a lightbox. He looks up at my words, a smirk on his face.

"Yeah, that's the room there, but all of us are qualified." He points to a closed door off to the side. "Why, Harlow? Would you like to get something pierced?" His eyes hold a challenge, but I don't rise to the bait.

"Maybe. I always wanted to get my belly-button pierced." Maybe a couple of other things too, but never had the time. "Do you have any?" He smiles smugly.

"Wouldn't you like to know?" With that, he goes back to his printing. *Damn right, I'd like to know.*

In front of the counter is a nicely set up waiting area. There's a black leather couch and a coffee table with artist portfolios sitting on it for clients to look through. There's also a vending machine for coffee and a water cooler.

Before I can ask another question, there's a knock at the front door, and Oliver nods to it. "Can you get that for me?" I nod my head and walk toward it. "Oh, and Harlow?" I turn back to look at him, and there's heat in his eyes. "Pretend to be my girlfriend, please?"

His words couldn't have shocked me more. I feel my face flush with embarrassment, and with that level of heat, there's no way he's missing the flash of color. "What? Why?"

"I want to know if this chick will hit on a taken man. I've seen it happen before; they flirt with their client even if their partner is with them. It happens with both sexes, and I think that's bad manners and bad business, and I won't have it in my store."

My eyes widen in shock, but I nod my head, and a heated smile slowly crosses his face.

"Good girl. Now go." He nods as the girl bangs on the glass again. *What am I getting myself into?*

## Chapter Twenty-Three

**Harlow**

When I open the glass door, the woman standing there looks at me in surprise, her eyes going wide and lips parting. "Oh, hey, I have an appointment with Oliver. My name's Lisa." She's got red, shoulder-length hair that has been artfully styled into pin-up curls. Her ruby lips stand out against her pale skin, and her eye makeup is dramatic and sets off the smattering of stars she has tattooed on the side of her face. It looks familiar, but I can't quite place where I've seen it before.

She's wearing a 50s-style dress that's covered in skulls and bleeding hearts, and it lifts her breasts sky high before flaring out at the waist. Whatever client she bends over will get an eyeful before they're smothered to death if she's tattooing above their chest. On her feet are a pair of high heels that not even Max would dare to walk in. I'm not sure if this girl is dressed for seduction, or if that's what her everyday look is, but surely it can't be what she tattoos in day to day. I remember Tasha saying she likes to wear comfy, loose-fitting clothes when she has to be bent over for hours at a time. Stepping out of the way, I wave her inside the shop. Oliver is walking around the counter as she steps in, and a huge smile crosses her face.

"Hi. I'm Oliver Summers, thanks for coming in to interview with us, Lisa." He reaches out a hand for her to shake. She grabs it and moves it up and down enthusiastically.

"Oh hi, Oliver, thanks so much for seeing me," she gushes, her portfolio slipping from under her other arm in her enthusiasm. It starts to head for the floor, but Oliver is quick and manages to grab it before it hits the ground. He hands it back to her, and she looks at him like he's just saved her cat from up a tree. Annoyance starts to build, the feeling almost like when you have an itch that you can't scratch, and she hasn't even really started flirting. But then I smack myself internally. *No reason to feel jealous. You're only pretending, Harlow.*

"Thanks," she says, the words breathy and low. Oliver's answering smile is professional and welcoming but not overboard, just what you'd expect from someone conducting an interview. My opinion of him rises in that moment, liking that it doesn't seem as though he's going to take advantage of how much she's obviously overwhelmed by his mere presence.

"Did you meet my girlfriend, Harlow?" He gestures to me before sliding his arm around my waist and giving me a squeeze and a kiss on the cheek. My heart starts to gallop at the physical contact, and I realize, for the millionth time, that I haven't been laid in way too long. Her eyebrows crease in a frown as she watches his hand on me, but she quickly replaces that with a smile. *Well, I guess that's one small warning sign so far.*

"Why don't we have a seat, and we'll look through your portfolio, and you can tell me about your experiences." He waves to the leather couch, and they both move toward it, leaving me standing there still in shock from his contact.

"Harlow, honey, why don't you put the coffee machine on in the back?" He turns to Lisa. "Would you like a coffee?"

Again, her face lights up. "Yeah, sure, that would be great!" Her enthusiasm is beginning to grate on my nerves; no one can be *that* perky all the time, so I'm pretty sure it's more about getting rid of me than actually wanting a coffee, especially with the way she keeps eye-fucking him.

"Sure, babe, of course I can," I say, gritting my teeth and smiling. His eyes heat at my words, and I can feel his eyes on me as I walk to the staff room.

Before I get there, I hear their conversation start up again.

Quickly looking around the room, I easily find the coffee machine on the kitchen counter. It's one of those drip filter things that isn't too bad when it first makes the coffee but tastes horrid and stale as can be within an hour or so sitting in the pot. Digging around in the cabinets, I find a filter, the coffee grounds, and a measuring spoon in one of the drawers.

Measuring out what looks like an alright amount, I fill the thing with water and flick the switch. The red light shows it's working, so while I wait for it to do its thing, I wander back out to the cubicles. Lisa's busy outlining her achievements to Oliver in her grating voice, and I unconsciously scrunch up my face as I pantomime her words, my inner kindergartener apparently getting the best of me.

Tuning them out, I look at all the framed artwork on the walls. Photographs of each artist's work make up most of them, and when I get to a stunning piece of a tiger across someone's shoulder, I stop and stare. The artwork is phenomenal, and the tiger looks like it could crawl off the body and eat you up.

"Harlow, baby, how's that coffee going?" Oliver's voice sounds slightly strained, so I plaster on a smile and walk back to the waiting area.

"Almost done. How do you take your coffee, Lisa?" My eyes lock onto the fact that she has her hand on his thigh, so I move over to them. Placing my ass down on the arm of the sofa, I nuzzle into the back of his neck, clearly staking my claim. Her hand moves, but not quick enough as far as I'm concerned. Even if I am the fake girlfriend, she has most definitely pushed the boundaries of what I consider acceptable behavior. A small groan escapes his mouth, and he moves away from me slightly, his body tight with tension.

"I like the look of your work, Lisa. What I'd like to see happen now is maybe you could set up your workstation how you prefer it, and then you're going to tattoo one of us." His tone is friendly, but I can hear the underlying strain I just caused, and a wicked part of me wants to almost purr with satisfaction at knowing I'm responsible for it.

"Yeah, ok, cool, that would be awesome." She looks at me. "What are we tattooing on you?"

I smile at her assumption and shake my head. "Oh no, honey, you're tattooing the boss man today." Her face pales slightly at my words, but I have to give her credit, she pulls it together quickly.

"Ok, awesome!" I roll my eyes at her enthusiasm again as I move off the sofa arm. I just hope she didn't see it; I couldn't hold that one in.

They both stand up, and Oliver leads her to a cubicle. "Everything you may need is in the workstation or the cabinets lining the wall. How about you get set up, and we'll go and get that coffee."

Before she can answer, he grabs my hand and tugs me to the back room. We don't even make it past the door of the kitchen before he has my back slammed against the wall, and his mouth is on mine. It's a wild clashing of teeth and tongues as we fight for dominance, but once his hand cups my boob and starts caressing it, his fingers pinching my nipple, I pant like a bitch in heat and give him everything he's demanding.

His hands move to my ass, lifting me so I've got my legs wrapped around him, his hardness grinding against my soaked panties. With my back pinned against the wall to hold me in place, he removes his hands from my ass and runs a finger over the seam of my pussy, my panties the only thing separating him from bare skin. My dress has been pushed up around my hips, giving him easy access. A groan escapes my mouth as his finger finds my clit, circling it, my core tightening with delight.

His mouth leaves mine, and, sucking and nipping, he moves toward my breasts. But before he can get any further, I hear Lisa call out, "Ah, Oliver? I can't find any tape."

"Fuckkkk," he groans, his head resting against mine, our eyes meeting, and I'm sure mine are as turned on and as needy as his. Before I can say anything, he steps away, letting my legs fall to the ground. Once I'm stable, he turns quickly and strides away, not another word said.

I collapse into a nearby chair, resting my head

on the table. *Holy fuck! What was that?* My skin is tight and lust is heavy in my bones as I try to get my body under control. I've never felt like that before except for that one time with Jaxon at the club.

With that realization, I sit up in shock. *Fuck, they're right about me. That's two brothers I've made out with and would have gone further if we hadn't been interrupted.* A slight prick of guilt joins those thoughts, but I shake it off. No. If Jilly can have different lovers in every city, and the characters in my book can have multiple partners, then me kissing two different guys is no big deal. Or that's what I try to convince myself as I get up and pour three cups of coffee.

Carrying the cups out and hoping I don't look freshly ravished, I set a cup down next to each of them. They're standing at the counter, the lightbox on, and the printer ready. Lisa thanks me with a smile, a funny look entering her eye as she examines my neck. *Crap, do I have stubble rash?*

"So, Harlow, Oliver tells me you're in charge of picking his tattoo. What are we doing?" My eyes meet Oliver's, and he has a smile on his face, but I can see the frayed edges that he's trying to hide. *Good, I hope he's as affected as I am.*

"Oh, he's not allowed to know until it's done. It's a surprise between the two of us. Go and take your pants off, sexy, and lay down on the table," I demand, looking down at his groin. Whoops, poor bastard still has a raging hard-on. Lisa's eyes follow mine, so before they can get to his crotch, I turn her around and tow her in the direction of the client bathroom.

"Hey, what are you doing?" she cries, trying to shake me off.

"Oh, I want to tell you about the tattoo, just somewhere he can't hear," I say, giving her a flimsy excuse that both of them may believe. For whatever deep-seated reason, I don't want her eyes roving over his body right now, and besides, I really do want to show her my penguin tattoo. That's right; he made a mention of it the other day, so I think it's only fair that he gets one of his own to match.

By the time we finish in the bathroom and she knows what it needs to look like, we go back out to the cubicle. She heads over to the counter and sketches it up real quick, shows me for my approval, prints it on a stencil, and I join Oliver at his table.

He's got on a pair of tight boxer-briefs, and while it looks like he's got his dick under control, it's still mouth-watering behind the material.

"Uh uh, no! Not going to happen," he snarls at me. "You need to leave. There is no way that I can't not get an erection if you stand there, looking at me like that. Go and wait in the staff lounge. One of the guys should be in to open the shop up soon." He waves his hand, actually shooing me away.

"You're going to have to remove your briefs," I tell him with a smug smile, and his mouth drops open in shock. "Shall I get you a towel to preserve your modesty, good sir?"

He growls at me but nods his head as I go and grab one out of the storeroom and bring it back, draping it over him so he can remove them without flashing Lisa whose heels are clicking on the floorboards as she walks back to us.

"Close your eyes and no peeking," I order, and with a resigned look, he nods, shooing me away again.

## Oliver

Her ass sways as she walks away from me, the movement hypnotic and alluring, and my cock is hard as a steel rod from kissing her before. God, the woman undoes me. I'm so attracted to her, in a way I never thought I would be. I mean, she's the enemy, right? She's the one who's trying to break up our happy family. Or that's how Jacinta, Jaxon, and Declan tell it...but I'm not so sure. I think back to our conversation in the car and how I told her things that I haven't ever told another woman before. Mind you, none of them have really asked me about that kind of stuff either. All were more interested in whether I had tattooed anyone famous or if I would do one on them for free. I'm not sure if I've ever really had an actual relationship. But Harlow...I'd opened up, and it all seemed to pour out.

What is it about her? Is it that she gives off that vibe of being a kindred spirit, one abandoned child to another? The attraction I feel toward her is not only on a physical level but an emotional and spiritual one. I can't say that I was really looking for something like this, but with her here, right in front of me, there's a part of me that says I'd be an idiot not to see where it could go. As my brain starts to think about what the future could hold for us, I think about what my sister has planned for Harlow, and it's enough to make my cock soften. While I don't appreciate the reminder that my future with Harlow might rightfully end tonight, it's definitely good timing because Lisa pops in front of me suddenly.

"Are you ready? I just need to put the stencil on, and we can get started," she tells me a little too enthusiastically. I'm getting a little more excited college cheerleader and less professional tattoo artist. "Now, she said just in from the crease of your thigh." She starts to rip the towel off my lower regions, but I quickly hold it in place.

"Yeah, you don't need to remove the towel. Let me just hold it back for you. Always give the client the option of more modesty until you know their preference," I explain to her, already a little disgruntled with how this interview is going. The last thing I need is my potential new artist getting an eyeful of my cock. So I peel the towel back as far as it needs to go while keeping it secure over the rest of my goodies.

"I hope you don't hold this against me," she whines as she places it. "She assured me you were okay with her choosing. I mean, I wouldn't put this on you normally. I'd like to think that I have a much better grasp on what would be fitting for a man like you. Maybe her taste just isn't as good." She's trying so hard to shit on Harlow with her not so thinly veiled words, so I tell her firmly, "I lost a bet, and I stand by my words. I'm sure it's not horrible; Harlow wouldn't do that to me."

She purses her lips in disapproval and starts up the gun, but I'm not even paying attention, my words having struck a chord with me that honestly makes me a little bit uncomfortable.

Harlow's not a bad person, so why are we trying to get rid of her? I really need to speak to my siblings, see if I can change their minds, especially before tonight.

I close my eyes, and the gun drones on as she carefully outlines my tattoo. "So, how long have you and Harlow been together?" she probes conversationally. *Strike two, not reading her client. Clearly, I'm not in the mood for mindless chit chat.*

I roll my eyes behind my lids at her obvious question. "A while," I lie, hoping she doesn't ask anymore, but of course I can't be that lucky.

"And how did you meet?" she fires back, but I have a way of warding off the questions.

"Look, when I get tattooed, I like the silence," I explain to her. "I like to sink into the sensation and block out everything around me. You should probably check with your client about whether they're the same or are happy to hold a conversation." I chastise her gently, trying to change the subject, and when I open my eyes to gauge whether she understands, pink stains her cheeks, so I guess she does. She's quiet for a little while longer before more words flow out of her mouth, and those seal her fate.

## Harlow

I take myself and my cup of coffee back to the staff lounge and curl up on the couch there. Pulling my book out of my backpack, I hear the tattoo gun start-up and the low murmured voices of the two of them. Tuning it all out, I get sucked into my story, and phew, it is heating up. The main female character has five mates, and she is *seriously* being taken care of sexually in every kind of delicious way. This is so not what I needed after Oliver had already gotten me all hot and bothered.

Looking at the door of the bathroom, I wonder if I can just sneak in there and finish the job he started with a little TLC self-service. But before I can do that, the back door opens, and a huge hulking guy covered in tats and leather walks through the door. He's holding a motorcycle helmet in his hand, and his dark brown hair is messy from wearing it.

Stopping suddenly at the sight of me, he frowns, blinking his steel-blue eyes once, then twice, before asking, "Who are you?"

"I'm Harlow," I tell him, standing up, smoothing out my dress, and running a hand through my hair. Shit, is Oliver like Jacinta, not wanting anyone to know who I am?

His eyes run the length of my body and back before a small smile crosses his face. "Ah, Brad's daughter. Nice!" He steps further into the room, his tall body looming over mine as he reaches out one huge paw.

"I'm Jonah, one of the tattoo artists here at NPI." My hand is engulfed in his, but it feels warm and secure as we shake briefly before he drops it and moves away. Putting his keys in a cubby nearby and stripping off his leather jacket, placing both that and his helmet in there too, he moves on to the coffee machine.

"Oh, did you get this started, or is it old crap from yesterday?" he asks, looking at it dubiously.

"Fresh this morning," I exclaim, holding up my cup in demonstration, and he breathes a sigh of relief.

"Harlow, you just became my new favorite person," he tells me, pouring himself a mug and coming over to sit next to me on the couch. His large body takes up most of the room, but it's not intimidating. Instead, I get the vibe from him that he makes his clients feel comfortable, maybe even cozy, and I almost want to gravitate toward his energy. A huge sigh leaves his mouth as he leans back with his eyes closed, sipping the liquid.

"Oh yeah, like manna from the gods." His voice is rough but happy.

I can't help myself, and I snort out loud. "Rough night?" I ask him, and he turns to look at me with a serious look on his face.

"You would not believe it if I told you."

"Try me," I prompt, now desperate to know. A cheeky grin crosses his exhausted face as he chuckles.

"Well, I did warn you. I went out with some buddies and went home with twins last night," he tells me, sounding proud, and I roll my eyes, but his next words have my mouth dropping open in shock. "And let me tell you that brother and sister tag teamed me like a pro wrestling duo, and, well, I'm surprised I can even walk this morning." *Holy shit, did he just say, brother and sister?* He closes his eyes again, and I run my gaze over him. Seriously wouldn't have picked this dude as bi, but shit, that's hot.

"You know, I can just hear what you're thinking,

and yes, it was amazing, and yes, I will be keeping their number in my phone." Now he's just smug as shit.

"Fuck," I grumble, "some people have all the luck. I can't seem to get anywhere sexually *or* platonically."

His eyes pop open at my words, and he looks at me, shrewdly nodding toward the main room. "Go easy on him. People see the gloss on the outside and are envious, but every one of the Summers kids has scars of their own and walls a mile high. With a light and gentle touch, you may just get through to him. Hopefully, if you win over one, the rest will follow."

Huffing, I stand up and take my empty cup to the sink. "Somehow, I don't think I could get through those walls with a ton of dynamite." He stands up, and we both head toward the sound of the gun buzzing, but I stop suddenly as Lisa's words register in my ears.

"Oli, I saw the problem you had earlier. Would you like me to take care of that for you?" The offer is flirty and suggestive, and I hear a grunt come from his mouth and then a gasp. *Oh hell no, she didn't!*

Before Oliver can reply, I storm into their cubicle, seeing her hand without the gun in it straying to areas it doesn't need to be. So I reach out and pull the plug from the socket.

She shrieks as it comes to a stop. "What the hell

are you doing?" she shouts at me, standing up and coming over to me.

"Oh no, bitch, I heard you proposition my boyfriend. Pack up your shit, grab your portfolio, and get the hell out. There will *not* be a job available for you here or at any NPI in the future."

She turns to Oliver in shock, and he has an amused look on his face as he nods his head, chuckling slightly while he holds his towel to his groin, keeping his goods covered. "Sorry, Lisa, but if you're going to hit on me with my girlfriend in the next room, I can't trust you not to hit on clients. Better do what Harlow says."

"But- but- the tattoo?" She gestures to his groin, and I wave Jonah forward.

"It's fine. Jonah will finish it up. Get the fuck out!" My words end in a growl, and she squeaks as I step toward her. Abandoning the gun on the station, she hurries to grab her bag and portfolio.

"Don't let the door hit you in the ass on the way out!" I shout after her, and Jonah and Oliver both chuckle with laughter.

"Wow, my girlfriend is feisty," Oliver says, trying to get a look at his new ink.

"Eyes up here, bucko," I demand, and they meet mine, amusement in them.

"Sorry, Jonah. I know I didn't ask, but if I show you a picture on my phone, do you think you could finish it up?"

"You bet, sweetheart. Anything for you. I think I

just fell in love. My heart is pounding after that performance." He grabs at his chest playfully, and I have a moment where I wish I'd be able to stick around for more than just today; I wouldn't mind having another friend, and Jonah seems perfect for that.

"Dude, I think maybe it's a left-over reaction from last night." I giggle as I walk off to the back to grab my phone and quickly snap a shot of my penguin. I hear Oliver ask about Jonah's night, and I smile when he starts to retell his story.

## Chapter Twenty-Four

**Harlow**

The buzzing of the gun is a soothing sound as Jonah finishes off Oliver's tattoo. He'd finished telling him about his night, and Oliver had started telling us about Lisa. "She was pushy and unprofessional from the very start. Kept asking me personal questions about you and me, Harlow, while she was shaving my skin. She didn't put gloves on to apply the stencil, and when she put the oil on for the transfer, she tried to cop a feel of my cock."

Jonah snorts. "Lucky you, man, you should have gone for it. Why do you keep calling Harlow your girlfriend, anyway?" He looks at me, raising his eyebrow and giving me a bright smile. "No offense." I just laugh.

"I wanted to test her professionalism. I don't

want her hitting on clients' partners if they come in with them." Jonah stops the gun for a moment, looking thoughtful but eyeing Oliver with suspicion.

"That's actually a good idea. I've seen that happen quite a bit with some of the artists I've worked with in the past, and that's *so* not cool. But are you sure that's the only reason?" Oliver ignores the question, and Jonah starts the gun up again as he continues telling us about Lisa.

"She also kept pushing the towel back further and further, and I ended up having to cup my junk to hold it there." He sounds pissed now. "And you heard her words at the end. If I had told her to blow me for the job, she would have right then and there. I'm a lot of things, but that's crossing the line as far as I'm concerned. The worst part is she's a talented artist, and she would have benefited the business, but her behavior was reprehensible."

Jonah has his tongue sticking out slightly as he finishes the shading of the penguin. "I don't know, man, it might have made good drama for the TV show."

Oliver grimaces. "Yeah, but I'd rather it got by on its merit and the talent of the artists as opposed to the drama the artist can stir up. I'm sure the client stories are going to be dramatic enough."

Jonah shrugs, wiping one more time and pulling away. "Okay, Miss Harlow, check out the handi-work." He gestures at Oliver's crotch, and I blush at the thought that I'd like to check out more than just the tattoo. My eye catches Oliver's, and he winks slowly at me like he knows what I'm thinking. His hand goes down to cup his crotch as Jonah puts the gun down.

"Can you break this down? I got to get set up for my first client; they should be here very soon." Oliver nods, but his eyes don't leave mine, and Jonah walks away.

"Well, are you going to take a look?" he pushes, and I move around to where Jonah had been sitting. Peering down, a smile crosses my lips at the matching penguin. *It's perfect!* Just as I'm about to say something, Oliver moves his hand, and the towel shifts as his cock stands at attention. I can't see anything but the outline, but it looks long and thick.

My eyes dart to his as he smiles lazily at me. "Didn't have this problem with Lisa." His eyes drop down, and I follow them. As I bend over, the maxi-dress gapes in front, and he's got a good view of the top of my breasts. "Pass me that mirror there." He points to one on the workstation. Reaching, I hand it to him and back away, waiting for the fallout.

"Fucking hell, Harlow!" he bellows, and I collapse onto Jonah's vacated chair in hysterics. Jonah's chuckles join mine from the next cubicle.

"What's wrong, Oli?" I tease, and his eyes heat at my use of his nickname. "You were admiring mine so much I thought you needed a matching one." He sits up, dropping his towel, his thick cock erect and twitching and *holy shit*, look at those piercings.

The underside of Oliver's cock is lined with three metal bars, a Jacob's Ladder. That has my laughter stopping instantly as I watch him grab a piece of cling wrap that he places over the penguin before taping it down and pulling his briefs back on. My eyes stay glued to his thick length the whole time, thinking about the things he could do to me with it. My nipples pebble, and my panties grow damp again. He pulls on his jeans and starts stripping the table and wiping over it with disinfectant before setting it up again.

"Your turn, Harlow. I want you on the table, on your back, and pull up your dress. I'm adding to your thigh tattoo with the mystical creatures." He's all business suddenly, like he doesn't even want to address the tension flowing between us.

"Don't you have other clients coming in today?" I ask him, and he shakes his head, changing out the gun and the chords and ditching the old ink pots. "Nope. I rescheduled them all after dinner last night. I'm all yours today, and we should get this finished before we need to go back and get changed for the premiere. You up to it?" There's a hint of a challenge in his voice, but that doesn't bother me.

"Sure, you've seen my tattoos. I've got a high pain threshold and staying power. You'll probably cave before I do." His eyes heat even more, and he runs his tongue across his lip, causing a shiver to travel down my spine. He doesn't say anything, just pats the table, so I follow his instructions and climb up.

"Oh, hang on, wait." I stop and run for the back room to grab my phone and my book before heading back out and climbing up on the table. Lying back, I pull my dress up and tuck it through my legs, so the back is now in front, sort of like a big diaper. That keeps it up out of Oliver's way, and I won't flash my panties to anyone who may walk by.

Oliver starts to dry shave my thigh over my other tattoo. He's business-like and focused now, all signs of teasing and desire gone. I just hope he gets it done in time for tonight. That makes me think of something.

"Oliver, what's the deal with Cecelia and Brad? Are they a couple? I was surprised to see her at breakfast this morning." His forehead wrinkles in a frown, and he snorts.

"She wishes. She stays in a spare room if they've been working late at night, and he uses her to ward off all the gold-diggers at social functions. She may have gotten the idea that it's more than that, but I can assure you it's not." He looks up and meets my eyes. "I've got a feeling she may find herself replaced by you from now on."

He rubs some oil onto my leg and lays the transfer down. I try to sit up and look as he puts a hand in the middle of my chest, but he holds me down. "Uh uh, same rules go, no peeking." So I stay flat, and he goes back to the transfer, smoothing it across my skin.

"Harlow, if you have no intention of building a relationship with Dad, I suggest you go home.'" His sudden sullen words surprise me, though there's less hostility in his words than there would be if one of the others had spoken. I blink at the ceiling and wait to see if he says anything else.

"You could probably ask for the world, and he would give it to you. It's not that he loves you any more than he loves us. It's just he has so much guilt. Guilt from not knowing that you existed and for you having to grow up as you did. Guilt that he wasn't able to save you like he saved all of us. Please, Harlow, don't break my dad's heart. You will not survive the onslaught from my siblings if you do. We will do anything to protect that man because he did everything to protect us." He includes himself in that last sentence, and my heartbeat rises in panic. Reaching down, I stop his hand against the stencil.

"I don't know what's going to happen between Brad and me, but I'm enjoying getting to know him, not that we've had much chance to, though I'm hoping tonight changes that. But if anything does go wrong, you and your siblings have only got yourselves to blame. Most of them have been cold and hostile toward me since day one, and I have done *nothing* to warrant it. Me coming from where I did is not a valid reason. From what I understand, none of you were in better situations when Brad adopted you."

Oliver comes to stand by my head, looking down at me. "No, you're right, but Jaxon and Jacinta are hostile because they've been with Dad the longest. They don't know any better; they were young, and they only have vague memories of their birth mother, and nobody knows about their father. They have a deep-seated fear that you're going to replace them in his heart. Jacinta's spent so long as the only princess of the family that she'd be this upset at any other woman who came in, not just you."

I snort my disbelief. "Somehow, I doubt that. Listen, Oliver, I don't care about any of that at the moment. I'm a big girl, and I've dealt with much worse than what your siblings can dish out, but I swear you better not fuck up my tattoo in some act of revenge."

He growls in anger, that last statement getting more of a rise out of him than anything else we've said so far. "I wouldn't do that, I promise. It's my reputation on the line." He stomps back to the end of the table and pulls the stencil up. Obviously happy with the positioning, he starts to fill little cups with ink and proceeds to ignore me. *That's fine with me.* I pick up my book and open it to where I left off, but Jonah's voice draws my attention.

"So what is it you do, Harlow, when you're back home?" I try to answer him, but Oliver butts in.

"She rides horses," he says, his voice filled with scorn, and I frown at his words. Do they seriously not know that I'm a vet? Fuck it. I'm not going to enlighten him. And how dare he judge me.

"My foster family trains horses for movies, and I've helped them with that," I hedge slightly.

"That's cool! Will I have seen any of the movies?" he asks, sounding excited, and I have to think hard about it. Once they leave for a set, I don't tend to pay any attention unless I'm watching an actual movie and recognize one of the horses.

"We had a couple on the *Game of Thrones* set. Oh, and the new Selena Cross movie that she's filming at the moment has some of ours, and my friend Max is her stunt double."

"Selena Cross is smoking hot." Jonah sighs as he sets up his station.

Oliver snorts. "And a lying, gold-digging whore. She thinks Declan is her ticket to mega-stardom, and he might have been, but she blew it. She made Declan look bad. I'm not sure if I'd want to be in her shoes at the moment. She's supposed to be his date for the premiere tonight. It'll be interesting to see if he brings her or not."

I roll my eyes at his words. I've got a feeling that the Summers boys think all women are gold-digging whores. Someone or someone's really did a number on them. My heart sinks at the thought that he's bringing such a beautiful date, but then I kick myself. *He's been nothing but hostile, and you were making out with his brother not five minutes ago, not to mention you've made out with another brother, and then there's the fact you're attracted to, well, all of his brothers.* I close my eyes. *Harlow, it may be time to go back to your therapist. It seems you have such a deep-seated need to be wanted that you're latching onto multiple men no matter how horrible they are.*

Oliver rolls his chair over to the table, gun in hand. Behind his black-framed glasses, his eyes are focused. "You ready? It's going to take a while. Make sure you let me know if you need a break for the toilet, or if you start to feel light-headed."

I wave my hand at him. "I'm fine, just get started; I don't want to be late tonight and let Brad down." He nods his head once, and the gun starts up.

The droning humming noise is a soothing balm against my battered soul. He starts the tattoo, and like normal, I flinch slightly at the pain, squeezing my eyes shut and gritting my teeth. I know it's coming and how it's going to feel, but the first swipe of the gun is jarring. But within five minutes of him working, I've sunk into the feeling, and the pain just washes over me, nothing more than a slight annoyance. Relaxing back, I pick up my book and read. The door of the shop opens, and a buzzer sounds out as a perky blonde with her own array of tattoos and piercings pops into the cubicle.

"Hi, boss. How's it going today?" She's much

too cheery and enthusiastic, and Jonah's groan easily travels across the small space between us.

"God, Beth, not so loud and happy first thing this morning," he complains, still suffering his night's after-effects. I smile to myself.

The gun stops, and Oliver looks up. "Hey, Beth, how are you? I've canceled all my appointments for this morning. Can you look at the book and reschedule them for me?"

Her eyebrows turn down in a frown, and she looks at me.

"Oh, why?" I can see she's trying to figure out how I fit into things, but I just pretend to go back to my book, not acknowledging her. She's as bad as Lisa, panting after Oliver like he's a cool drink of water, and she's thirsty as hell. Not that I blame her, the man is smoking hot.

"Harlow lost a bet, and now she's paying up." His words are smug, so I put my book down again.

"Ah, I believe we *both* lost, and you've already paid up," I remind him, and he frowns down at his lap. That's right, girls; he's marked by me now—a permanent reminder. I'm feeling pretty fucking pleased about that.

"Oh, okay, I'll get on that. I've got a couple of piercing clients today, but they're not coming in until later."

"Didn't you say you wouldn't mind getting something pierced?" His words are full of laughter like he doesn't think I would go through with it. But then my mind instantly wonders if she pierced him, and I almost growl out loud with jealousy, barely managing to hold it in.

"Yeah, but I think I'll stick to the tattoo for now. I'm already worried that it will get stuck to whatever Nana has for me to wear to the premiere tonight."

"Oh, that's right! That's tonight. Do you have a date for it, Oliver?" she asks, fishing for an invite and possible information on who I am.

"Nope. I think we're all going stag tonight except Declan was supposed to be escorting Selena. She makes a guest appearance in the movie, so she needs to be there, but who knows if that's still happening."

"Oh, no one else is bringing a date?" I ask curiously, and he shakes his head.

"No, I don't think so, but Jaxon has been known to flaunt Nana's requests, Holden too."

The gun starts up again and cuts off anything that Beth was going to say. Her face falls, covered in disappointment, before she plasters on another smile. "Well, okay, I hope you have fun."

No more words are exchanged between us. I spend my time reading and watching the goings-on in the shop, unable to throw myself back into my book. Jonah seems to be the only other artist working since Beth seems to be the receptionist and piercer. The shop stays busy with a constant flow of people in and out, making inquiries, appointments, and getting piercings. Jonah has two clients during the time my tattoo has been going on.

After about two hours, Oliver shuts off the gun and places it down; he groans in pain, stretching his whole body and standing up. "Okay, I need a break."

He tapes some plastic over the tattoo and pulls my dress down for me. "Why don't you go and get a drink and use the bathroom if you need it." He walks in that direction himself, leaving me on my own, and Beth must see it as an opportunity to grill me because as I stand up and stretch myself, she bounds over.

"So, what kind of bet did you lose?" she asks. "And how do you know Oliver?"

"None of your damn business, Beth," Jonah growls from over his client. "Go back up the front and worry about your own shit." She blanches, and then she disappears. Mouthing thank you to Jonah, grateful for his interference, I head toward the bathroom, half-hoping to run into Oliver and half-not.

## Chapter Twenty-Five

**Harlow**

The next couple of hours pass quickly with few words spoken between us. A couple of times he had to go and talk to potential clients up the front, but I resisted the urge to peek. Another artist had arrived—shaved head and tattoos over every exposed piece of skin I can see. Large gauges in both ears and a ring through his eyebrow, he has a slightly Middle-Eastern look to him, but no accent when I get introduced.

"Harlow, this is Ramsey." Oliver waves in my direction. "This is Harlow." I try to smile, but I'm at that point of the tattoo where my whole skin feels like it's on fire from the shading, and I don't know how friendly it looks.

He comes around to look at Oliver's work, and his eyes widen with surprise when he sees it. His gaze goes from my tattoo to Oliver, where it lingers for a moment before moving to me. He seems to make some kind of internal decision, and a smile crosses his face, turning him from a fairly intimidating man to super hot. *Wow.*

"Nice work, man." He slaps Oliver on the back before moving into one of the other cubicles. Oliver raises the gun, wiping over my skin, his gaze giving nothing away.

"All done," he announces, and he dribbles something over it and gives it a thorough wipe so I can look at it in the mirror. "Hop up and have a look." I'm half-excited, half-worried, so I don't think about how quickly I'm moving, and just as my feet hit the ground, all the blood rushes to my head, and I start to tip sideways.

"Whoa!" Oliver grabs for me, holding me tight against him and steadying me. My brain is foggy and unclear, so I just lean against him until I get my bearings. His citrus scent penetrates my senses first, and I breathe it in deeply.

"Are you *sniffing* me?" He sounds amused, and now that I'm okay again, I pull away quickly, embarrassment imminent.

"No?" My denial sounds like a question. *Damn.* I may not entirely be back to my senses. He holds my arm as we walk across the cubicle to a full-length mirror, and when I see the tattoo, my mouth drops open in shock.

To my other mythical creatures, he's added a

mermaid. But not just any mermaid. This is in fact a merman, with shimmery blue and green scales and a bare torso with rippling stomach muscles and impressive pecs. He even has a piercing through one of his nipples. He's holding a trident, *Aquaman* style, and his hair is a flowing turquoise blue. My eyes drag up to his face, and it looks familiar somehow. Staring at it, I suddenly realize why and start to giggle. Familiar whiskey brown eyes are sparkling with mischief, but they're missing black-rimmed glasses. He's tattooed me with a merman in the image of himself. I start to laugh uncontrollably and need to lean against the mirror for support. His actual eyes meet mine in the reflection, and they look concerned like he's worried I don't like it.

"Oh, Oliver, it's the best fucking tattoo I've ever had!" Spinning, I throw my arms around his shoulders and give him a huge hug and a kiss on the cheek. Our eyes meet and hold, but just as I think he's going to lean in and kiss me, Jonah calls to me.

"Come over here and show me, Harlow. I'm dying to see what he did." Oliver pulls away first and starts cleaning up his station and stripping down the table, so, holding up my dress, I walk over to where Jonah is and show him.

He looks, blinks, and his mouth drops open in shock. "Did he... Is that..?" He seems to be speechless, but all of a sudden, great big booming laughter explodes from his mouth, and he has to step away from his client and put his gun down. He bends over, holding his stomach, and I giggle along with him while his poor client looks bewildered.

"I can't believe you did that," he calls to Oliver when he gets himself under control. "Looks like you both had similar ideas about putting your marks on the other."

That has my giggling cutting off instantly, and Oliver stops what he's doing.

Our eyes meet as Jonah goes back to his client, and we stare at each other, his eyes are saying so many things to me. There's heat and desire, but also wariness. He breaks the stare as his phone beeps in his pocket. Pulling it out, he looks at the message on it, a deep frown appearing like he's just received bad news. After a moment, he shakes his head, stuffing it back into his pocket.

"Come over here and let me wrap it." His voice is flat and impersonal; he sounds like he's giving me a standard speech now, any warmth we'd gained between us suddenly gone, fast enough to make my head spin. "By the time you get home, you should be able to take it off. Make sure you put some of this on it after you shower before you get dressed." He hands me some cream, and I put it with my phone and book. His hands are soft and gentle against my skin as he places some cling wrap over it and tapes it down, but this just feels like the mark of a good tattoo artist, not someone who's taking care of me in particular.

"Grab a seat, I won't be long. Beth!" he calls,

and she comes bounding over. I do as he says, confused over his demeanor.

"Oh, you're done! Can I see it?" she asks with an excited look on her face, but I point to the covering.

"He's already covered it, sorry." Her face drops, and she shrugs.

"Oh well. What can I do for you, boss?" Her sparkly shiny self is once again all perky and compliant.

"Can you finish this? Harlow and I need to get moving." He pulls off his gloves and throws them in the trash. He's done some cleanup but has left the rest for her.

She wrinkles her nose at his request, but she pulls on a pair of gloves and gets to it without argument.

"Come on, we need to go." Oliver's voice is abrupt, and he won't even look at me. *What happened in the last few minutes that made him like this?* He starts out of the shop without saying a word to anyone, not returning Jonah's goodbye. I grab my things and say goodbye to Beth, who just looks at me but doesn't respond. *Whatever, bitch.*

I say goodbye to Ramsey and wish Jonah good luck with his twins. He shoots me a wink, and I follow quickly after Oliver, grabbing my backpack from the staffroom. By the time I get to the car, he's sitting in it, and it's already running. The throaty purr is sexy in itself, but combined with the man sitting in it, it's deadly.

When we arrive home, I follow him inside, only to have him disappear  into their wing without another word. He's left me standing in the foyer, gaping at his back and wondering what happened, and that's where Nana finds me.

"Oh, good, Harlow, you're back. You just have time to have a shower before the stylist is ready for you."

I blink a couple of times, feeling a little bewildered, but Nana is already dragging me along. "Stylist?" I manage to get out.

"Cecelia organized one to come to the house. Jacinta is already done as she and Jaxon went on ahead. They're unveiling the billboard tonight before we go into the premiere, so they wanted to be there early to make sure the details are finalized. They'll meet us on the red carpet. Cecelia is getting done now, and I'm next while you have a shower and put your dress on; it's hanging in your closet. Then when you're done, we'll be taking one of the choppers into the city, and from Neighpalm Industries building, we'll go by limo." This information Nana's throwing at me is almost too much, and combined with Oliver's sudden cold shoulder, I'm getting pretty overwhelmed.

We get to my room, and she leaves me, telling me not to take too long. In a daze, I walk into my room. Princess is asleep on my bed again, so I just put my backpack next to her and strip off my dress and underwear.

Moving into the bathroom, I turn on the shower, peeling off the plastic wrap from my tattoo before stepping under the water. A cry escapes my mouth, and a shudder wracks my body as I wrap my arms around myself, rocking back and forth. My tears start, joining the flow of water. The gut-wrenching sorrow I feel almost brings me to my knees, and it's like all the pressure of Diane dying, finding out about Brad, being rejected by my siblings, and now Oliver's hot and cold act have just added up to be too much. *What the hell happened? What did I do wrong?* I sit down, curling up my legs, and sob.

My mind is a chaos of thoughts, running things over in my head. *What did I do?* I thought we had been finally making some inroads to a semi-decent relationship. Hell, I thought the sparks were flying. I thought I might finally have an ally or at least some support in this fucked up situation, but I guess I'm just a fool. I sit there until my tears have run their course, then I rebuild my walls because something tells me I'm going to need them tonight.

Standing up, I quickly wash my body, taking care of my beautiful new tattoo. I was honest when I said it's the best one I've ever had. Tasha does excellent work, but Oliver's is exceptional. It looks like he's ready to leap out of the water and ravish me. Unfortunately, the new-tattoo high has diminished a bit with my fit of tears, and I try not to focus too hard on the merman's face.

Washing my hair with the products already in there, I quickly climb out and dry myself off, wrapping a towel around my body and hair. I wander back into my room to find a robe on my bed. *Nana must have popped back in,* I think, a smile crossing my face, but that quickly slips into a frown. *Gosh, I hope she didn't hear me crying.*

Ditching the towel around my body, I've pulled on the robe and started rubbing at my hair when there is a knock at my door. "Come in!" I call, not looking up, assuming it's Nana, but when she doesn't say anything, I move the towel. Standing there in an emerald green gown is Brad's PA, Cecelia. She's got a funny look on her face, and I can't think what she may want.

"Hi. What can I do for you?" I question when she doesn't say anything.

"Don't get too comfortable," she says quietly.

"Excuse me?" I ask, bewildered.

"Being Brad's escort. Don't get too comfortable with it. It won't be happening for long. I've almost got a ring on my finger, and don't you think for a second I'm going to let some trumped-up daughter of a whore come in and steal my place," she hisses, her words scathing and hurtful as her eyes flash with venom.

I can't help it; my mouth drops open in shock.

"Steal your place? Eww, he's my father." *What the fuck has this woman been smoking?*

"You may be new and pretty and shiny now, but he *always* comes back to me. You better watch your back." With that last threat she flounces from the room, and I collapse onto the bed. Looking at Princess, I wave a hand at the door. *Is everyone bat shit crazy here? What the fuck else can happen in the next thirty minutes?*

"Did that just happen?" She just blinks tired eyes at me and starts purring as I stroke her between the ears. I have no words, so I'm just going to ignore that whole tirade. The woman is obviously a few sandwiches short of a picnic, but I'll keep an eye on her; I wouldn't want her to become a problem.

I go in search of Nana and the stylist, and I find them in the little living area of this wing. Similar to the main floor, this wing has a space for hanging out to read or play a game of chess. The stylist has her gear set up in there.

"Ah, there you are, Harlow, great timing! I'm done." She gets up and waves me to the seat. "I'm just going to get dressed. Now we don't have much time left, so just let Marissa weave her magic."

Nana leaves then, and the stylist gets to work. She doesn't talk, and to be honest, that's a huge relief. I'm not sure I could cope with small talk. I need to fortify myself with whatever strength I have left to make it through this premiere.

She quickly blows out my hair and twists it up into a stylish updo. Then she skillfully applies my makeup, giving me a smokey eye and some deep plum lipstick. She hands me the tube to stash in my clutch for touch-ups and says, "All done!"

I take it, thanking her, and she starts to pack away her stuff, so I head back to my room for my dress. Pulling the bag out of the wardrobe, I open it and reveal this beautiful, deep purple sheath. Unzipping it, I carefully step into it and pull it up my body, making sure not to rub over the tattoo as I do. The fabric molds itself to my figure like it was made especially for me. Inch-wide straps cover my shoulders; the neckline plunges deep, showing my cleavage to a spectacular degree before the dress skims my figure to flare out the bottom, mermaid style. I can't quite reach the zip, so I step into the shoes that I found with them, some four-inch black high heels, and grab the little clutch, throwing in my lipstick, phone, and my bank card before I go in search of Nana. I find her, Poppy, and Brad in the area where the stylist was, but she's now gone. *Wow, she was efficient.*

"Nana, can you help me with this?" She stands up and clasps her hands together.

"Oh, Harlow, I knew that was the right dress! You look gorgeous." The three of them are grinning like fools, and a matching one crosses my face.

"Thanks. I feel a little like Cinderella."

"Well, does that make the kids the ugly step-siblings?" Nana's laughing, but her voice has a hint of worry. Damn it, she must have heard me crying in the shower when she dropped off the dress.

"Harlow, you look beautiful. Thank you for agreeing to come with me," Brad says, stepping closer to me. "I hope this is the first of many times that I'll get to proudly escort you on my arm."

I take a deep breath. "No, thank you for inviting me, Dad." The three of them stop abruptly, surprise on their faces before those huge grins are back, and Dad wraps his arms around me and pulls me close.

"Thank you," he whispers in my ear, and it allows my heart to start to heal.

## Oliver

Standing there as I watch Harlow giggling with Jonah, a warmth flows through my body. I really like this girl, and I think that maybe, just maybe we were wrong about her. The feel of her in my arms was like nothing I've ever experienced, and her kiss had me harder than a schoolboy. If Lisa hadn't interrupted us, I would've had her up against the wall. An incoming message on my iPhone has me pulling it out of my pocket and looking down. My heart sinks when I read it.

**Jacinta:** All set and ready to go, don't be late.

God, I don't think what Jacinta has planned is

such a good idea anymore. I was happy supporting it at first, but now that I've gotten to know her a little more, I can't deny our chemistry, and I don't want it to happen. Fuck, she's never going to forgive me after this, but I can't go against my sister. *Family first.*

So I shove my phone deep into my pocket and do the same thing with my feelings. I tape up her tattoo and ask Beth to clean up and bolt out of the store without saying goodbye to any of my employees. The car ride home is riddled with tension, but I just can't be her friend and then watch tonight as Jacinta's plan unfolds. Ignoring her, I head inside to have a shower. Half an hour later, Nana's at my door as I'm putting on my suit, her face a thundercloud, and if I were small again, I know I would be getting a whooping.

"I don't know what the hell you did to her, but she is crying her eyes out at the bottom of her shower. You need to fix this because if she goes home and your father finds out you or any of the others had anything to do with it, he will never forgive you." Her words are sharp enough to cut, and there are barely a handful of times in my life that I can remember Nana speaking to anyone like this, let alone one of her grandchildren. We might be spoiled...okay, definitely *are* spoiled, but there's always been an easy love in her voice even the times she's been raging mad. This, right now, this is very, very bad.

She sighs and some of the anger leaves her as she sits down on my bed and pats it so I'll sit next to her.

"I know this is such an adjustment for all of you and a huge shock, but have you ever thought about the positive possibilities?" she says gently, but I just shake my head, having no clue what she's talking about.

"Did you know that Poppy and I had every intention of introducing you all to Harlow anyway?" Her question has my ears pricking up, and I turn to her much too quickly to disguise my interest in her words. "We were going to convince her to come and visit us once she had finished college because we think she would be a perfect solution to a problem all you boys are having."

"What problem, what do you mean?" I ask in return, and I can feel the frown on my face as confusion rises in equal measure with suspicion.

"Well, the fact is none of you can find a woman who's not a gold-digging whore." I flinch at my Nana's language, but she's not wrong. "I don't know where we went wrong, but you all have *horrible* taste in women. Harlow is the exact opposite to all of that despite what you all may be feeling at the moment." As the confusion starts to lessen, the suspicion doesn't go away. Nana's come up with some crazy shit in our lives, so God only knows where this is going.

"And who exactly were you planning on setting her up with?" I ask, half-hoping it was me.

"All of you!" she announces calmly like she's not suggesting that my brothers and I share a woman, not that it would be the first time for some of us. I scoff, but her face hardens as she grabs me by the chin.

"Now you hear me, boy. None of you are very good at relationships because you are all so busy, and you've got enough trust issues to fill the Grand Canyon. Lord knows you all wouldn't know the perfect woman if she walked right in front of you, holding a sign! So, I figured I would do you all the favor of bringing you a Nana-approved girl whose character is beyond question. Harlow is the perfect solution! She's woman enough and wonderful enough to keep you all happy, and she doesn't care about money or status or being seen. In fact, she would be happier curled up on the couch watching a movie or having a picnic somewhere on the estate than being seen at restaurant openings and movie premieres. There isn't an ounce of pretentiousness in that woman, and if you would all stop being such morons and pull your heads out of your asses, you might see what you've got right in front of you. Maybe your sister could even have a real friend for once instead of those leeches she usually finds herself surrounded by."

She stands up and brushes off her dress before stalking to the door, not waiting for my reply. Before she leaves, she turns to make one last jab. "Fix it, Oliver. You don't want to miss this opportunity." Her words sink in, and the more I think about them, the more I like the sound of them, but my heart sinks as I remember what's about to happen.

I try to call Jacinta to tell her to abort, but she doesn't answer, and neither do any of my other brothers. *Fuck!*

## Chapter Twenty-Six

**Jaxon**

My phone beeps, and when I look at the screen, I can see a message from Oliver is waiting. Swiping my finger across the screen, I ignore it, shoving my phone back into my pocket. I'm sure he's trying to talk us out of the plan. He and Kai are both soft on the bitch and don't think we should be doing what we are. At the moment I have no time for either of them; they're either with us, or I don't want to know about it. A crowd is just starting to gather around the red carpet as my sister giggles with glee when the billboard contractor hands her the curtain remote.

"If you just press the big red button, the curtain will drop, and the billboard will be revealed," he explains to her, showing her the right button and giving her a narrow-eyed look. I mean, I would too. I doubt anyone's ever been as excited as my sister to get a remote for a billboard.

"Thank you so much," she gushes in reply, "for rushing the job for me. I really appreciate it." She flashes a wide smile at him, and he blinks at the megawatts she's putting out, his ruddy cheeks turning even redder, before muttering his goodbyes and hurrying away.

Laughing, I nudge my sister. "Let's dim the glee a little bit, or someone, namely Dad or the grand-parents, are going to suspect something."

She places the remote in her clutch and closes it before looking up at me. "Hopefully this will send that tramp back to where she came from." We walk toward the theater and find a seat in some of the plush couches, waiting for the rest of our family to arrive so we can meet them out on the carpet.

"Yeah, I'm not sure if this will," I tell her, and her eyes frost over. I know it's not directed at me, but it's a little weird to see that look on my sister's face when it's just the two of us. I'm the one that Jacinta hides nothing from; we love all of our broth-ers, but there's something about the twin bond that they've never been able to touch.

"You're not going soft on me, are you?" she snaps, and I quickly hold my hands up in defense.

"No, no, God, calm down. I'm just saying I

think she's got more of a backbone than you've ever come up against before. This might knock her down for a minute, but I bet she comes back swinging. Do you really want to risk tanking your company?" I play the devil's advocate because when my sister has a bee in her bonnet, she tends to have tunnel vision. And it's true, so far I haven't seen any of the usual conniving tricks women use when they have an opportunity with one of us. In fact, I would go as far as saying she's pretty much avoided us all, and I can't say I'm not a little intrigued. Is this a new ploy to win us all over, or is she genuinely not interested in any of us? I'm almost starting to feel sorry about the way I bombarded her in her room that first night...*almost*. There's a part of me that's still pretty pissed off that she made me look like a fool. Jacinta shifts those frosty eyes to me, but this time they soften from cold anger into annoyance.

She scoffs in response. "Please, Neighpalm Couture is solid. This won't even be a bump in the road, and hopefully by this time tomorrow, Harlow will be back in Connecticut and far away from us all so that Dad can move on. He hasn't had time to develop a bond with her yet, so I'm sure he'll get over this quickly. Plus, people will be talking about this for weeks; imagine the spike in publicity!"

My sister waves her hand at a nearby waiter who has a tray of champagne glasses. As she grabs one and hands me another, she raises her glass. "To another successful job at getting rid of another gold-digger." I clink mine against hers and take a sip of the effervescent liquid, desperately hoping that she's right and Dad hasn't grown attached...otherwise, we may be in more trouble than she can comprehend.

## Harlow

Cecelia arrives, and Brad rushes us out to the helicopter pad. That's right, the back lawn behind the deck has a helicopter sitting on it, and Oliver, Holden, Kai, and Thomas are already sitting in it. We take the remaining seats, me finding one next to Kai, and the pilot in the cockpit flicks a few switches. The engine starts up, and rotor blades start to spin.

Kai tries to offer me a headset, but I don't want to mess my hair, nor do I want to join in their conversation, so I shake my head, using my hair as a convenient excuse. Oliver hasn't even looked my way since I sat down, and the sorrow that had gotten the best of me in the shower threatens to rear its ugly head again. Both Nana and Cecelia follow my lead, but I can see that the guys have a conversation taking place. I turn to look out the window instead, hiding any visible trace of the burning in my eyes. It's almost dark outside, but I'm hoping to get an aerial view of the abandoned mansion.

The rotors must finally reach the right speed as the helicopter starts to rise into the air. My stomach dips, and I clench my clutch hand against my chest and close my eyes. A hand suddenly presses against mine, and looking down, I see Kai has reached out and grabbed it. Folding mine into his, he doesn't even look my way as he continues the conversation with the others. A small smile crosses my face, and I leave it there, but I don't want to read anything into it. For all I know, Poppy told him to distract me; I won't make the same mistake of overestimating his kindness like I did Oliver's.

As the chopper starts to move toward the city, I peer out the window, straining my neck to get a good look. Poppy sees me, and he must say something because the pilot does a quick lap around the building. From the top, it looks like a medieval fortress with spires and buttresses, and is that a moat wrapping around it? But before I can make out anything else, the helicopter moves on. The sun dips behind the clouds, and the sky has turned dark by the time we get to the city and land on the towering Neighpalm Industries building.

We wait for it to power down as to not mess up our hair and then make our way down in the elevator to a waiting limo. It's huge and fits all of us, and again, I find myself sitting next to Kai. My hearing is still a little off from the helicopter, but his voice breaks through, clear as day.

He nudges me slightly, though even a slight push from a guy his size makes me feel like I could fly halfway across the limo. "You're quiet tonight. Do you not like your new tattoo?" he asks teasingly, but I think there's a hint of seriousness behind it. That stops the conversation in the car, and everyone turns to look at me, except Oliver.

"Actually, I love it. I wish the dress had a slit so I could show you all," I tell them, getting varying reactions, but my eyes are on Oliver, and my words don't get a single response from him.

*Well, fuck him.* "Nana, are Alex and Shane meeting us there?" I ask her, and that gets a reaction. Not much, but I can see him flinch slightly at my words. Good! At least I know he's a little bit affected by today.

"Yes, sweetheart, they said they would wait at the end for us."

As she finishes, the limo starts to slow, and the crowd begins to grow. People are lining the streets, shouting and waving signs with words on them. It comes to a halt, the doors open, and cameras start flashing as everyone climbs out until I'm the last one. Dad holds his hand out to me; I think he can see my nerves. "Come on, honey, it will be fine." So, taking a deep breath, I grab his hand and step out into the spotlight.

It feels like all eyes look to me, then the whispers and speculation start. "Who's that?"

"Is she one of the dates?"

"No, it looks like she's with Brad Summers." I catch the word girlfriend and gold-digger and a whole range of horrible things.

Voices are shouting questions, and my shoulders hunch as I try to make myself less conspicuous. Nana tuts, the noise somehow breaking through the clamor around us. "Don't do that, Harlow. Who cares what they're saying? We know who you are, and that's what is important."

Just as she says that Jacinta, Jaxon, and Declan approach us. Selena Cross is wrapped around Declan, and Jaxon has a model I now recognize as Astor Minchin. And something occurs to me; this is the woman I replaced at the shoot, who had been too ill to make it. My eyes run the length of her body. She's tall and slim to the point of gaunt, and her clothes drape over her like a sack of cloth, but she's holding onto Jaxon like he's her last port in the storm. His cruel eyes meet mine, a mocking smile crossing his face.

"Awesome, everyone's here." Jacinta is overly excited about something, and my heart sinks. I watch as Oliver tries to speak into her ear, but she pushes him away, and his shoulders slump in defeat. For the briefest of moments, our eyes meet, and I see a glimpse of pain in them, the same flash that I'd seen when he told me about what he was like as a boy. *Whatever happens next isn't going to be good.* She turns and points at something. Behind the crowd of people across the street is a covered billboard.

"Is everyone ready to see the new Neighpalm Couture lingerie campaign?" a voice announces to the crowd, and they cheer even louder. "Let's have a countdown... Ten. Nine. Eight..."

The crowd chants, and Jacinta grabs me by the arm. "Come on, Harlow, you don't want to miss this!" There's an almost frantic glee in her voice that I've never heard before, and something in me already starts to flip upside down, nerves rising to the point of almost nausea. She pulls me to the front of the family. When the countdown hits one, she holds up a remote of some kind and presses a button. The sheet detaches and falls to the ground, and what I see has me just about vomiting on the red carpet as the crowd's cries rise to a fever pitch.

It's the same photo that Shane had sent to me, but with the Neighpalm Couture logo on it and the caption "Lingerie for that gold-digging mistress in your life" emblazoned across it in big, bold red letters.

The crowd falls silent, and as I look around in horror, I can see the conclusion they've all reached. Jacinta has made it look like *I'm* Brad's gold-digging mistress. The noise explodes into more questions and laughter and finger-pointing, and a wave of dizziness overtakes me, my body completely unprepared for this level of manic scrutiny.

I slap my hand over my mouth to stop myself from screaming, but the tears well in my eyes. "Oh my God!"

Looking around at the family, I see various reactions. Jacinta, Jaxon, Declan, their two dates, Thomas, and Holden, are all laughing. Kai has his fists clenched, his eyes flashing with fury and his brow creased in a frown as he rounds to face the others and words start to pour out of his mouth. I'm pretty sure he wasn't on board with the plan, and he's now telling them off. While I'm sure I'll appreciate that later, his reaction does nothing to make me feel any better at this moment. My gaze drifts to Oliver, who is standing slightly apart, hands jammed into pant pockets, shoulders hunched in on themselves, looking decidedly uncomfortable. *Good, I hope he's suffering.* I thought we'd made progress today, not to mention the kiss against the wall. My eyes then find Nana's, and her mouth is open in shock, the formidable woman speechless for once. Dad and Poppy look as furious as Kai, but Cecelia seems to be smothering a laugh. Looking around, I search for an exit, but I'm frozen to the spot.

"Harlow, Harlow!" My name has me looking around for who's calling me. Alex and Shane push their way through the crowd of people still on the red carpet.

Alex wraps his arms around me. "We've got you, babe." He ushers me in the direction of another limo whose passengers have just left.

Shoving my head down, he helps me in before climbing in after me. Looking out the window, I see Shane having stern words with both my father and Jacinta, whose face has dropped into a bitter scowl, before he hurries after us. When he climbs in, the limo moves away, and I let the tears fall.

"Fuck, how could she do that? Not just to me, but to my dad." Shane surprises me and wraps an arm around me, pulling me against his chest, where my tears proceed to soak his shirt.

"I'm not making excuses for her, but I don't think she's been thinking very clearly recently. She obviously doesn't cope well with change and upheaval, and she's lashing out. It's not fair that you're getting the brunt of it."

"I don't belong here. I want to go home, but I can't. I promised Chuck I would look after his horses, and I can't bear the thought of letting down *both* of my dads." My sobs have my voice all uneven, and I'm impressed that they even seem to understand me.

"I'm sure he would understand if you told him what happened," he suggests, and Alex nods his head but stays quiet. He, too, seems to have tears in his eyes.

"No, I'm *not* telling them. You're not to tell them either. I'm so embarrassed." I fall silent as the limo moves through the city, finally pulling up in front of an apartment building, and they help me out. Shane is still supporting me while Alex holds the door open. They hurry me through the foyer to the elevator, which goes to the top floor once we've gotten in. They proceed to hurry me through an apartment, but I'm so out of it I can't take in any of the details.

Somehow I find myself showered and dressed in a big t-shirt and squashed into bed between Shane and Alex. I'm not sure how that happened, but it seems I may have blanked out from the stress. Maybe that's not a bad thing. I don't think I could cope, knowing they had to remove my makeup and change my clothes.

For the first time since it happened, I start to comprehend how much damage she's done. My reputation is mud, and in the age of social media, there'll never be a way to truly scrub the memory of this billboard from the world's eyes. I'm never going to be able to get a reputable job. The scenario runs through my mind of an internship coordinator asking me about the billboard, my nerves morphing it into a nightmarish moment where the interviewer shoves their phone into my face, an image of the billboard and its caption in vivid color.

*What could she have been thinking?* After a few more minutes of a flurry of dizzying thoughts, the warmth and security of being surrounded by my two friends has my eyes drifting closed and my heart rate slowing for the first time. Alex's fingers running through my hair cause a deep drowsy feeling that is so much preferable to everything else I'm going through right now.

"Sleep, Harlow, all will look so much better in the morning." His voice fades, and the bliss of darkness surrounds me.

## Jacinta

The movie premiere seemed to drag on forever, but by the time it finished, I had no fingernails left, and Cecelia had everything organized for a small press conference.

My brothers and I stand behind my father as he takes the podium, his and our grandparents in a state of frosty silence, something none of us have ever experienced before. Dad won't even look at me. I've barely managed to keep my nausea under control the whole time, and my worry about his reaction has been so bad I can't even tell you what the film was about.

He and Nana and Poppy hadn't watched the movie, instead commandeering a small meeting room to discuss a plan of action on how to play off the billboard. I tried to convince them that it had been a mistake by the marketing department, but I can tell by the look in their eyes they didn't believe me.

Turning to look at the billboard, I can see that it

is now blank, the ad having been ripped down while we were watching the movie. My dad has enough pull that it probably took one phone call to get it done so quickly. My attention switches back to the podium when he clears his throat, drawing the press' attention to him as well. "Good evening and thank you for attending. We will be making a short statement to clear the air but won't be taking any questions today. You may direct any questions you have to Neighpalm Industries PR department."

"Firstly, I'd like to address the subject of the bill-board. When a marketing department tries to come up with a campaign, they throw everything on the table, the good, the bad, and the ugly. Unfortunately, this one, which was a joke and a rejected idea, seems to have made its way to the printers by accident. We have now removed it and will be replacing it as quickly as possible. We know that the age of social media gives new life to things that are better left forgotten, but we'd like to request that the press treat this incident as it was, a mistake, and not rampantly publicize an ad that's disrespectful to our line and the models in the photo."

The reporters start to shout questions, but he ignores them as he continues. "As for the girl on the billboard and my date this evening, do not make the mistake in thinking that she is what the poster made her out to be. That girl is actually my biological daughter. We've recently discovered each other's existence, not having known previously, and she is out here to see if we can develop a relationship, something that I'm hoping will not be hurt by tonight's mistake."

I snort quietly, but my stomach rolls again at his words, and I barely resist rolling my eyes, knowing full well the cameras are focused on me and my brothers. Turning my head slightly, I look down the line and can see they all have their game faces on. *I better not blow it.*

"Lastly, my daughter Jacinta will be taking a step down from CEO of Neighpalm Couture, and my mother Grace will be sliding into the position temporarily. Jacinta is going to be taking some personal time to work on next season's line." I flinch at his words. *Oh fuck!* He just smacked me publicly. If I didn't realize he was upset before, I do now, and I have no idea how I'm going to be able to make it better. Well, I do, but I'd rather swallow rusty knives than apologize.

Jaxon, standing next to me, grabs my hand and gives it a hard squeeze. "Don't worry, we'll figure something out," he whispers out the side of his mouth.

Dad thanks the press, and he and Nana and Poppy start to leave as more questions fly at them. When they see they're not going to get any response from them, they start on us, but we've all become pros at ignoring them. We all pile into the nearby limo and head for the NI building. The ride is silent and full of tension, and I shift repeatedly in my seat, wanting to break that silence but not knowing how. When we get to the building, Nana and Poppy and Dad get out of the limo, but as we start to follow, Dad pops his head back in.

"I think maybe you should take this time to think about your actions," he commands, his voice somber, and there's a sheen in his eyes that tells me I just might have broken something inside my father. The man who's given me *everything* is barely holding himself together, and I don't know what to say to him.

"You should probably all check into one of our hotels. I'm not sure I wouldn't say something that would hurt us all if you come home tonight. Maybe use this time to come up with some kind of explanation for this fiasco because I have never been as disappointed in someone as I am now. Maybe we'll talk tomorrow. Your grandparents and I need time to figure out how we feel about all this."

His head moves out of the way, and the door slamming shut is like the lid sealing on a coffin. The limo starts to move away from the NI building and heads toward the Neighpalm Hotel, the silence oppressive as we're all stuck in our own minds.

"Guys, I think I fucked up," I say into the quiet.

"You think?" Kai snorts, and nothing else is said for the rest of the drive. *How am I going to fix this?* Not only have I lost my job, I've disappointed and upset the one man who's never let me down. I run my hands through my hair in frustration, desperately wishing my brothers could swoop in and fix this. As I run various ideas through my mind, I feel a wetness on my cheeks, and it's only then I realize I'm crying. God, I hope it's not too late to make things better and as for Harlow, that bitch is going to pay.

Thank you for reading!
I hope you enjoyed the book. It would be super awesome if you could leave a review wherever you bought it, because I love to hear what you thought of the story.

**Want more of Harlow and the gang?**
**Pre order Broken Girl book two here**
Broken Girl

And Book Three pre order here
Tormented Girl

Want to keep up to date with new books coming soon? Sign up to my newsletter here
Newsletter

Another way to do that is to join me Facebook group. I drop teasers and giveaways in there all the time. Here's the link
Lexie's Ladygarden

Visit my webpage and check out reading orders and what else I've written.
www.lexiewinston.com

## Acknowledgments

Thank you to all the normal crew this book wouldn't be possible without you all.

Michelle for your invaluable editing.

Emma for all the late night and early morning chats.

Infinity Book Designs for the cover

My beta team for being super awesome as usual.

Grace for being a great sounding board, you rock

Hope and Mollie for their pimping prowess and a very special thanks to Leslie Arnett my veterinary advisor who made sure I hadn't made any blaring blunders when it came to Harlow.

Lexie

Check out something else by me. This one is a reverse harem paranormal romance.
Guardian
Collectors Division 1

## Prologue

Quiet, gentle snores drag me out of the darkness of sleep. Rolling over, I study the naked body of the man lying beside me. The long sleek lines and muscular backside of a golden Adonis who had done so many delicious things to me last night. He was a perfect distraction from the nervous energy filling my body in anticipation of the coming day, and found creative ways to use it. So much so that I was able to rest peacefully for a few hours.

But that was then, and this is now, and the incessant sexual need, awakened not long after the loss of my virginity, is building in my body again. A never-ending line of no-strings-attached fuck buddies, male or female—I'm not fussy—has been able to keep the need at bay, but not for long periods of time. And although my body's needs can be temporarily appeased, my heart and soul ache for more. Aches for love and acceptance. To be needed and wanted.

Something I thought I'd found once. A group of boys I had formed a big attachment with. Boys who had promised to wait. Boys who had broken that promise and callously stomped all over it. Boys who had caused my heart to harden.

Boys I would never have been able to choose between anyway.

A nagging, buzzing sound drags me from my thoughts. Pulling my naked body out of bed, I hunt for my communicator. Searching through our clothes, which we had dumped haphazardly in our pursuit of pleasure, I find it under my undies, now torn to shreds and useless. I throw them at a bin in the corner of the room before checking the messages on my screen. Across the screen scrolls a message from my roommate and best friend Olivia.

*Mina, where the fuck are you?*

*Mina, we've got The Gauntlet run in two hours. Get your ass home and ready.*

Shit. My heart thumps hard in shock. I never expected to fall asleep and certainly not long enough that I would need to be reminded about today's challenge. Rushing quietly around the room, I throw on my clothes. Luckily, the man in the bed is also a student at the Academy and has an apartment in the same building as me, though he's a year behind and not participating today. I leave him sleeping peacefully as I make my way quickly back to my apartment. Bursting through the door, my roommates' surprised looks greet me as I rush in.

"Thanks, Livie, I just need a quick shower," I tell them both as I run past them, noticing James' sly grin.

He shouts after me, "Washing off the sex smell are you, Mina?" I throw up a one-finger salute as I duck into the bathroom and hear an oomph. Livie must've smacked him for the comment.

They both know about my problem. I've talked to them about it in the past. It's not like I could hide the amount of sex I have from my roommates, and, well, I didn't want them to think I had become careless with my body. They both suggested I speak to the Academy doctors about it, but I just wasn't comfortable sharing it. What if there was something wrong with me?

Shrugging all that off, I shower quickly and pull on my Academy uniform, focusing on the task today. The most critical challenge of the last four years. Today is the day I finally achieve my dream.

Get it here Guardian

This one is a M/F Paranormal Romance

## Prologue

"This meeting of the Matrons of Morbank Island may come to order." Prudence Miller announces as she bangs her gravel on the podium in front of her. She peers out at the rest of the ladies in the large room of the town hall. "Come now, settle down." The noise of the room slowly quietens, the other nine women look up with curiosity.

"Prudence, what's this meeting about?" Victoria Digby questions. "You know I love meeting with you ladies, but usually drinks and nibbles are involved."

"Town affairs *are* better solved with a Mojito in hand." Glenda La Croix adds with a laugh and a wave of her hand. A tittering of giggles explodes from the ladies, but when they see that Prudence is not laughing and has a very somber look on her face, they all quieten down quickly.

"Ladies, I think we all know why we are meeting here. The portal is fading, and there's not enough power generation to hold it open anymore. We are failing the realms. Action needs to be taken. If not, the council could very well appoint another coven in charge of Morbank, and we'll get kicked off our ancestral island." Prudence says with a look of sadness on her face. "It's time for the next generation to step up and take their rightful place at the head of the family businesses. We're all ready to retire, and the creative ideas just aren't flowing like they used to." The women all nod their heads in agreement. Prudence continues with a hitch in her voice, "There's also something else that I have to tell you."

"Oh, Prudence dear, what's wrong?" Lucille Crane asks as she gets up and puts her arm around Prudence. "What's making you so sad?"

"Don't you think it's strange that all of our oldest daughters have left town? Even though every single one of them is following in the family business." She asks, looking at the ladies. The ladies start talking amongst themselves.

"I did think it strange that they all decided to leave town and learn from other artists, but they're young and independent," Laura Woods exclaims, shrugging.

"Yes." adds in Fiona Blackwood, looking down at her hands, "I understand why Tia went to China. But I always thought she'd come back when she finished learning what he wanted. Instead, she stays." Fiona's face is covered in sadness. "I keep trying to get her to come home, but she avoids the topic."

"I have similar conversations with Tatiana," Lucille adds. "She's so busy with that boyfriend of hers." The sneer on her face when she says this makes it visible she isn't too keen on him.

"Ladies, Ladies," Prudence says, hugging Lucille and encouraging her to sit back down. She straightens her shoulders and takes a big breath. "When Susan the slut ran off and left Regan," she starts, looking very sad.

"May she suffer pox on her pussy." The other nine ladies chime in unison—one of them spitting to the side.

A small smile appears on Prudence's face. "Amen, my loyal ladies. When this happened, and Ruby didn't come home to help her brother and his babies out, I knew there was something very wrong. Not only that. When I hired someone else to run the shop, she didn't even bat an eyelid. Once upon a time, that would have made her come home on the warpath. Nobody was allowed to run her shop except her. So, I conducted some research. What I have discovered may surprise you."

The women look on eagerly, waiting for her to continue.

"Well, don't make us wait, what have you found out?" questions Laura

"The girls are under a powerful repulsion spell." She announces. Gasps and shocked chatter erupt. She talks over them, and they calm down to listen. "The signs were all there; we didn't acknowledge them. One, they all suddenly left town around the same time. Two, none have shown any interest in coming home. I know for sure; it was Ruby's dream to take over the candy store. For her to up and leave all of a sudden, it was suspicious. She's been gone for eighteen months now and has shown no interest in coming home." She says, wringing her hands together.

"I think part of the dwindling power problem is we are all getting older, and the businesses need a new influx of power. With the lack of new creative inspiration, the tourists have lost interest. All of us are looking to retire, if the girls don't come home and take over, we will have to sell the businesses or close them down. An artisan village with no artisans has no draw. So, with my suspicions, I cast a detection spell. I have discovered that this town and, in particular our places of business and homes, have a repelling spell on them specifically aimed at the girls."

More gasps and outrageous cries fill the hall.

"Who could have done such a thing, and why?" Marie Payne questions out loud; a look of sadness haunts her eyes; her skin is sallow, and she looks like she has lost weight. Pru makes a note to visit her soon.

"Well, that's the all-important question, isn't it?" Prudence says with a glare in her gray eyes and steel in her voice. "I will be informing Sheriff Crimson of my findings, but that is not going to solve our problem."

"I see by the look on your face you have a plan." Victoria says with a smile on her face, "Don't be coy, share."

"You bet your ass I have a plan." Prudence says with a determined look on her face, "I have found a spell to counteract it, but there may be some negative side effects. I need all of you ladies to think about this quite carefully, because once done, there's no going back. The negative impacts could affect you directly."

"I don't know about everyone else, but if someone is messing with my girl and that's why she won't come home to visit her Mama, then I'm in!" shouts Beatrix Shadowsoul getting to her feet.

"That's right," agrees Marie also getting to her feet, "Nobody messes with our kids or town and gets away with it."

By this time, all the ladies are on their feet and agreeing to the spell. A tear appears in the corner of Prudence's eye. She smiles, looking around at the other women in the room.

"My sisters, I knew I could count on you, just as we have been counting on each other since we first formed this coven so many years ago."

"That's right, witches for life," shouts Denise.

"Or bitches as the case may be, Hey Denise," Lucille says cheekily, bumping her hip against Denise's.

"Well, you would know," Denise says back with a grin.

"Ok, ladies settle down. We will meet in the clearing behind the Manor at midnight tomorrow night. It is a full moon and the best time to fulfill the spell. Please bring something from your girls with you to go into the spell. It must be something that means a lot to them." Prudence announces with a satisfied smile. "I don't know who did this, but the backlash when we break the spell will let them know we are onto them. We must prepare to ward off a takeover."

"We will have to be more vigilant. We have grown complacent. Although we know most people in town, there are always people coming and going." Minerva Crowe muses out loud. "Someone is trying to start trouble, maybe a coven from another town."

"Let keep this to ourselves for now or at least until I can speak to Sheriff Crimson. Now go, and don't forget to perform your purification rituals, and I will see you all tomorrow night." Prudence shoos the ladies away.

The ladies all make their way out of the hall, go back to their business's or go on with their daily routines. Prudence collapses in a chair. She rubs her head to ward off the pounding behind her eyes.

The counter-spell could have some far-flung and dire consequences, but it is needed to break such a strong aversion. But saying that, there isn't much these ladies wouldn't do for their oldest daughters. Picking up her handbag, she places it over her shoulder. She straightens her shirt and smooths down her skirt before reaching to do the same with her hair. Then with a deep breath and head held high, she strides out of the hall towards the Sheriff's office to have a quiet and confidential conversation with Sheriff Crimson.

The moon is high and round in the sky, the night has a bite of cold to it, with that sharp smell of the coming fall. The trees are losing their leaves, and the leaf litter is scattered all over the floor of the clearing. Back through the trees, a single light in the manor can be seen, left on for late-night visitors and portal users.

The Manor Bed and Breakfast is the location of the supernatural portal linking all the realms to Earth for the US region. All kinds of creatures pass through. That being said, it doesn't mean you won't find humans staying there; the supernatural world is a new curiosity.

One by one, the ladies drift out from amongst the trees from different directions. All ten of them are wearing their coven robes. Scarlett red with gold thread woven throughout in intricate designs. Hoods pulled up to cover their heads, hands clasping lit white candles. They make a circle in the clearing. Prudence reaches under her robe and pulls out a satchel from over her shoulder; the other ladies follow suit.

Out of the bag, she pulls an athame and her spell book. She places them next to her, then walks to the center of the clearing. There is a fire pit with a cauldron, filled with salt and water, sitting over the top. With one word and gesture from Pru, the fire burst to life and starts crackling, the blue and red flames flickering, casting an eerie light around the clearing. The ladies blow out their candles and place them into their bags, putting them to the side. Prudence grabs the athame and moves back to the cauldron.

"Please move forward, bring the object precious to your daughter, and place it into the cauldron. We will need a few drops of your blood as well. Then let us join hands for the incantation."

Each lady places the object into the cauldron. Using the athame, they drip a couple of drops of their blood into the water. The steam drifting off the top takes on a red hue. They all step back and join hands. Prudence adds a handful of bay and sage leaves to the water and moves back to join hands, starting the chant

*"Oh Hecate, hear us now, I call upon thee to hear our pleas.*

*Come forth and cleanse our first-born daughters of all evil and alien magics intending harm, and restore them to balance, health, and home. We thank you and by our wills combined, so mote it be."*

"So mote it be" repeats the rest of the coven.

With a loud boom, a flash of purple bursts outwards from the cauldron, flowing through all the women in the circle and continuing outward. When the light has disappeared, the flame has gone out of the fire, and the spell is complete.

"Now all we can do is wait," announces Prudence.

"Well, I don't know about anyone else, but that was thirsty work. Who's up for a drink?" Asks Marie as she walks back to where she has left her bag. Pulling out a couple of bottles of wine, she hands them out before opening one and taking a swig.

Once the tense atmosphere breaks, the ladies laugh. They all take seats around the cauldron, more bottles of wine appear, as do a couple of joints. Smoke drifts on the breeze, pungent and pervasive. They are all talking quite loudly and joyously when a rustle through the trees causes them to drop into silence.

"What was that?" asks Lucille.

Victoria jumps, grabbing the athame from near the cauldron and brandishing it in front of herself. "I don't know, but they are going to have to go through me to get to you!" she says ferociously.

The ladies all look at each other and burst into laughter. Out of the trees walks Regan, Prudence's son, the man who lives in and runs the Manor bed-and-breakfast, and polices the beings that come and go.

He has a wry look on his face, "Evening ladies, mother," he nods his head at them all. "I could hear you all from inside and felt the pressure wave from the spell." He raises an eyebrow at Victoria. "Did you forget you could use magic to defend yourself?" He laughs, gesturing to the athame.

She blushes and puts the athame back where she grabbed it from before retaking a seat, as he continues.

"That's what you get for addling your brains with wine and herbs, aren't you all a little old for partying hard?" He chuckles, as they all squirm like teenagers caught out. Looking around he asks, "I notice there are no men from the coven at this little ceremony? You certainly didn't send me the invite." Pru sputters at the question.

"This spell needed a purely maternal energy to it." He raises his eyebrow skeptically.

"Did it, Mom? Or did you ladies want to have a little full moon party without the old ball and chains? Keys are to go into the bowl." He gestures to them, holding out a fruit bowl. "Your loved ones will thank me in the morning. Beds are all made up for you in the manor. Try to not wake my children or the few guests I do have when you come in. Also, make sure you magic those room clean, I don't have enough staff at the moment to be picking up after grown-ass women."

The ladies sheepishly pull their keys out and drop them in the bowl.

He walks back towards the manor. "Have a good evening ladies; I really hope the spell worked."

"So do we, Regan, so do we," his mother says as he walks away.

**Want to read more?**
**Get it here**
**Candy Conniptions**